DRAGON SEED

The Archemi Online Chronicles

Volume 1

By James Osiris Baldwin

A Gift Horse Productions Novel

Copyright Notice

For permission requests, please contact James Osiris Baldwin: author@jamesosiris.com

A huge thanks to Stacy Schonhardt and her excellent copyediting!

Layout and design by James Osiris Baldwin.

ISBN: 9781980382706

Table of Contents

BOOK ONE

The Herald of the Hidden Seed

Chapter 1

The coughing fit kicked me upright before I was even awake. Strangling, eyes throbbing from the pressure in my head, I coughed and heaved and flailed around, unable to see anything but dancing black and white spots. My lungs were burning by the time I pitched back onto my pillows, exhausted and shaking with lingering terror. Not just terror of the present: terror of the future that awaited me. I was now at Stage Two of the HEX virus – in three days' time, I'd be dead.

There were no nurses in our quarantine tent. Everyone here was already sicker than me, moaning and rattling in their sleep. Still wheezing, I fumbled across for the box of bleach wipes next to my Army cot and used them to clean up my face and hands. The smell made my throat burn raw, and I shook with unfamiliar weakness. I hurt all over. My joints felt like angry dwarves had been pounding them with hammers while I slept... and it was only my second day of being sick.

My tent bunked eleven other soldiers, all infected, all of us in the prime of our lives. My conscript's uniform only had three badges on it: my platoon, my rank - Private - and my name badge, which was just my surname, 'Park'. I was twenty-seven, fit despite my chronic gaming habit, used to bouncing around the world with a pack and rifle. When I rolled up a sleeve and looked down at the inside of my arm, the smooth tan skin I was used to seeing was mottled with a spreading red rash.

HEX was like clockwork. The first day hits you like a train, and five days later, you're toast. By tomorrow, I wouldn't be able to walk. Day Three was the worst day, because you were still aware of everything that was happening to your body. I'd watched people cough until the veins in their eyes ruptured and they began to cry blood. If I did nothing, if I followed orders and stayed in bed to die, that was all I had to look forward to. But as Baldrick from *Black Adder* would say: "I have a cunning plan."

Assuming I could find the strength to get my ass out of bed.

My hands were shaking with fever as I pulled up my ration of medications and fumbled them out into my palm, clenching my teeth while I tried not to drop them everywhere. The cocktail of tablets were all anyone had to fight HEX, the common name of the H5N1-X virus: a lab-made super-flu unleashed on the world as a weapon of war. The tablets would take down the fever, keep my lungs from filling up, help the cough, and manage some of the pain. When I stood up, my head began to pound even harder. I pinched the bridge of my nose, willing the pain to stop, and then got dressed. A t-shirt, BDU pants, boots, then my sidearm. Last but not least, I struggled my pack on, took one last look at the other men in the tent, and hobbled outside. I'd packed the most important things I needed, just one small bag for me and my brother. There wasn't much need for ordinance where we were going.

I forced myself to a clumsy jog outside, moving past ripped and dirty tents full of coughing, moaning people. We had started with a division between soldiers and civilians, but that division had broken down entirely. The only armed patrols on duty were PALADIN sentry robots: each one seven feet tall, loud, clunky, with sensor arrays instead of faces. They prowled the ragged rows of tents and manned the perimeter gates, standing watch or marching in set patrol routes no longer directed by a human controller. The bots' reflexes were starting to slow as their batteries wound down. When we were healthier, me and the other lepers in quarantine had had fun throwing things onto them in the yard. Hats, scarves... we even uploaded a few videos we called 'Stuff on Our Robot Overlords'.

Unlike human guards, PALs could stand watch at full attention for forty-eight hours – provided they were at full charge. With no one to top up their juice, the ones that were still moving were sluggish, like humans who hadn't had any sleep. Sweat poured down my face in the early morning chill as I broke from cover to cover to keep out of their sight. I focused on putting one foot after the other. My heart was pounding, my guts were cold and twisted with fear. Not only fear of dying, either.

I'd received a text on an old civilian cell phone I'd kept, but now only used for morning alarms. It was a message from my brother, Steve. He hadn't spoken to me in five years. The last time I'd seen him was during the big knockdown, drag-out fight that had ended in me stalking out of his house and out of his life. But three nights ago, Steve had contacted me. He'd sent me only two awful words. "*Mom's dead.*"

Then, ten minutes later. "*I'm sick. If you're alive and uninfected, get to Washington D.C. You're named in my will... there's a place for you in the Capitol Shard. If you're sick... please come home. PLEASE.*"

I was sick, so I was up for Plan B. Guilt tore at me as I waited for a PAL to turn around, and then staggered out from cover and through the ramshackle wire perimeter of the quarantine camp. The robot's rear sensors were covered by a USMC cap that hung at a jaunty angle over the thermal lens. There had been a method to our madness.

My mission was to reach the base's A-Block garage and reunite with the love of my life, Mona. She was waiting for me in the parking lot in spot A-457, concealed by a large locked tarpaulin.

"Hi, baby. How are you doing under there?" I tried to croon to her, but my voice came out as a harsh croak. I unlocked the tarp and pulled it off, throwing it carelessly to the side. Underneath it was a stripped down, banged up Ducati 996X. Mona's bare steel frame hadn't been painted in a while, and her fuel tank had a couple of dents and scratched paint, battle scars from the stunts we did together. Like most motorcycle stuntmen, I'd started on a little 250cc bike, a Ninja, which had enough power to do the job but hadn't punished me when I'd screwed up. I'd worked my way to stunting and racing the Ducati. If you screwed up on an 996X, it *would* punish you. It was the closest thing to a dragon I would ever ride outside of a video game.

I normally enjoyed the ritual of putting on my motorcycle gear, my suit of armor. Kevlar jeans, boots, jacket, helmet, gloves, in that order. Today, I only had gloves and goggles, my sweat-soaked uniform, and a bag. I swung a leg over and took a moment to catch my breath before turning the key. The bike came to life with a deep booming purr, and for a couple of seconds I just sat with it and drank in the way the machine made my body rumble. It would be the second-last time I'd ever ride her.

The first leg was to find my brother. We'd make peace, I hoped, and then I'd take Mona out to the highway and ride as long and as far and as fast as I could. We'd tear up the Big Sur at a hundred and twenty until we were almost out of gas. When the needle touched Empty, the plan was to wheelie jump the bike off a cliff overlooking the Pacific, because screw this whole 'drowning on your own lungs' goat fuckery. I was a stuntman. When I died, it was going to be *spectacular.*

I walked my bike backwards, turning her to line up with the exit ramp, and then threw it into gear. The purr turned into a snarl as the chassis kicked underneath me, the front of the bike briefly lifting as I turned the throttle and screeched off.

The only way in or out of Fort Richard was the main boom gate, but I wasn't the first to desert and I wasn't going to be the last. One of my buddies had given me directions to a section of unmanned fence where waves of soldiers and desperate refugees had cut holes in the wire and poured in and out. As I drew up on it, I could see that he'd been correct, in that the hole was there, but it was now manned. Two PALADINs waited on either side of the gap, which was big enough to admit an elephant. The railguns in their hands and heaps of dead – some in uniform – strewn on the ground around them was testament to why no one was no longer going in or out.

"Shitballs." Resigned to an untimely demise, I threw my bike into third gear, and hunkered down as the Ducati howled. I spun the back wheel, raised a fist, and energetically rasped a battle cry. "PORK CHOP SANDWICHES!"

The robots saw me coming, visored helmets swiveling. They aimed, and I swerved hard and low to the ground. I came out of the zig and zagged as they opened fire where my motorcycle had been only a second before. Any panic I felt in the face of being fired on had been beaten out of me in Indonesia and Syria. I kept my focus and leaned the bike over until the ground tore open the knee of my pants, swooping along the ground and then righting up as I blasted through the hole and sailed out over the embankment below. The robots fired at me during the jump, and several rounds blew by close enough that I felt the sting on my arms, but they were no longer fast enough.

My stomach swooped as the rush hit.

"Sayonara, bitches!" I found myself laughing, giddiness breaking through the cold focus as I rode the heavy machine to the ground, clutching at it with knees and thighs. We hit the dirt, fishtailed, and kept roaring forward.

I nearly ran several civilians down as they stumbled to get out of the way. There were people everywhere out here, a camp much less organized than the one inside of the Fort. Fellow victims of HEX stood around coughing, or staring at me with dead, confused eyes. There were a lot of kids, many without parents. The hard summer ground had somehow been churned to mud, and the air hung heavy with the smells of human misery.

I pulled over to catch breath, which only resulted in a coughing fit that felt like it was going to send my eyeballs shooting out of my head. When I pulled the cloth away from my mouth, it was bloody. I stared at it in impotent rage, and then, with anger burning a hole through my gut, at the huge silhouette in the sky. Looming above us all from the bay was the Golden Gate Shard, a mile-high megastructure that jutted up from the water like a glittering crystal spike. The Generals and Colonels were up in there along with the rest of California's elite, sealed away from HEX and protected from the war they had started.

"Fuckers." Aching, my breath rattling in my chest, I started the motorcycle and set the GPS for my family home on Hyde Street.

Despite not being Chinese, our parents had bought a house on the fringes of San Francisco's Chinatown at a time when housing was still remotely affordable. It was a small rowhouse at the end of a strip of larger rowhouses, with a big parking lot on one side that was always crammed with cars. Now, the lot was abandoned. The chaos and rioting had been and gone, and everyone who'd survived had fled the city to try and escape the spread of HEX. I was shaking with fatigue by the time I pulled up, running on nothing but adrenaline and the cocktail of drugs I'd taken an hour and a half before. It was by will alone that I swung my leg over and stumbled toward the dark green front door. It was the home where Steve and I had grown up. I hadn't been here in seven years.

I pressed a shaking hand to the palm lock, barely believing it would work after all this time. When the lock flashed green and clicked, my legs nearly went out from me. Mom and Dad hadn't completely erased me from their lives after all.

"Steve? Steve, you alive?" I called as I opened the door.

The stench that billowed out of the house was like a slap to the face. I recoiled, struggling not to vomit. Breathing in that dead smell on the battlefield was one thing. Breathing it in at your family home was enough to make me want to run away a second time, as far and as fast as I could.

"Hector?" My brother's voice was a dry rasp, but I could still hear the surprise in it.

Bracing myself, I pushed through the stench and went inside, freezing up for a moment as the old instinct to take my shoes off at the door kicked in. I shook it off and followed Steve's voice to the den. He was propped up on the sofa, a bloody blanket half-fallen over his lap. I knew by looking at him that he well into Day Three. HEX had made a ruin of my tall, handsome brother. His skin was mottled with bruises, his eyes sunken and his face gray. He already looked like a corpse. I stopped in the doorway, too shocked to move or speak.

"Hec... Hector." He wheezed on the 'H', trying to sit up higher. "You made it. Thank God. You look... so fit."

"I call it the 'Forced Conscription Jungle Warfare Diet." My mouth was moving way ahead of my brain at this point. I checked myself. "And apparently I'm a snarky asshole when I'm sick. Sorry."

"Hah." He almost let himself laugh. "You've... you've changed so much."

And you probably haven't. I didn't say it out loud: just forced a smile. "So have you."

"How did... how did you... get here? You were in the Army?"

"I deserted," I said. My voice was cracked, too, and it hurt to speak. But I wasn't as bad as Steve, not yet. "About fucking time, too."

Steve was so exhausted he didn't even notice that I'd sworn. As I came closer, he searched over me in shocked relief. "Deserted? But you... you shouldn't have deserted. Why didn't you ask for leave?"

Typical Steve. "From who? There's hardly anyone left. We were on the front lines for HEX. And I'm dying, Steve - what's the worst they could do, shoot me?"

His eyes focused on the rash on my arms, and then it seemed to finally click. "Oh no. Not you, too."

"Of course, I'm sick," I replied. I sat down on the floor. Sweat poured down my face and down my back. "Everyone's sick. Dead or dying. The city's deserted. We might be the last ones here, bro."

He closed his eyes, as if struggling to process the enormity of it.

"Hey. I brought something for you." I struggled the backpack off and pulled it around.

"What?"

"My RetroConnect," I said. "And granddad's library of games. I know you've been working on those fancy VR rigs and everything, but we used to play together and I thought, 'Fuck it: might as well go out making up stupid Latin words for the Sephiroth theme song one last time'. You know how it goes: 'French frogs, big cherries..."

"Peter Pan, magic cheese. Sephiroth!" He croaked. He couldn't quite get the dramatic chorus falsetto going, but I busted up laughing and coughing anyway.

Steve and I were chalk and cheese in every significant way, and always had been. Games had been the one thing that had brought us together. The sounds of us hacking and wheezing were obliterated by the roar of a helicopter passing by overhead, low to the ground. By the time I could hear anything else, I was wheezing and gasping for air.

"I figure we can do at least one speed run of most of these before we croak," I continued once I got my voice and hand-eye coordination back, taking out the box and the chip with the games, and then the other things I'd brought: candy bars of every shape and size, chips, and energy drinks. "Remember that time we went trick or treating and told dad we were at cram school, and we ate ourselves sick?"

"He nearly killed us," Steve said hoarsely.

He actually had nearly killed me. Dad hadn't just been any normal kind of asshole: he had been a whacko-religious dentist who forbade sugar in the house, especially on Halloween. One year, we'd snuck in a bag of candy and gorged on chocolate and taffy until we'd puked. Dad beat me with a folded electrical cord. Even Steve had gotten a few lashes for that one.

"Here." I passed him some chocolate.

"No," he said. He shook his head, struggling up a little more. "Hector, listen to me. I asked... asked you to come for a reason. Listen-"

"Hear me out, first," I said, unwrapping a candy bar for myself. It helped cover up just how much my hands were shaking. "I came to like... apologize. I hate that we spent so much time fighting. I hate that I was jealous of you and I hate that dad used you to make me feel bad. I hate it that you and him trashtalked me all the way through school. I'm sorry I was such a jerk to you. We don't have much time... and I just want to hear you're sorry for treating me the way you did, then move on and play Secret of Mana until we croak, okay?"

"Hector. Listen," he rasped. "I know this. I know it all. You being alive, being here ch-changes everything. Listen to me. They're coming for me. I'm going to make them take you with me."

"Who? What?" I frowned, trying not to hold my breath. Even though HEX was working its way through my body, I still felt weird about breathing in the air around the infected. Steve had been bright with health not even a week ago. It seemed like the flu took him faster than the others... or maybe I just noticed more.

"Ryuko." He fixed me with a fever glare.

Ryuko? Ryuko was the AI systems company he worked for. I sort of nodded and shook my head at the same time, not sure what he was trying to say.

He reached out his hand for mine. "They're late, but they're coming for me. I'll tell them when they come that... that... I'll make them...make them take you. You go with them, Hector."

"Ryuko? I don't understand." He was babbling, and it creeped me out. I'd never known Steve to talk like this, but he was serious about whatever he was trying to get across to me. His agitation beat against my skin. I squeezed his hand in both of mine. "It's okay, man. You need to rest."

"It's secret... it's..." His eyes wandered past me, and I saw something flash at his temple: a small blue light. His Brain-to-Interface link.

"Ryuko," he whispered, staring at something behind me.

There was a bang on the door, and then another as the wood splintered and then crashed in under the weight of a battering ram. Five years of training and experience kicked in instantly. Coughing, I was up on my feet with my pistol aimed before I'd even had time to think.

"Hector, no!" Steve hissed.

My grip on the pistol sagged at his command, but I was still in firing position as soldiers poured in through the door. Not ordinary soldiers. They were all identical: the same height, the same matte-black bioarmor, the same oversized rifles and terrifying stillness when they came to a stop. The guns were pointed at my face, and I froze in fear and confusion. There were no eyes behind those featureless black visors. They were androids. Machines.

"No fire. No fire!" Steve cringed back into the sofa, lifting his voice until it broke.

"No fire." A woman's voice broke through in the sudden silence.

I eased down as the unseen woman rounded the corner and stood in the doorway, and dropped the pistol down as my eyes widened. She was tall, supermodel perfect, like a vision out of Viking myth. Lean, long legs, a sculpted face like an avenging angel, golden blonde hair pinned up behind her head in a twist underneath a clear, HAZMAT-style helmet. The rest of her outfit looked to me like a fancy white spacesuit, and I wasn't too sick not to notice how the thick leather-like material hugged her curves. I blinked several times, not convinced that I wasn't tripping balls.

The woman looked between the pair of us. "Mister Park?"

"Park One and Park Two, at your service." Every breath hurt like hell, but sassiness was just as incurable as HEX. "Bro, is this-"

"You informed the company that you had no living relatives, Mister Park." She didn't bat an eye. Angel Lady's voice was cool, crisp, and matched her elegant face and hair. Now that she was up close, something was pinging at my uncanny valley reflex. There was something not quite right about this lady. "Has the status of your family changed?"

"Yes," Steve croaked.

"What in the ever-loving fuck is going on?" I asked the room.

Steve shuffled behind me, and I turned to see him sitting upright. He was trembling with the effort, his jaw tense, eyes wild and hot. With a glance at the others, I went to him and helped him to stay up. His hand grasped my forearm, tight and inhumanly strong.

"T-Temperance. This... this is my brother. Little brother." His breath bubbled on every exhalation. "Do... background check under... Park Jeong-Ho."

I flinched at the sound of my birth name.

"Sir, Ms. Hashimoto ordered me to bring *you-*"

"You're too late." Steve retorted, and for a moment, he looked more like himself. He'd always had a fire burning deep inside, a fire he'd manifested by powering through achievement after achievement, scholarship after scholarship. He'd won local and state awards for mathematics and linguistics, joined Mensa, and had gone on to work for Ryuko Entertainment as one of the best AI immersion developers on the United States' side of the Pacific.

"I'm very sorry we weren't here yesterday as we planned, Mister Park," Temperance replied. She didn't sound very sorry. "My transport was delayed by rogue aircraft. If you cannot travel, I am afraid we cannot honor the contract."

"I can travel, and yes, you will honor the contract. Hector is my next of kin," he said, straightening his back. "I want to forfeit my place to him."

"I'm afraid that's not possible," Temperance said. "My orders were to bring you..."

"Get Akari on a BCI channel," Steve said, his voice firm with authority. "Now."

"Yes, sir."

"Steve, what the *fuck* is going on?" I turned on him, suddenly angry.

He glared at me with blood-shot eyes. "Hector. Not now."

Steve's BCI flashed, and then Temperance's. They gazed at each other in silence with faraway expressions for several moments as they exchanged information. Once it was done, Steve sagged back into the sofa, and Temperance stood there like a shop mannequin, inhumanly still. She wasn't breathing.

A gynoid, I realized. Holy shit. There were only a handful of real androids 'alive' in the world, so to speak. The woman in front of me was the real deal - an artificial life form. A walking supercomputer.

"Thank you, Mister Park. Ms. Hashimoto is revising her orders," Temperance said. "I will perform the requested background check. Please look directly at me, Mister Park Jeong-Ho."

"My preferred name is Hector. No 'mister'," I grunted. More out of surprise than anything, I looked up and met her eyes. They were as wide and blue as the Caribbean Sea, a perfect crystalline color that seemed to dance with light.

"Thank you, Mister Park. Management has approved your appeal," she said, after five minutes or so.

Steve shuddered. "Thank God."

I scowled, glancing between them, and got to my feet. "Would either of you like to tell me what the hell is going on?"

"Hector, I am here to execute your brother's contract with the Ryuko Virtual Reality Corporation," the gynoid replied. "Your brother was an employee involved with a project that is being repurposed. Mister Steven Park, if I understand your uploaded testimony, do you vouch that this man is qualified for the trial and you wish to include him under the terms of your contract?"

"Hey, wait a second." I stood, alarmed. "What contract?"

"Yes." Steve choked. "Take him. Please."

Intellectually, I knew Steve was doing something to try and save my ass. What, exactly, I wasn't sure – but I was starting to get pissed off. I'd never had control of my life because of our parents, and now he was trying to control me, too. "Wait! Take me where? To do what?"

"I am the Executive Assistant of Akari Hashimoto, the CEO of Ryuko Corporation," Temperance replied. "I have been ordered to make you an offer as requested by your brother, Ryuko's Senior Virtual Intelligence Developer, Steven Park. The offer must be made in a secure facility, and you are under no obligation to accept the terms and conditions... but it may very well save your life. Would you like to accompany me to discuss your future?"

Chapter 2

This had to be some kind of sick joke. "I've got HEX. I don't have a future."

Temperance tilted her head on her long neck. "Ms. Hashimoto did not send us out here for a prank, Mister Park."

While I boggled, she turned to my brother, who was fighting to not throw up from coughing. "Mister Steven Park, please hold while the medivac assembles." She looked back to me. "Hector, your brother will be removed from this building regardless of your decision. Do you wish to accompany us?"

I looked over at the black-clad troopers. None of them had moved since they'd come into the room and taken position, frozen like statues with perfect trigger discipline. "Why? Are you guys working on a cure, or...?"

"We're working on a lateral solution that may save millions of lives in as soon as ten days' time," Temperance said calmly. "Your brother was part of the project, and has volunteered to help us test it. He has extended his invitation to you."

Millions of lives? What the hell had my brother been working on? It took longer than usual to process everything through the headache and fever, barely controlled by the fistful of meds I'd taken. "If Steve goes, I'll go. But what-"

"I'm not at liberty to discuss anything more outside of company property."

Three more uniformed androids filtered in with what looked like clear glass coffins on rolling trays.

"You are fortunate. Another trial subject passed during the delay we suffered last night." Temperance nodded, her arms loosely folded underneath her breasts. "Because of this, we had a spare containment pod when we received Steven's request."

Whatever it was we were supposed to be doing, I didn't feel fortunate: not when it was at the expense of someone else's death. "Jesus, lady. Did they forget to slot your emotion chip in this morning or something? People are dying. My brother is *dying.* I don't feel 'fortunate'. I feel like an asshole."

"Hector," my brother said warningly.

The gynoid regarded me coolly, her eyes half lidded, lips parted. "My controller disabled my emotional responses for the purposes of this mission. He was concerned that I would not be able to function if I was fully capable of empathy and affect. It would be too distressing to be surrounded by the dead and dying, knowing that you can do nothing to help them, and our mission relies on the speedy and effective recovery of very sick people."

"Oh." Suddenly, I felt even more like a shithead. "Sorry."

"No apology is required. I am also currently incapable of feeling offended." She motioned to the containment pod. "Please stand aside. We will see to your brother first."

The androids clustered around Steve while I waited anxiously on the sidelines. They got a respirator on him, took out his IV, and inserted a new needle into his elbow that was attached to a small portable tank.

Then they lifted him, blankets and all, into one of the pods. When he was inside, it began to hum, and the inside frosted over. The last thing I saw were his eyes looking out at me before they disappeared behind a wall of frost.

"Sir, please hand over all weapons and other gear."

I startled up, looking into the impassive black mask of one of the troopers. No, definitely not human. In a battlefield, he would have passed for human until you'd had a chance to stop and look. I'd never seen robots this advanced before.

Coughing, I removed all of my kit and handed it over, left in nothing but my dirty fatigues. I was given a respirator, a portable IV, and was then guided into the empty pod.

Small spaces have never been my deal. I get claustrophobic in cars, let alone in a glass box roughly the size and shape of a casket. My heart was thundering in my ears as I lay down, beating faster and faster as they shut the lid and a cool cloud of gas puffed out around me. It smelled like disinfectant. There was a click, and then a sudden cold sensation... my head spun and I relaxed. The pain in my joints and skin receded, and as the mask pumped oxygen into my inflamed lungs, I could think again.

Ryuko. I knew who they were, but not why they were here - or where they were taking me and Steve. They were a Japanese-American *zaibatsu*, the biggest developer of virtual reality technology in the world. The company had ascended with the First Total War during the 2030s. That War had been a drone war, and the pilots with the best tech had been the winners: Us, fortunately.

Like other World Wars through history, the years after the First Total War resulted in a technology boom. The VR games I liked to play - adventure games, RPGs, shooting and racing - were all based on the tech developed during that time. And that's what I thought of, when I thought of Ryuko: wargames, drone systems, and RPGs. I'd known Steve had been working his way through the ranks, but not that he'd ascended to the level where he was on first-name terms with the CEO.

We were wheeled out of the house and onto the street, where more super troopers waited to escort us. They fell in around us as we bumped our way down the road, and I twisted to see my motorcycle one last time before we turned the corner of Hyde Street. The helicopter I had heard earlier was sitting right in the middle of the street, and it was a beauty – a sleek black bio-drone with a giant faceted eye in place of a windshield, like a dragonfly's eye. It was already idling, and the blades sped as we were carried into the bright, clinical cabin and taken to the rear of the ship. There was a bank of autosurgery pods back there, the bases ready to receive our glass-fronted Snow White coffins. Another half dozen men and women were laid out there already. All of them were sedated. My brother's coworkers? I didn't recognize any of them.

I watched anxiously as Steve was lowered onto his bed. Almost immediately, the surgical machine got to work. The glass rippled as tools came out to tap his new IV and feed him a cocktail of drugs I could only guess at. Mine did the same: I lay back and tried to relax as whirs and soft clicks echoed around me.

Temperance sat down next to my pod with her legs crossed, her back straight and chest lifted. It was easy to imagine her in a secretary's blouse, pumps and pencil skirt. She seemed to know how to effortlessly position her body for maximum attractiveness, like something out of a movie – or a hentai. Too perfect to be real.

"Hector." Her lips moved, but her voice came from a hidden speaker near my ear. "Given the abrupt change in plans, I regret that we could not give you a more detailed explanation of why we are airlifting you, but I assure you that all will be explained."

"Can you..." I trailed off to swallow, not entirely convinced I wasn't tripping balls after being dosed up with who-knows-what drugs straight into the vein. "Ma'am, can you give me, like, the summary version?"

Temperance turned to watch me with dulcet blue eyes. "When we are in the air."

That wasn't going to be far off. I lay back and focused on my breathing while the doors to the chopper racked shut. It began to hum like a hive of angry hornets. Within ten minutes, we were clear for takeoff, and my stomach lurched as we picked up off the ground, swaying, then angled as the chopper headed for the sky.

"If it's an experimental treatment, my answer is yes." Soldiers developed a high tolerance for getting jabbed and pumped full of strange shots. "I'll do it. I don't care if it kills me."

"We are not offering drug treatments," Temperance said. She blinked, lowering her chin toward her chest. "As you may know, Ryuko is the world's leading manufacturer of virtual reality solutions, both for entertainment and utility purposes. This helicopter, the autosurgery units, and my protection team are all being remotely guided by AIs. I myself am in constant contact with my Controller, who was evacuated to the Meridian Shard. Like everyone else, we have committed our resources to saving as many people as we can. It is obvious that we face a bottleneck extinction event."

I coughed, hacking up phlegm that was delicately suctioned up by a soft tube. "No shit."

"The Shard arcologies are completely full. The European-Near East Union has evacuated the maximum number of citizens to the Yetzirah space station, but artificial biospheres are unstable and have a very limited capacity. It's simply not possible to evacuate everyone still healthy, which means that we must find a cure, or think spatially about ways to preserve life."

Ugh, Shards. I hated the Shards and everything they symbolized. They were super-skyscrapers, huge crystal and carbon spires that towered above cloud height. Each one could support about a hundred thousand people, give or take. Politicians, corporate executives, and military officers, the elites who'd never shed blood on the battlefield, got the first pickings at salvation. A lot of them were guys my age, rich draft dodgers. The rest of us were left to cough our lungs out, literally. In chunks. "No way-" I paused to do just that for a second. "N-No way will they find a cure in time."

Temperance nodded. "No. That is the consensus."

"Then what are we doing up here?"

"The information you are about to receive is top secret." Temperance folded her hands in her lap, her head turned toward me. Traceries of azure light flickered through her eyes as she processed and thought about whatever it was she was going to say. "Ryuko has two divisions: a civilian division, and a contracted military division. The divisions exchange technological innovations, repackaging military applications for civilian use, and vice-versa. Our military division works on a number of systems for the Air Force and the 101st Powered Armor Division, and over the course of the Second Total War, we developed the technologies that turned the tide against the Pacific Alliance... true brain-to-interface hardware, and software capable of managing full-contact, full-immersion connections... and systems that are capable of storing the information transmitted by the brain to a network."

I swallowed, grimacing at the dry, itchy discomfort. "You can copy things from people's minds?"

"And *to* people's minds." Temperance smiled. "And even more than that: we have been able to replicate consciousness. A copy of a person's mind can become a self-functioning 'AI' within a network. Or a virtual reality scenario. We call this technology *GNOSIS*, and the supervisory AI system *OUROS*. With these systems, we have been able to create functioning 'copies' of our best drone pilots. So rather than one flying ace, we have ten – all of whom can remotely pilot a machine in formation, while communicating instantly with each other."

THAT'S what Steve had been working on? I listened on in rapt silence as Temperance continued.

"Besides the military applications, we also had a side project: a 'lite' version of OUROS and its accompanying systems were being repurposed for the world's first full-immersion videogame engine," she said. "Entertainment is still important during war-time, after all. The first game using this engine was scheduled for release early next year. A full sensory immersion VR-RPG, with the working title of 'Archemi Online'."

My chest rattled as I breathed in. Even the strong mix of pain meds and anti-inflammatories I was getting wasn't taking the fluid out of my lungs. And by tomorrow... I really didn't want to think about it. "An MMO?"

"Archemi is, in every way, a true virtual world." Temperance's lips quirked. "It's not really a MMORPG... it's orientated toward single-player or small-group play, much like real life. We had hoped to give people a release from all the horror in the world. There were going to be limitations on log-in time and many other failsafes, but after HEX began to spread, President Hashimoto decided to repurpose the Archemi project to something more beneficial. We have now integrated the system with our BigBrain Cloud AI and have established near unlimited storage. The goal was to create a limitless population of human minds, experience, and personalities."

Well... shit. "That's a lot to digest. What does Steve have to do with it?"

"Your brother was a senior project developer on the civilian OUROS project," she replied. "All of the people working on these projects were given the opportunity to sign a contract with us that would allow them to participate in innovative research. Essentially, the employee had the option to be uploaded to BigBrain if they ever developed a terminal condition, to see if their consciousness would persist if the body ceased to work. The problem with GNOSIS is that the upload process is still unreliable. OUROS needs at least a thousand uploads before it really learns how to do it flawlessly. We were willing to work that out over the next century with willing volunteers, but..."

"HEX happened," I finished.

"HEX, and the ongoing nuclear threat to Japan and the USA," Temperance replied. "Everyone has scrambled to finish Archemi and refine the upload process, but we still need that first thousand or so, the vanguard of volunteers. Without them, we can't make GNOSIS stable enough to reliably upload the unique brain patterns of millions of people as fast as we need to. And that, Hector, is the basis of the agreement we made with your brother and will hopefully make with yourself."

I licked my lips and frowned up at the frosty surface of my capsule. "What kind of setting is Archemi?"

"Open world fantasy with steampunk and 'dark fantasy' elements. Archemi is part of a paracosm. Do you know what that means?"

"Nope."

"A paracosm is a complete, self-contained reality which encompasses its own physics, mythos, characters, cultures, and environs beyond a planetary scale. Famous examples of paracosms include Discworld, Middle Earth, the Forgotten Realms and Elder Scrolls. Are you familiar with them?"

Now, *that* was a list of names that brought back good memories – the time I spent with my grandparents before they died. Dad's parents had grown up reading and playing all those games, along with Korean and American MMOs. They only had memories of those MMORPGs – but their collections of single-player games were something they'd shared with me and Steve. My *Halbi* and *Halmon* had cared about me in a way dad never had.

"Yeah. I had... *have* a thing for old games. My grandad used to play Elder Scrolls." I had to pause to catch my breath. "Steve volunteered for this? To be uploaded to Archemi?"

"Yes. Along with many others involved with the project. As I've said, Archemi is in early beta. There are bugs and in-game issues we must resolve before we risk giving false hope to the public."

And I was lucky enough to be one of the guinea pigs. "What's the catch, ma'am?"

She sighed. "At present, we cannot upload people who are in advanced stages of illness. However, with every successful upload, the GNOSIS-OUROS system learns and we increase our odds by percentage. Once we have processed another two hundred uploads, the system should be stable enough to attempt the first mass immigration."

"Okay. By failure, you mean death, right?"

Temperance nodded.

"What are the odds?"

"For people at your stage of infection, one in eight."

I swallowed hard, shuddering. One in eight wasn't great odds, but that was a... what? 87.5 percent chance to survive? Not bad. I was currently running at 100 percent toward an early mass grave.

My brow broke out in a sheen of sweat that had nothing to do with the flu. I rubbed some more fog off so I could see Temperance's face. "What's it like? Archemi? What... options do I have there?"

To my surprise, Temperance smiled. Maybe they'd re-enabled her empathy features now we were off base. "The world has both original and familiar features common to medieval fantasy and steampunk. The world itself is beautiful. Stunning. The best artists in the world have been laboring on it for more than five years. The game itself is quite open-ended. For the purposes of the refugee program, many of the major threats and challenges players expect will not be present, but there will still be some conflict available for more martial players."

Beautiful, huh? I had no idea what kind of life I could expect as a virtual avatar in a virtual paracosm - if you could consider it a life - but it had to be better than this shit. The process might kill me, maybe, but my brother was willing to do it. And he'd included me at the end. No matter what he thought of my chocolate-binging, motorcycle riding worthless ass... he'd wanted to help me. He'd probably been sitting on this for months.

I closed my eyes, drew as deep a breath as I was able to, and sighed it out with a wheeze that made my chest ache. "Okay. Count me in. For science."

Chapter 3

By the time we reached the facility, I knew I was dying. I was consumed by the horrible, powerless sensation of my body tearing itself apart while an army of millions of viruses replicated explosively through my cells. The pod had been managing me so well that I'd almost forgotten how sick I was for a couple of hours, until I went to sleep... and woke up strangling and panicked, coughing blood as I heaved for air and found only pain.

The helicopter landed on a helipad that then sunk down into a building with a deep underground basement. Or sub-basement. I couldn't tell where we were, exactly - east of the Cascades, that was for sure. My pod was carried out by the men in black, Temperance following behind as we were loaded onto a transport truck. It rumbled off down a dark corridor of rough stone. I lost track then, fading in and out of consciousness.

When I woke up again, I was sitting upright and everything around me was white - blinding white. The room hummed with voices speaking softly at a distance, and it smelled like clean, new plastic. I was in a chair I could only describe as a throne. It was huge. I felt like Alice in fucking Wonderland.

The chair was connected to a tower pulsing with blue light. 'Ryuko Industries BigBrain' was emblazoned across the side. It took me a little while longer to realize that I'd been pulled out of my clothes and put into plain white pajamas, and that I was inside of an inflatable bubble that sealed me off from the rest of the room. The people outside of the bubble were all in the same slinky HAZMAT that Temperance wore.

My chest was rattling and I was barely able to sit, but I wasn't in pain any more. More curiously, I had a HUD. The holographic display hovered in front of me, a round blue portal roughly the size of a door. It was monitoring my vitals, all of which were shit. On instinct, I reached back, and touched something metallic behind my head. A cold, rounded surface with a thin edge, floating. Like a halo, but rotating behind my skull instead over it. *What in the shit...?*

I jumped as I caught movement out of the corner of my eye, flinching with a soldier's instincts. It was Temperance. She'd changed into a different frogsuit. IT was jet black, a startling contrast to the rest of the room.

"Good afternoon, Hector," she said. "And thank you for volunteering. I'll be here to walk you through everything."

"Where's Steve? Where's my brother?" I gripped the arms of the BigBrain Throne, glancing back and forth between her and the HUD. I was used to them - every game with a headset used a floating menu just like this one, as did a lot of military tech - but I wasn't wearing a headset. That was the weird part.

"Mister Steven Park has agreed to attempt upload despite his advanced illness and low odds of success. He is in a separate laboratory doing this very same exercise. Are you ready to be walked through what will happen?"

"Hit me," I said.

"You have been fitted with an upgraded Brain-to-Computer interface: a Ryuko PRISM Corona which is capable of utilizing the experimental GNOSIS system. I explained GNOSIS to you earlier," she said, walking over to stand in front of me. She had a corona of her own, completing her angelic beauty. "Coronae greatly improve GNOSIS outcomes. They are the absolute peak of our technology, Hector – computers comprised entirely of nanorobots engaged in constant exchange."

"Right." I nodded, exhaling heavily on every shallow breath. As far as I was concerned, nanotech was sorcery. I preferred machines you could see.

"We require you to sign the same waivers and other documents as your brother," Temperance said. "I will assist you to call them to your heads-up display. You may sign simply by uploading the document, and then thinking of your name when the document has been digested and you are prompted to do so."

Nervously, I sat back and rested my hands on my knees to keep them from trembling. I'd never had anything uploaded via BCI before. "Go ahead."

My head pulsed, and suddenly, I knew all the details of Ryuko's waivers and liability policies. Just like that.

"SHIT!" If I'd had any strength left, I'd have leapt out of my chair. Because I didn't, I sort of flailed around like an angry jellyfish and then slumped back, wheezing with effort. "*Dude!* Fuck!"

"Do you hereby agree to remove all liability of damages from Ryuko Virtual Solutions, its corporate affiliates, subsidiaries, and partners?" Temperance asked... Inside my head. She didn't speak out loud. Too weird.

"Yes...?" I spoke aloud out of habit. That seemed to work, because a word suddenly popped into my head. 'Signature'. I thought of my name in reply, and that was that. Other than a warm sensation behind my eyes, I was no worse for wear after the info-dump.

Temperance flashed me a sympathetic smile. It reached her brilliant eyes this time – someone had their empathy chip back in. "Alright. When you're ready, we'll begin the upload. You will be put into twilight anesthesia for this step, and then full anesthesia to induce a coma. Are you ready to begin?"

Was I? I couldn't shake the feeling that I was missing something thanks to the virus... that everything was going too fast, that I was setting myself up for something. I felt like I'd only just walked through my family's front door, and the stench of death was still in my nostrils. I searched back through the waiver, but the information seemed to be getting tangled up with my fear. What was going to happen to my body? I'd always been a physical guy... motorcycles, parkour, martial arts, stuff that engaged the senses. The thought of losing all of that was suddenly terrifying.

"Hector?"

I closed my eyes, struggling for a moment. At least I knew what was going to happen with HEX. "Before I say anything... tell me what's going to happen to my body when I die. And my brother's."

"When you have successfully uploaded, we will induce your body into a coma and support you for the duration of your natural life. After you have passed, your remains will be cryogenically preserved for research by Ryuko and its affiliated companies. One of our first partnerships involves developing a cure for the H5N1-X virus."

Body. Remains. Numbly, I checked through the tangle of information uploaded by the waiver, and sighed. It was there, right in the contract. "Alright. Do it."

"Please confirm again: you are ready to begin?"

My heart hurt, spasming painfully in my chest. It was inflamed already, but now it was rattling along at high speed. At this rate, I was going to have a heart attack before I, or my virtual clone, reached Archemi.

"Yes. I'm ready." I replied firmly.

The white suits outside of our bubble flew into motion, working at virtual terminals and doing things that made the blue-glowing tower thrum and surge to life. All the scientists had coronas too.

Temperance crouched in front of me, visible through the glowing blue HUD. Her expression was one of calm compassion, but no breath fogged the inside of her helmet. "Look at me, Mister Park, and watch my lips. I'm going to count down from ten, and when I reach one, you will be sent on your way."

I licked the sweat off my lip, and tried to compose myself. The Norse had this old myth about warriors being carried off the battlefield by beautiful Valkyries. I was a warrior, and my Valkyrie was Temperance: six feet in heels, long legs, porcelain pale skin. She had a full mouth... it looked surprisingly soft.

"Ten." Her lips framed the word like a blessing.

Beautiful as she was, I closed my eyes. This was the best thing I could do for myself and everyone else. My family was gone. My parents were dead, my brother, too... maybe.

"Nine."

At least one of my family could live on. Me or Steve, maybe both of us. I was sure that I wasn't going to be that one of guys that died doing this. I wasn't going to be afraid.

"Eight."

... But I wasn't ready. A whine built in my ears, and my stomach tensed horribly, a sensation I'd only felt once before: the gut twist of terror when I'd first been set out to the front lines. The IV was pushing something warm into the vein in my elbow now, and it was spreading through me in a wave, turning my limbs to jelly. Was I dying? Distantly, I realized that I couldn't move any more.

"*Seven.*"

I was bracing for six, but it never came. The reddish darkness of my eyelids inverted into roaring white. I was pulled up toward something with crushing speed. My heartbeat was there one moment, and then it was gone. A roar built in my ears, thunderous and terrifying.

This is what I imagined being the passenger in a plane crash felt like. For all I knew, I was clutching the arms of my chair and pushing back into it while the corona and GNOSIS did their work, ripping a duplicate of my brain like a bootlegged movie. I might have been in pain - there was no way to tell. Same with time. As it ticked on without even a heartbeat to count by, I was more and more convinced that something had gone wrong, that I hadn't made it. I was about to die or... was I already dead? What if this was it? Maybe the end was just this. Nothing.

Then the white turned to green, and the howling pressure stopped and rushed away. My consciousness spread out like a web through my nerves. I could feel again, though I couldn't see any limbs. There was nothing but a green field when I tried to look down and around.

"Hey... can any of you hear me out there?" There was no sound when I spoke, which was bizarre, because I *felt* the words come out. My throat worked, my lungs drew air, but there was no body I could see. I'd just made up my mind to start screaming until someone paid attention to their monitor when the blank environment turned black, and then opened up onto the biggest battlefield I'd ever seen.

Chaos. That was the only way to describe it. The stench, the screams, the whine of magical bolts impacting against shields and barriers that flashed and crackled when struck, the roar of warriors surging in formation against one another. My breathing sped, mostly out of surprise that I could feel the wind, smell the reek of medieval warfare, and I *still* didn't have a body. But I sure as hell had ears, because when a huge black dragon tore through the sky over my 'head', bugling a harsh, hateful cry, I flinched down out of pure reflex.

The thing was the size of an airliner, with a blunt, T-Rex-like head, long horns, and hard black scales covered in spines. I gaped after it as a V-formation of armored dragoons followed on its tail, ruffling my skin with the wind as their griffin-like mounts screeched above and around me. The dragoons split as the dragon wheeled and backwinged in mid-air, barking gouts of blue fire as they surrounded it. One of the fireballs caught a dragoon full on, incinerating mount and rider. My nose seared with the smell of ozone and cooked flesh as the convulsing, charred beast began a lazy death spiral toward the ground, the skeletonized rider still tied into their saddle.

"The shores of the Terenthal continent, on a world whose name has long been forgotten." A clear female voice heavy with grief spoke from right beside me, and when I looked across, I saw the flickering outline of something that looked like a ghost without distinct features or form. *"Just over a hundred years ago, the Vrath'kha Drachan - the Void Dragons - opened a portal to this place and began their conquest. The Terenthali were the last to fall. This was their final stand, the stragglers who had managed to escape the Drachan and their servant-children, the Rostori. I wish I could say it ended in victory. It did not."*

The scene shifted. We hung over a massive volcano, the edge of which was ringed by screeching, snapping black and red Drachan who carried riders: The Rostori. They were tall, proud, vaguely reptilian horned people in ebony and steel plate armor. The core of the volcano was blue with magic, not orange with lava. It was a brilliant white-blue, burning and surging like the core of a star. The Rostori were throwing captives off the backs of their mounts into the caldera. My stomach turned at the callousness of it... then clenched tightly as a rumbling growl bent the sky around us, shaking the ground. I looked back and forth for the source of the sound, not seeing anything until the heads of the dragons all turned in the same direction and bowed in prostration to the monster that flew in overhead like a rotting jumbo jet.

This dragon was dead. It was a skeleton, the tattered rags of its wing membranes and skin turned to leather that trailed behind it like banners. A flexing field of dark light crawled and spat through its bones, an effect which left me feeling queasy as it circled the volcano in eerie silence. The wind tore over it... it was huge, and its riders were tiny by comparison. I saw them when the beast glided down to land gracefully in the space that had been cleared for it by the other dragons. The tallest man wore a suit of fluted death's head armor and a crimson cloak, his face masked. The other two had their helmets off. One was a woman with swept back horns and vivid red markings on her skin. The other was a man with the same horns, but no birthmarks. They both had scarlet-red hair of the same deep wine color.

"The Rostori triumphed over this world as they had many others, draining the land dry for their magic. For magic is not endless... it is drawn from the earth itself, and when unnatural creatures like this dracolich drain it to sustain their undeath, the earth is dead within five hundred years."

"Damn," I said, more to myself than anything. "You'd think you'd learn after the first time."

"You presume they have the desire," the Narrator replied.

I nearly jumped out of my skin. I had *not* been expecting a reply.

"The Drachan and Rostori destroyed their home planet long ago, and are never satisfied by what they have. They do not learn from their mistakes. That is the nature of greed and narcissism. The greatest of the Elder Drachan sustain themselves by pillaging planets of their magic. They teach that mercy is weakness, and cruelty is strength."

Just as I opened my mouth to speak, the undead dragon reared up and raised its foreclaws, posing them in a series of arcane gestures as it began a rumbling chant. Its voice was like boulders tumbling down a dry mountain. The Rostori continued the sacrifices, and soon, the thunderous volcano drowned out the victim's screams.

"To move from one world to the next, the Drachan use the Dragon Gates, vast wells of mana, the stuff of magic," *the narrator continued on calmly. "They gathered the last of the magic of this world and used it to travel to the next. Our world... the world of Archemi."*

The volcano erupted with a column of white fire, and I nearly wrenched my neck following it as it shot into the sky, illuminating the massive dark army I hadn't seen in the valley below. The light drowned out sound and vision, throwing me around like a leaf. The indistinct sensation of floating was replaced by the swooping, giddy momentum of flight.

I broke out of the blinding light into a sweep of massive forested mountains. My stomach dropped out as the ground sped beneath me. I could feel *everything.* The wind, the hot sun on my back, the turbulence of the air. It was the freshest air I'd ever smelled. We'd long ago trashed Earth, even before the Total Wars and HEX and everything, and I'd ever only seen places like this in History class. It was brilliant and bright, tainted only by the knowledge of what I'd just seen before. It was almost too bright, like they'd turned the saturation up on the blue of the sky and the green of the forest. I crested a ridge, and came up over a huge walled city that faded off into farmland as the valley wound off between the mountain peaks.

"Archemi, however, is different to the worlds that the Drachan and their slaves conquered in the past for two powerful reasons," my narrator said. *"Archemi has dragons of its own, a wise and sophisticated*

race wholly different to the greedy Drachan. Not only does it have dragons, it has you, and people like you."

"Because every world needs more angry, dyslexic Korean washouts," I joked.

"Do not be so quick to disparage yourself, Hector. You are Starborn, one of the immortal Souls of Fate incarnated on Archemi in times of crisis. An age ago, when the ocean split and the Drachan entered our world, they brought monsters with them. The Starborn appeared, and with the help of the native dragons of our world, the invaders suffered their first defeat – but at great cost. The first races of Archemi were all but destroyed. Huge swathes of land were Stranged with magic, becoming twisted wastelands crawling with monsters where there were none before - but we did win. The Drachan were forced into an unquiet sleep, the Rostori bound to the frigid wastes of the far North. They are trapped there by the Caul of Ancestors, a powerful magical barrier called into beings by the sages of all Archemi's races. Archemi has known peace ever since... but the Rostori have not forgotten their mission, and they know that greed is infectious. It is only a matter of time before they find their way free. As that risk increases, more Starborn will appear... but it is up to them whether they help or hinder the threat to Archemi. Which brings us back to the now. You, Hector, are a Starborn: a soul waiting for a body. And you have a unique and difficult choice ahead of you."

I startled from the story trance and turned to the narrator-ghost, who looked back at me with a face like liquid light.

"Hector, it is time for you to choose your place here. Will you remain a soldier, fighting for a king or nation? Will you give into your rebellious nature and become a criminal, or an assassin? Will you become a priest of your people, worshipping and working with the local gods? Will you become a dragon knight and fly the skies, or a hedge knight who wanders the land?"

My heart skipped. *...A dragon knight? As in, a knight on an actual dragon?*

I thought I saw the narrator smile. "*Your destiny is in your own hands, Hector, and you have complete freedom to decide your path... but choose wisely, because your decisions may not just affect you, but the course of history.*"

Chapter 4

The valley and city faded out, and I found myself standing in a neutrally lit room surrounded by a ring of enormous, fancy mirrors. My reflection looked like me. I was medium-height, with a stocky build that had leaned towards fat before the Army and was now mostly muscle. I had a crewcut, a hard jaw, wide cheekbones, dark eyes that blinked when I blinked. They'd even included my acne scars, but fortunately, not the deathly, rashy skin or hollow cheeks caused by HEX. I looked down at myself, and saw I had all five appendages intact. Curious, I reached out and touched the glass in front of me. It was cold, smooth... whatever the hell tech they were using to generate this level of neural feedback, I was seriously impressed.

"As you've guessed already, this is the character creation room," the ghostly narrator said. She sounded happier now. "First things first. Due to the emergency repurposing of the game, you have the option of creating an adventure-ready player character suitable for combat quest roles, or defaulting to a simplified creation process which draws on your natural strengths and experience. We recommend that people who wish to participate in civilian Life Skill paths - such as craftsmen, farmers, merchants or other non-combative occupations - select the simplified character creation stream."

"No thanks," I said. "I want adventurer creation."

A detailed HUD scrawled into view. It was ornate, in a subtle, elegant way, but otherwise a pretty standard UI... all the meaty RPG stats, inventories, skill trees, and suchlike.

"Archemi's menu system is underpinned by an encyclopedic archive. Navigate the menus and archives by thought. It doesn't matter if you decide to use voice or gesture at first - as time goes on, you'll train the menu to react with your intentions and needs," the narrator said. "The first thing you'll want to do it to choose your race and sub-race. Archemi is large and diverse, with civilizations and nations with distinct cultures. Try thinking *'show race menu'.*"

Open race menu. I changed her words in my head, interested to see how it responded.

A tab popped up, spooling into a short list of playable races, each one with a sub-menu:

+Artanese

+Meewfolk

+Mercurion

+Dauntan

Only four races? That was a bit of a letdown. Frowning, I opened the +Artanese sub-category, and suddenly faced another list of options:

++Dakhari

++ Vlachian

++Sharet

++Sathbari Plainsman

++Hercynian

++Khago

++Okinevan

++Jeunan

Artanese humans - they were humans - were tall and vaguely elf-like. They didn't have pointed ears, but they had large, expressive eyes, no matter their skin color or other features. The Dakhari were dark-skinned, the warm ochre-brown you saw in India and the Middle East; the Sathbari were even darker. The sample Hercynian characters looked mostly Caucasian or Mediterranean, and the Jeun were the most elf-like: tall, lithe, elegant, and Asiatic.

When I thought 'Dakhari', a much longer list and a short description opened:

Dakhari (Artanese, Race)

"The Dakhari are the dominant human people in Dakhdir, a large nation in The Shalid, a region in the South of Artana, which is the largest continent of Archemi. They have a caste-based culture divided into nobility, merchants, warriors, and peasantry (or the townsman ancestors of peasantry). In addition, there are two 'outcaste' groups: sorcerers and untouchables, who are both known as 'Shallatu', or Fireblooded."

Huh. I whistled as the complexity of the character creation really began to dawn on me. If I went Dakhari, I could choose my general social starting position, whether or not I was urban or rural, and a bunch of other variables. Each one had their pros and cons, stacking into a complete character picture. If you played a higher caste, you didn't get any special physical perks, but you got the perks of that caste. Shallatu started off with fantastic physical stats, but steep social and economic impediments. There was a lot of reading to do, but I wanted to get a general idea of the main race options before I started drilling down too far. The Fireblooded had me curious, though. My curiosity was obviously enough of a prompt, because I got an explanation:

Fireblooded (Dakhari)

Dakhari Fireblooded are so called because of their coloration and unique relationship to magic. They are universally tall, strong and good-looking, with vivid red or orange hair and gold or red eyes. Fireblood always runs true – every child who has one Fireblooded parent will themselves be Fireblooded. However, rates of fertility are very low, with only one in every ten adults able to have children. Men and women are of equal height and near-equal strength.

Believed to be the descendants of demons, they are pariahs within their country and culture - though not necessarily outside of it. They start with a -10 social penalty (-15 with Caste-loyal Dakhari) and severely reduced resources, but they are immune to Stranging and take reduced damage from all magic.

"What's Stranging?" I'd barely formed the question when a tooltip opened.

Stranging

When living creatures are exposed to raw mana, the toxic effects of liquid magic will mutate and/or harm them. Stranging is a phenomenon which ranges from radiation burns to dementia, infertility, sickness, and in extreme cases, mutation and division into monsters. All Starborn (player characters) have limited resistance to Stranging, but not complete immunity.

Infertility? That implied fertility as well, which meant... I could father babies here? Jeez. Hopefully they had condoms as well. Stranging definitely sounded like something I wanted to avoid... it made me wonder how mages didn't curl up and die with their first spells. And dementia? Given this was a beta, who the hell knew what would happen if you got dementia in a video game?

The Sathbari were basically dino-riding plains warriors, proud Afro-Asian people who dressed in buckskins, furs, and hard leather armor tanned from hookwings, dinosaurs that looked pretty much like oviraptors with feathers. The Hercynians were European-esque, divided into nationals who ranged from swarthy Grecian people to moon-cheese-marshmallow white. As my tooltips helpfully informed me, Hercynia comprised a region of six unique, economically powerful nations on a peninsula on the far West point of Artana.

I found I was able to bookmark things of interest while I waded through the database and learned more about the world and its cultures. The Jeun Empire was cool - kind of like ancient Korea plus magitech as far as I could tell - but mostly orientated toward magic users and artificers. Not really my bag. I respected magic classes, but I wasn't any good with them.

"Show me the Dauntans." I spoke aloud before remembering I was supposed to be thinking my way around the menu.

The menu faithfully appeared. There were only two sub-races of Dauntan: Tungaant and Lysidian. The Lysidian WERE elves: gracile, urbane, orientated towards ranged combat and magic, with long pointed ears and a skin color palette that ranged from coal black (in the equatorial nations) to an interesting pale blue-gray. Judging by what I read, the city I'd seen in the intro was one of theirs. Elves weren't really my schtick - I preferred races that were a bit rougher around the edges, and that's what I got with the Tuun.

The Tuun were basically Tibetan Vikings. They were craggy humans who wore dark colors and crossover jackets, heavy fleece, leather, and cleated boots. They had a Eurasian look about them, with the tanned skin and the rosy cheeks of people constantly exposed to the wind and sun. They were tall and strong featured, with clear, piercing eyes and unusual square pupils.

Tuun (Daun, Race)

The Tuun are the rugged, independent people of the Nima Plateau, from the north of Daun. Tough, resourceful and stoic, they live a semi-nomadic lifestyle with their dinosaur herds and circulate through several ancient mountain cities. The nation is loosely ruled by a council of three abbots, the Chitahbach (Songmaster or 'Disciple of the Tongue'), the Dragahbach (Skymaster, 'Disciple of Sky') and Kanachba (Stonemaster, 'Disciple of the Ground'). They each head one of the three main orders within the Tuun religious tradition, which is known as Ruhebah (The Way, literally 'Path-finding'). As one of the oldest contiguous civilizations in Archemi, they have a unique relationship with dragonkind, and dragons were once an important bridge between their far-flung communities.

Dragons? Hell yes. As I read through the options, I began to feel that stirring excitement you get when you've hit on the right character. Tuun were tough, a bit anti-social, and they basically grew up on horseback - well, dino-back. They had some heavy resistances to disease and bonuses to mobility and riding, but no protection from magic. They had some features that would make a good dragon knight character, if that was a real class. I bookmarked them as well.

The Meewfolk – that was their 'common' name, not the name they called themselves - were pretty much walking, talking Siamese cats.

They weren't particularly anthropomorphized, looking more like cats than people, with elegant long digitigrade legs and long fingers with toe-bean pads. I was surprised to find that Meewfolk probably made for the best fast combat builds in the game. Female Meewfolk, anyway - they were intensely sex-segregated, with females taking on the warrior and lore-keeping duty in cities, and males leaning towards rogue and bard classes in nomadic gangs. If I wanted to play a Swordsman or Monk/Striker class, they'd be the one I'd go for.

Then it was time for the Mercurions. I opened them up, and my breath caught. I'd seen images of two of each race: male and female. There were six example Mercurions. They ranged from a short, muscular, very masculine guy through to a very tall androgynous person who was clearly neither male or female. But they were gorgeous. The Mercurions had smooth silver skin and swept back wings made of crystal in place of ears. Their hair looked like spun glass: translucent, but flexible. Their faces were exquisitely beautiful, the kind of heavy, sweet beauty I associated with angels and renaissance paintings.

Mercurions (Zaunt, Race)

Strange living constructs created to fight dragons, Mercurions painstakingly craft each new generation of their kind. The foundation of Mercurion society is the family. Their clans are called Tlaxican ('Lineages') which vary extensively in size and power. Tlaxican measure their wealth in the number of children they have, the quality of those children, and the reserves of mana they have to create them.

To reproduce, Mercurions sculpt their children with a mana-treated elastomer, glass, silicon-carbonite (which is relatively common in Zaunt, their island homeland) and specially treated metals. Their techniques are derived from the technological processes used by the Aesari and Drachan nearly 4000 years ago, and are one of the closest-kept secrets in Archemi. They are known for their haunting music, their expertise as Artificers and Assassins, and their level-headedness. Mercurions live in subterranean cities which are deadly to living beings due to the poison gases and raw mana in the air.

As constructs, Mercurions are sexless and genderless. Instead, there are six types of Mercurions made to fulfill certain social roles, such as combat, music or magic. They are also painfully short-lived, though this is not so much of a concern for the rare Starborn among them.

Their pages were pretty detailed: just as well, given how alien they were. I queried 'Aesari' out of curiosity, but nothing came up. A mystery, then.

I was really tempted by the *Joh* build Mercurion - described as tall, muscular and masculine - but I wanted to play someone who was on good terms with dragonkind, not purpose-made to kill them. My eyes were drawn back to the Tuun. When I thought about the male avatar, he appeared in the mirror in front. I liked the compact, tough, confident look about him. He looked like someone who could build something for himself, make his own way in the world. He looked *free.*

My whole life had been spent in a cage of other people's needs. My parents had pushed me and Steve both to the limit at school. He'd done well, while I had my first breakdown in late elementary school. My dad said I got bad grades were because I was a lazy sinner who played videogames instead of working. In reality, I just couldn't read. My eyes would skip over the words, and I couldn't concentrate on them unless I was moving. Neither of my parents believed me, because *their* son couldn't have a learning disability. I was just supposed to pray more.

I got into VR games as an escape from the pressure and batshit religion, because games had text-to-speech options and the freedom of swinging a sword, riding a horse, owning a house. And I was good at it, just like I was good at riding. In the months before the war, I'd found freedom in motorcycles and had started auditioning for stunt work in Los Angeles. I rode Mona in stunt competitions, and had just made a friend in the racing business when the Second Total War broke out and they called the draft. Steve hadn't had to serve, because he was working for Ryuko and the corp filed a petition for him.

I didn't have anyone on my side with that kind of money. I was a dyslexic revhead who was good with bikes and games and not much else. It was the rank and file for me... and the brief taste of freedom I'd had vanished forever.

The reflection in the mirror shifted, and suddenly, I was looking at a cleverly blended composite of my face and body meshed with that of a Tuun. The AI had even selected my preferred hairstyle. Tuun men had varying hairstyles with a common theme: two thin braids that started from the back of the neck, wrapped in red cloth and bound with metal rings. They could be worn down the back or front. The one I liked had them at the front, while the rest of my hair was shaved along the sides and braided along the top like a mohawk. I chose that one, and my hair changed to match.

Overall, my character looked... well, pretty damn awesome. Ripped in a natural warrior-fit kind of way; masculine, energetic. I changed my eye color to a dark storm blue, made myself a bit taller - around five eleven - and that was that. But I hesitated to confirm my selection. Character creation was usually the fun lull before the challenges of the game, but this felt serious. Like, *really* serious. What if I'd picked wrong? Tuun didn't start out with much money. Just how 'real' was this going to be? For all I knew, I'd just signed up for *Oregon Trail: The Next Generation,* and if I died here... what then? My body was gone, probably. It's not like I could take off the headset, get out of my cryofreeze tank, and head back home to Base.

No. I wouldn't hesitate. Maybe it was life or death, but it was still just a game. They wouldn't go to all the trouble to bring me here just to knock me off.

The Narrator lady's voice came back online as my resolve to play the Tuun cemented.

"*Now that you have chosen your race, it's time to choose your starting class. New adventurers can choose from four basic starting classes: Warrior, Specialist, Artificer and Mage. Each Class has multiple Paths, which become available at Level 5. You can explore Paths in your Paths menu. At Level 15, you may acquire a second Class and a second Path: but remember, you only have so much EXP!*

There are special Advanced Path (AP) skill trees which can be unlocked through certain Class and Path combinations. For example, if you take Warrior at Level 1 and Specialist at Level 15, you gain access to the Ninja Advanced Path. You can explore the Paths menu to discover some Advanced Paths and their requirements. Others might come as a surprise!

The Class starter packs all seemed pretty balanced, and the Paths were quite diverse. Warrior covered all your essential non-ranged combat Paths, while Specialist led to Rogue, Scout, Ranger, Gunslinger, and other squishy and ranged DPS Paths. Artificers used magic to build attack and defense units and artifacts. Mages had a variety of Paths, nearly all of them related to elemental specialization.

I normally played Warrior/Fighter types mixed up with the occasional Rogue, but the former was more appealing. I skimmed the Warrior Paths that would be available to me later on, which was fairly extensive: Swordsman, Barbarian, Duelist, Monk, Lancer, Knight, and a number of others. I played around with combinations, looking at the advanced paths. There were some specialized Racial Advanced Paths for Tuun, which included the *Baru* class - a kind of assassin-healer monk with some badass stamina-based abilities. There well as more general APs, too: Mounted Archer, Assassin, Lancer... Dragon Knight.

Dragon Knight? I could actually be a freaking Dragon Knight? Hopefully they meant actual dragons, and not just some cheesy dragon-themed character. My mouth actually went dry as I brought up the description of the Path:

Dragon Knight (Advanced Path)

The undisputed masters of Archemi's skies, Dragon Knights are warriors who have undergone and survived the grueling rites required both by the Orders who train these warriors in the arts of honorable combat, chivalry and skycraft, and by the dragons themselves. To gain levels in this Path, you must choose the Knight Path and undergo the ordeals to bond with the dragon who will serve as your life companion and mount. When your dragon reaches the Young Adult stage, this AP becomes available. But be warned: only the chosen few can become true Dragon Knights.

My heart hammered. "Hey, lady - where do I sign up for dragon school?"

I waited in hopeful anticipation for a couple of seconds, but there was no reply from the Narrator, so I selected Warrior and had a look over my sheet. I got a couple of starting Combat Abilities by default - Basic Weapons Training and Armor Mobility - plus a free selection, plus my native Racial Abilities.

I went straight to Combat Abilities and had a look through. The ones you could start with were fairly basic: Power Attack, Charge Weapon, blah blah... my own fighting style was based on a philosophy of 'hit it as few times as possible as hard as possible until it's dead', so I selected the scalable extra-damage ability, Doubletap. It would be meh at low levels - it allowed you to five of your Adrenaline points to do double damage on a single strike - but at higher levels and stacked with other bonuses...? 19,998-point damage strikes, here I come.

At the end of it all, I got to review my sheet and get a good look at my new avatar:

Hector - Level 1 Dauntan (Tuun)

Level 1 Warrior

==Stats==

Strength: 12

Dexterity: 14

Stamina: 12

Will: 8

Wisdom: 11

Intelligence: 12

HP: 140

XP: 0

Adrenaline Points: 100

==Abilities==

=Racial=

Blessing of Burna: +10% bonus to resist disease; +5% Stamina bonus to recover from illnesses. Immune to Pox and Lockjaw. +10% cold resistance. All physical needs accrue 2% slower.

Plateau Native: No Stamina penalties in thin air, -2 Stamina penalty at sea level.

Saddle Born: All Riding skills increase 5% faster.

Sun-sight: No vision penalties in bright or very bright light, -5% penalty in dark environments.

Blessing of Tarn: +15% movement speed.

Blessing of Hrrun: No airsickness, reduced inertia at high altitudes, no vertigo.

=Traits=

Curiosity: The player is an open-minded and engaged person, willing to question their modes of thinking and doing and readily accept new ideas. Combat, craft and class skills gain 5% more quickly.

Introvert: With a preference for their own company or small groups of loyal friends, the player gains a 5% bonus to accumulate skills in solitude provided they are not disturbed. Fatigue accumulates 10% faster in large groups and crowds outside of combat situations.

Dyslexic: The written word is something of a mystery to the player. Books take longer to read, and all language-related skills gain -%5 slower.

=Combat Abilities=

Basic Weapons Training

You are trained in the arts of war, and fight unarmed and use all simple and martial hand-to-hand weapons without penalty. Does not include exotic weapons. Train with specific weapons to develop specializations.

Armor Mobility

You are used to wearing armor and bearing heavy loads. +10 Defense in armor (L,M or H), no penalty to Inventory weight.

Doubletap

Required Level: Warrior 1

Required AP: 5

150 x 2 Damage

Cooldown: 2s

Increases Accuracy +10% for 5s

Adrenaline Recovery +10 every good hit

Pushes Enemy

Flow combinations possible

=Path Abilities=

None.

==Skills==

=Combat Skills=

Martial Arts 1

Polearms 1

Swords 1

Daggers 1

Clubs 1

=General Skills=

Riding 1

Navigation 1

=Crafting Skills (Common)=

Foraging 1

=Crafting Skills (Advanced)=

None.

There was no mention was made of starting equipment, but that was fine. I'd sort that out once I spawned in whatever starting town they dumped noobs into. I breathed in, and my chest lifted. My hands balled into fists, and so did the work-worn hands of the character in front of me.

"Confirm character."

Chapter 5

There was a sound like a set of massive studio lights turning off, and the room went dark. For several seconds there was nothing... but then a haunting song sung by several voices broke through the darkness, a hypnotic multilayered chant in a language I didn't understand... until I did. They were singing in *Tuunhar*, the native language of my character. And with the song came memories: the taste of thin soured milk flavored with a sweet floral syrup, like smooth yogurt; the feel of the wind on my face, the sight of a million birds migrating through a mountain pass, and weirdly, a memory of hiking along a trial and coming up over a bare bluff of stone that was covered in giant metallic red flies the size of small dogs. They weren't monsters: they were something important to the Tuun, something I still didn't know the full significance of. They weren't my memories. But they could have been.

I was still wondering how the fuck I knew this stuff when I woke up to the stench of human filth.

My wrists hurt. Everything hurt. My teeth, knees, muscles. I felt like I'd run a marathon... or that I was, well, deathly ill, and had just come out of a very bad fever. The room was smoky, the air tinted with a deep brownish haze, and it stunk like hell. My head was pounding and hot, my guts cramped with real hunger and real thirst.

There was a thump beneath me, and creaking, and then my stomach dropped out from under me with a very familiar sensation: Air pockets. The wall I was slumped against began to rumble and shudder, jostling me back and forth in the nest of heavy iron chains that were snapped around my limbs. People around me began to moan: some in fear, some in pain. Worse, some of them began to cough, and my head began to pound for another reason. Pure animal terror.

I was in the hold of a flying ship, sitting on the floor among a crowd of other people. It was too dark for me to make out much in the way of features, but we all looked pretty miserable. I was dressed in what looked like torn buckskin rags. I was cold, and people were sick. I'd agreed to this to get away from dying of some horrible illness, and I'd ended up stuck with a bunch of sick people. *What the actual fuck, Steve?!*

My first instinct was to test the strength of the manacles on my wrists, ankles and neck. They were looped onto long chains that ran through stout eyelets on the hull behind me, connecting me to the other people in my row. To my left, another Tuun man slept an unquiet sleep, frowning even as he snored. To my right was an elf woman with brilliant platinum hair. Her restraints were even more severe than mine: a leather mask that only left her nose bare and that laced tightly around her jaw. Her hands were encased in cages that followed the shape of her fingers and didn't allow her to move them. Her clothes were torn and dirty, like mine, the collar of her tunic ripped down to her chest. Only the collar and mask stopped her shirt from falling down around her waist. A captured spellcaster?

Magic, right. This sensory hell is a game.

Normally, you spawned somewhere kind of neutral in an MMO. The bunny slopes, or a tutorial garden... some kind of cutesy village or the Altar of Recombobulation or something - not a crowded slave ship.

It felt so real that it was actually weird to call up the menu, but sure enough, my HUD came up on prompt.

"Do you want to set up auto-alerts?" A message appeared over the HUD display.

"Sure." I agreed aloud before I thought about what I was doing. The bound mage's head turned toward me for a moment, but then she fell back and curled against the wall as best she could.

"Auto alerts enabled." The message cleared, showing me my main tabs: Inventory, Character, Crafting, Quests, Options, Artificing, and World Map. The Path menu was greyed out.

If nothing else, my predicament gave me time to have a look through everything. The UI was gorgeous: light on dark, clear layout. Seeing my blank inventory and being able to remind myself that this was, in fact, meant to be fun made me feel a little calmer. No matter how much everything stank and how realistically my stomach lurched, this world was a game. There was a way out of this situation - somehow.

I thought across through the tabs. Nothing happened. Annoyed, I tried to manually select something by thinking the name. Still nothing. I couldn't interact with the menu at all.

Before the panic really had time to set in, an alert pushed its way into my vision:

New Quest!0021FETCHNUMBER?
Escape the Slave Ship... or Die Trying

The Arabella, an airship contracted to carry slaves, is headed for the dangerous mana mines of the frozen North! Slaves live out their brief, miserable lives digging mana from the earth before their mutated bodies are cast into the crushing waves of the Sea of Blades. You must escape before the ship makes landfall. Look around for tools to ***Difficulty:*** *??72m4q24fphttttodsl-0021FETCHNUMBER?*

Reward: *myj3thkoark120kslz—0021FETCHNUMBER?*

"What in the holy fuck...?" I muttered to myself. I tried closing the Quest Journal, but it was frozen. So was the HUD.

Shitballs.

Calm down, Hector. Calmity calm calm. As my limbs thrummed with fear, I took a deep breath of stinking humid air and took stock of my manacles, shaking and pulling at them. The iron cuffs weren't budging. I could use my hands and move my feet, though I wouldn't be able to stand. The cuffs had crude padlocks holding them closed, but I wasn't getting them off without tools.

Well, fine. Okay. I looked around the floor for anything I could use to try and pick a lock, squinting through the frozen HUD, and came up short. No tools. The guy beside me had turned over, so he was no help, but the elf woman was now sitting up stiffly. She looked... undefeated, somehow, despite the hood. Now THAT was something I could work with.

"Hey, miss," I said. My voice came out as a heavily-accented gravelly rasp that threw me off for just a moment. "Uh... can you hear me?"

Her head and shoulders turned toward me, but she couldn't really nod or properly shake her head. The hood was tied onto what looked like some kind of posture collar. Kinky.

"Want me to try and get that mask off?" I asked. "Just, uh... wiggle your nose once for yes, twice for no?"

The way her cheeks bunched, she might have smiled. She twitched her nose once.

"Alright. Hang on." I struggled up as the hull continued to jolt up and down with turbulence, and yanked my chains in to give me a bit of room to move my arms. They pulled on the limbs of the guy beside me, but he just rolled with it and continued snoring away.

The mask was laced to the collar with tight knots, but my fingers were callused, nails thick and strong. I sawed and picked at them until they came away, zoning in on the work until I was able to get a look at the collar. It had a bolt instead of a padlock. When I touched it, the metal and the ends of my fingers both turned ice-cold. Some kind of magic. We weren't getting that off in here.

I pulled the mask from her eyes first, and then her mouth. The mouth part had a gag attached to the inside, and she had to work it past her teeth to spit it out. This woman was very pale. Her beautiful silver hair was snarled, but glossy and bright with health. Her mouth was full and sensuous, her violet eyes fierce in the dimness of the hold. Her lower lip was split and puffy, flaked with dried blood.

"Thank you." Her voice sounded as dry as mine, parched but sweet. She had a British accent, the kind that made me think of *Pride and Prejudice* and strict boarding schools. "That was a kindness you didn't have to offer."

"Can't agree with that," I said. "That looked seriously uncomfortable."

She smiled faintly, but it was pained. "Not all men are so honorable. Not that it will go far... the bastards will lock me up in it again as soon as we reach land."

"You know where we are?" I felt a stir of hope, something clearly not reflected in my companion.

She sighed, and rolled her shoulders with a grimace of pain. "No, but I have a terrible feeling we're headed north toward Zaunt."

"Zaunt? Where the fuck is Zaunt? Why?"

"As slaves," the woman said matter-of-factly. "Zaunt is the homeland of the Mercurions. Strange people. You, they will work to death in some bluecrystal mine or another. Me... well, take one guess what will become of me."

Ahh, yes. Beautiful, charming, escapist Archemi. I wanted to log out and punch Temperance in her plastic face, but I was stuck here, so I forced a smile instead. "I don't remember how I got here."

The sorceress's expression was grave. "I don't remember much, either. I was searching for someone, and I activated the Star..."

She trailed off, and her brow furrowed.

"The Star?" I cocked an eyebrow.

"Never mind." She shook her head, and winced a little. "Ah, godsblood. There's no way out of this."

"Look, I don't know how I ended up here, but I'm not spending the rest of my lives digging for rocks," I said. "We have to get off this ship somehow."

"Impossible." The woman shook her head. "We're over the ocean. Can't you hear it? Feel it?"

I'd assumed the rumbling in the background was engines powering whatever flying craft we were on, but now that she mentioned it, it did sound an awful lot like the ocean. But... deeper? Louder?

"We'll be fortunate if this blasted hulk doesn't wreck." She swallowed, and glanced down at her bound hands. "If I had my magic..."

"No point wishing for what we don't have." I shrugged. "What's your name?"

"I am Rutha of Vasteau," she replied. "And you?"

"Hector. Dragozin Hector. Of... Tuungant."

Rutha smiled a wan, bitter smile. "Well, Hector, I suggest you sleep. I doubt very much that we will be relieved of our fate by the time we reach land. You'll need all your strength."

Frustrated, I tried to banish my quest journal to the HUD again, but the window was still firmly locked in place. Fucking piece of crap game. Fuming silently, I tried to pick out objects from the background, searching for ways out of the bind. The devs had to have given this situation some kind of resolution that didn't involve me getting worked to death or getting sick. But it *was* a beta... and there was something wrong with the quest. The Journal entry told me to search for tools, but there were no tools to be seen.

What if something had gone wrong, and the items I'd supposed to be able to find hadn't spawned? And now that I'd been spawned here... what would happen if I died? Would I spawn back on this ship? Or would the bug extend into a faulty reincarnation as well? What if my file got corrupted, or I was deleted? I remembered Temperance's calm warning about people who were too far gone with HEX not making it. What if it was that they reached the start of the game, bugged, then died when the game crashed?

I felt lightheaded as I sat back, stomach churning. I swallowed nervously. "Yeah... sleep, I guess."

"Thank you for at least making my journey more comfortable, Hector." Rutha glanced over me. Her eyelashes were the same brilliant white as her hair. "Rest well, as much as one can in this circumstance."

She might have been tired, but I wasn't. I was worried - and pissed. As Rutha turned away, I wrapped my arms around my knees and frowned. I didn't need sleep – I needed a way out of these chains and off this ship. I needed to find Steve and check that he'd made it, and I needed to learn what the hell I was supposed to do here.

I closed my eyes, listening to the ship creak and the ocean roar, a relentless drone of sound that went on, and on... and that didn't vary or change. The ship was creaking over and over again at the exact same pitch, too quickly. *Ree-ree-ree-ree-ree,* like an alarm.

My gut tightened, and I sat bolt upright, looking around as realization dawned. Everyone around me had frozen. All the sounds that had been going on in that moment were either skipping, or had blurred into the one constant roar. Sweat beaded on my forehead as I shifted in my chains, looking around. Rutha had frozen, her eyes only half-closed, lips slightly parted, her head not quite touching her shoulder.

"Oh fuck." It WAS a bug.

There was a strange tugging sensation inside my head, like something was pulling at the inside of my skull, and my heartbeat stuttered as fresh terror flooded my chest. My hands and nose began to buzz.

Then I heard footsteps.

My head whipped around so fast I nearly wrenched my neck. A tall, shadowy figure was picking its way through the crowd of human cargo, effortlessly avoiding legs, out-flung hands, and crates. It was heading straight for me.

"Greetings, Hector." The shadows resolved into a man with a light, even-toned voice. It carried through the hold in a way that felt unnatural, and the hairs on the back of my neck crawled. "It seems the Architects have cast you a cruel lot yet again."

"Who are you?" My eyes narrowed, but I couldn't really do much. The chains on my wrists weren't making the right noises any more, but they sure as hell felt real.

""You may call me Matir." The man stopped six feet or so from where I sat. He was dressed in all black: black breeches, black boots, a hooded half-cape, a black tunic, all of which shifted and bled sparkling static into the air. His face... he didn't have a face. All I saw was a pit of darkness underneath the hood, with one point of light burning like a star in the center. "I thought that perhaps you could use a helping hand."

Chapter 6

My eyes narrowed. "Who and *what* the hell are you?"

"I told you. I am Matir. And I am here to encourage your potential." Matir looked down at me, his 'face' a void of sucking darkness, like a black hole. "Your arrival did not go as planned."

Swallowing nervously, I tried to tune out the repetitive soundbytes playing over and over again. It was like being trapped in a cell with a giant box of cicadas. "No shit."

"A great force is at work, seeking to unbalance the world," Matir said. "And it seems you were caught up in the discordance it is creating. It is my gift to sense such things... and thus, I am here."

"So, you're a literal Deus Ex Machina?" I sighed. "Fine. What do you want?"

"As you are aware, you are on a slave ship. Specifically, you are a prisoner of war," Matir said. "This isn't usually a problem for Starborn, but there's a problem. You aren't Starborn."

"But Starborn are players, right? What do you mean I'm not Starborn?" My stomach clenched.

"You were meant to be." The dark figure spread its hands. "You have all the prerequisites... but something went wrong between the time you chose your fate and the time you descended to begin your life on Archemi."

"I'm not in the mood for this," I said. "Just give it to me straight. What does that *mean*?"

"Starborn are what they are because they return to life when slain. You will not return. You will die with finality, like all other men. Those who could recognize you as Starborn will not know you for what you are, and will not offer you the adventures your spirit craves. In the rare event you obtain a quest, it will cause time and reality to warp around you, as it did here. You carry the seed of fate, but it has Stranged and cannot blossom... and if you die and join the Caul of Souls, your spirit will be sucked into it and destroyed."

Well, that explained the HUD freeze and the weird 'numberfetch' stuff. "Then I guess I'll be doing my part to keep the Drachan out of Archemi," I said, sourly.

Matir laughed. "What fire you have! The Drachan are already here, boy. Why do you think you're in the bowels of this hulk?"

"I figured we were doing one of those mystery murder cruise things."

"Murder and mystery indeed," Matir said. "So, will you let me help you?"

No lie: this guy creeped me the hell out. I fought the urge to hunch back against the wall. If he wasn't a dev or a mod or something, what *was* he? Something generated by the AI, some kind of failsafe to bail players who got stuck in impossible starting sequences and accidentally got turned into NPCs? "What can you do to get me out of here?"

"Oh, this and that." If Matir had a face, he'd have smirked. "But first, I must know something. I can and *will* help you, but my favor must be repaid. Do you agree?"

Of course. Something told me this was a really bad idea, but what choice did I have? I didn't want to spend eternity here. "Depends on the favor."

"Nothing that you cannot rightfully accomplish. Do you want my help?"

I hesitated for a moment. "Sure."

"Then we have a deal." Matir stood back from me, clapping his hands together. "And a bargain, I might add. You shall be Starborn... but you shall be born under a dark star, Dragozin Hector. And when you are ready, you will come to the Thunderstones near the village of Myszno in Vlachia. Take your time, though... there's no rush. The passing of the Dark Star is a ways off yet, and you will need to realize some of your potential before we can settle up. For now, I will give you a memento to make sure you remember me."

Before I could reply, the hooded man lifted a gloved hand, and a sudden searing, cold pain shot through my right arm. I hissed, jerking away, and looked down to see a strange symbol burning itself into my skin. A Chaos Star with nine irregular spokes, each spoke containing a pair of sigils that crawled with sparks of dark energy for a moment before settling into dark, seared lines.

"My mark." Matir lowered his hand, radiating satisfaction. "Now those with the eyes to see will be able to recognize you."

I was liking this less and less. The intense pain vanished as quickly as it arrived, leaving the brand etched into my skin. It was less like a tattoo and more like a black charred scar. I looked up at him, frowning. The environment was still glitching around us.

"What are you?" I demanded, straightening on the floor. "You're not meant to be here. This isn't part of the game."

He looked down at me. The darkness inside his hood seemed to suck in the visual snow that blurred the edges of his figure. "Everything and everyone are part of the game. Especially you."

Just like that, the game resumed. It was like I'd blinked: one moment, everything was screwed, and the next, we were back to rocking, thumping, and creaking. People around me shifted and dozed. Rutha's head was properly resting on her shoulder now, her hair tumbling over her face.

My HUD unfurled like a flower, automatically pulling up a rapid-fire series of alerts, new messages, and a quest journal entry all at once:

NUMBERFETCH 00-001A-TypeNew[[HeraldOfMT]]

Registration complete! Compiling profile...

Pain Threshold Detection: 76%

Visceral Tolerance: Med-High (Realistic)

Race: TuunM-0016

...

As the factors continued to download in a flashing wave, I had the feeling that I was seeing something I wasn't supposed to be able to see. It was like watching people putting a stage set together when you were supposed to be there to see the show.

Once it finished, the spool of alerts closed, and the first message opened automatically.

Welcome to Archemi!

Thank you for joining us in our mission to repurpose our Full Immersion Reality world, Archemi, and for assisting us with the BigBrain Virtual Consciousness Project! Your participation will clear the way for Ryuko to save tens of thousands of lives – the unique 'brain maps' of people who would otherwise be lost to HEX.

Due to the nature of this mission, Stranged and monstrous enemies over Level 12 are currently disabled, random mob (enemy) spawns will not occur in populated regions, and all potentially devastating world events have been suspended. Leveling is currently reduced, and there will be a Level 10 cap until we have realized the full scope of the evacuation and surrounding policy. We are working as fast as we can to strike a balance between making Archemi an escape for the adventurous as well as a refuge for people who may not be gamers, so please bear with us as we assess what features will remain and what features we'll have to put on ice.

The Mod Team will currently be logging in and out as we continue to refine BCI networking and storage. You can use your menu to view a list of online Mods at any time.

Despite the caps, there's still plenty to do, and plenty of baddies to fight at lower levels. So don't rush – explore your city or town, have fun, and relax. You're immortal, baby!

–Your Friendly Neighborhood Devs.

Ahh... the message I probably should have gotten during a normal upload. So Matir had been right, unfortunately. All things being well, I should have landed in a Tuun city with some starting gear and a couple of fetch quests, not in the belly of a slave ship. Maybe it wasn't all bad, then. I hated fetch quests.

I tooled over to the Quest Journal to see what quest Matir had inflicted on me:

New Quest: The Shrine of the Elder Gods

When the Dark Star passes in front of the Moon, journey to the Thunderstones at Mysząno, a village in the east of Vlachia.

Reward: ???

Difficulty: Level 12-15

Level 12? But the maximum level cap is 10, right? I was still staring stupidly at the quest window when the hull began to vibrate in a way it hadn't before, then jolted so hard that people woke with short, startled screams. Rutha started up, as did the man next to me.

"Whu-what?" She looked around as much as her collar allowed for. "Are we docking already?"

There was another jolt through the hull, and this time, people screamed for real. It felt like a giant foot was kicking us from underneath, making the chains rattle and bang against the walls. Fear made my skin hum, but my combat training was kicking in. This was a battlefield, just like the ones I'd fought IRL, and maybe even less dangerous - assuming I *could* respawn. Rutha scrambled up, tugging on our line of chains as, down the end of the ship, a trapdoor opened up and a pair of men clattered down into the hold. They carried torches and whips, and began yelling at the other slaves in a language that sounded like Italian, but harsher. Small prompts floated over their heads, identifying each man as ⟦Slave Guard⟧ - Level 2.

Our chance had come.

Chapter 7

"Hey brother." I turned to the man on my left. He was awake now, and like me, he was Tuun. We spoke the same language. "When they come this way, give me slack on the chains. I want to try and get the keys."

Any other person probably would have laughed in my face or told me I was crazy, but this man's eyes narrowed with dark humor. He was older than me, shorter, with a wide, chiseled face and narrow eyes. His hair was a short bristle of spikes on top, braids like mine down the back. "Not if I get the keys first. Let's have some fun."

As he spoke, a health ring - like a corona - appeared behind his head, identifying him as [[Tuun Warrior]]. My first NPC party member.

I nudged Rutha next. "Me and Psycho here are going to get up when those two come this way. Can you help us get slack in the chains?"

"Are you insane?" Rutha boggled at me.

"Like live lizard in fire," the other Tuun grunted in an accent thicker than mine. "They took us like cowards, when we were fallen. Now, we are awake. There cannot be many guards. More of us than them, if we seize ship."

One of the [[Slave Guards]] was beating on someone on the ground: someone small, maybe old or very young. I began to shout and curse at them, thumping my manacles against the floor and making a ruckus. "Hey! Dickcheese! Come here and give me some of that!"

One of the pair of slavers, a thin guy with a thick mustache, barked something at his companion and ran back upstairs. Going for reinforcements, I bet - they knew they were outnumbered down here.

The Tuun was warning the woman on his other side, a thin girl with huge eyes, who nodded and turned to her left to do the same. The slaver was picking his way toward us, features contorted in fury.

"Shut up! Shut up!" He barked. "Or we'll dump you all in the ocean right now, you worms!"

"If they have to lighten the ballast of the ship to make it through this storm, they will anyway," Rutha murmured.

I was trembling now, but not from fear: from excitement. Adrenaline was my friend. It had been a while since I'd been able to get into a fight and not have to worry about getting my ass handed to me by an officer. Time to put these newly chiseled biceps to good use.

The [[Slave Guard]] came up near us, striking indiscriminately across the rows of people chained down, while five more came down into the hold from the trapdoor. I saw him raise his weapon to bring it down onto the frail girl, and that was it. "Go go go!"

"HuuRAH!" Rutha hauled toward me on one side, throwing her weight in, and the girl and her neighbor did the same on the other side. Suddenly, me and the other Tuun had enough room to get our feet under us. We surged up, surrounding the isolated slaver with a collective twelve feet of pissed off beefcake. The guard yelled an alarm and shoved the hissing torch in my face: I smacked it aside with my cuffed wrists, while the other Tuun belted him over the back of the head with his manacles. The torch dropped and rolled, and immediately began to smoke on the dry wooden floor of the ship.

"Put it out! Put it out!" The Tuun Warrior roared.

The newly arrived ⟦Slave Guards⟧ were running for us, but a wave of excitement had ripped through the hold. I saw people trying to trip them up, sticking out legs and ramming their bodies into them. The stir was greatest in our row, and we had all the chain we could ask for as everyone pulled their links in toward us to give us room to fight. I kicked the sputtering torch toward the old woman in front of us and stomped on the embers, swearing a storm as the embers burned the soles of my bare feet. She groped forward for it, trying to pick it up and get it off the ground before the ship caught fire.

The other Tuun beat the guard down to the floor with the shackles, ripped the keys off his belt, and began to hurriedly unlock his manacles. The five ⟦Slave Guards⟧ were getting closer: I could see green translucent health rings now. They'd entered the range of combat.

"You better make it fast!" I turned to the fallen guard and searched him for weapons. A Loot inventory popped up. He had a ⟦Curved Knife⟧ on his belt, a ⟦Whip⟧, and ⟦3 Copper Lintz⟧. I looted him bare, equipped the knife, and set it between my teeth.

My new ally got his cuffs off, threw me the keys, and faced off against the five new enemies headed toward us. The extra slack in the chain meant that others could now stand, but I struggled to keep my balance between the rocking ship and the game of tug of war going on to either side.

"*Tarn takhrah*!" The Tuun Warrior bellowed, just before he charged into the fray.

I got the first manacle off my foot and dropped it, and was just getting started on the second when the ship rolled and then dropped, sending me sprawling. Everyone left the ground for a moment, then crashed back down. Shrieks of terror pealed out in the chaos.

"Fuck this piece of shit!" I struggled with the lock, muttering around the knife as the combatants picked themselves up again, and eventually felt the rusty thing turn with a click. The Tuun was up before the Guards were, fists raised. He kicked one in the side of the head so hard that the man's health dropped fifty percent, just like that. It was five against one, though - and they had knives.

The Tuun took a hit to his shoulder, grunting with pain, but the little girl beside him kicked the Guard in the back of the knee and pitched him forward. I threw off my manacle, and lunged forward, still attached to the chain gang by one arm. The others had caught on and were helping us now, though, a forest of HP rings now bristling in the air around us. They were ALL entering combat.

"Come on! We can take them!" I called out to the other prisoners.

Three [[Slave Guards]] mobbed the Tuun and took him down to the floor, roaring like a bear. The other two had swords and were screaming for backup. I stabbed one guy in the neck until his HP dropped and he fell, his bar gray, his body a bloody mess, and jumped into the fray before they killed my new comrade-in-arms.

[[You slash Slave Guard for 5 Damage!]]

[[You slash Slave Guard for 7 Damage!]]

[[You have killed a Slave Guard! You gain 15 EXP!]]

The fight was close and messy, dark and smoky, and I had to trust in my character's build and my own martial reflexes to parry knives, turn away from fists and feet, slash at a hand groping for my eyes. The slavers fell back, their health flashing orange, and I reached down to help my bleeding companion back up to his feet. He was down in the red zone, fifteen percent health and dropping, but his face was grim with determination. I gave him the knife and fumbled with my cuff while he held the wary guards at bay.

"Give me the keys! I can fight!" A Lysidian woman called out to me from across the row. She looked fit and fierce, with a fall of black braids and dark gray skin. I nodded to her, dropped my cuff, and threw her the ring of keys just as more men clattered down into the hold. These [[Elite Guards]] were Level 3, and they had crossbows. Shit.

The other downed Guards had keys as well, and one of them had a [[Mint Potion]]. I ransacked their inventories, screwing up once in my excitement, and pulled the keys off them to hand to fellow prisoners. But we were too late: the injured [[Slave Guards]] were retreating, and before I could find cover, the crossbow-wielding [[Elite Guards]] began to fire into the agitated crowd.

It didn't matter to me now that the people around me were NPCs. Some of them were just children, and they and the weaker adults could die with a single hit. I handed my Tuun companion the potion, which he threw back like a shot. We each seized a sword, and then pair of us roared our challenge and charged in like angry bulls.

I took a bolt to the leg, and stumbled down to one knee as pain tore through my leg. *Fuck! That hurt!* My HP dropped from 140 to 94 points, but I snarled and powered on through the pain toward the Guards until we were within striking range. The archers had to reload, and that was our chance. I focused on the weakened [[Slave Guards]] first: they'd been drinking potions, but those only healed 15 points and they were still in the yellow. The other Tuun went for the ranged attackers to distract them. We were now at ten mob and counting, all of them over our levels, and my health was going down with every hit.

I took down two of the weak Guards, earning another hit of EXP, but took a blow to the head that knocked me down to 86 HP and staggered dizzily to one side. I saw an [[Elite Guard]] train on me, but before he could fire the shot, the gray-skinned woman with the long black braids materialized out of the air behind him and plunged a stolen knife into his neck with a precise blow. Her Backstab was a one hit KO: he dropped the crossbow and crumpled to the rocking floor.

The Tuun Warrior took another bolt and sunk down to his knees, his health flashing in warning, but then whoops and cries echoed from behind us as more people - young, old, men and women - ran up to join in the fray. A few of them got taken down, but as the Tuun had said, there was more of us than there was of them, and the nine guards were soon overwhelmed by at least twenty angry ex-slaves, who beat them with fists, their cuffs, extinguished torches, anything that came to hand.

The guards had crappy starting gear, but I stripped them bare via my menu and managed to find myself a ⟦Leather Helmet⟧, a pair of boots, a ⟦Rusty Spear⟧ - a piercing weapon, good against armor - as well as another potion. I took that one myself. It went down with a cool, light minty flavor, and I felt instant relief as my HP jumped back to 101 points.

"Hey you, take the keys and free everyone!" I called to the injured Tuun Warrior as he dragged himself up to his feet. "I'll lead the others upstairs and we'll seize this hunk of junk!"

He grunted in agreement, pulling a crossbow bolt out of his upper arm. He was back into the red zone, sweating and bleeding profusely from several cuts and punctures. The man was keeping himself upright by force of will alone. "Go. What is your name?"

"Hector," I said. "You?"

"Bobayer," he replied. "Be blessed by Burna's sickle. Beware the storm."

"No worries, Bob." I nodded, jaw set, and cast around to take stock of who we had. The rogue woman came up to me, hand outstretched. I shook it, and she clasped it, warrior to warrior, before turning to regard another tall, light-skinned man with a short red ponytail of hair, and Rutha, who was now free of most of her restraining leather gear. Other people were gathering with us, too. Stony-faced commoners, most of them.

"We need to get up there and take them out with anything we can find," I said. "Loot what weapons you can. Let's go give them Hell!"

"Oceans take these bastard slavers," the red-head said. His identifier was 'Escaped Convict'. "Were you the first to stand?"

"Me and Bob here." I nodded toward Bobayer, who was unshackling an older woman from her chain gang. "I'm Hector."

"Louis," the man replied. His identifier changed accordingly.

"And I am Wikati," the gray-skinned woman said. She sounded Jamaican to me. "We need to keep the captain and navigators alive, unless someone here knows how to fly a Skycutter."

"Leave the Captain to me," Rutha said crisply. "All we have to do is get to the bridge."

"Alright! Let's do this." Spear in hand, I motioned to the stairs, and led my first party up into the pounding rain: my first entrance into the world which was to be my new home.

Chapter 8

We emerged out of the trapdoor into a bitterly cold, howling wind that threatened to blow us right off the skyship. The deck was bucking and rolling as the Arabella bounced with the turbulence of the storm. Sails arched overhead in a multilayered canopy that was keeping the worst of the rain off the deck, though it still lashed the wooden surface in waves. Out here, the sound of the ocean below us was thunderous.

"We should sneak past," Rutha said. "If we have to fight, we're not going to make it through all these sailors."

She was right. I was still Level 1, a noob without armor and a shoddy [[Rusty Spear]] with a 10-45 damage range. The sailors and remaining guards were all level-appropriate and seemed to be manageable, but there was a lot of them and only four of us. "Good idea. By the time we get to the bridge, all the other prisoners will be released. We can mob the crew after that."

Louis and Wikati nodded. It was the woman who spoke. "Let me scout ahead. I have training in stealth."

"Go. We'll be right behind you," I said.

"Okay. When you move, stay low to the ground. Watch how I do it." Wikati smiled thinly, then dropped into a half-crouch and stealing gracefully across the deck, moving into the shadows and staying there. I followed behind, trying to copy her posture and light cross-step.

We stuck to cover: masts, the boxes lashed down with nets. Sailors were yelling at one another as they struggled with ropes. The sails were horizontal, arching over us like sheets instead of standing up from the masts. Wikati stayed ahead as we got closer and closer to the back of the ship. As I crossed from one shadow to another, a prompt flashed up in the corner of my eye:

[[You have learned a new Skill: Stealth]]

Skill: Stealth

You have learned how to move through cover, concealing your presence from enemies... provided you don't trip over your own feet.

- 5% concealment chance from enemies

- Move at half speed on normal and fast terrain, one quarter speed on difficult terrain.

Skill Type: Active (requires Focus)

Duration: Active until canceled.

The game rewarded my experimentation with a sudden burst of insight, and suddenly I knew exactly how to move, now and every other time in the future, if I wanted that five percent bonus. It was cool, but also creepy. It also made me want to try new things - a lot of new things. Was there a Parkour skill? I could do parkour!

Wikati fell to a crouch behind the forward mast, waving us back as I prepared to follow her. She shook her head and pointed toward the door leading to the bridge, which took up the forward part of the deck. The shape reminded me of a jetfighter cockpit. There was a solid wall with a heavy airlock door facing us, but the rest of the room was made of thick reinforced glass. Two men wearing intricate steel and crystal gauntlets held their hands above what looked like magical control panels, glowing spheres that spooled crawling feeds of sigils into the air. The mages worked with frantic concentration. The Captain - a tall, olive-complected man with a shaved head, a single forelock, and a huge mustache and thin goatee - alternated between barking orders at them and talking angrily into something he held in his hand.

Most of the guards were down at the other end of the ship trying to put down the slave mob, but two of them remained outside the entry to the bridge. They were enormous Cossack warriors, muscles straining against their shirtsleeves. These [[Captain's Guard]] carried sabers nearly as long as I was tall, and they had small, burning red skull symbols smoldering next to their HP rings. They were a much higher level than me, dangerously so.

There was a sudden uproar from behind us. Looking back, I saw the other prisoners pour out of the hold. The Captain's face contorted and he began to yell at his crew, gesturing angrily to the deck. Wikati stole back to us under the cover of chaos.

"If we work together, we can take them out. Wikati, do you have like..." it felt strange to ask her this question. "Rogue attack skills? Backstab, anything like that?"

She grinned, flashing dainty fangs. I hadn't seen those in character creation. "If you can distract them, I can sneak behind one and stick him in the kidney, if that is what you mean?"

"I can do that," Louis replied, quietly reloading his crossbow as we talked.

"Sounds good. If we focus on one at a time, we can halve the threat and then focus our attentions on the other guy." I nodded. "Can you do magic, Rutha?"

"Not without spellgloves," she replied. "About the best I could do is push the mana around in the ship engines, but the engines are struggling as it is. I don't dare try and interfere with the navigators."

How the hell did magic actually work here? Time to test out the game glossary. I focused for a moment, and thought the words 'Mana Definition':

Mana (also called Seid, Sanghar)
Every culture in Archemi has myths about mana, the physical form of raw magic. Mana is naturally distributed through reality as the 'fluid' which binds matter into cohesive forms, but can be extracted from powerful sites of magic known as spirit wells or star wells. It is a physical substance. Highly volatile and dangerous to most living organisms in its pure form, mana must be handled carefully.

Pressurized liquid or gaseous mana is required by mages to perform magic, who use specially crafted gloves, gauntlets, wands and other focusing devices to shape spells. Artificers use mana to make a range of magical artifacts: skyships, horseless carriages, weapons, home furnishings, and more. Mana extraction depletes the land or creature from which it is taken, resulting in premature aging or death.

Mages had their work cut out for them, then. I'd never played a game where they faced a resource limit beyond an innate supply of magical energy. "Any idea where they might be keeping your spellgloves?"

"They're expensive artifacts," Rutha replied. "If they survived my capture, then they're likely in whatever they use for a treasury on board this ship."

I guess that was where I came from, though I had no memory of the place and no idea where it was. "Right. What makes you think you can handle the Captain?"

"Because they have enough available mana in there that I can and will boil his brain in his skull once I get into that room," she replied firmly.

Oh. Woah. I blinked several times. "Righty-oh. Ready, Wikati?"

She nodded, brandishing her knife. Louis went to a crouch, bracing the crossbow against his shoulder, and sighted down. "Alright. I'll count to fifteen and fire. Right or left?"

Left," I said. "Let's do this."

Wikati and I dropped to a crouch and scuttled toward the rear mast like a pair of crabs. The door guards were hopped up, grinding their teeth as they strove to make out what was happening at the other end of the *Arabella*, but it was clear they weren't allowed to leave their post. I was going to have to kill these men. When I thought about it, I felt... well, like an ass, really. The fighting down in the hold had been so fast and so desperate that I hadn't had any time to see or think about what I was doing. I couldn't remember seeing any guts or gore, just blood. This was different - it was premeditated. I'd hoped to get used to this full-immersion VR thing by killing some monsters. Instead, I was about to jump a couple of guys following orders and doing their jobs, without any idea why, exactly, we were all being taken to the Caul to begin with. Matir had said we were POWs, but a guy had to have a face - not a hole - for me to take him at face value. For all I knew, I'd just teamed up with three war criminals while rapists and looters ran around on the ship.

Ten seconds had passed already. I shifted nervously, and tried to think calm thoughts. Battlefield thoughts. *They're enemy mob. You're supposed to kill them, Hector.*

Still, even battlefield training and experience only took me so far. Killing someone with a rifle from a distance was very different to jamming your spear into their lung.

"Go!" Wikati dashed forward just as the crossbow clicked.

A bolt whipped over my shoulder. I couldn't fault Louis's aim: the bolt took the Cossack in the gut, knocking him down a good seventy points with his flanking bonus. Wikati was on him like a shot, but the man roared and swung with the hilt of his sword, striking her so hard that he knocked her over and she tumbled. So much for Backstab.

"*Tarn takhar!*" I called it out before I even realized what I was saying, charging in with the spear. I hadn't really ever used a spear before, but I'd fought with a bayonet once or twice and it was enough to get me through. We clashed, and the first thing I noticed was that this guard was monstrously strong. The second thing was the yellowish tinge to my Vitality meter. I was operating on two thirds of my hitpoints against a guy with full health, who was at least a couple of levels above my class rating. I got in three jabs, whittling him down, but he blocked the fourth and planted a heavy boot into my gut before I could defend. It sent me staggering into the back of the other man, who whirled on me and slammed his fist right across the side of my head.

Everything whirled and turned white for a second. I was dimly aware of Wikati's battlecry as she made to assist, and sensed motion to my left. I brought the spear around, turning the next blow that would have taken me from 10% to zero, one hit. Head throbbing, I dropped and rolled away from the sudden rain of blows that came from above, and I was suddenly very glad that Tuun didn't experience vertigo. I'd be puking my guts out if I did. This VR pain stuff could go die in a fire.

A deep male voice roared from somewhere close by, and I stumbled up to my knee to see Bob charge in past me, face dark with bloodlust. He'd made a club out of a thick plank of wood, and he laid into the less-injured guard with his full, renewed strength. He was back to full health, and he parried the guard's baton and headbutted him, shoving him away so that I could get to my feet on the lurching deck of the ship and rejoin the fray. I was more than happy to let Bob tank while I circled around, struggling to see through the red haze of blood and concussion. This wasn't something I'd ever had to deal with before - fighting an NPC while managing real pain, real exhaustion, actual freezing cold wind, the jerks and jolts of turbulence on a really real airship. But this was life or death, so I made it around while he focused on Bob, triggered Doubletap, and ran the [[Captain's Guard]] with my spear from behind.

The [[Rusty Spear]] went through his body with a sick soft feeling, like stabbing a carving knife into raw beef. He got out one gurgling cry, and then dropped to his knees, clawing at the polearm that was trapped in his guts. As my Adrenaline burned down, I twisted and jerked the weapon up into his body as he screamed in pain.

[[You land a critical hit on Captain's Guard!]]

[[You do 17 Piercing damage!]]

[[You do 17 Doubletap damage!]]

A critical hit! I should have been happy at the massive damage combo - instead, I felt disgust as I hung on tight, holding the thrashing man in place as Wikati leaped on him from the front and stabbed him in the neck and shoulders. I felt him slump around the head of the spear as the life drained out of him.

[[You have killed Captain's Guard!]]

[[You gain 35 XP!]]

Almost at Level 2 already. Kind of a sick way to think of it. I pulled the spear from the Guard's body and kicked him to convulse and bleed out on the deck. The other guard was a sitting duck for the five of us, alone in a semi-circle of blades. He fell back from us, hands raised. His face was a bloody mask. "Please, I yield! Mercy!"

"Slaver dog!" Bob snapped back. "Where was your mercy for us?"

Wikati was breathing hard, but she was staring at the Cossack with hard, predatory eyes. "My thoughts exactly. Who did you plan to sell me to? Some slumlord who'd keep me locked up in his brothel? A lord wanting an exotic fuckdoll? A legion? Hard labor?"

"I don't know!" He was looking between us, eyes wide and white, as Rutha and Louis joined us from the shadows of the mast. There was a riot going on down on the rest of the ship. "I am a mercenary, hired on at Taltos! I have a family-"

"Leave off." I stepped forward, his friend's saber loose in my hand. "He's surrendered."

"He's honorless scum!" Bob snarled at me in Tuun.

"He's a mercenary. He doesn't believe in honor, just coin," I said. "Different gods for different men. He surrendered. He knows we're his masters now. There's no honor in putting him down."

I got an auto-prompt. You have learned a new skill: Negotiation.

Both Wikati and Bob turned on me to argue, but Rutha stepped forward, hand raised. "This is pointless. The man was doing his job and following orders, however loathsome they might be. Slavery is not illegal in Vlachia."

I held up a hand, staring down at the shaken guard. "How did we get here?"

The Captain's Guard frowned. "You were purchased. My Guildmaster assigns jobs to us. I was rostered for Captain Melint's ship this cycle. We left Gilheim... we are going to Zaunt."

"So, you are trading slaves to the Mercurions," Rutha said. Her voice was like a whip. "North or South?"

"South." The big man cringed.

A collective gasp went around the others.

"What does that mean?" I said, looking around.

"South Zaunt is the home of the Phaedran Mercurion clans. Our fate there is even worse than being worked in the mines," Rutha said. "Zaunt has been embroiled in a civil war of attrition between north and south for nearly five hundred years. The Phaedra fight with machines that extract mana from the bodies of living things. They call them Sanghar'tak."

"Cursed things," Louis said hoarsely. "Machines that shred people on the battlefield and feed on their blood."

The Captain's Guard shook his head. "Please, m'Lady... I was hired on. I don't get a say in where the Guild sends us."

"I am Rutha of Vasteau, Court Sorceress of Ilia." Rutha drew herself up. "This ship is being taken over in the name of His Lordship Eduard Scandiva, Protector of Ilia and Warden of the Realm. Swear you'll lay down your sword for the duration of the mutiny, and face the Warden's justice."

The Cossack dropped his blade, glancing down at his dead comrade. "I surrender, lady."

"Then it is done. Come with us to confront your Captain." Even in rags, her skin sluiced with dirt and thin mud, Rutha had the air of a noblewoman: or at least someone who was used to being listened to and obeyed. Wikati looked reproachfully to me, then Bob and Louis.

"The lady and the mountain man have the right of it," Louis said.

Bob made a heavy sound. Reluctant agreement.

I nodded. ⟦Negotiation success!⟧

"Come. Let us finish this," Rutha said. "The sooner I get access to mana, the sooner we can be off this stinking hulk. You there - unlock this door."

"On the honor of my Guild, I cannot assist you," the guard said, speaking quickly. "They'll execute me as soon as you all will. Take the key from my neck. I can say I defended myself and did not cooperate with a mutiny in good conscience."

"This is not worth another life, indeed." Rutha turned her face to me. "Hector? Will you do the honor?"

I shrugged and walked up. The others tensed as I frisked the big guardsman, but he didn't lash out at me. I pulled a ⟦Bridge Key⟧ off from a necklace he was wearing. It appeared in my Inventory, under Quest Items.

"Okay, move to the sides of the door in case there's projectiles." I slot the key in the lock and turned it, squeezing the handle. "Get ready."

The party assembled: whatever 'Starborn' meant, apparently it made them inclined to listen to me. I cracked the door open, and yelled in through the gap. "This is a takeover! Surrender and drop your weapons!"

⟦You have learned a new Skill: Intimidate. While you may catch more flies with honey, you won't have any flies to begin with if word gets out you have a bug zapper.⟧

⟦Intimidate failed!⟧

"Go dunk your head, you goatfucking savage!" A man's voice roared back. "This is MY ship. Drop the forward rudders! Hit the rear flaps!"

"Is he crazy!?" Wikati's eyes widened, huge in her dark face. I was about to reply when the rudders dropped and the flaps... flapped?... and the ship suddenly pitched forward. It bodyslammed us all into the wall, including the guard, and sent unsecured cargo sliding across the deck to slam and shatter into the masts. And we were at the *front* of the ship, where the turbulence was least. Screams pealed from the back as rioting slaves and sailors were thrown off their feet into the air.

"Crazy as a shithouse rat!" I shouted over the din.

The ship pitched up and down as I kicked in the door, and it nearly slammed back on me as an explosion rang out inside the cabin, the crack of a pistol in a small room. The slug hit the hardwood and bounced, and I burst into the room just to see one of the Navigators take the ricochet right to the throat.

"Hold it, asshole!" I leveled my spear at the Captain, who was backed up into the other end of the bridge, where the rounded bubble windows converged into a soft point. "Freeze, or I'll run you through!

[[Intimidate failed!]]

The Captain snarled in frustration, frantically reloading as his Navigator slumped off his chair and fell limply to the ground. I tensed for the charge, only to be thrown off my feet as the ship lurched to one side. The Captain, wedged into the tight corner, was able to stay upright.

"Hold it right there!" Rutha stalked in past me to the abandoned navigation panel, which flared to life in her presence. "Or I'll burn you alive in here!"

At her command, the Captain finally faltered. "Who in the Hell are you people?!"

"I am the Court Sorceress of the Protectorate of Ilia, and I *demand* that you put down your weapon. Now." Rutha held her hand out over the Navigation sphere, causing the blue-white globe to swirl and the ship to shudder.

"Sir, please! Lucas is dying!" The other Navigator called back, panicked.

Rutha had told me she couldn't do anything without her spell gloves. I knew she was bluffing, but the Captain didn't. He licked his lip, face beaded with sweat, and dropped his pistol.

"Good man. Now. We're going to land as soon as we reach a coast," Rutha said. "How far off are we?"

"Not far. Abou' twenty leagues off of South Zaunt," The Captain growled, looking alongside at his other navigator.

"Then we're going to steer our way there, very nicely, and drop anchor," Rutha said sweetly. "And pray to the gods the Phaedran Mercurions don't find us before I can summon help, because they'll be just as happy to grind you through their blood-engine machines."

The Captain grunted, looking down along my bloody spear, then at his injured Navigator. "Lucas is out. You're a witch: can you work a navglobe?"

"I'm a fast learner," Rutha replied.

"Good. Because we're already off course." The Captain was tense, with the bated, high-strung air of a vicious dog in a cage. "You there: take my man downstairs and get him healing afore he dies."

I was in half a mind to argue, given that the fuckwit had shot his own crew member, but if we were going to make land... "Fine. But you better hold your end of the bargain, Captain."

I pulled Lucas outside by the armpits, where my team and a few escaped slaves were waiting.

"What's happening?" Louis asked.

"We're headed for land, and they're going to anchor and let us go. Wikati, Bob - do you think you can watch over the bridge? Make sure the Captain doesn't get any funny ideas about Rutha? I have to go take care of our Navigator and get some rest, or I'm going to keel over."

Bob grunted, and went inside without another word. Wikati nodded. "Sure."

"Alright. Good luck." And then I continued on my way, taking Lucas the Navigator - semi-conscious and bleeding - down below decks for a brisk drag to the medical bay.

Chapter 9

I got Lucas sorted out - they had the right tools in the medical bay that meant this NPC probably wasn't going to bleed to death - and commandeered an officer's bunk for myself. Every conscripted soldier dreamed of doing something like this at least once, right?

Once I bunked down, I tried to sleep - 'tried' being the operative word. My first problem was fear. What happened if I went to sleep in a world like this? When I'd played VR games before, you logged out and took the gear off when you got tired. The sensation of being fatigued and hungry inside of a video game was weird, and made more surreal because I was getting prompts warning me about fatigue and hunger penalties to my skill stats every now and then. Besides that, just because we had the Captain hostage and were headed for land didn't mean there weren't people on this ship who still wanted to kill me. The encounter with Matir – and my weird status in the game - also loomed large in my memory.

The nine-pointed star symbol no longer burned. It had faded into a raised scar with thin black lines just under the skin, like a Maori tattoo. While studying it, I discovered a feature of Archemi I hadn't known about - you could look at items and people and call up information on them, like an 'info' command. They ranged from the commonplace (Table: An ordinary table.) to the sarcastic (Chamber Pot: Step 1:

Apply butt to seat 2: ??? 3: Nightsoil!) and the cryptic (Vase: can be used as a murder weapon. Please be careful.).

When I looked at the tattoo, I got a blank translucent window. No text, no title, and no GNOSIS information input. Nothing. For some reason, the empty window made me more nervous than if there'd been no effect at all. The tattoo clearly had some kind of item/inventory number assigned to it, but no reference. Like 'missingno', or a glitch.

Or a virus, a small voice in the back of my mind whispered.

That thought woke me up enough to make me act. I called up my Message center, and rattled off a quick email to the Mod team with a description of what had happened. The reading and writing process was strange: I could basically compose by thinking of what I wanted to say. IRL, reading had been slow and painful thanks to my old friend dyslexia. Here, the system filled in the blanks and turned letters around the right way, allowing me to 'read' as quickly as anyone else might have normally done.

Once that was finished, the knot of tension between my shoulders finally eased off, and I began to get drowsy as the ship rocked on. I half-dropped off at one point, only to startle up when I realized I was falling asleep. Eventually, I couldn't keep my eyes open. When sleep came, it was like a door slammed shut. No dreams, no sense of time passing, just what felt like a long moment of darkness, and then the sound of something hard being beaten against wood and my name being called, over and over again.

"Hector! Hector!?"

I woke with a snort, confused, and groaned as a sharp, hot sensation lanced through my head. Suddenly, I was surrounded by HUD prompts.

[[Message from Temperance: "Are you alright?"]]

[[Sleep restored full HP!]]

[[You are hungry! HP will no longer regenerate!]]

"Urgh... wait, I'm coming!" I called to Wikati - it was her panicked voice outside - and then waved the alerts away like flies. "Auto-alerts off, for fuck's sakes!"

The little messages all disappeared, except for the message from Temperance. It was an Urgent Admin Message, and throbbed red when I tried to close it.

"Shit." Rubbing my eyes, I cued the message to display.

Hello, Hector - I have been trying to message you for the last five hours or so, so please open this message as soon as it arrives. We cannot find your character ID and believed your transfer had failed, so we were quite shocked to receive a report from you. It's fantastic that you are safe, but this is a first for us and we need to follow up to make sure you're alright. If you can get this note, please check in ASAP. You can reply to this message or whisper with username 'Temperance'.

Thank you,

Temperance.

So Matir hadn't been bullshitting me after all? I got to the edge of the bed and rubbed my hands over my face, frowning. I was too groggy to trust myself to think correctly, so I spoke aloud. "Menu: Message Temperance."

The HUD whirled and opened a rectangular message screen with a blinking cursor.

"Hector!" Wikati cried outside the door.

"Hang on!" I called back, and the cursor obediently typed what I'd said. "No, goddammit. Scratch that. *'Hi Temperance, I'm fine. Things are a little weird, but I think the game sorted itself out. I'll check in properly soon, but I have to run: there's an IC emergency over here. Is Steve okay? Thanks, Hector.* 'Send."

The message window flashed blue and then vanished. I staggered out of the bunk, still mostly undressed, and unlocked the door to reveal Wikati: bloodied, the armor she'd taken from the guards dented and torn.

"The bridge," she blurted. "The prisoners stormed the bridge. They dragged the Captain out!"

"What?!" I left the door open, and lunged back to the chair where I'd left my own clothes and weapons. "What the fuck happened? Where's Rutha?"

"She's trying to calm them down." Wikati's voice was high-pitched with stress. "They won't let the Navigators get to the console... I think they're trying to turn the ship around to go back to Daun."

"But that's fucking ridiculous. We were almost at the delivery port, weren't we?"

"Yes. We sighted land this morning, and when they saw that it wasn't a green coastline and we were North, and there were icebergs..."

"Where are they?"

"Near the bridge. There's a big crowd. Bobayer and Louis are trying to hold them off while Rutha steers, but-"

I sighed. "Go back out there, and I'll be right behind you."

The Lysidian woman nodded and broke off down the rocking corridor at a run.

I equipped my armor and sorted through my scanty pile of loot, but there was nothing any better than what I had. Just as I picked up my spear, something occurred to me. I could probably message Steve the same way I'd messaged Temperance. My spirits lifted a little as I dashed out the door, calling the HUD the same way I had for the gynoid. "Menu: Whisper Steven Park."

No such player found, came the reply.

His old MMO handle was SP_Mikklos, so I tried that.

[[No such player found.]]

My stomach twisted nastily in a way that had nothing to do with food. I tried several different variants of the 'Mikklos' name before giving up in a cold sweat. Steve probably had chosen name I didn't recognize, and that was why I couldn't tag him. I was about to try something else when the ship jolted, and then dropped what felt like about three feet.

"Fuck!" My feet left the deck, and I crashed against the wall as it listed hard toward the left, and then shuddered. My ears popped as the timbers around me groaned. I ran as fast as I could, catching myself every time the ship bucked, and burst out into a full-scale riot on the upper deck. Ex-slaves were battling sailors and each other in the early morning light. The nexus of the chaos was near the bridge.

"Hey! Move it! What's going on!?" I shouted over the noise as I got to the edge of the crowd, pulling people away, ducking a fist that swung at my head, and shoving back the man who'd taken a shot at me. I broke through to the front, where Bobayer was arguing down a semi-circle of angry Tuun.

"What else do we want? What kind of question is *that?*! Turn it around and kill the devil dog over there! That's what we want!" One man was leading the shouting, stabbing his finger past Bob toward Louis. Louis was standing in front of the Captain, who was slumped against the wall. The medic who'd cared for Lucas the night before was assisting him. The women were inside the bridge. Rutha was bent over a navglobe, disheveled and pale as milk.

"He lied to us!" Another older man at the front of the pack snarled, slashing a hand toward the bleeding Captain. "This isn't Gilheim!"

"Of course it's not sodding Gilheim! We don't have enough food or fuel to turn around!" Bobayer shot back. "We will land, and the Witch can use the engines to call for help from-"

He was drowned out by the rising rage of the people in front of us, and I was suddenly reminded of my own wisdom. Individuals could be smart, but mobs were always dumb.

"We ain't getting no help from the Witch!" Someone else howled from within the crowd.

"Look!" I waved a hand, resting the butt of my spear on the ground. "We're all in this together, and-"

"We'll be killed!" A Lysidian woman closer to the front cried out, her voice shrill with hysteria. "I don't want to die here!"

"Turn it around!"

"Give us the Captain!"

"You're working for *them!*"

"Throw them overboard!"

"Stop this! Stop this!" The old woman who had been chained in the row across from me was trying to calm people down, her voice drowned out by the growing hum of rage. I began to feel it, the air of menace. These people had been only the most tenuous of allies, and they were rapidly turning into their own worst enemies.

"This is stupid!" I said, unable to think of anything that could amp them down. "Please, calm down!"

A jar sailed over the heads of the people near the door, sending a few screaming and scattering as it smashed against the door to the bridge. It smelled like... lamp oil?

"You stupid pack of dogs!" The Captain roared, staggering up with the help of his surgeon. "Back it up!"

The surgeon paled. "Sir, please don't-"

"No!" Louis reached back, trying to grab his arm as another jar flew over our heads, shattering with a bang. The Captain snarled and brushed him off, pulling out his pistol from a hidden holster behind his back.

That was all it took for us to lose the little bit of control we had over the crowd. They overran us in an angry wave, boiling over so fast that I barely had time to put my spear up. We were swamped by at least thirty people, all of whom suddenly sprouted a rainbow of HP bars and ⟦Angry Mob⟧ enemy tags. Individually, the freed prisoners weren't very strong. As a group, they were as unstoppable as the tide.

I was forced to fight with my spear held like a staff, beating people off as they swarmed me with daggers, shivs, bottles and their fists, taking damage every time they landed a blow. It was death by a thousand cuts - five, six HP at a time, I fell back. I saw the old woman fall and cry out as she was trampled in the rush.

Fear flashed through me as I kicked away an enraged man with a guard's sword, parried a blow on reflex, and had to headbutt someone who got up in my face. "Wikati! Bob! Don't let them get into the bridge!"

The Captain shot into the crowd, and rage turned to screams of horror as someone went down with a gut full of lead. I dropped my spear, cracked a pair of skulls together, and tried to worm my way to where Wikati and Louis were fighting back-to-back near the door. I was almost there when someone leaped onto my back and took me to one knee. I threw them off with a roar, but it was too late. Someone booted me square to the head, and I went down until the collective power of twelve fists and feet, HP flashing orange. I heard smashing glass, female screams... and then the ship groaned, as if in pain, and began to tilt forward.

"You fucking idiots!" I shouted, blocking the blows to my face with my arms. "We're going to die if you kill her!"

But it was too late. The ship yawed as the rudders began to stroke the air unevenly, slowly building into an unstable pitching motion, back and forward and side to side. Half the mob was now trying to stop the other half, pulling the looters out of the bridge by their trousers and hair. I swayed up to my feet, bloodied and bruised, only to be thrown down by the motion of the ship. The sails snapped and loosened, wood moaning as the airship lurched and dropped. The powerful magical engines were surging, the regular thrumming sound becoming erratic as the deck angled up, sending everyone tumbling toward the back, then down, flinging the unlucky souls too close to the railings over the side.

I slid on my belly like a wet fish across the polished deck, flailing out desperately for something to grab. My native Tuun ability to withstand high altitudes and motion sickness was all that saved me from falling off the ship: I was able to stay orientated enough to catch the mast as I flew past it, hanging on as my HUD flashed in alarm.

Whatever had happened in the bridge, there was no recovering from it. I'd seen enough planes crash to know what a fatal angle of attack looked like, and now, I knew what it felt like, too. Surprisingly, not as terrifying as I'd expected. I'd thought I'd feel... something. Anything but cool self-control, a core of resignation that jelled as the ship groaned like a dying animal and rolled over. Whoever was at the controls was trying to save it by alternating thrust on either side, but it was too little, too late.

I hung onto the mast with all my strength, which became easier when the ship flipped and I could swing my legs up and wrap them around the mast, too. We tumbled toward the frozen ground below. If we landed on the hull, there was a chance I'd survive. If we landed on the deck...

Quest Update: Escape the Slave Ship... Or Die Trying
remember to find me in Mwszno

Exp: 150 EXP

[[Congratulations! You are Level 2!]]

[[You take 2500 points of impact damage!]]

[[You have died.]]

Chapter 10

I respawned in the slave hold with my shoulder impaled by a shard of wood. It would have been less horrifying if it had hurt, or if it had been a visible injury of some sort, but there was no pain and no blood. My body had just formed around it like playdough, and I was stuck.

"Har har. Morning wood... I get it." Groaning, I looked around. The *Arabella*'s hold was smashed, a landscape of wreckage jutting toward the sky, and I couldn't see much. My head was thick, my limbs tired and heavy. I tried to recall what had happened, and came up blank. There had been the sensation of falling, the rip and roar of the wind, and then a black rumbling through my bones before... nothing. Death had come so suddenly I hadn't even really had time to be afraid.

My HP was only a quarter full, the meter throbbing with a dull red pulse. A lot of small icons were flashing for attention in my HUD: messages, quest updates, status alerts.

[[You are starving! -1 HP per 5 minutes, no HP regeneration.]]

[[You are parched! -1 HP per 5 minutes, no HP regeneration.]]

[[You have a message! Temperance writes: RE: Are you alright?!]]

That wasn't good. I only had 45 HP left, which gave me just under an hour to find water and food, assuming I could extract the wood from my clipped arm without bleeding to death. Grimacing, I sat up, careful in case the shard was secretly attached to something. Then, I pulled up Temperance's message – it was short and to the point.

Hello, Hector: Please get in contact as soon as you're able. We have news re: Steven Park. Temperance.

My head swooped. 'News'. A tactful way of saying 'he didn't make it'.

I went back to the main menu and opened a private chat with Temperance. "I'm alive and checking in, ma'am. What can you tell me about Steve?"

After a couple of seconds, her window brightened, and a video feed opened. I saw her face neatly positioned within the frame, her expression carefully styled into a mask of concern. "Hector: thank you for getting back to us. We were beginning to worry again."

"I'm still worried," I replied. "What about my brother?"

"We would like to offer our condolences," Temperance said. "He did not successfully transfer."

I looked away, throat tightening.

In response to my silence, Temperance began to speak again. "You and your brother were both in the critical phase of HEX. Previously, we had only attempted uploads of people with Stage One and Two. He was our first Stage Four. It... decreased his odds substantially."

"He might have made it. You didn't know I was here." My voice was still steady. "He could be alive, and we just don't know it."

"We knew you had reached the character creation and neural duplication stage. There is no record of him ever getting that far. No psychological or neural profile was created for him. We waited to see if the system would produce another anomaly, but there were no results. I'm sorry, Hector."

I clenched my jaws, looking down at the tattoo branded into my flesh. I couldn't even think about my big brother being dead - really dead - right now. He'd been my last family, my last link to the real world. It just... no. Not now, when I was stuck somewhere like this. I had to survive, push on. Then, I could think, digest the news... and mourn.

"Do you know what this symbol is about?" I lifted my arm to show Temperance the tattoo.

"It appears to be one of the elemental faction symbols. The Darkness faction," she said. "Where did you get it?"

"Guy calling himself Matir. He helped me out of the bug."

Temperance pressed her lips together in a thin line. She looked puzzled. "Matir is a feature in the game's mythos and storyline, but not an active character. None of the draconic pantheon is. It was probably a contrivance of the AI. The game's systems try to keep the world in-character at all times, so it made an auto-correction with something within the scope of the lore."

Matir was a dragon god? Interesting. "What can you tell me about him? He gave me a quest."

"Not very much. You would have to ask one of the developers," Temperance replied. "But given that Matir is part of Archemi's lore, they may be reluctant to tell you much."

"Okay. One thing, though: is he a good or evil-aligned character?"

"The elements are fundamentally neutral," Temperance replied. "But I am not connected to the game's database. I have spent most of my time as the CEO's personal assistant since I was deployed two years ago."

Only two? I was about to say something sassy when something inside of the ship's belly collapsed, and the smell of smoke drifted to my nose. "I'm stuck and about to burn to death. I'll touch base again later."

"Alright. We are very sorry to have to deliver-"

"I'm a soldier. I'll cope." I was an unwilling conscript, really, but I'd been through the dissociation training everyone else had. Before she could press me into the breakdown I was holding off, I cut the link and refocused on my predicament.

"Okay, game." I reached up, seized the piece of wood, and let out a steadying breath. "Let's see if you autocorrect this shit."

I hauled on the shard for about a second, until pain blinded me and I let go with a yelp.

⟦You have taken 3 points of piercing damage!⟧

"Oh, fuck you." I picked myself up, and cautiously rolled my shoulder. As long as I didn't try to pull the wood out, it acted like it was part of my body. With a sigh, I called up an empty Dev Report, and dutifully filled it in. I mentioned that I'd spawned without any tools or inventory, but left out the part with Matir. I'd gotten a quest from him, so he was an NPC and part of the game. A creepy NPC with a creepy-ass quest, but a quest none the less.

Once the message was sent, I looked over my other alerts and my character sheets. As I was contemplating how my stats had gone up, I heard a sharp *bang!* and then the crumpling sound of collapsing wood overhead. The air was hazy, and it was getting harder to breathe.

Cursing, I looked around for my gear and weapon. It was at that moment that I realized I was stark naked, save for the addition of the wood. I picked my way over crumbling timbers, halting in disgust when I encountered the first crumpled body. It was a girl, and her bones had been smashed in so many places that her limbs were barely recognizable as arms and legs. The carnage only grew worse the farther I went, climbing naked *down* toward the deck through the gaps created from the crash.

I stumbled on the contorted corpse of the [[Captain's Guard]] we'd spared near the bridge, and stopped numbly, blinking as my brain tried to put the pieces of him back together. As I did, his loot list appeared, waiting patiently to my left while I struggled with shock. I looked past him, and realized that the deck had split from the sides of the ship and rammed up into its belly on an angle. Among the people tangled with the wreckage was Louis. Well... half of Louis. Sure enough, staring at him brought up the same menu. He was equipped with nothing except a [[Torn Shirt]].

Head ringing, I lurched to one side, fell to my knees, and threw up. With the Starving status in place, I didn't produce anything except water, but it felt - and hurt - just like puking, only without the hydrochloric acid chaser. I could feel each one of these things piling up on me like weights. The ship crashing, Steven dead, the carnage around me... the death of hundreds, maybe because of my decisions.

"No!" I slammed a fist on the deck, struggling for breath. "No! Fuck this! I won't let this fucking stop me!"

Anger replaced numbness as I pushed myself up, panting, and weaved my way to the wall of the ship. It arched over us like a giant fireplace full of tumbled kindling. I began to feel along it in the near-darkness, searching for a weak patch of wall until I found it.

The rumbling sound of the sea and a frosty ocean wind blasted my face as I kicked through a couple of shattered planks and squeezed through the hole. We had crash-landed on top of a cliff, sliding over the hard ground before coming to a stop against a snowbank. It wasn't snowing right now, but the sky overhead was dark with swirling clouds. It was beautiful, in a stark, crystalline way.

[[Warning: Temperature is dangerously low. Find clothing or armor for protection!]]

"Alright! Jesus!" I wasn't going back into the hold to pull clothes off the dead - no way. Instead, I pulled myself out, hung onto the edge of the hole, and dropped down to the ground. It wasn't too far, only about twelve feet, but a long enough fall that I jarred my knees and feet when I landed. A pale blue ring joined my red HP corona: my hypothermia bar. Great.

I rubbed my arms briskly, looking around. There were dead people everywhere, some of them already attracting ravens. The birds were massive, larger than cats. Reluctantly, I found a corpse who was wearing heavier clothing - a jacket, shirt, pants and boots - and looted them bare. When I equipped the [[Ill-Fitting Clothes]], the pale blue bar disappeared. They weren't the kind of clothes that could have protected someone in the real world, not unless they were a supernaturally tough Tibetan-Viking badass like me. I was feeling more nationalistic about Tungaant by the day.

As I turned back to the ship, I got a Quest prompt. Curious, I opened it up.

New Quest! (Optional): Find the Survivors

The slaver airship Arabella has crashed on the coast of the Northern Wastelands. You managed to survive - but what about the others? Pull people from the wreckage and prevent them from freezing.

Special: This quest is timed (120 min)

Rescued people: 0/???

Difficulty: Average

Reward: 20 EXP per rescued person and Renown.

I nodded and accepted, grimly surveying the destruction around me. For all I'd resented the draft, there was something to be said for military training. It gave you a different way of looking at the world, turning 'hopeless disaster' into objectives, situations and challenges.

My first challenges were to find something to eat and drink, then set up a place to take the wounded - there was no point in dragging them out of the wreckage only to have them freeze to death, and it was clear that this game was as much a survival game as it was an RPG. The key was the snow bank that had been created by the weight of the skidding skyship. The ship had split into three parts: the end of the ship was nothing but blasted debris that had exploded near the edge of the cliff. The burning, collapsed middle section and most of the deck was where I'd come from, while the remaining part of the deck, the bridge and prow had slid along the ground and driven snow up in an arched wall around it. That part of the ship wasn't burning, and the snow formed a ready-made overhang that could be reinforced and used as a staging area for the injured.

Resolved, I stormed over and began to pick up useful-looking pieces of wood and tinder, belatedly realizing that the clipped piece stuck in my arm had finally vanished. The place where it had stuck still felt weird, so I turned away from the wind and opened my jacket to have a look at my shoulder. What I saw made me blanch. There was a black... scar? Wound? When I touched it, I felt nothing. The area was numb, and my fingers didn't feel anything as I felt over it. I couldn't push them through, but there was no sensation at all. The skin around it felt fine: It was just that jagged, triangular patch where the spike had jutted from my body.

Shivering, I closed my jacket up against the weather, and turned back to get to work. I stored firewood under the overhang, then began to pack down the walls, compressing the snow to make it firmer. Cold flakes rained around me as I worked, and the lip of it crumbled and showered me, but the majority of the impromptu cave was already solid from the impact. I used a timber to scrape away a hole at the back of the cave, and then built up a fire pit from packed snow, clearing it down until I reached the grass underneath. Snow was a surprisingly good insulator, when you were in a cold environment like this: if there was enough room between the fire and the side of the pit, it wouldn't melt the snow and put itself out.

As I assembled the shelter, I got progressive alerts scrolling in the corner of my eye.

⟦Congratulations! You have learned Survival 1!⟧

⟦You have learned Survival 2!⟧

⟦Congratulations! You have learned your first Common Craft Skill: Improvise Shelter! Would you like to learn more about Crafting?⟧

"Sure. Why the hell not?" I was getting better at reading and-or absorbing knowledge from the prompts as I went about my business, so I set the message to read out as I angrily heaved firewood into the pit.

Crafting

Craft Skills in Archemi can be divided into two families: Common Crafts and Advanced Crafts. Common Crafts are craft skills which can be easily studied or discovered without the aid of special training or rare tools. They include Improvisional Crafting Skills (Shelters, Mending, Foraging), Gardening, Cooking, Prospecting, and Animal Husbandry. To learn Common Craft skills, you can talk to experts, experiment with the ingredients and tools you find, pull apart weapons and armor, read books or expose yourself to special Skill Runes.

Based on your unique cognitive profile, you may learn any Common Craft to Journeyman level and fourteen common crafts to Master level.

Advanced Craft Skills, (Armoring, Alchemy, Gastronomy or Astrology, to name a few) require specialized tools and workspaces, as well as training. All Advanced Crafts require a working knowledge of synergized Common Craft skills to become available. For example, to gain access to Alchemy tuition or use Alchemy Skill Runes, you must have a basic working knowledge of collecting useful plants (Herbalism), and where to find them (Foraging). The higher your Common Craft skills, the faster you will advance in your chosen Advanced Crafts.

There are hundreds of Advanced Crafts to choose from, but you can only Master a maximum of fourteen, so choose wisely!

Crafting checks are based on your Intelligence + Perception + the most relevant physical stat to the craft. They also synergize with non-crafting skills, if those skills are available. For example, the general skill Survival synergizes with crafting Shelters, Foraging for food, and Mending your items. These General Skills give you bonuses to your Crafting attempts.

You will find it difficult to improve some Craft skills if you do not have supporting general knowledge - for example, Botany for Alchemy. In addition, some teachers may refuse to instruct you if you have not shown sufficient interest in your field by gaining knowledge or experience-based skills in their area of expertise.

I nodded along as I listened, dumping wood into the firepit and checking the time left on the countdown. I'd burned about 30 minutes setting up - not bad, given the circumstances. I decided to light the fire from some wood that was already burning instead of starting from scratch: there were plenty of embers to get a fire started, and drilling - rubbing a hard stick into a softer piece of firewood - took longer than it would for me to jog down and get wood that was already burning. I was shaky, still losing HP, but my Tuun toughness was standing me in good stead.

I thawed snow in my gloves and ate the slush as I went to collect embers from the burning middle section of the ship. I got a helmet from one of the dead - lot of good it had done him - and scooped in a mixture of hot rocks and wood crawling with small, intensely hot flames. As I did, I heard a groan from somewhere inside the hulk, not far away. A human groan.

"Hang on in there!" I called out, pulling away with my precious cargo of hot wood. It felt callous, but without fire warming the snow cave, anyone I managed to free could go into shock and die. Most games didn't go that far, but I wasn't willing to assume Archemi did anything by halves.

Once the fire flickered to life, I dusted out the hot inside of the helmet and put snow in it, leaving it to thaw beside the fire as I stumbled back to where I'd heard the voice. There, I pulled a tattered coat off a body and used it to dig out around the edge of the ship, ignoring the warning flashes of my health ring. "Can you hear me in there!?"

"Nngh... yes?" A woman's voice.

"Can you move?"

"... I... I think so?"

I dug harder, shuddering with exertion as snow and dirt flew aside. Eventually, I broke through and stuck my head in to look around at what was around the other side. Through the smoke and dust, I saw a head stir from under a pile of debris. Long silver hair, lean pale limbs. Her clothes were torn, but... "Rutha? Is that you?"

Chapter 11

"Hector?" Rutha looked up at me in shock, and her eyes darkened. It was like she was seeing me for the first time.

"Sure is." I grabbed a broken timber and started digging around her. "Can you feel your legs?"

"Yes." The elfin woman grimaced. "Unfortunately. But something's caught... I'm stuck."

"That's good. I'm going to need you to start wiggling from side to side, okay?" I scraped away soil and snow, sweat pouring down my forehead. "One, two, three. Wiggle wiggle wiggle!"

Even with the dire circumstance, the order was still funny. Rutha choked back pained laughter, wiggling as commanded, and the trench began to widen around her as I scraped with the timber. When she began to be able to inch forward, I wedged the timber in beside her until I felt it jam, then linked arms with her and pulled her free. Rutha yelped as cloth and skin tore, but the cut she took was better than what happened once the wreckage was destabilized. It crumpled and crashed in where she had been laying, a giant bear trap made of splintered wood.

Rutha had been wearing rough fabric trousers, which were now torn from just over her knee all the way to her foot. Pulling her out had drawn a long gash up her calf. Before I could intervene, she seized the ripped cuff, and tore it around, using the cast-off material to put pressure on the bleeding wound.

"Tie it on. We have to get out," I said. "There's other people here and not much time to get them free. Think you can walk if I help you?"

"Yes." Her voice was tired, but firm. She held out an arm, and slung it around my offered shoulder. "Are you-?"

I shook my head. "I really need something to eat and to sit down. But I'll live, and so will you."

"You're Starborn," Rutha murmured. "Aren't you?"

It was the first time anyone other than Matir had mentioned it, and I glanced at her sharply as I helped her to her feet. The god's whole 'born under a dark star' part of being Starborn probably wasn't necessary information. "That's what I've been led to believe."

"Then it's true. The Starborn *are* returning." The sorceress winced, but she had an iron will, and she was more than capable of keeping up with me as we squeezed out of the wreckage and picked our way to the now-warm snow cave.

There was only 40 minutes left in the quest. I tried not to worry about the timer as I helped Rutha to sit. "Can you find a way to make some water here?"

"Yes, go help the others." Huffing with effort, she found a way to make herself comfortable. "Hector, be careful. Don't overexert yourself. If you feel weak..."

"Don't worry. I'll be back." I nodded, and scrambled out again.

Rutha had a point, though:

My stomach was gnawing at itself - and at me - leaving me nauseous and lightheaded. I steeled myself, and trudged over anyway, scanning the scattered cargo for anything edible. As I focused on my search, item tags came into view around me. Shattered trunks, boxes, crates... wait. Crates and boxes were lootable, weren't they?

"Hold on! I'll be right there!" I called to the other rescuers, turning toward the tattered trail of broken wood, torn cloth, and smoldering cargo that led to the edge of the cliffs. Sure enough, the containers had loot in them. I found string, wire, linen, and then, to my great relief, food.

Hard Tack

A hard, plain cracker made of compressed flour, water and salt. Slightly more palatable than wood, but about as nutritious. Prevents starvation. Heals 2 HP.

Dried Fish

Chewy, salty, and very fishy. Heals 10 HP

I inhaled three fish without tasting them as my nausea turned to ravenous hunger, and then stuck a piece of hard tack between my teeth and gnawed on it as I looted what other food I could carry. I didn't have a pack, so I was only able to take a half a dozen fish and three or four pieces of hard tack - all that could fit in the pockets of the [[Ill fitting clothes]]. That put me bac to 52/180, which was a lot better than I had been.

[[Warning: 20 minutes left in Quest: Rescue the Survivors!]]

Feeling stronger, I ran back to the gaping hole in the side of the ship and joined in the search and rescue, helping the two strangers dig out whoever and whatever we found. I was able to pick up an [[Iron Dagger]], which I used to dig. We pulled out five people in nineteen minutes, three of whom were alive. The sixth was an unconscious man trapped face-down underneath timbers that were hot to touch. The fire was almost on us, and I was hot inside of my heavy clothes.

"Come on! We can get him!" I called to the others, leaning all my weight down on a heavy beam we were using to lever the debris on top of him. "Grab his hands and pull!"

There was a crash from back inside the belly of the ship, and then the roar of flames as something flammable burst and accelerated the mana fire. The ozone fumes of magic clung to everything like bleach.

[[Quest Warning! One minute left!]]

I growled, hauling down until my shoulders popped as the others clambered in around me, grabbing the unconscious man's hands and pulling him out on his belly. I dropped the lever once his feet were clear, and that section of the wreckage simply collapsed. Panting, I wiped my forehead, and then yelped as a gout of blue-tinged flame erupted from the tangle of broken wood and metal in front of me, stumbling back. I turned that into a run through the path we'd cleared, jumping a broken chair. When I landed, the hulk moaned... a sound followed by the crumpling sound of shattering charcoal as the ship caved in on itself.

"Out out out!" One of the other rescuers - a thin man with big teeth, his face deeply lined with soot and sweat - shouted as we hauled the survivor out into the open and jumped with him to the ground. The timer ran out while I gathered myself for the leap from the hole, and I was alarmed to feel the hull move under my feet, turning inward like a dying spider as the magic-fueled fire consumed the wreckage.

Quest Complete! Rescue the Survivors

You have managed to rescue 7 people out of the wreckage of the Arabella!

Reward: 140 EXP

Bonus: Talk to Rutha.

Congratulations! You reached Level 3!

The mission could have gone better. We'd only pulled out four living people. Plus me, the pair of men I was working with, and Rutha, that made eight adult survivors out of a couple hundred. Blah.

My heart sank as I watched the ship cave and burn. "Bobayer... Wikati. God dammit."

I tried telling myself that they were just NPCs, but the feeling of loss was real. I hadn't even really gotten time to get to know them, but they'd been brave and willing and... other than Rutha, I was alone.

Memories of Steve and my family were trying to fight themselves in past the fatigue and the necessity of being disciplined, cold, rational. Frustrated, I turned away and joined the other survivors, who were trying to get the unconscious man to wake up. "Hey, guys: I'm going to go get some of those scattered planks to use as sleds. If we take a body each, we can get everyone together in the shelter and plan our next move."

"As you say." The second rescuer was a Lysidian man with long pointed ears. He held up a hand with his thumb and middle finger pinched together, some kind of 'okay' symbol, and got back to what he was doing.

Rutha was tending the fire when we got back, helping the other stragglers with sleds and improvised crutches. There were more people near the shelter now - three women who huddled together around the fire.

I pushed my makeshift sled all the way inside, and turned to the women. "Any of you able to help me with these? Some of these men are wounded."

Without a word, the women picked themselves up and began to assist. They were mute with cold and shock, but like me, they worked mechanically, dissociated from their feelings by the needs of the moment.

"Hector, we have to go back out as soon as we can," Rutha said. She had made a splint for her leg out of torn cloth and broken wood. "I need your help to find the ship's engines."

"One of them is completely screwed," I said. "Cracked open and on fire. The other is... uh..."

I wracked my memory for the other engine, but couldn't actually recall having seen it.

"It has to be close by." Rutha shifted with a grimace, and held up her good arm. She was still wearing the intact glass, metal and leather gauntlet she needed for magic. "If I can find some mana, then I can call my kingdom for aid."

That's right: she'd said something about being the Court Magician of the Regency of Something-or-Other. "Aren't we like... really far north? Like, middle of nowhere territory?"

"As I understand it, yes." Rutha gestured to the sled. "If you can use that to get me to the other engine, I can siphon the mana and use it to bring help."

I regarded her blankly for a moment, then shrugged and sighed. "How far away is help?"

"Ilia is quite far away, but physical distance is irrelevant," the sorceress replied crisply. "The light is growing shorter, Hector, and we risk being swept out to sea by the wind at night: if we are going to do this and survive, we should go."

Chapter 12

After ten minutes or so of experimentation at base camp, I managed to find a way to get rope on the sled so I could pull it along behind me instead of pushing it over the snow. Rutha was done with her fish and crackers and one other survivor had arrived by then, bringing more looted food with them. Rutha got on board, and I got my first real look at Archemi.

There were a number of things that told me that this truly was an alien world. Archemi's sun was not yellow: it was blue-white, and looked much smaller than the Earth's sun. The temperature felt about the same, but the light was a very pure white. I could see in the snow without any issues, but Rutha covered her eyes and grimaced as we left the shade of the snow cave. That white light was the reason Archemi looked as clear and vibrant as it did. I knew fuck-all about astronomy, but I'd worn blue-tinted glasses before, and remembered how the lenses had made trees and grass look greener.

Even more striking was the moon. It was rising over the land-side horizon from what I assumed was the east like a giant yellow eye. It was huge compared to the blue pin-point sun - easily four or five times the size of the moon I was used to seeing at night, and it was rising while the sun was still up. I slowed to a stop to get a better look at it, and realized after a moment that the moon had *clouds.*

"Hector? Is something the matter?"

"Woah," I said, looking back. "Archemi is a moon?"

Rutha blinked. "Pardon?"

"That." I pointed at the edge of the massive planet shimmering over the snow and gravel. "That's a bigger planet than this place, right? Like a binary planet, maybe?"

"That's Erruku," she replied, "Archemi's moon, the Palace of Kyrie."

I sighed. "Alright... never mind. So, where do you think this engine bounced off to?"

I expected a snarky answer, but instead, Rutha pressed the palm of her good hand against her brow and concentrated, eyes closed. "Toward the north-west. Closer to..."

"What?"

Rutha shuddered. She drew an hourglass symbol across her chest, like how a Catholic would cross themselves. "The ocean."

"What's the matter with the ocean?" I caught the sled ropes and resolutely dragged her toward the edge of the cliffs, looking around for anything resembling magical engine parts. "I mean-"

"You're from the high mountains, aren't you? I don't suppose you've ever really seen the ocean before."

"In my, uh, other lifetime, I saw it plenty of times," I said. "Blue, lots of waves. Kind of salty. I liked to go to the beach and swim or surf."

"You ARE Starborn," she said, with what might have been a touch of awe. "You do not fear death."

"It's more that I don't associate the beach with death." But I trailed off when we crested a small hill, and I finally got a view past the cliffs to the source of the thunderous noise that had been my constant companion since spawning in the guts of the Arabella. "Oh. Wow."

Monstrous. That was the only word for what I saw raging beneath the very high, very steep granite cliffs where we'd stranded. The water was a blue so dark it was almost black. My eyes tried to trick me into seeing a snow-capped mountain range that was bobbing up and down, because the waves that were lashing the sides of the cliffs were at least a hundred feet high. They peaked into charging white volcanoes of water that folded into yawning black pits, which in turn snapped shut like jaws rimmed with white teeth. Whirlpools raged wherever the waves and downdraft converged, sending up huge vertical plumes of foam. The waves smashed icebergs together further out, mashing them into pale blue rubble. Even the toughest aircraft carrier would have been ripped apart in that water.

"The ocean is a place for the dead." Rutha hunched her shoulders. "And Erruku has only just begun to rise. Once it is at its peak and the tide comes in..."

"This is *low* tide?" The waves were already reaching most of the way up the cliffs as it was.

The sorceress nodded grimly.

Guess that explained why there wasn't a huge amount of snow cover up here, and no trees or... any plants, really. "So! You were saying about that engine? How soon can help arrive?"

"Hopefully soon enough. Otherwise, we will have to trek inland until we find sanctuary from water."

I shook my head, scanning the field of debris, and paused as a flash caught my eye. Searching for items in an environment created a kind of augmented reality state, where highlights appeared around items of note. In this case, it was a breadcrumb trail of metal shards sparkling in the sunlight. The ground had been torn up around them, skid marks leading into a bank of powdered snow over a large disk-like shape, like a huge ice-hockey puck.

"Is that it?" I pointed.

"Yes. The resonance is strong enough."

I pulled Rutha in that direction, kicking things out of my way as we made our way there. I dropped the rope, and was about to close the distance to brush the snow away when her voice halted me.

"Wait! Hector, come back!"

"Huh?" I turned, confused, and then alarmed as I watched her struggle up onto her uninjured leg, face contorted with pain. "Wait, what's the matter?"

"Magic is dangerous." She was huffing through her nose as she hopped over. "The engine runs off a late system."

"What? You mean it doesn't run on time?"

"L.A.E.H.T." She spelled out the letters. "A Liquid Azurine-Emeraldine Hybrid Transmutation system, if I'm sensing everything correctly."

I squinted. "Just so you know, I heard you say something like: 'The engine probably hurped an azurine transmajiggy', okay? Just so we're clear on my level of magitech literacy."

"Azurine is... well, don't worry. The point is there could still be volatile mana gas trapped in the crucibus. Stay back."

"I hate it when I get gas stuck in my crucibus." I didn't like leaving Rutha in agony like this, but I was willing to admit I didn't know a thing about magic - or magical jet engines. "Seriously, though. What's a crucibus?"

"A crucibus is an artifact that can safely combine azurine, which is highly refined, neutrally-charged liquid mana, with ground emeraldine, which is a crystallized form of mana contaminated with copper," Rutha said distractedly. "Umm... the higher the purity, the more potential *animus* in the mana, but the more difficult it is to attune with and control. Because of the alchemical properties of copper, emeraldine has lower animus but is highly responsive to a mage's control, so it holds well in runes and sigils. A longhauler like this ship needs the power and sensitivity of azurine but also a great deal of control to be able to keep it flying, so it uses a hybrid engine."

I blinked a couple of times. "Every part of that is above my paygrade."

Rutha limped to the edge of the disk and brushed the scattered snow and dirt off the surface, revealing a pane of cracked quartz that crawled with acid-etched sigils. "*This* is the crucibus, which processes azurine and emeraldine into liquid fuel and gas. The gas is mostly azurine, so it's the most psionically active form of mana the ship expels. That's how the Navigators feel the air around the ship and adjust the position of all the rudders and flaps."

"Of course it is," I replied. "Silly me."

"I only hope I have enough energy to properly assess it and start the siphon." Rutha waved me back further, and held her gauntleted hand over the exposed crystal pane. She took a breath, let it out, and then made a series of gestures with her fingers. The gauntlet flared to life, blue light pulsing softly along the flowing lines of script engraved into different parts and pieces of it. What looked like electricity snapped between her fingers and the pane. I watched her curiously as her lips parted and she shuddered. I smelled ozone... and then something that smelled very much like blood. The odor bore into my sinuses, a coppery taste that made me recoil.

The snow trembled and danced on the surface of the engine, dancing with colors that formed whorls and crawling lines. All the technobabble had kind of disguised the magic part of what Rutha had been talking about, but as her hair lifted and her arm glowed, I began to see the other side of what she was talking about. Sure enough, the glow connecting her with the machine was blue and gaseous, if I understood it correctly - and the green glow was her fooling around with symbols written in the machine. How she did it... that was between her and the crucibus. And the transmajiggy, which was definitely the most important part.

A rippling wave of raw power washed over my skin. I hung back, burning with curiosity, but wary of the tingling, radiation-wash feeling I was getting from the magic. Rutha was mouthing a silent chant as she brought her other hand in like a conductor. The crawling lines of power resolved first into patterns, and then, to my surprise, script of some kind. The crack in the quartz was spewing boiling gas into the air, but it parted and swirled around Rutha in a slow vortex as she did whatever the hell she was doing, and-

There was a *thump* through the air around us, as if everything had lifted slightly and then dropped. I felt myself rise off the ground for a second, just before a flash of light threw me back on my ass. I slid away, staring as a column of raw energy exploded up from the center of the engine and Rutha cried out in pain - or ecstasy - as it funneled into a straight pillar into the sky above us.

"Rutha!" I flipped up to my feet, halted by the appearance of a new teal bar and a flashing alert: *Warning! You are in danger of dying from mana poisoning!*

The teal bar was decreasing rapidly, like a suffocation meter. Coughing, eyes watering, I fled from the overpowering metallic stench - and Rutha. The light was too bright to stare at, like a magnesium flare, so I ran with a hand over my eyes until the teal bar disappeared, the light faded, and I could breathe again.

I looked back. Rutha was floating. Her hair had lifted, fluttering around her like a veil of liquid mercury as she regained command of her magic. The mana had formed a slow vortex around her and the engine. It was like trying to look at someone through blue stained glass.

I was boggling so hard I almost didn't notice the amber quest alert. I final did when it turned red and jumped, startled.

New Quest: Protect the Sorceress!

In order to summon help, Rutha, Court Sorceress of Ilia, must sustain a beacon of energy to guide her allies to your location. Unfortunately, magic also attracts unwanted attention: monsters and other Stranged creatures who hunger for mana and the magically-charged flesh of mages. Protect Rutha until help arrives, but don't get too close - or you could end up Stranged yourself!

Timed Quest: 5 minutes

Reward: EXP and Renown

Rolling my shoulders, I cracked my neck and blew out a tight breath. Sure, why not? A 'Protect the Flag' quest, right now, while I was languishing on less than half HP and without any good healing items? Let's rock.

No sooner had I accepted than there was a shriek from overhead. I watched with a sinking heart as four huge winged shadows circled us, and shaded my eyes to look up at the sky. It was that moment that I remembered I didn't have a spear any more: just a somewhat blunt dagger that I'd been damaged by using it to dig people out of the ship. I didn't have any armor, either, save for my wet leather helmet.

Scowling, I shook the soupy water out of my helmet, pulled it on, and thumped it down onto my head. "Harpies. Why the *fuck* does it have to be harpies?"

Chapter 13

The first harpy dove with a seagull-like shriek, clawed hands extended for Rutha's back. I shook my head, knife in hand, and charged it from behind as it pulled up to harass her, tawny wings flapping furiously.

"HuuuRRAH!" I leapt from the ground and jumped onto the spindly creature's back, stabbing at its neck and shoulder. The harpy was a skinny humanoid, vaguely vulture-like, and naked. It screeched as my dagger plunged into its flesh, spraying indigo-dark blood from the wound every time it beat its wings. The blood burned my skin where it landed.

[[You stab a Harpy for 10 points of piercing damage!]]

[[Harpy is bleeding!]]

[[You are poisoned!]]

"What!? Since when in the fuck are harpies *poisonous?!*" I shouted, dismayed, as a sick feeling of nausea washed through me. The harpy threw me off, clumsily retreating into the air, just as two more dived. I snarled, slashing wildly, dealing damage here and there as I lost HP from the harpy's toxic blood and the odd scratch. The knife was really the wrong weapon to be using on the damn things. I hadn't killed any, but so far, I was keeping them away from Rutha.

"Hector! Can you hear me?"

The woman's voice was in my mind, the words forming out of my own thoughts, but in Rutha's voice. *"Uhh... yes?"*

"Hold them off just a little longer! The Skyrdon are on their way!"

I had no idea what a Skyrdon was, but I hoped they had better weapons and armor than I did. I was back to a quarter HP and sinking. I still had a Dried Fish and a piece of Hard Tack: in battle, consumed food items vanished from your Inventory and folded straight into your HP, instead of you having to eat them. Twelve points wasn't much, but every point counted in this fight.

I Doubletapped a Harpy as she flew into my face, raking me with her hind claws. I took 5 damage, but my stabs landed like hammerblows in her ribs. She screamed, and I kicked her away from me before she could bleed onto my exposed skin. The harpy flopped away across the hard ground in a tangle of wings, but there was no time to celebrate. As I recovered from the blow, two more shadows plummeted toward me. I slashed out at the one to my right, teeth gritted against the pain of the slashes the first monster had given me. The wounds faded as my HP struggled up, regenerating as I fought off clutching hands, and then abruptly halting when blue blood splashed across my face.

⟦You are poisoned!⟧

"I fucking know!" I snarled, fighting not to be lifted from the ground. Once you were poisoned, you couldn't be double-poisoned, so I laid into the screeching harpies without pause, throwing one off and killing the other. The only good thing about the Poison status was that the continuous damage made my Adrenaline Points charge faster, and that meant more Doubletaps.

⟦Warning! You are at 10 HP!⟧

⟦30 seconds remaining.⟧

I don't know what it was: the countdown, the grating screech of the monsters I was fighting, or the fact they were monsters, not humans... but something cut loose in me. All the rage and fear I'd been holding back since learning that my parents were trapped inside the HEX quarantine zone ruptured out past the walls I'd put up around it.

"JUST FUCKING DIE!" I felt a wave of cold fire twist up through my right arm, the arm that Matir had branded, and as I slammed the knife into the Harpy's skull, a brief look of surprise passed over its ugly face before tendrils of dark energy tunneled through it and blew its head apart. My adrenaline drained to zero, but my HP bar suddenly jumped 30 points.

I roared wordlessly as harpies mobbed me from the sky: four of them, then eight, as their attention tore away from the column of magic. As the timer turned red, counting down the last ten seconds of the quest, the Mana beacon turned blue, then green, then violet. Rutha shouted something I didn't understand, flinging her arms open... and the pillar became a field, then a field of twinkling purple gas.

5... 4...

[[Warning! You are at 10 HP!]]

3... 2... 1...

[[You are poisoned!]]

I was pushed down, bleeding from a dozen cuts, and slashed out weakly at the squabbling bird-women trying to tear me apart. The world turned dark with a rushing sound, and I braced for death - again - as a huge cold shadow fell over us. The harpies screeched in alarm and suddenly took wing like a flock of pigeons, only to scream as a straight bolt of lightning split through the air overhead and incinerated them. The couple who managed to scatter outside of the fire shrilled, winging off to the side. One got clear: the other was snatched by a huge talon as an enormous winged blur shot by us, barrel-rolling at speed.

Dragons.

There were four of them, and as they flew back over us, the air thundered. They were at least a hundred feet long, from the tips of their elegant, aquiline snouts to the ends of their whip-like tails. My mouth hung open, pain forgotten, and I struggled up onto my elbow as the blue dragon and his rider came out of their roll and strove for height, revealing the pure white dragon I hadn't seen.

⟦Quest Completed! Protect the Sorceress⟧

⟦You earn 120 EXP!⟧

"Hector!" Rutha hobbled over to me and knelt down. She looked exhausted, even gaunt, her cheekbones like knives set underneath her skin. Her long, pointed ears drooped with fatigue. "Oh no... the harpies! Their toxin!"

"Whuh?" Awe had pushed aside the pain. "Oh, right. Poison. Do you still have any fish?"

"Yes?" She fumbled back on her scavenged pouch, pulling out the dried fish I'd given her. I grabbed it off her, and as she watched, bemused, crammed it into my mouth. I didn't even have to chew it - it just vanished, and the sliver left on my HP jumped back up ten points.

"I-I don't think fish is a cure for harpy blood..." she said, uncertainly, and then looked down at my wounds. They were healing rapidly. Her eyes widened.

"Must be a Starborn thing." The poison was now competing with the HP regen from the food. I dropped a point, gained a point, but it was relatively stable. "I'll live. These... these are Skyrdon? Dragons?"

The dragons formed a disciplined formation above, turning on their wingtips and arrowing back toward us from over the ocean. As a unit, they backwinged and touched down, sending snow flying. The lead dragon was a brilliant white and silver creature whose scales flexed like mercury. There were two blues and a green, only slightly smaller than their squadron leader.

They were... beautiful. Most dragons were either six-limbed – wings, plus four legs – or the four-limbed 'wyvern' type dragons. These dragons were the six-limbed variety, but they looked more like velociraptors than traditional dragons. Graceful, with a cat-like quality to the way they moved, their hides shimmered and flexed with holographic color. They had smaller forelimbs, with expressive, dexterous claw-tipped 'hands' that they carried off the ground. Their necks were S-shaped and sinuous, their heads almost greyhound-like in shape. Everything about them was streamlined for speed: The backswept horns and barbells, their long, narrow wings, the blades-edge forward profile of their bodies.

I was gawping at the dragons so hard that I only belatedly noticed the riders. They were tied to their saddles with quick-release point harnesses connected to long braided leather cables. Like their dragons, they were armored for aerodynamic speed. The knights wore swept-back helmets, close-fitting shoulder guards and bracers, and more leather than metal. The armor was well-made and elegant, giving them good protection and mobility while protecting the most vulnerable areas of their bodies.

The dragons crouched, putting their hands down on the cold ground, and their riders slid down with their lances in hand. Their faces were distorted by their helmets. The lead knight's visor was solid metal, and my first thought was that there was no way they could possibly see through them, until I noticed the way that the steel smoldered with crawling blue embers... embers that followed a complex sigil pattern.

I groaned, fighting to sit up as the group of dragon knights jogged over to us. The man in the lead – tall, built like a quarterback - had white-and-steel armor with gold trim, while the others had only blue. He pushed his visor up to reveal a long, hard, starkly handsome face. There was no visible hair around the edge of his helmet, but this man's eyebrows were golden-blond, and his eyes... his eyes were weird. I couldn't exactly say why, but he looked like a blond Prince Charming serial killer, until a smile flashed over his mouth and his features softened. Slightly.

"My Lady Rutha." The guy in white and gold - Skyr Arnaud? - had a deep, smooth voice. "I'm grateful to find you alive and talking. His Highness has been beside himself since you ceased contact. You're injured, terribly."

"I maintain both my honor and my ability, in no small part due to this man here." Rutha turned in a swirl of silver hair, looking at me with concern as I leaned against the shoulder of the Skyr who'd helped me to my feet. "Hector, this is Knight-Commander Yoren Arnaud, one of our finest Skyrdon and a champion of the realm."

The knight looked me over, and I had the distinct feeling he was unimpressed by what he saw but was too polite to say what was on his mind. He bowed very slightly from the neck. "A pleasure. Hector of...?"

Rutha's smile faded a little.

"Tungaant," I replied tersely. "A warrior of Tungaant."

The knight-commander arched both eyebrows. "Titleless? A *commoner*, are you?"

"We don't have peerage in Tungaant." The fact was part of the racial knowledge I'd downloaded during character creation. "No noble class."

"No nobility? Then who holds the land?" A tiny, condescending smile twitched at the corners of the man's mouth. I found myself liking him less by the second.

"Everyone owns the land," I replied. "There are boundaries set by the temples which are respected, but the steppe is not easily controlled by any kind of elite. We share all things evenly, or we die."

"How disorderly," Arnaud said, biting each word off cleanly.

"Hector is Starborn, Commander. One of the Stars of Destiny." Rutha spoke before I could retort. Her words made all of the Skyrdon stand up a little straighter.

"Starborn?" Arnaud blinked, and for a moment, the patronizing arrogance left his voice and face. "Impossible."

The sorceress leaned on my shoulder. "He came back from the dead. He heals wounds in battle... he has all the signs."

'He' had a name and could speak for himself, thank you very much, but mystique was to my advantage in such esteemed company. I tried to look heroic and serious, and let Rutha talk. Unfortunately, the knight-commander didn't suddenly smile and nod. He looked worried... maybe even disgusted.

"Starborn incarnate in *our* land. That is how it has always been," he said, glancing at Rutha's hand on my shoulder.

Rutha's brow creased. She was holding herself together, but it was clear she was reaching the end of her rope. "Well, there are stories of them in Lysian lands, good Skyr. I don't see why there wouldn't be representatives among the Tuun."

"Hmmph." Skyr Arnaud said. "Forgive me, lady: we have been talking while you are hurt. Tabetha, Pior: you will transport the survivors to Lys and arrange them hospitality at the Skiathan Orden's Eyrie. Make sure they are questioned, and held there until they can be seen safely to their homes."

Two of the knights: the woman who'd helped me up and one of the other men, both bowed. "Yes, commander."

I watched Tabetha go to her blue dragon mount, reaching up to the creature's muzzle with her hands as the dragon bent down. She rubbed his jaw with obvious affection, and the dragon rumbled with pleasure. The connection between them was palpable, powerful. It made my chest lift and tighten a little, that feeling you got when you were a little bit in love with something.

"As for you." He turned his attention back to me. "I don't think we can take you to your homeland, Hector – there are no known waypoints. But we can send you to any of the Warden's outposts in-"

"I want to go with you and Rutha," I said quickly. "To Ilia."

Arnaud did the eyebrow thing again. "Lady?"

"That suits me just fine," she replied. She was still leaning on me. "Hector did everything in his power to aid me. He led the slave revolt, and bought the ship into our hands through honorable combat. I watched him pull people from the wreckage, even though he was badly hurt, and he fought again on my behalf just now. I vouch for his honor, and I will provide a Writ of Good Standing for him to carry in Ilia."

"I cannot see the Warden approving of such a Writ, but as the Lady says." Arnaud forced a stiff smile. "Come, barbarian. We shall see if you faint on takeoff."

Chapter 14

There's nothing quite like your first time.

I still remember what it felt like to sit on my first motorcycle. It was raining, and the air was heavy with the smell of wet leather and exhaust as I kicked the engine to life. I sat there with the engine rumbling through my bones, letting it warm while the instructor led us through the next steps. Even before we'd done our first circuit around the course, I knew that that was *it.* No matter what else I did, riding these machines was the thing I wanted to do for the rest of my life. I was having the same feelings a second time, but this time, it was for the dragons.

"His name is Talenth," Commander Arnaud said, boots crunching over the snow. His dragon was crouched with his tail held high and stiff in the air behind him, the great white breastbone resting in the snow so that the commander could step up on his forearm, reach up to grasp the sharp protrusion of the forward wing shoulder, hook an ankle over the edge of Talenth's wing, and pull himself up onto it. "Ever been in the air, outlander?"

"Not like this, Sir." I studied the way he moved up along the great beast's body. He walked up Talenth's wing until he reached the saddle – a scalloped seat of leather nine feet long, strapped around his chest like a backpack and cinched low around his belly through a scarred hole in his wing membrane.

"Don't worry, boy. We won't be doing anything too spectacular on this journey." Arnaud threw me a harness from Talenth's back. It tumbled down, bounced off the dragon's shoulder, and landed in my hands with enough speed I nearly fumbled it. It looked like a rock climber's harness. It belted around the waist, pelvis and thighs, like a rock climber's harness. "Make sure this is snug, but not too snug. You don't want it too tight. Once it's done, pull up on the front ring and down on the back to see if it slips at all. Then see if you can get up here."

"Yes sir." I was actually shaking as I put it on. Not only because of the anticipation of flying, but because of the intermittent Mana Poisoning alert that flashed in the corner of my eye. Now and then, my HP started to drain... and I couldn't help but notice that it was timed with the dragon's breath, each time it frosted the air and blew back toward me.

Not quite believing what I was about to do, I put a hand on the dragon's arm and started my way up, following the same path that the commander had. Talenth wasn't cold and pebbly, like a reptile: his scaled skin was as smooth as polished metal, and intensely hot, like someone with a raging fever. When I reached the saddle, the Commander offered a hand and pulled me up with inhuman strength. There, I saw his eyes up close for the first time – and realized what made them so strange. His irises were huge, barely leaving any room for the whites, and so were his pupils. The usual rim of pink that surrounded a normal person's eye was dark gray. The dragonrider had literal eagle eyes.

"Just noticed, did you?" He said.

I cleared my throat. "Sorry, I didn't mean to stare."

"Most sane people do stare, and fear. The Skyrdon are a breed apart from normal men," Commander Arnaud said with a downward twist of his mouth. "Now, help me with Lady Rutha."

Two of the other knights had to help the exhausted, injured sorceress onto Talenth's back. The huge beast crooned encouragement every time Rutha winced and cried out, but after some careful adjustment, we got her onto the saddle. I watched as Arnaud helped Rutha into a harness, then guided her into a side-saddle position. He used straps on the saddle to belt the harness down in place, keeping her rooted to the saddle surface. I moved to the opposite side and matched the straps. "Can Talenth understand us? Hear us?"

"Of course. But he only speaks to me." Arnaud replied. "Mind to mind. While I assist the lady, go buckle yourself down. You'll either figure out the straps or you won't."

I had the distinct impression he would be just fine if I blew off the back of his dragon into the sea. Still, I'd dealt with enough pompous officers to know when to put on the poker face and salute, so I did exactly that and went to sort myself out.

The saddle had plenty of room for passengers, and as I unwound the tangle of straps, it began to make more sense. You had to half-sit, half-kneel to the side of the dragon's neck, with the harness belted to rings on three points. You hooked one foot under a loop of leather, and held on to another pair of stiff loops with your hands, one to each side. I found my place, and while I waited, I experimentally tried to think out toward the dragon. "*Any advice for me? Anything that would help you feel comfortable?*"

I wasn't expecting a reply, and didn't get one. Still, I smiled, and hunched into my jacket while others buckled in.

When we were ready, Arnaud went to the front, between Talenth's shoulders, and dropped to one knee as the dragon reared his head and stretched his wings, using them and his forearms to push himself up to his hind feet, and I found myself grinning as he turned and faced the ocean. The saddle was warm from the heat of his back. I could feel the incredible power in him as he turned and stretched.

"Ready?" The Skyr called back.

"Yes." Rutha was lying down on her stomach, her leg and arm splinted and braced in the kneeling grooves. She was bound flat to the saddle – there was no way she could have held on.

Talenth rumbled, lowered his head, and began to run. I slid back along the saddle, my limbs catching and holding in the grooves molded into the leather as he gained momentum. The wind whistled past us, and I watched over his shoulder with huge eyes as the cliff's edge and the waves grew closer. My heart was pounding, swelling as I felt the air catch over his wings and the tension grow in the huge body underneath us.

The dragon leaned his body forward, picking up speed, then leaped out into the choppy wind. Rutha cried out with alarm as the creature seemed to drop out from underneath us, lifting clothes and hair. He rose again on the first downbeat as we slammed back against the saddle. It was like a hand had pushed me flat: my head snapped down, and I instinctively tucked in and hunched as Talenth scooped the rough air and gained height. I looked up to see the ground rushing away from us, and I felt that same sense of wonder I'd felt all those years ago on my first motorcycle, but more intense, more... complete. This was *it*. I could never get sick of this feeling: the rush of takeoff, the awe found in watching the ocean thunder beneath us, the moment of dizzy, delicious excitement as the dragon dipped a wingtip and lifted the other to circle up on the wind generated by the sea.

The *Arabella* came into view, and I was able to see the full extent of the wreckage. We'd hit the ground upside down and bounced, by the look of it. I was staring at it in amazement when I felt a ripple of hot energy wash over us, like steam, and then the air flared blue and everything vanished.

For the first time since seeing the dragons, I was afraid. I couldn't feel my hands clutching the saddle, or Talenth beneath me. The only sense I had was hearing, and I could hear what sounded like twin hearts laboring, pounding in the minute or so of nothingness that seemed to stretch into eternity until we teleported back into existence. I cried out in alarm, this time, as we erupted into warmer, sweeter air and fell, only to swoop back into controlled flight toward a gleaming white city below.

My eyes widened. As we glided in over the city walls, I tried my hardest to see everything. The outer walls encircled a large portion of the buildings all the way to the cliff-side, where airships - made tiny by height and distance - hung at sky docks. The walls sheltered a huge sprawl of manors and granaries, docks and warehouses, narrow stone houses and soaring towers. From above, we could see how broad roads branched off into jagged alleys and elegant courtyards and parks. There were many bridges. They crossed twin rivers that wound through the city. To the north, the rivers wound away into the smoky horizon. To the south, they turned into massive waterfalls that spilled over the towering cliffs facing the ocean.

Nearly all of the buildings were made of white stone that gleamed under the sun. At one end of the city, forming a bulwark against the cliffside waves, a magnificent amber-spired cathedral soared into the air. There was a wide, straight road that ran from it, all the way to the center of town. There, where the rivers surrounded a tall island, was a grand ivory palace with the fine architecture of a gothic French cathedral. The palace had its own protective walls, which contained both the palace and other, smaller manors and towers. Like everything else, it looked small from a distance, but the closer we got, the bigger it became... until I realized that the island was more like a small mountain than a hill, and that Talenth was like the size of a cat compared to a house as he swooped down toward it. This was a castle that had been made for a world with large creatures like dragons - and maybe giants, as well.

We landed on the castle roof, an airfield for flying creatures. We were the largest to arrive, but the airfield clamored with different kind of flying critters and their rides. There were huge gulls with forty-foot wingspans bickering as their riders saddled them up, and feathered dinosaur-like animals that walked on their wing 'hands' and long, scaly back legs. They all scattered out of the way as Talenth glided in, and carefully back winged to come to a precise halt in the center of the largest circle.

"Get a Sister!" The knight-commander called to the three young squires who rushed up to greet us. "Get a Sister and a litter, with strong bearers! We have an injured lady!"

I unbuckled myself from the saddle and moved over to help. Rutha was wincing as she tried to sit up. The commander and I helped her to rise while the squires ran off, shouting for aid.

The sorceress's ankle and knee were now both very swollen, dark with bruising. She clutched at my sleeve to sit up once we freed her from the saddle straps. Fortunately, we didn't have to slide her down the dragon's arm. When the squires came back, they brought a mounting platform and two strong men, as well as the litter and a woman in long, gray robes that I assumed was the Sister. We helped Rutha to the ladder, and between the four of us, we were able to help her down without bumping her injured leg.

"What happened to her?" The Sister demanded. "The Warden has been mad with worry ever since you left Liren, my lady. He was sure that rebels –"

"It's a long story, but the short version is that I was captured by slavers and nearly crushed to death by a ship," Rutha said through gritted teeth. "It had nothing to do with the rebellion and everything to do with raiders. Come: take me to the hospice and let's get this over with. I'm sure there's bones that I need reset and I'd rather get it over and done with before they heal too much more."

We helped her to lie down, and then she was carried off before we could even really say goodbye. She was in too much pain now to do anything other than cover her eyes with her arm and let her servants bear her off.

"So," the knight-commander sighed, "I suppose you'll be off to tour the city. Have you ever seen a place this grand before?"

"Not quite like this," I replied. "But that's not what I want. I want to join your order."

"Come again?" His face stiffened.

"I want to learn how to fly." I held his gaze. I want to learn to be a Dragon Knight."

I'd expected some resistance, but what I didn't expect was the way that Arnaud's face morphed into a mask of disdain.

"There are no barbarians in the ranks of St. Grigori's Skyrdon," he said coldly.

Anger rose inside me with every word. "Then I'll be the first. That's what Starborn do, right? Go on adventures, brave danger, break new ground."

He continued to look down his nose at me. "You really have no idea how common you are, do you?"

"You've been making it clear that you think I'm lower than whaleshit, sir," I replied agreeably.

He snorted, his lips twisting into a wry smile. "No, boy. I don't mean your social standing. In all honesty, your being a barbarian is nothing more than a variation of the same old story. No... You're common because you are nothing but a creature of lust. You lust for my dragon. For power. For freedom. Your heart is beating faster just looking at Talenth, isn't it?"

He was right, but I decided to try what had gotten me through the Army: salute and play dumb. "I failed Philosophy in school, sir."

"Really, now. Why do you want to come with me?"

I pressed my lips together while I gathered the right words. "I want to make something of myself, sir."

"And what does that mean?"

I did my best to look through him, standing to attention. "It means I never had a real chance at a life. I can't read, and I have trouble concentrating on anything if I'm not moving around. My family wasn't rich, but they were proud. And I..."

The Commander arched an eyebrow.

I'm tired of being different, being told that I'm wrong because of who I am. I'm tired of being alone. I'm exhausted by how powerless I feel, and by my inability to change things. Dad. Steve. Mom. HEX. Watching my buddies die. I want to fly away from it all, become someone new. I don't want to be alone any more. The bitter truths marched through my mind, but damn if I was going to admit any of that to this smarmy bastard.

"I didn't get to choose whether or not I became a soldier, but I was good at it," I said firmly. "And I might be dumber than a stack of bricks, but I know that when you're good at something, you keep doing it. I'll be a soldier, if that's what it takes. But this time, I'm going to choose what I do and where I go."

The knight-commander considered me for close to half a minute. Long enough that I'd started to get my hopes up.

"We are more than soldiers. We are a holy order in service to the realm. The *realm,* boy. We are patriots. Men of honor. But most of all, we are Ilian. You are not committed to the realm, and you cannot possibly understand what you would be risking, even if you were a viable candidate. There is no room within our order for mercenaries. I suggest that you spend some time here learning our ways and the basics of courtesy, and at least learn to read before you aspire to a greater station, 'Starborn'."

Was this guy for real? "I'm already courteous enough not to call people I don't know 'barbarians'. Sir."

"It is not intended as an insult," the commander told me. "It is a matter of fact that you are a common peasant warrior from a different land – and, in fact, an entirely different breed from us. Lady Rutha may have some sympathy for you because you come from the same continent her people do, but I have men in Lys, and they tell me that in contrast to the elves, the Tuun are little more than leather-clad savages. If I were you, I would go to the port and catch a ship home. *After* a bath."

"Yeah, now you mention it, I *do* need a bath after this salt," I said, miming brushing stuff off my sleeves and chest.

"You did the realm a service by helping Lady Rutha, I'll acknowledge that." Arnaud's eyes narrowed, and he pulled his gauntlets up along his wrists. "Fair day to you, barbarian. I sincerely hope you find something worthwhile to do that is within your means."

I sincerely hoped that he would fall off his dragon after this, but I was too polite to say so. I grinned, baring teeth, and watched as he walked back to his dragon like a smug asshole.

Talenth was watching us both as his rider returned, staring at me with one brilliant white blue eye. Momentarily, I felt something like sorrow. This seemed... Unfair. Not just to me, but to the dragon as well. The knight-commander banged on Talenth's leg with a fist to get them to drop down so that he could mount him. The dragon assumed the same forward bow posture that he had in Zaunt, but this time, I noticed that there was a reluctance in the way he moved. I didn't like watching a creature like this be treated like a glorified, hundred-foot-long horse. It didn't feel right.

I bowed from the neck to him, and tried thinking my speech in Talenth's direction. "*You and your squad saved our lives. I know flying is what you do... but thanks. For the effort, and for letting me fly on you. It was an honor.*"

The white dragon rumbled, a sound that vibrated through his deep chest. To my surprise, I felt a kind of mental push just before a deep baritone voice reverberated through my mind. "*In truth, it is this one's privilege to witness the arrival of the Herald of the Hidden Seed.*"

"Umm." I blinked a couple of times. I had NOT been expecting a reply. "*Sorry, what?*"

The Dragon straightened his head as his rider reached his shoulder and began to attach himself back into the saddle. "*My blood hears the words of power written into yours, Herald. Your arrival is foretold by a story whispered by my Mother to me when I was but an egg, and from her Mother to my Mother, all the way back in time to the creation of the Seals.*"

"*The Seals?*" I fought the urge to step forward again and go to him. "*What Seals?*"

"*I cannot speak of them.*" Talenth replied. "*But this is a truth. Besides the dragons, there are those at Fort Palewing who will recognize the mark you bear, and know its significance.*"

"*You mean the Mark of Matir?*"

"Of course. The Black God has not chosen a champion in nearly five thousand years," the dragon replied. *"But I know the smell of it as surely as I would know my own issue. Do not give up. But this one advises you to trust carefully, and keep the Mark of the Hidden Seed... well hidden."*

My skin came up in goosebumps. I stepped back, swallowing, and bobbed my head in a sort of awkward bow as the dragon bunched, then threw himself into the air. The downwind was almost enough to push me to one knee, but I held my feet, shading my eyes and watching as Talenth rose into the air, wheeled into a glide, and then disappeared in a blue flash.

"Welp. The commander's a cunt." I muttered, dusting myself off. Now that I was on the ground, I realized just how bad I smelled. If nothing else, I *smelled* like a barbarian. Maybe he'd like me more if I was cleaned up.

At least Rutha didn't hate me. If I was nice, I probably get at least some starting equipment, a map and food... Hopefully enough to start me North on the road to Fort Palewing. Because if the knight-commander wouldn't take me there, I'd find my way to the dragons myself.

Chapter 15

With the help of the people attending the airfield, I was able to find an escort into the sprawling palace and locate the hospice where the Sister and the litter-bearers had taken Rutha. It was just as well I had a guide. The place was enormous, an ornate maze of marble, eerie pale blue wood, inlaid pearl and warm birch.

The hospice was a miniature complex unto itself. The main hospital was a large, rectangular room with a high frescoed ceiling. Sisters in gray robes moved between several sick people, treating their wounds with bandages and poultices and helping the ill to drink potions. Beyond the hospital were individual suites. Rutha was in one of these, her leg propped up on a stack of soft pillows. The silver-haired elf lay on a large, soft bed, shadowed by the fine silk curtains hanging in the open balcony doors. I walked in to see them dancing in the warm breeze as she downed a bright green potion, her throat working with long swallows.

"Healing magic?" I hung back near the door, watching her.

Rutha held up a finger, eyes closed. When she was done drinking, she made a face and set the empty flask on a table beside her. "There's no such thing as healing magic. This is plain old medicine."

"No such thing as healing magic?"

"True healing magic was an art lost eons ago. Some say it never existed at all, or that only the Aesari were able to use mana for that purpose."

"Huh." A world without healing magic – that was new. "How's your leg?"

"Well, the Sisters had to reset some broken bones. I'm glad you weren't here to listen." Rutha motioned me over, patting the edge of the bed. "But the worst is over. These potions aren't 'magic', exactly, but they do speed the healing process considerably."

I couldn't help but smile as I came over – not too close. "I'd sit, but if I do, I'm going to stink up your bed. I was wondering if I could ask for a bath and something to eat here? Sir Asshat gave me my marching orders when I asked to go with him."

Rutha's lips twitched, pouting a little in surprise. "You asked to join the Order of Saint Grigori?"

"I don't think I've ever wanted anything more." From a few feet away, I couldn't help but notice the curves of her body underneath the blankets that covered everything except her legs. "No offense to you, Lady."

The elf bit her lip. Now that I had time to see her and no one was trying to kill us, I noticed that she had silverish freckles across her nose and cheeks. Her eyes were deep violet that contrasted with the white-silver of her hair. "No offense taken. The dragons are magnificent, but as I'm sure you realized, knight commander Arnaud can be somewhat abrasive. He's a bastard."

"Yeah, he's definitely kind of dick." I paused for a moment. "Wait. You mean, like, an actual bastard? Like-"

"The product of an affair outside the marital chamber, yes," Rutha said delicately. "And all bastards are prickly, you'll find. His birth was a scandal: his father is one of the great Lords of the realm, and was a member of the Kingsguard. He was removed from his post and stripped of his titles by the Mad King when his infidelity was discovered, casting the family down into poverty. Perhaps because of that, Arnaud played a major role in the Civil War and is greatly invested in the new regime."

"Forgive me for sounding like a blunt barbarian," I said. "But I don't care whether or not someone's parents are married or not. He's an elitist asshole. He went on some rant about 'leather clad savages'. I know I need a bath, but really? Does he think slave ships smell like roses and unicorn farts?"

The sorceress laughed, a high tinkling sound that echoed through the hospital suite. "He really can be overbearing, but that stubborn nature helped him survive before he joined the Skyrdon. And yes, you could do with a bath. If you go behind that screen over there, there is a bathtub. It even has hot water."

"As in, *running* hot water?" I began to move in that direction. The ornate screen she was indicating had some measure of privacy. The area behind it was shadowed.

"No, even better. The water runs cold, but there is a sigil that heats it to an agreeable temperature." I heard her sigh happily. "I'm so glad to be back in civilization."

"Me too." Curious, I went to see what she meant. A large stone tub was set into the floor with a single faucet, which I opened. Water gushed into the bath, and soon it was full enough for me to consider stripping down and getting in. "How do I activate the sigil?"

"Just speak the word of power. *Orfailen.*"

"Orfai-len?" I said uncertainly. I crouched down, and stuck my hand in the water. It was ice cold. "Orfailen! Orrr-fai-len?"

Rutha's laughter echoed out from beyond the privacy screen. "Or-*fai*--len. Say it as if it were three words."

"Or-*fai*-len." I tried mimicking her, fighting the urge to roll my eyes, and yelped when a yellow tracery of lines flared on the bottom of the tub and the water was suddenly hot. More out of shock than anything, I jerked my hand out and nearly fell over on my ass. Rutha's laughter grew louder.

"I do *not* live for sorcery." Grumbling, I stood up and began to strip. Only then did I remember the Mark of Matir, and Talenth's warning that I shouldn't show it to anyone that wasn't a 'friend of the old gods'. It had been hidden under the long sleeve of my jacket. "See? This is why I'm a leather-clad savage. I'm too dumb to be a mage."

"Nonsense. You're terribly clever."

"That's not what my grades said. You know what I read on every single one of my school reports? 'Hector could try harder in class'. 'Hector needs to pay better attention'. All of it code for 'Hector is a dumbass'." Before I got into the tub, I searched for a towel and made sure it was close at hand.

"Well, there are different kinds of intelligence, you know," Rutha called back to me as I finished undressing. "Some people are good with their minds, some are good with their hands. Some are good with other parts of their body."

I chuckled, easing into the water. "So, what you're saying is that you feel better after that potion?"

"Quite a bit better," she said, in that same English schoolmistress voice. "Healing draughts like this get the blood moving, you know."

I glanced ruefully at the Mark. Goddamn cockblocking ancient gods of darkness. More alarming, though – the gap in my shoulder was still there. The place where the wood had been sticking out was a black void where my flesh should have been, but when I touched it, it felt like warm skin. Still... Rutha was making her intentions clear, if I was reading her right. Swallowing, I gathered my nerves and tried to sound confident. "Feel well enough for a bath? There's room in here for two."

"You know, warm water and some very careful positioning might actually be good for my leg," she replied. "Let me get my cane."

I kinda hadn't actually expected her to agree. Suddenly frantic, I grabbed a handful of soap – a kind of fine sandy stuff, heavy with perfume, and threw it in the water. Then I sloshed it around and churned it up into bubbles... bubbles that I submerged my branded hand under as Rutha came around the screen. She had a sheet clasped around her hips, naked from the waist up, and my eyebrows nearly hit my hairline.

"Mmhmm." The elf rolled her lip under her teeth as her gaze roamed from my chest, up along my neck, to my face. "*Very* careful positioning. With my back to your front in your lap, perhaps?"

"As the lady wishes." My heart was hammering, and my blood was warming, too. But I couldn't suppress a passing concern that Archemi would have some weird sex system I was going to have to figure out on the fly. *Tap this circle to make her cum!* Or worse, a fade to black session with no actual relief. *Fuck. I have no idea what I'm doing. What the hell have I gotten myself into?*

As if reading my mind, Rutha flashed me a crooked little smile and let go of the sheet she had held around her waist. Like every elf I'd ever seen illustrated, she was small-breasted, slim and smooth, but not completely hairless. She did have some wisps of hair down there... a very fine, straight dusting of it, as pale as the pour of silver down her back.

My eyes widened. Okay... *that* was what I was getting into.

"You're gawping like a boy who's never seen a woman before," she teased.

"Umm." So much for being 'terribly clever'. "If you... umm... come over here, I'll give you a hand in?"

Getting into the tub was difficult for her, but I was able to assist – mostly with one hand – and nervously guide her onto my lap. She had to tilt her head back to kiss me, but that was fine... while she nibbled and panted against my lips, my hands could roam, slippery with soap, until the woman's kisses turned to moans of pleasure and she threw her head back against my shoulder.

"Feeling better?" I asked hoarsely.

"Much better." She rolled her hips against mine, suggesting what was to come... and when it came, it was everything I had ever imagined.

Sometime later, Rutha dozed in the still-hot water against my chest, slippery and warm, while I relaxed back with a lingering high, a slowly replenishing Stamina bar, and mild concern that I hadn't asked her about birth control. She didn't seem to be worried about it. When I fingered a long strand of her hair, she smiled and kissed my neck with a soft sound of satisfaction.

"See?" Rutha said. " *Very* clever."

I chuffed, almost a laugh, and flushed. "That... uhh... that was my first time, actually."

Her eyebrows nearly hit her hairline, and it was my turn to laugh.

"You're joking!" She nearly squealed. "Don't tell me I just-!"

"Yes ma'am," I replied soberly. "You did."

It was Rutha's turn to flush. She whapped me on the chest. "Why didn't you say something? I'd have been a bit more careful, or, or... gentle, or *something*."

Sheepish now, I shrugged. "Well, you know... it got going, and then *I* got going, then *you* got going. And, well, I wasn't about to stop you and blurt out 'by the way, I'm a virgin'."

She looked me up and down, lips pursed. I had my branded hand hidden behind my back, practically sitting on my left hand. "A virgin? I really find that hard to believe."

"Well, it's true. Just never happened for one reason or another." I shrugged again. "I mean, I had girlfriends, but we never went beyond kissing and fumbling. Never liked brothels... and if you're in the army, you either visit the camp girls, swap brojobs with the bi or gay guys, or become a monk and be completely celibate. I chose option three."

"I see." She seemed to consider that for a moment. "Well... hopefully I haven't scarred you with my forwardness."

"Are you joking? I've been grinning for half an hour now. My face is going to end up stuck like this."

Rutha laughed, and settled back against my chest again.

"Say... you have the brain-smarts, so maybe you can tell me a story." I reached around with my right arm, caressing her stomach. "Who or what, exactly, are the Aesari?"

"Talking dirty, are we?" Rutha tipped her head back with a sigh, before her NPC instincts to provide information took over. "Very well. The Aesari are one of the Elder Races. They, the dragons, and the Meewfolk are the oldest races of our world. Humans, Elves and the Mercurions didn't appear until after the First Cataclysm."

"The Drachan." I slowly ran my hand up over one of her breasts, listening.

"Mmhmm. They brought Humans and Elves to this world as slaves. The Aesari were the greatest civilization of all time – they were somewhat human in appearance, but with wings and other strange features. They were also great mages, the greatest artificers the world has ever known. They created at least one new race - the Mercurions - as soldiers against the Drachan, and they created the Caul of Souls. But after sealing the Drachan away, they were corrupted by their power. They enslaved humans, elves, and the other races as well. Instead of using their own reserves of power to feed the Caul, they sacrificed our bodies and souls to it... and eventually, the oppressed races rose against them, destroying them, their gods and their wonders and casting them into the ocean. They say that they still live there under the waves... demons who used twisted magic to build great cities underwater."

"With waves like what we saw? No way." I shook my head, amused.

"Well, the ones who say that are the priests and preachers," Rutha said, mischief in her voice. "So make of that what you will. But speaking of the Aesari... I have something you might like."

"Something else? I dunno... I think I'd be pretty hard pressed to find anything better than this right now." I tweaked her nipple with expression of great concentration, and she laughed and shoved playfully at my leg.

"Help me up and out of here, will you?" Rutha asked, looking back over her shoulder.

"Only if you close your eyes."

"What? Why? The woman rubbed back against me under the water. "If you're feeling shy, I'm certain I've already got the measure of you."

"Because if I'm going to start feeling weird about this, it's going to be when I'm standing up buck-ass naked in front of a beautiful woman for the first time." I smiled down at her.

She quirked her eyebrows, sighed, and closed her eyes. I lay a small towel over my branded arm, threw another dry one over my shoulder, then scooped her up and carried her out. The floor wasn't carpeted, fortunately, because water went everywhere. I sat her down on a stone bench and toweled her dry, careful to be gentle with her injuries.

"Can I open my eyes yet?"

"Not yet."

She scrunched her nose up, but when I began to gently rub her dry in more sensitive places, she made a soft sound of appreciation. I was most of the way done when the door to the suite flung open and a Sister walked in on me, naked, toweling off Rutha's foot while she rested it against my chest. The nun screamed, I screamed, we all screamed. I threw the towel over my arm, and the Sister backed out of the door with a sharp scandalized yelp, and Rutha cracked up with helpless laughter.

Chapter 16

Thirty minutes or so later, I was back in my filthy clothes, Rutha was dressed in a much nicer scarlet shift that clung to her body in interesting ways, and I was being led away from her and through the airy gothic corridors of the Dinant Palace by a nervous Chamberlain. He took me to a huge pair of double doors made of the strange, pale, blue-tinged wood that comprised so much of the decoration in this place.

"This is one of our guest quarters," the Chamberlain said. He was a tall, plump man with sour features and pale, papery skin. He had a flat, slightly nasal voice, and was dressed in a stiff, plain doublet and breeches, with no ornamentation or embroidery. "I can prepare you a bath, though I'm afraid we don't have any of this dust bathing nonsense that they do on the plains. Water and soap only, I'm afraid."

"We prefer mud baths where I'm from. But don't worry, I just had one." Admittedly, my clothes still did smell pretty bad. Still, I wasn't entirely sure everyone was being such an asshole about it. "All I need is a change of clothes."

"Very good, *missiure*. I do have clothes in here that ought to fit you." The Chamberlain threw open the doors into a modest but attractive suite. Like the rest of the palace, it was open and airy, with high Gothic ceilings and big blue and crystal stained-glass windows. There was a bed, a chair, a chest, a writing desk, a wardrobe, drawers, and a trunk. A copper tub sat behind a screen. The Chamberlain went to the wardrobe, opened it, and began to shuffle through the rows of clothing.

"I don't suppose you can get me some armor?" I hung back, watching him as he pulled out tunics and gloves and trousers. "Light armor, heavy on leather, preferably black."

"If the gentleman desires," he replied, laying out the clothing over the desk next to the wardrobe. "Though I would advise that you let me shave you and trim your hair before you try putting on armor."

"The hair stays. All I need is a comb and maybe some oil." I sat down and began to unbraid the central mohawk-like length of hair and the two long braids to brush them out. The hair reached down almost to the backs of my knees. IRL, I'd always had short hair, but I'd adjusted to the braid pretty quickly.

"It is highly irregular for men to have long hair," the Chamberlain replied stiffly.

"Maybe it is here, but where I'm from, the length of your hair tells people how badass you are." I looked over the clothes he picked out for me. A plain gray and white tunic with a square collar, pants, black boots, a Celtic style loop belt, and gauntlets long enough for me to tuck the sleeves of the tunic into them.

He sighed a long-suffering sigh, and handed me a hairbrush from his grooming kit. "I will go and see what armor I can find in your size, *missiure*. Will you let me shave you, at least?"

I took the brush, then reached up and felt my face. Stubble. I kind of hoped shaving was one of those things I wouldn't have to do inside of the game, but no. "Sure. But if you touch my hair with anything sharp, I'll pull your lungs out through your asshole."

"How vivid of you, *missiure*," the Chamberlain said dryly.

He made something of a show of stropping his razor before carefully trimming the hair on my face. Once he was done, he left to find my armor and I sat down on my bed and redid my mohawk-braid. Somehow, I knew how to do it: how to plait my hair down the center, then split it off into two braids and weave them with the strips of red cloth tied into them. I'd never braided anything in my life, but provided I didn't think too hard about what I was doing, I could twist it all up with the same kind of effortless skill that came from years of practice.

Beaky McPrissyface returned after nearly an hour had passed. I was napping when he knocked and entered, followed by a guardsman who was carrying armor inside of a bundle. I sat up, yawned, and watched as he laid out the pieces on top of the desk. As I had requested, it was mostly black leather, and what appeared to be a close-fitting tunic of dark, heavy cloth stitched over metal plates:

Jack of Plates

50 armor

+10% resistance to slashing damage

+10% resistance to bludgeoning damage

+30% resistance to piercing damage

Light armor

Body slot

100% durability

Hunting Breeches

15 armor

+2% resistance to slashing damage

+2% resistance to piercing damage

light armor

legs slot

100% durability

Reinforced boots

15 armor

+3% resistance to piercing damage

+3% resistance to bludgeoning damage

+3% resistance to slashing damage

light armor

feet slot

100% durability

Light Vambrace

15 armor

+3% resistance to piercing damage

+3% resistance to bludgeoning damage

+3% resistance to slashing damage

light armor

100% durability

"Are these suitable, sir?" The Chamberlain asked with an arched brow.

To me, the stats looked like decent starting armor, probably better than what I would've gotten had I started normally in a town and not ended up here. I loaded the armor into my inventory, then equipped it. I didn't have to physically change into these clothes. As soon as I equipped them, they appeared on my body and fit as if they had been tailored for me. And just like that, my Defense rose from 25 to 95.

"Absolutely. This is fantastic." I stretched, did a couple of squats, then pushed the screen aside so I could see myself in the mirror over the tub. I looked... Well, kind of awesome. It was only low-level equipment, but it fit well and looked great.

The Chamberlain inclined his head. "When you are ready, the lady wishes to see you."

My first impulse was to rush off to see what Rutha wanted, but then I abruptly remembered where I *really* was. Archemi was a game, with game mechanics... and a quick glance at my character sheet told me that I had a level to consolidate, unspent skill points, and a bunch of skills and abilities that needed training. It was easy to think of Rutha as a real person... but she was really an NPC. Hot as hell, but an NPC. Whatever item she was going to give me, there was a good chance it would come with a quest or a job.

"In a few hours," I said. "What's the time now?"

"Two hours past midday."

I nodded. "Please tell Rutha I have some business to attend to and will be at her laboratory at six."

"As you wish." The Chamberlain bowed from the neck, and turned to sweep out of the room.

"Sorry, before you go, I need to ask something," I said. "Do you have a blacksmith here?"

The man turned, looking at me down his nose. I don't think he meant to, he was just one of those guys who was effortlessly arrogant. "Yes, we do. Do you need something altered?"

"Sort of." I nodded. "I want to talk to the smith and get some supplies to maintain this armor."

"Ah. Well... here." The Chamberlain pulled a small scroll from his pocket and handed it to me. When I opened it, I saw a map.

⟦New Map Added: Dinant Palace⟧

"The smith can be found in the outbuildings near the stables," he said. "And Lady Rutha's laboratory and quarters are in the underground level of the East Tower."

"Thanks." Satisfied, I tucked the map into a pocket. I felt it dissolve, and then saw the notification as it transferred to 'Quest Items' in my Inventory.

It wasn't until the Chamberlain left that something else occurred to me. I didn't have any money, and I hadn't really collected any useful items while I was on the slave ship. My inventory was limited to ten slots and five of them were empty. I had a curved knife, the sword I looted from the Captain's Guard, the clothing and other odds and ends I looted from the wreck. Altogether, I'd probably be able to buy some basic equipment to maintain my armor, and hopefully some raw materials to start learning the Armor Smithing and Self-Repair skills.

I eyed the wardrobe, the desk and trunk. Then I went over to go and have a look inside of them.

As I thought, nearly all of the lootable items were categorized as 'Junk' and only worth coppers, but enough coppers added up to a silver piece, and enough silver pieces would eventually add up to a gold piece. However, when I took the clothes and other bits and bobs, their inventory entries were surrounded by a thin red border marking them as stolen.

"Hmm." I didn't really have a problem with the stealing part, to be honest. This was a palace after all – it wasn't like they couldn't replace watch pieces, spoons, and clothing. But I was guessing that none of this could be fenced to the smithy. Resigned, I put the items back and left the room to go and see what else I could do.

I headed for the outbuildings where the smithy was supposed to be, and sure enough, I heard the sound of the hammer striking iron in the distance. Palace guards were drilling in the big open space that separated the palace from the rest of the buildings, and the stables – which were visible from the exit – were not full of horses. The building was full of dinosaurs. They snipped and snarled at one another, brandishing their scythe-like front claws if their neighbors got too close. Their feathered forelimbs were neither hands or wings. The bones had fused into a single long claw that was held back along their ribs. Superficially, they strongly resembled velociraptors. They had sharp teeth, brilliant gold or white eyes, long stiff tails, and high, straight backs. My HUD identified the creatures as 'hookwings':

Hookwings (also known as Ghora, Myinn)

The favored destrier mount of most warriors in Artana (the Eastern Continent of Archemi), the ferocious dinosaurs known as hookwings are known for their intense loyalty and fearlessness in battle. Naturally bold, curious and pack-orientated, they can cope in conditions that would send even the best-trained herd animal mounts into a panicked retreat.

Hookwings are named for their specialized forelimbs – vestigial wings that have fused into long, powerful claws. The finest hookwings are said to be bred in Vlachia, where they are known as Ghora, but the oldest lines of domesticated mounts are found in Prrupt'meew, home of the Meewfolk, where they are known as Myinn.

"What are you doing standing around, soldier!"

I jumped in my skin as a mustachioed man riding one of the hookwings pulled up beside me. He was carrying a whip and wore a saber at his belt.

"Where's your pack?" He looked me over, frowning. "Hold on, wait: You're one of those foreign legionnaires, aren't you?"

"I..."

"Go and see the quartermaster," he said before I had a chance to really reply. "Assuming you understand what I'm saying."

"Of course, I understand what you're saying," I replied. "And I'm not one of your soldiers, so-"

The man's mustache bristled. "Then what are you, then?"

"A guest of the court sorceress. I am a warrior, though."

"Oh. Well, in that case, I'd advise you not to be walking around the training yard. Not unless you fancy yourself good with a sword or spear, and want to train with us."

That actually wasn't a bad idea. My only weapon was currently the shittiest dagger in the world. "Sure. Do you have a sparring session or dummy that I could train with?"

"Across the yard there." The officer gave me a curt nod. He pointed to the other side of the courtyard, where three soldiers were hacking and slashing at straw dummies wearing armor. "I'm sure my men would be interested in sparring with a foreigner. Go over there and see how you go."

⟦New Quest: Training with the Soldiers (Reward: 20 Skill EXP)⟧

While he rode his dinosaur into the stables, I accepted the quest and headed over to the training area. Like all soldiers, I had some training in hand-to-hand combat, but basic training and my frontline combat in Indonesia hadn't covered swords and spears. I wasn't sure which weapon I preferred yet, and this was a good time to start developing a specialization.

As I walked up, the three soldiers stopped beating on the dummies and turned to look at me.

"Who's this, then?" The man closest to me, his doughy face framed by a round helmet, planted the butt of his spear on the ground.

"Hector," I replied. "I came to train."

"You a recruit?" He eyed my new armor with some suspicion. All of the soldiers here wore the same uniform - plain steel armor with a purple surcoat emblazoned with a white gull.

I shook my head. "No. Just visiting. Your officer over there recommended I come and learn with you. Said you might be interested in fighting someone with a different style. Either that, or I guess I can stand here and beat on one of the dummies for a month or two while everyone stares at me."

"Sure we would. Be good for when we get sent to the front. I'm Franco." The guard with the spear nodded. "Come on, then. What have you got?"

Literally one crappy dagger. "I've had more experience with a spear than anything else, but I'll try a sword."

Franco nodded. "There's practice swords over there. Pol, you go in. We'll watch."

Pol - the tallest of the three - nodded and stepped forward. He drew his sword, which had a blunt edge like the practice sword I picked up. The others stepped back, and we got to sparring.

The yard soon rang with the sound of steel on steel. Within a minute, I was sweating. Pol pressed the attack relentlessly, swinging his sword like a hammer, and forcing me to defend myself. I swung up to clumsily defend myself from an overhead blow, only to trip and fall when he swept my legs out from under me. The other two soldiers laughed.

"Like I said, no real practice with swords," I said as I picked myself up. I could either be humiliated or energized by what was happening here, and decided that I wasn't going to let these men humiliate me. "Again."

With a grin, Pol came at me again, and once again, I lost. But every time his blade struck mine, and with every bruise and stumble, my sword fighting skill was going up. It wasn't long until I got the notification – I'd reached Sword Fighting 2.

"Okay," I said. My arm was burning from the weight of the longsword. "I'll try with a spear instead."

"You can't be any worse with a spear," Franco chortled. "Spear versus sword, do you think?"

I nodded, and held a hand out for the practice spear he was carrying. He gave it to me without a word of complaint, smiling with more than a little malice as I took it and faced off Pol again.

"Let's try this again, shall we?" He lifted the sword and faced off with me.

This time, steel struck wood. He pressed the offense, but his down cut was twisted aside by the staff of the spear as I instinctively blocked it and then kicked him in the gut. He stumbled back, and I swung the butt of the spear up to tap him on the edge of the jaw before spinning it and lunging forward with the point resting in the join of his armor between his helmet and his gorget.

"Nice, nice," Franco said. "I'll try next. Leo, go get us another spear."

I rested and allowed myself a small moment to savor the victory. I was already at Polearms 3. Maybe it was just that the ⟦Rusty Spear⟧ had been my first weapon in the game, but the polearm felt more natural in my hands than the sword had.

Leo was a compact man in his early 40s with the spare, hard face of a soldier who had seen many battles. He handed Franco the second practice spear and then stood back so that the two of us could face off.

"Look sharp!" That was all the warning Franco gave me before he charged in, spear first.

The weapons clacked, and he struck mine with almost enough force to knock it from my hands. I managed to hold onto it, spinning and ducking as he jabbed it toward my neck. I hit him in the back with the end of it, sending him stumbling forward in his heavy armor, and when he turned around, he found the tip of the spear resting in his armpit.

"Not bad." He grinned, and this time it wasn't mocking. "I'm glad you're better with this than you are with a sword."

"Me too," I said. "I think about the only thing I could do with a sword is fall on it."

That made them chuckle. Franco nodded at the weapon. "You can keep that, if you want."

I looked down at it. This was also a ⟦Rusty Spear⟧, with exactly the same stats as the one I'd used on the ship. "Sure. Thanks."

The four of us paired off, and as the hours ticked by, my skill meter rose. I was tired and trembling by the time we called it quits, but I'd leveled my Polearms skill to 4, and the quest gave me Skill EXP on top of that. I saved it for now – I needed time to review my build before I started spending points.

"All right, gentlemen," I said. "I think that's about all for me. Is there a place I can get something to eat here?"

"I was just thinking the same thing," Franco said. "The mess should be open, if you want to come and grab a bite."

"Sure." I folded the spear into my inventory and resigned myself to relying on it for the time being. Skills worked strangely in this game: Sword 2 was better than Sword 1, but my natural aptitude for the Spear not only made it level faster, but better.

I was comfortable in mess halls. Sitting alongside the palace soldiers, I was able to eat and drink without worrying about offending anyone. Dinner wasn't fancy, but it was delicious: some kind of hearty meat with berry sauce, roasted leeks, butter on hunks of coarse, flavorsome bread, and fruit ale on tap. The stuff was called *lambic*, and it was probably the best beer I'd ever had: thick, frothy, and intensely flavored with fresh raspberries. I wanted to drink a lot more of it, but I still had to go and see Rutha and I didn't fancy doing that while drunk.

It was dark by the time I reached Rutha's laboratory, which took up the ground and basement levels of the eastern tower. There were a pair of guards waiting outside the entry, both dressed in ornate silver armor and carrying halberds.

"The lady is expecting you," one of them said. "Enter. You will find her downstairs."

The first room was a deceptively normal-looking solar, with a sofa, firepit, and floor-to-ceiling bookshelves. The intricately tiled floor reminded me of Middle Eastern mosaics, except that this room's mosaics were sealed with a glassy material that crawled and sparked with magic. No sooner had I stepped in than Rutha's voice echoed out of thin air. She sounded pleased. "Hector! Head through the left door and meet me downstairs?"

"Uhh... sure?" I looked around for the source of her voice, but there was nothing resembling speakers. Shrugging, I followed her directions and headed down a steep flight of stairs, idly wondering how she'd gotten down them with her wheelchair.

The wheelchair was nowhere to be seen in the rooms below. It was a solid rectangle of stone, blazing with mage lights and a fire in the hearth. Shelves lined the walls, but there were fewer books and more vials, flasks, and other equipment. A huge hutch held jars of herbs and ingredients for potion making. Diagrams hung on the wall; another cabinet displayed Rutha's magical gauntlets. Special books lay under glass or rested on reading stands. In contrast to the rest of the palace, the furnishings here were all dark, rich wood and brown leather, and it smelled of parchment and spices.

Rutha was seated on a fainting-couch style sofa with a book in her lap. She smiled at me, cat-like, and stretched as she sat upright to greet me.

"Feeling better?" I asked.

"Much," she said. "Help me up. I have something I want to show you, a gift, and perhaps also something to explain."

"Like how you got your wheelchair down here?" I went to Rutha and scooped her up. "Someone carry it down?"

"Yes. Arnaud did." The elf motioned to a door across the room with a languid hand. "And if you would bear me to my chamber, mighty steed, I shall reveal mysteries beyond counting."

Chapter 17

Rutha gestured with a hand, and the door to her study opened as I carried her toward it. A desk crowded with papers took up one side of the room, and a tinker's bench covered in parts took up the other. It was stacked with crates full of metal pieces and racks of tools. This room was messy, even chaotic. There was only one notably clear space: a strange, alien-looking altar sculpted from metal feathers. Suspended over it was a glowing sphere made up of floating rings, like an old-fashioned atom symbol. At the core of the rings was a perfectly round, dark red jewel. It was currently throbbing like a racing heart.

I set the sorceress down on a chair, and she motioned to the altar. "This is why I was on the *Arabella* - and possibly why you were there, too. This artifact is the Star of Destiny, used to find Starborn like yourself. The process of using it is... complicated... and until recently, it was dormant."

"What made it activate?" I studied it curiously, but didn't get too close.

"The reappearance of Starborn on Archemi." The sorceress gestured expressively with her hands as she spoke, motioning to me. "You, and possibly others as well. You're very rare."

"Not for long," I replied. "There'll be a huge wave of us soon."

She regarded me with some surprise. "You know this? How?"

I didn't really feel comfortable saying 'because this is a fake digital world being used as an emergency refugee program for victims of a bio-weaponized plague', so I shrugged. "I just know."

"I see." She nodded, then sighed. "Well, I've recovered enough of my memory to be able to tell you how I ended up a slave. About three weeks ago, I was able to divine that there were Starborn being incarnated in Gilheim. I went north with a company of six men... all of whom were all slaughtered when we were attacked by Reavers. We fought, but one of them landed an unlucky blow on my head, and that was the end of that. The Reavers who sold me onto that ship."

"Right." I frowned. "Why were you looking for Starborn?"

"A very serious matter, unfortunately. One which I was just discussing with Commander Arnaud." The sorceress sat back, her injured leg resting stiffly in front of her. "The Caul of Souls is failing."

She'd been talking to Arnaud, alone? I crossed my arms. "You mean-"

"The barrier in the North which seals the great evil bound away by the Aesari." Rutha watched me with violet eyes, drawn and serious. "Year by year, the magic that holds the barrier together is becoming more unstable. It could be that the demons sealed in the Caul have awoken, and they are struggling against it from the inside. It could be that the Artifacts that bind the Caul are corrupting with time. My former master tracked the decline over his career by measuring the resonance of the Caul, and I have done the same since his passing. Every season, it frays a little more. In the past, the decay was not measurable... but it is accelerating."

"Well, shit." I rubbed a hand over my mouth, scowling. "That isn't good."

"No, it's not." Rutha glanced down at the floor, pursing her lips. "The Drachan are bound by the Caul, but they are deathless. That which cannot die does not wither. They are behind this, I'm sure of it."

"You say this barrier is failing." I crouched down on my heels, linking my fingers between my knees. "What can we do about it?"

"Before he died, my master found an incredible artifact," Rutha said. "Go over there, and unwrap that bundle on the table."

I rose and went over, untied the bindings on the cloth, and opened it up to reveal an ornate glaive-like weapon, battered and rusty. Once, it would have been magnificent... but now, it was a ruin. The weapon was deeply tarnished, the metal pitted, and there were nine round holes bored into the haft. My HUD read it simply as ⟦Ruined Spear⟧.

"Aww shit," I said. "You're about to give me the Mana Sword, aren't you?"

There was a pregnant pause.

"Pardon me?" Rutha finally said.

"Don't worry." But I was grinning now. I knew what was coming, and I didn't mind it at all. This was classic RPG, right here. Final Fantasy. Terranigma. With the recent horrors of life still churning around in the back of my head, there was something comforting about discovering something like this. Some kinds of stories had just been around forever. This was one of them. "What is this?"

"That is very likely to be the Spear of Nine Spheres," Rutha replied. I heard her shuffle the chair back, and looked over to see her very carefully rising to stand. "I say 'likely' because it's possible that a weapon like this could be a very good fake. With the level of magic in the modern age, we can never be entirely sure... A good Aesari fake may well still read to someone like me as a very powerful magical artifact."

"Assuming it's real, what does it do?"

"The Spear was the weapon used to bind the spirits of The Nine - the old gods - to the Dragon Gates, which are mana nodes used to sustain the Caul," she replied. "But it can only be used by a Starborn with the willpower and inner strength to control the energies it commands."

I held out a hand over the Spear, and when my fingertips were almost close enough to touch it, the Mark of Matir burned underneath my glove with cold fire. I hissed, and jerked my hand away. "Yeah, I think you found the real one."

"You know? How can you tell?"

"It's a Starborn thing," I said, rubbing the back of my hand. It felt like someone had dripped liquid nitrogen on my skin. "But I don't think it likes me very much."

"The Spear is reputed to be a difficult weapon, and the magic that remains in it is heavily corrupted by time and wear, but it is necessary for restoring the integrity of the Caul of Souls," Rutha said. "My master wrote that the wielder of the Spear must find someone who is capable of re-forging it, and then take it to each one of the Dragon Gates, rebalance the energies in the Gate, and restore the words of power if any of the artificing has degraded with time. The Aesari left songs and prayers that spoke of a heroic Triad... A Paragon, who is the one to wield the Spear and bind the energy of the gods; an Artist, who is the one to reforge the Spear and repair the words of power, and some kind of protector who assists them and keeps them safe. We translated the word to 'Warsinger', but that doesn't make a great deal of sense. The problem is, we don't know where any of the Dragon Gates are, or exactly who or what the 'Artist' or the 'Warsinger' is. My guess is the Artist is a Starborn Artificer."

I stroked my hand up over the Spear's worn blade. "What makes you think this is for me?"

"I'm not terribly religious, but I *do* believe in fate. Even though I went to Gilheim, I somehow managed to end up on the same ship as you." Rutha hobbled over to stand next to me, putting her weight onto her hands as she drew close to the workbench. "And there is... Something about you. I don't say that just because I like you, and to tell you the truth, if you asked me, I wouldn't have the words to describe what I see in you. Willpower, or... strength of will. The same thing I know is driving you north to put it to Commander Arnaud."

I laughed briefly, and Rutha's face flooded with a smile. My HUD activated then, displaying the formal quest notification I'd been expecting.

New Quest: Restore the Spear of Nine Spheres

The Spear of Nine Spheres, an ancient Aesari relic, was used to create the Caul of Souls - the great magical seal that protects all of Archemi from the Drachan. The Court Sorceress of Ilia, Rutha, believes you can become a hero worthy of wilding the spear and revitilizing the Caul.

Reward: ??? (Varies)

Difficulty: Epic

Special: This is a unique quest.

Special: This quest relates to a world event.

Special: This is an evolving quest. Updates will appear in your log.

'*Wilding the spear and revitilizing'?* I was dyslexic, but even I knew that those errors must have slipped through the copyediting software somehow. My amusement at the typo was brief, because spelling errors or not, this was a big fucking deal. The most responsibility I'd ever had was my duty to the Army. World-shattering, world-changing events were way, way beyond the scope of my reasoning. But as I stared at the HUD notification, the fear began to shift, turning toward determination. Maybe the game had generated this quest for me, sensing my hunger to life a life of purpose and meaning. With work, self-improvement... could I be that kind of person? Not only a dragonrider, but someone able to help my new world?

I tried to take the spear again, and this time I didn't hesitate in touching it. The mark flared a second time, burning with sharp, icy pain, but as soon as I touched the haft, the pain stopped. When I lifted it, I was surprised to find that it was much lighter than normal spear. The curved, sword-like blade was elegant, but streaked with burn marks, bent and dull. I took a look at its stats while holding it:

Ruined Spear

Soul-Bound Weapon

Slot: Two-handed

Item Class: Relic

Item Quality: Ruined

Damage: 25-55 Slashing or Piercing

Durability: 36% (-5% damage)

Weight: 1 lb.

Special: +2 Dexterity, Soul Bound, +50 HP, +2 Defense

Quest Updated: Reforge the Spear of Nine Spheres. You will need to find a Mastersmith capable of reforging Lazula (Bluesteel) magical artifacts.

Even with the damage penalty, the Spear was easily the strongest weapon I'd come across in Archemi so far. I slashed it a couple of times, testing its balance and weight, and my doubts began to recede. For a polearm, it was extremely light... and it felt right in my hands. I felt better just holding it. Stronger, faster, imbued with a growing sense of purpose and responsibility.

"Thank you," I said. And I meant it. "Quest accepted. But I'm still traveling north to become a Dragon Knight."

Rutha nodded. "I had no doubt of that. You have the bearing of someone who wants to make something of themselves. I wouldn't call it ambition, exactly..."

"I never thought of myself as ambitious, yeah. But it'd be nice to make something of my life," I replied, palming the spear thoughtfully. "My entire family is dead. My brother... the last thing my brother did was save my ass. I want to do something that would make him proud."

The sorceress's expression softened. "Did your family perish in war?"

"Kind of." I couldn't look at her while I was speaking, so I looked at the weapon instead.

"Well... then my second gift should sit well with you." Rutha tilted her head, a motion that caught my eye.

"Yeah?" I looked back over at her. "What's that?"

"You'll see," she replied. "Tomorrow morning, after we eventually get out of bed."

I rose an eyebrow. "Eventually?"

Rutha smiled prettily. "Eventually."

Chapter 18

I spent a very pleasant evening with Rutha in her quarters, and once she fell asleep, I lay there in the dark, basking in my afterglow while I marveled at several things all at once. Firstly, that I'd met someone like Rutha by accident after years of being awkward around women. Dating had been weird and – more often than not – embarrassing. I was too much of a geek to attract normal girls, but looked too much like a dumb jock to have a chance with cute nerdy girls. I'd spent a lot of time admiring women from afar, trying not to be a creep... which led to Rutha. She was an NPC. She wasn't a real person... or was she? If I'd met a woman like her in a bar, I couldn't have guessed she wasn't human. Rutha laughed when she was amused, conversed spontaneously and not always perfectly, felt pleasure and pain. It was the stumbles and caught words that arrested me the most. Robots didn't make mistakes like that. They didn't correct themselves. They didn't murmur and snort in their sleep.

Rutha didn't know she was an AI, an algorithm, that there was a physical reality beyond Archemi. She didn't know there was a world without elves, or hit points. This was her universe. Given my previous difficulties with women, it led to some uncomfortable questions. Like most NPCs in all the games I'd ever played, was she programmed to serve the heroes and heroines that came her way? Could she love, or was she executing a program designed to please me? Did it matter?

After brooding pointlessly on the existential nature of humanity for a while, I pulled Rutha in against my side and brought up my character sheet for what felt like the first time in months:

Hector - Dauntan (Tuun)
Level 3 Warrior

==Stats==

Strength: 14

Dexterity: 18

Stamina: 14

Will: 13

Insight: 11

Intelligence: 12

HP: 212

XP: 348 (182 to Next Level)

Adrenaline: 22

(New) Renown: Mildly notable

==Abilities==

=Racial=

Blessing of Burna: +10% bonus to resist disease; +5% Stamina bonus to recover from illnesses. Immune to Pox and Lockjaw. +10% cold resistance. All physical needs accrue 2% slower.

Plateau Native: No Stamina penalties in thin air, -2 Stamina penalty at sea level.

Saddle Born: All Riding skills increase 5% faster.

Sun-sight: No vision penalties in bright or very bright light, -5% penalty in dark environments.

Blessing of Tarn: +15% movement speed.

Blessing of Hrrun: No airsickness, reduced inertia, no vertigo.

=Traits=

Curiosity: The player is an open-minded and engaged person, willing to question their modes of thinking and doing and readily accept new ideas. Combat, craft and class skills gain 5% more quickly.

Introvert: With a preference for their own company or small groups of loyal friends, the player gains a 5% bonus to accumulate skills in solitude provided they are not disturbed. Fatigue accumulates 10% faster in large groups and crowds outside of combat situations.

Dyslexic: The written word is something of a mystery to the player. Books take longer to read, and all language-related skills gain -%5 slower.

(New) Natural Leader: You have a natural inclination to take charge. Social skills increase +2% faster when engaged in leadership activities.

(New) Endurance: You are becoming accustomed to pushing yourself, even when you are exhausted. You may spend adrenaline to offset starvation, fatigue or bleeding for +1 minutes x your Stamina.

(New) Mark of Matir: May convey special abilities at higher levels. When Mark is activated, drain health from enemies on a critical hit. HP regained is equal to remaining AP + Will bonus. 300 second cooldown. You are immune to undead fear effects. – 500 Infamy in places hostile to worship of Matir.

=Combat Abilities=

Basic Weapons Training: Passive -You are trained in the arts of war, and fight unarmed and use all simple and martial hand-to-hand weapons without penalty. Does not include exotic weapons.

Armor Mobility: Passive - You are used to wearing armor and bearing heavy loads. +10 Defense in armor (L,M or H), no penalty to carrying.

Doubletap: Active, -75% Adrenaline - You strike the target, and as they reel from the blow, bring your weapon around like a snake to strike again. Deal double weapon damage.

Fury Drain: When your HP falls below 20%, you can drain 10 HP per good hit from a single enemy (Cost: 5 AP. Cooldown: 10 sec).

=Path Abilities=

None.

==Skills==

=Combat Skills=

Martial Arts 2

Polearms 4

Swords 1

Daggers 1

Clubs 1

=General Skills=

Riding 1

- (New) Riding Specialization (Dragon) 1

Navigation 2

(New) Stealth 1

(New) Negotiation 2

(New) Intimidate 1

(New) Survival 2

=Crafting Skills (Common)=
Foraging 3

(New) Improvise Shelter 3

=Crafting Skills (Advanced)=
None.

It... wasn't looking great. I hadn't had a chance to really start grinding any skills, let alone levels. If I'd started normally, there'd have been tutorials, easy quests, training grounds, and so on. As it stood, I had a fuzzy quest of undefined difficulty and a bunch of hoops to jump through. Still, I had two unspent ability points and all the time in the world to catch up.

The first thing I needed to do was learn some shit. With a view to the future, the first thing I did was search the game glossary for anything on dragons I could find. There was nothing about dragon riding, and the main article only had a summary of them:

Dragons (Solonkratsu)
Archemi's native dragons, the Solonkratsu (literally 'People of the Sun') are perhaps the oldest race of sentient beings on Archemi, along with the Aesari and the Meewfolk. Unlike those two other ancient species, dragons are not monument builders: free-spirited, fierce and sociable, they live out their long lives as lorekeepers, hunters, and in partnership with Archemi's terrestrial races.

Dragons have been a vital part of Archemi's development across millennia. Due to Archemi's impassably rough oceans, dragons were for a long time the only transport between the continents. The mana in their blood and their natural grasp of the 784 Names means they are able to perform advanced magic that is difficult for other species, such as teleportation.

Dragon society is complex, based around large clans who operate in smaller bands or 'wings'. Wings are usually led by a dominant male and female breeding pair, but all of the wings within a single clan answer to the authority of a single Queen dragon. Male dragons are typically larger than ordinary females, and both come in an ordinary array of colors: red, blue, white, green, silver and gold being the most common. Queen dragons have exceptional colors and are generally much larger than even the strongest males, though they grow more slowly.

Dragons speak their own language, Solonkratzi. Because they hatch with the ability to fluently speak this tongue, human sages believe that Solonkratzi is the true 'language' of magic.

I frowned. "*What the fuck are the '784 Names'?*

The 784 Names of Power

The 784 Names of Power are the foundation of all magic on Archemi: words which are spoken, thought and written - either directly in the Aesari script or in a symbolic coded form as sigils or runes - to control, transmute, or sublimate mana. Every Name is comprised of three phonetic letter-sounds (Words) which lend the Name its power. The Words give a name its quality, associating it with one or more of the seven elements (water, fire, air, earth, light, darkness and time) and its relationship with the four modes (temperature, structure, dynamism, entropy).

It is estimated that there are millions of useful combinations of Words and Names, most of which remain undiscovered, and research into the Names is a vital branch of magical discipline.

And that, right there, was why I wasn't playing a mage. I'd probably read a Name backwards and summon Cthulhu.

I had unspent skill points and the option to select two more abilities from the Warrior combat ability tree. Thinking about 'upgrading skills' brought up a list of my current general and combat skills.

"At every level, you gain bonus skill points that you can assign to different skills," a light female voice spoke in my mind. The Narrator again. *"General Skills, Combat Skills, Traits, and Basic and Advanced Crafting skills all interlink with Paths and with each other. Focusing on certain skills and abilities will create 'chains', linking and strengthening your skills and abilities. Compare and contrast skills, abilities, traits, and Paths to discover which abilities chain."*

"Mmm. Min-maxing." I spoke aloud, before I remembered I wasn't alone. Rutha mumbled in her sleep, and I froze, waiting to see if I'd woken her... but she simply snuggled deeper into the warm sheets and resumed snoozing.

The Warrior tree ended at Level 5, where it branched off into six possible Paths: Ranger, Rogue, Lancer, Berserker, Swordfighter, and Knight. The Dragon Knight advanced Path was one of the visible advanced Paths that branched off of Knight at Level 10 and up. I wasn't thrilled: The Knight Path was a solid defensive class, but kind of boring.

There were two main combat branches on the Knight tree, an offensive path that was heavily focused on power attacks and heavy blows with two-handed weapons, and a defensive path that relied on a shield and sword combination. There was some cool vorpal head-chopping and paladin-like buff abilities going on at later levels, but I didn't get tingly from any of it. I supposed the dragon was the tingly part, and the Knight Path surely changed quite a bit once you acquired a flying mount. The Passive Skills branch, which all Knights acquired, were related to leadership and riding, which was also likely to change after bonding with a dragon. Decent grunty-tanky stuff early on in the game, but likely to fall flat at later levels unless you weaseled your way into positions of social leadership.

The Path I *wanted* was the Lancer. Sword and shield and defensive, low-mobility tanking was not my preferred style of play. I liked high damage, high crowd control, high-speed classes that made up for their lack of defense with mobility. Depending on the game, that class was something like Dark Knight, Lancer, or Ninja. Now that I'd acquired the Spear of Nine Spears, it just made sense for me to go with Lancer.

As the name implied, Lancer was extremely specialized - spears, glaives, and scythes all the way – with a range of high-DPS crowd control abilities that hit things hard and chewed up a lot of Adrenaline Points: gravity-defying leaps, multiple strikes, bleeding and wounding attacks. There were good offensive AoE combos at later levels. The Advanced Paths for the Lancer were grayed out, though – I would have to discover them. That was a problem, because there was no Dragon Knight equivalent after level 10. I had no idea how strict the game was when it came to class specialization. It was possible that if I didn't take the Dragon Knight class label, no dragon would obey my command.

I grimaced, and closed the Path menu. Maybe something would open up for me, and I could avoid committing to the boring sword-and-board build. That was something to ask when I reached the fort and had the chance to talk to someone less up their own ass than Knight Commander Arnaud.

On top of skills, I also had some basic Warrior abilities to choose from. I decided on two offensive abilities with damage that would work well with Doubletap: Power Attack and Bluster:

Power Attack

Required Level: Warrior 3

Required AP: 5

Damage: 200%

Max 2 Targets

Attack Speed +10% for 5 sec

Stun on good hits

Chain with ***Doubletap***

Can be used in combination with other attacks.

Bluster I

Required Level: Warrior 3

1s action to regenerate 5 AP + 10HP per level

Cooldown: 25s

The journey to Fort Palewing would give plenty of opportunities for me to skill grind, so I put my failings out of mind for the time being, closed my sheet, and lay down. Now that I thought about it, I *did* feel stronger. My arms and chest were a little thicker, my limbs a bit more flexible than I remembered them being. I'd taken it in stride, but they were changes that the game had made to me. You didn't assign stat points in Archemi, so the game was only reacting to the ways I'd been exerting myself. It made me wonder what would happen if, say, a mage locked themselves in their study and didn't come out for a year. Could stats go down as well as up? Hrrm.

Sometime in the middle of these deep philosophical thoughts, I fell asleep again... and this time, I did dream.

I chased the flickering black tail of a dragon's shadow as it streaked across the earth, battling faceless creatures with Power Attacks and Doubletap lunges. They looked like weak shades with translucent limbs crawling with script, unraveling whenever my staff struck them. They spoke in small, whispering voices I didn't understand, as if they were trying to tell me something in the moment before they vanished.

We rose with the sun, and Rutha called for breakfast to be brought to our room while I prepared for the journey north. I hadn't realized the importance of her position until then: the way the servants acted around her, and the deference of the guards and the quartermaster when she and I went to visit. He was practically tripping over himself to get me the gear that I would need for the long ride into the mountains. Whoever ruled here – King or Queen, I hadn't asked – they held Rutha in high regard and basically let her have run of the place.

I traded in my saber – given my performance in the training yard and the new spear that I just received, I'd already given up on swords – and got some basic cooking gear instead. They let me keep the armor, and in exchange for the useful but cheap items I'd looted off the ship, I was able to get a pack with 30 slots and an array of survival and camping gear, plus the gear I needed to keep my armor mended and my spear as sharp as possible.

"Thanks," I spoke aside to the quartermaster once everything was packed. "This will help on the long walk. How long does it take to reach this fort?"

"Well, *missiure*..." The quartermaster watched me shoulder the pack. "Actually, the Lady has instructed me to give you a hookwing to carry you. I made arrangements, but..."

"But?" I shuffled the pack from side to side once it was on, checking the items against my weight limit. I could carry about four hundred pounds without difficulty, thanks to game physics. The pack put me at about 150, with plenty of slots left over for loot.

"Nearly all of our hookwings are in the north, or are being requisitioned for the civil war defense army," he said sheepishly. "We have a very limited stable to choose from... and by that, I mean the captain was only willing to part with... well, the mount we have for you has some 'issues'."

That was likely because I didn't have any amity with the captain, or much fame in Ilia. I raised an eyebrow. "Which is it? Lame, or retarded?"

The quartermaster rubbed the back of his neck. "Not exactly, no. Actually, quite the opposite, on both counts."

"Great." Smiling ruefully, I tightened the pack's strap around my waist. "Let's go."

The quartermaster reluctantly rounded the counter where he worked, and led the way toward the stables. Rutha was waiting for me there. She was leaning on a cane, her leg splinted and wrapped in bandages, and was watching two young squires in full plate armor trying to wrangle the biggest, meanest, scarred-up hookwing I had ever seen.

The animal was the color of coal, with cruel gold eyes and an iron muzzle that encased most of her face. The squires had their visors down and were hanging on for dear life while the big raptor lunged like a snake at one of them. She couldn't open her jaws, but the collision of muzzle and helmet knocked the boy over onto the ground.

"This is, uhh..." The quartermaster stopped well back from chaos as other stablehands ran over to bring the enormous dino-bird under control. "This is Curvena, *missiure*. Though everyone calls her Cutthroat."

"Faaantastic," I said flatly.

"She comes from champion destrier bloodlines," the man said quickly. "I mean, bred for battle for generations, and worth a fortune... but unfortunately, she never properly imprinted, and she takes the battle to her rider more often than not. To be blunt, *missiure*, you may be better off walking."

I went in closer, and the hookwing reared her head up, fixing me with one baleful yellow eye. She had a silver icon over her head that allowed me to look at her character sheet.

Cutthroat
Level 6 Hookwing Female

Reputation: -400

HP: 250

Age: 7

==Abilities==
Gore: A hookwing's kick does double damage and causes Bleeding.

Disembowel: A power attack with the front claws with a 1% chance of instant death.

Bite: 40-75 damage

Special: Berserk Rage: When injured, all attacks do +50% damage, but the mount becomes uncontrollable by all except the most experienced riders.

Description: A hookwing destrier bred to carry knights into battle, Cutthroat proved too temperamental to send into war. Unusually large, cunning, and bad-tempered, she hates other hookwings and strange riders. The Captain of the White Gulls uses her to haze new recruits.

While I wondered how Archemi's combat system would handle me breaking my neck if I was thrown from this thing, Rutha hobbled a wide circle around my mount-to-be, and came to stand by my left hand. "This hookwing is... very energetic, isn't she?"

"She's a psycho hose beast, is what she is." I replied.

"Can you handle her?"

Damn, she'd played the machismo card. Now I *had* to say yes. "Sure. I'm not letting this overgrown chicken get the best of me."

Cutthroat stomped her clawed feet as I approached, rattling in her throat. The muzzle kept her from biting me, but I was leery of the two and a half foot-long ebony spikes that gleamed between the feathers of her arms. They were as long as scythes and just as sharp.

This couldn't be much different than riding a bike during stunt work, could it? I drew a deep breath and planted my hands on my hips. "Okay, Hannibal the Cannibal. Either we get along, or I'm going to turn you into a turkey dinner." I turned to the shuddering stablehand near me, "Give me those reins."

The squire passed them over, and gratefully got out of the way.

Cutthroat's tried to bite me repeatedly as I pushed her hook arm in against her flank to stop her from skewering me, got a foot in the long stirrup and pulled myself up into the saddle. She hissed, and as I reached down to grab the stirrup so I could shorten it, she shook herself like a dog. I was pitched off her side onto the ground, far too close to her taloned feet.

[You have taken 5 points of impact damage!]

"SCREEE!" Cutthroat immediately seized on the chance to fuck me up. She began dancing and stomping around, forcing me to roll and scramble to my feet to avoid being mauled. Sweating and clutching my back, I rejoined Rutha. She had shrunk against the far wall. The quartermaster had disappeared like a fart in the wind.

"Too much to handle?" she asked, this time with her brows arched.

"Hell no." I straightened my back and winced. "But once I get on that saddle, you know as well as I do that she isn't going to stop... so I thought I had better say goodbye now, you know?"

Rutha smiled again, but this time it was a little sad. She reached up to cup my cheek with a delicate hand. "I had a terrible time on the *Arabella*, but I have to admit, it turned out well. May the Lord and Lady keep you on the road, Hector. It's dangerous beyond the city. The Civil War was decided here in the south three years ago, but it still rages in the north. There will be all manner of bandits and Stranged creatures."

"I'm pretty sure Cutthroat here eats nails and barbed wire for breakfast," I replied. "And if there's any monsters, I'll be able to test out this old stick. I'm an adventurer – sticking monsters is what we do."

"I know." She looked down, then back up to me. "I suppose this is goodbye for now?"

She really was a beautiful woman, but whatever bond had formed between us wasn't anything like love. Whatever it was, it still felt good, and I was okay with that. I patted her hand, the one on my face, then drew her into a careful hug. "For now. Next time you see me, I'll be a dragonrider."

She hugged me back. "I believe you."

Cutthroat sneered and tossed her head as I approached, pulling her lips back from twin rows of curved, dagger-like teeth. I tossed the Spear to the recovered squire while the other one hung on grimly to the hookwing's reins, then grabbed the saddle and pulled myself up. When she tried to shake me off this time, I was ready for it. I clung to the feathers on the back of her neck as she snapped and bucked. When I was sure I had my seat, I reached out a hand. The squire passed the reins to me, then got the hell out of the way.

The hookwing flapped her arms and screeched in rage, but I hung onto her back like a flea. When she lunged forward, I hauled back on the nose reins, forcing her to lift her head up and depriving her of forward vision. She shrilled angrily, trying to pull the reins from my hands, but the rings and muzzle stopped her from succeeding. The battle between us was decided – for now.

"Thanks for helping me with this, guys." I held a hand out for the Spear. The second squire rushed in and passed me my weapon.

When she realized she couldn't get me off her back, Cutthroat snarled and shifted from foot to foot. On a tight rein, she seemed to calm down... but still felt like sitting on top of a missile. With one hand white-knuckled on the leather straps, I arranged my things and then looked down to Rutha. She was solemn, her eyes wide with concern.

"Hector... I think you should know. A lot of recruits go to join the Skyrdon," she said. "Most of them never return. They keep their rites and training secret, as they have for thousands of years... but everyone knows it's dangerous and very few Skyrdon result from a great number of hopefuls. Historically, lords only sent their bastards there, because they either died or became a Skyr, usually the former. They'd never risk their trueborn children."

"I'm not too worried," I said. "I'm Starborn. I died on the *Arabella* and respaw... uhh, came back to life. Whatever they do there, I'll make it."

To my surprise and dismay, Rutha limped up to us, perilously close to Cutthroat's sickle arms. As the dinosaur bristled with rage, the sorceress reached back into the small leather satchel she'd brought with her to hand me up a pair of items: a scroll sealed with violet wax, and a small, hard object wrapped in a scarf that smelled like her perfume.

"Your Writ of Good Standing," she said. "And an artifact. The artifact is a Stone of Guiding... it will help you orient yourself to the north."

"Thank you." I loaded them into my inventory: ⟦The Writ of Good Standing⟧, the ⟦Stone of Guiding⟧, and ⟦Rutha's Token⟧. "And don't worry – this won't be the last time we see each other."

Her lips curled, and her eyes darkened as she stepped back. "I'm sure. *Hosca Kalin,* Hector. *Stay well.*"

That took me aback for a second... because I understood her. She'd spoken in Tuun.

"*Burnamarladik.* Burna spare yoOOOU! "My very serious and emotional farewell was cut short by Cutthroat, who had no time for this human nonsense. She spun around before I'd finished speaking, nearly throwing me off and almost knocking Rutha down with her tail. While I hauled on the reins and shouted obscenities, Cutthroat bulldozed her way out through the stable doors and into the yard, roaring and snapping at anything in her path.

"Brakes!" I shouted back toward the stable. "Where are the fucking brakes!?"

"Remember! You can't push with reins! Only pull!" Rutha called out helpfully, waving from the double doors.

Pulling on anything did very little as Cutthroat thundered forward, using her head like a battering ram to scatter soldiers and other, smaller hookwings as we headed for the gate, ploughed our way through it, and exited into the great open expanse of the world beyond.

Yay! Adventure!

Chapter 19

The Devs had advised us all that there weren't going to be much in the way of mob spawns in settled areas. However, the lack of encounters didn't matter – because my mount was a fucking monster.

"Will you just ffff- WILL YOU CALM YOUR TITS?!" Bouncing and flopping in the saddle, I roared at Cutthroat as she barreled down a village street. Townsfolk screamed and ran – or fell – out of the slavering hookwing's way.

The land beyond the city of Liren was taken up by farms and overcrowded, dirty, sprawling villages. The road had a lot of debris shuffled to the sides. Broken wagons, ripped tents, and other flotsam that suggested to me that there had been a lot of refugees here, and not long ago. Everything smelled like piss and hay, and the ground was muddy under my mount's feet. The stench clearly didn't agree with Cutthroat, because she took every opportunity to stop and counter-piss on things, like a territorial dog. And there was nothing I, the grand motorcycle virtuoso, could do to stop her.

Refugees were everywhere outside the city. They squatted under canvas lean-tos or shivered in tents. Others toiled in fields, commanded by overseers and watched by bored, sweating soldiers. Everything seemed fairly orderly, until I reached the end of the main thoroughfare and rode out past the final guideposts into the wilderness beyond. The turned-up earth and thin layer of long, brownish grass, the big pits and snapped off tree trunks where there had once been forest all spoke of the same thing. This had been a battlefield, and the war that had been fought here had merely been driven north.

After about fifteen miles, Cutthroat finally began to get tired. I, accordingly, relaxed my guard. This was a terrible mistake. She threw me twice: once so that she could run off and maul one of the few monsters we saw, an emaciated [[Ghoul]] that had been digging around in an old field, and once again when a loud explosion in the distance startled her into a homicidal rampage against the nearest tree. I had to battle my mount the entire day, and my Riding skill skyrocketed. I went from Beginner 1 to Apprentice 1 in barely forty miles. After that, I'd had enough. I got off and began to walk, leading Cutthroat by her reins until I found somewhere suitable for us to camp.

With my mount tied to a tree and out of my hair, I began to flex my Gathering skill, picking whatever I found, collecting wood, hunting small animals, and digging at interesting-looking surface veins of ore. As I practiced and my skills grew, the HUD began highlighting items of interest, making it easier to spot plants or ore that I would otherwise overlook. Rutha had given me some basic Alchemy collection tools: a siphon, to collect blood; jars and bottles, and a small, sharp skinning knife. Cutthroat got to eat her fill of fox and wolf and weasel, and I got to slowly grind up my overall level and some life skills. *Very* slowly. The EXP reduction and level cap thing was killing me.

I followed the map all the next day, the terrain becoming increasingly wasted the further north we rode. Toward the late afternoon, we hit the Ourthe River – but where there was supposed to be a bridge, there was only a ruin surrounded by an encampment of soldiers. It had burned from end to end, the remains trailing in the water on either side of the bank. The difference between the land on the south side of the river and the land to the north was stark. Across the water, the earth was barren and scorched. Dogs ran yelping across smoldering fields, while plumes of thin haze rose up into the sky.

Alarmed and alert, I guided my mount to the entry to the camp, where four Ilian soldiers were stationed: two halberdiers, two crossbowmen. They regarded me with suspicion.

"Halt! In the name of the Warden!" One of the men called out. "Who are you, and what do you want?"

"A traveler. I'm headed for Fort Palewing, to join the Skyrdon." I didn't dismount to speak with these men. They looked rough, unshaven, and pissed off.

"And me mother's a mermaid," the guard retorted. "The likes of you? Join the Skyrdon?"

My eyes narrowed. "Yeah, actually. Where's the best place to cross the river?"

"Lyrensgrove's the only place to cross now," the soldier replied. "Assuming it ain't been burned to the ground. There's still fighting on this side of the river to the west. This is the reserve camp."

And an impromptu prison, by the look of it. There were ranks of prisoners in locked and barred wagons, their arms hanging through the bars, voices raised as they begged, moaned, or shouted insults at the soldiers outside the doors.

"Right." I drew a deep breath to sigh, and immediately regretted it. The camp and the surrounding countryside reeked of burned wood and rotten meat. "What way do I follow the river?"

"Nor'east," the guard replied. "But you better have papers wiv you. You got a good sword hand?"

"Decent spear hand."

"Not bad. The boys at Lyrensgrove could probably do with some help, if you catch up with them. There's a modest reward in it for militia and mercenaries that jump in against these swinefucker rebels."

New Quest: Assist the Soldiers at Lyrensgrove
An expeditionary force of soldiers want to fortify the village of Lyrensgrove, which occupies a strategic position near one of the few remaining bridges over the Ourthe River.
Reward: EXP, 100 Florin bounty, Warden's Militia Mark, Bonebreak Poultice x 10

"Sure." I was desperate for real EXP and cash, and the quest seemed straightforward enough. I accepted and put the quest to the top of the queue in my HUD. "Thanks."

"Here- I'll mark your map. Now you should be set to go, aye? 'Ave fun." The guard nodded curtly, and his communication marker faded out as he resumed his watch.

Lyrensgrove was eleven miles northeast from the Riverbank Guard Camp. On the map, it was represented as a village node with tall palisade walls surrounded by forest. Cutthroat rounded the road and we saw plumes of smoke streaming off into the air through what trees were left. Screams filled the air. I could smell burning wood and flesh.

"Shit! Come on, girl! Let's go!" I kicked Cutthroat in the ribs and slapped the reins down, which was basically pointless because the dinosaur was charging toward the carnage anyway.

As we got closer, I heard the clash of steel on steel and more screams, women and children as well as men. Animals bellowed. We loped down the road, passing dead animals not dissimilar to small triceratopses. They were full of arrows, their bellies torn by swords.

The first people I saw were kids. Young peasant boys no older than ten, sobbing with terror as they ran from adult men brandishing a motley of weapons – clubs, swords, axes, even a lance. None of the three men were wearing uniforms or real armor. They were dressed in leather, and shabby homespun cloth, with cloth hoods and boots. My HUD read them as ⟦Marauders⟧.

Before I could even get my spear properly braced, Cutthroat screeched in challenge and took off at a sprint. I hauled back on the reins, but this only seemed to enrage her more. I had a second to realize that my Ride skill still wasn't enough. Maybe it would never be enough. Maybe this was Hell, and Cutthroat had been sent to torment me, forever.

The train wreck seemed to happen in slow motion. We ran one man down, my spear slicing his neck clean through and sending him tumbling to the ground in an arc of arterial blood. Cutthroat trampled the next, bowling him onto his back and running over him with razor sharp claws. But the one with the lance knew enough about what he was doing to set it against the ground as she charged him and jumped, heeding her instincts to leap and slash with her hind claws.

"*What is love?! Baby don't hurt me, don't-*FUCK!" I wasn't sure what threw me from the saddle: the jump that she made, or the horrible, shuddering impact of her body against the lance.

The hookwing screamed like a demon as her momentum skewered her through the shoulder. It wasn't a fatal blow, but the man holding the weapon couldn't say the same. Frothing in rage, Cutthroat pushed along the lance and plunged both of her front arm sickle claws into his shoulder and chest, her head darting forward. I'd taken the muzzle off earlier in the day, and now I understood why the Ilian Castle Guards had put it on. With hardly any effort at all, Cutthroat crushed the man's head and tore it from his shoulders, then tossed it aside to roll across the ground.

I ran to her, and while the raptor worried the twitching corpse, I seized the lance and pulled it free of her flesh. Cutthroat hissed and turned on me, claws raised. As she brought them down, I caught her by the reins, only to be nearly pulled off my feet as four more children ran past us into the forest, crying hysterically.

Cutthroat lunged for them, jaws agape, only to shriek and then moan when I yanked on her reins and punched her in her injured, bleeding shoulder at the same time. Dodging her snapping teeth, I pulled her forward by the nose to the nearest tree, where I tied her by all four reins. "No! Bad dinosaur! Bad! No biscuit!"

Cutthroat didn't notice or care that I was yelling at her. The children were long forgotten. She was now too busy trying to disembowel the tree trunk.

There were at least fifteen other men fighting beyond the village palisade. I bellowed a Tuun war cry and charged through the gate, jumping over the corpse of the now-headless bandit. Dead peasants lay sprawled in front of burning houses, while others faced off against the bandits. There was no sign of any Ilian soldiers – no plate armor, not even chain, and no flags or identifying markers to show they'd even been here. The ones closest to the gate glanced at me as I came rushing in, their eyes widening at the sudden appearance of an adventurer joining the rabble that was trying to fight them off. One of them got his sword up, but I activated Lunge. The maneuver closed the distance between us before he could get his guard up in this new direction, and my spear took him in the chest. I pulled it out, swung it around, and took the next marauder in the throat, knocking him back to kick his life out in the dirt.

"Quick! They locked up the alderman and the girls in the granary!" The man closest to me shouted. He was older, worn in the face, with dirt-speckled cheeks, rough hands, a crude shield, and a plain garden hoe that he was using to fight the bandits. "They'll burn the whole thing down and kill them all!"

"Fight with everything you've got! Form a line!" I dashed forward, uttering a cry as I used Power Attack, then Doubletap to cleave another bandit through the shoulder to the middle of his chest. Compared to the NPCs, my abilities were terrifying, executed with a power that none of them had. The marauders were Level 4, and after I dispatched a couple more of them, so was I.

My appearance rallied the peasants. Male and female, brandishing whatever weapons they could find, they tried to heed what I'd said and form a defensive line to avoid being surrounded and picked off by the bandits. I heard and saw them fall, but the bandits were spooked. I took a blow from a sword that slid across the front of my Jack of Plates and ripped the quilted fabric to bare the metal beneath. It took a quarter inch of my health, hurting enough to gain back adrenaline points and drive my next power attack. As he lunged for me again – snarling, eyes wild with hatred – I ducked and spun beneath his swing and rammed my spear up through his belly, punching through his rusty chain mail and lifting him up a good half foot before throwing him off the blade with a shout.

"Hyahh!" I was furious, driven by the sight of dead civilians sprawled in postures of agony around the well in the center of the village. Lyrensgrove was fairly large for a village, but out of the eighty or so people that had lived here, perhaps twenty were dead. The older man who had called to me back near the gate ran past me, heaving for breath as he headed toward the tallest building: the granary.

"My daughter is in there!" he cried, and the anguish and his voice was palpable. "Kira!"

The bandits fell back toward that same building, and as we closed in as a mob, me and the old man at the front, I heard someone shout: "Torch it! Torch it!"

"Well, shit." I followed him at a hard sprint.

Chapter 20

There were more of them than I'd thought. The remaining marauders, about twenty men, were gathered around the granary in a defensive group. Even as we closed in, a pair of them swung torches onto the thatched roofs of the outbuildings. The straw immediately began to smolder and then burn as the wave of angry peasants closed in and the lines clashed.

I was barely even aware of where I was: hacking, spinning, dodging, and thrusting, I took a solid blow to my back that knocked me forward and dealt critical damage. I turned to find my attacker wheeling around as a woman leapt on him, stabbing at his face and shoulders with a crude kitchen knife. I struck him across the back of his head with the butt of the Spear and he sunk to his knees. The woman stumbled back, and I saw that she had taken his sword all the way through her right shoulder. She went to the ground, pale with shock. Another man ran up behind her, sword raised.

"Down!" I kicked her away, before she had time to react, and lunged over her to parry the sword that was coming for her head. The edge of the blade struck my spear and slid down the haft, biting deep into my glove and the back of my hand before I could throw it off and close in. I headbutted the marauder, kneed him hard in the groin, and nearly took a dagger to the ribs as he pulled one from his belt and swung it toward my side. I saw it just in time, dodged it, and the old man with the hoe spun in from the side and slashed the tip across his throat. Gurgling, the marauder sunk to his knees, clawing at his throat. He fell on top of the woman, who began screaming as she tried to crawl out from under the bloody corpse.

"Kill these mangy dogs, you idiots! They're just sodding peasants!" The man in charge of the marauders was a tall, muscular, sharp-nosed thug with stringy, dark, shoulder length hair. He had a bow, and was shooting into the pack of the village defenders. I burned a healing poultice, jacking my HP back up into the green, and felt the surge of energy rush through me.

"*Tarn Takhar*, motherfuckers!" I bellowed and made a beeline for him – the commander.

"Whoever you are, this is none of your business!" The man snarled at me, nocking an arrow and aiming it at my head as I ran toward him. He tracked me as I dove and rolled, and I felt the point skim across my back. It took off a few HP, but it didn't penetrate my armor. When I rolled up, I sprang toward him, only to have the spear turned aside by the bow as he struck it.

"You know what's my business? People who murder children." I slashed back with bladed edge of the spear, and this time, the strange metal – shoddy as it was – snapped his bowstring and bit deeply into the wood. He pulled me forward with it, nearly jerking my weapon out of my hands, but I managed to hang on to it. As smoke filled the air, we spun. I freed my spear, and then plunged it underneath the edge of his helmet and into his neck.

[[Critical hit! You do 56 damage!]]

[[Raid Commander is bleeding!]]

"AAARRGH!" He clamped a hand down, and with blood pumping between his fingers, drew his sword with the other hand. "I'LL GUT YOU!"

Spear fighting had the advantage and disadvantage of reach. The raid commander seemed to know this, because he charged in at top speed, trying to get inside my guard. I turned his blade aside with a spinning parry, putting all of my upper body strength into it, but he continued his charge and drove his shoulder into my chest. I staggered, the breath driven out of me, and then barked a cry of pain as he rammed the hilt of his sword into the side of my face.

Stunned, I reeled away with a debuff flashing at the corner of my eye. He pressed the attack, sensing weakness. I felt the sword hit me in the chest, slide over the torn fabric and interlocked steel plates underneath, and bite deeply into my armpit. It hurt, and the strike ate up a fifth of my HP, which continued to drain as I clutched at it and clumsily dodged the next swipe.

⟦You are Stunned!⟧

⟦You are Bleeding!⟧

"Well at least I'm not fucking poisoned this time!" The next sword blows landed with bruising force, but my adrenaline points were full, driven up by the damage. I used the lunge maneuver, moving past him with superhuman speed. As the raid commander tried to follow my speed, I got a firm grip on the Spear and pivoted around in a low arc, stretching out in a wide, low stance that put me under his desperate roundhouse swipe. That took his leg off at the knee.

The raid commander screamed and toppled to the ground with his leg bleeding out in pumping spurts. He dropped the sword and blindly groped at it, rapidly draining of color and passing out before his HP bar turned black and he collapsed.

With the death of their leader, the remaining marauders began to run: five or six men, who were chased beyond the walls by the furious mob. I fought the urge to sink down from exhaustion, and spammed healing poultices. The Bonebreak poultices each healed twenty HP, and three of them brought me back to half health. In combat, the items worked instantly, like potions. Outside of combat, I had to pull them from my pack and slap them against the wound for them to take effect. Dizzy from combat, my world narrowed down to a dark tunnel. I was only vaguely aware of the heat on my back, but then the maelstrom of noise resolved into voices and words, and the details clicked.

The granary was burning, and the faint wailing I could hear were the people trapped inside. Worse, the peasants were losing.

"Fuck this fucking-!" I got to my feet, weaving drunkenly, and was promptly knocked down by a marauder. He hit me sword-first, driving his weapon into my arm.

"That *hurt*!" I snarled at him. I grabbed him by his shirt and headbutted him before shoving him back. He stumbled a few steps away, recovering just in time to take a Doubletap to the face. A couple more slashes and he was down, and I was sprinting for the granary.

The old man with the hoe and a couple of the other villagers were beating on the walls and doors with their tools. The bronze and iron tools were heavily damaged, dented and broken from contact with real sharpened steel. They weren't strong enough to break down the doors or crack the gigantic padlock that held them closed. I had a brief look at the durability of the Spear of Nine Spheres. It was still at 36%, not having degraded at all since I began using it in combat.

"Get out of the way!" I shouted, steeling myself, and then ran at the door. The peasants scattered out of the way. With a roar, I triggered a power attack and struck the heavy, old iron lock with the enchanted weapon.

The padlock didn't give way, but the fittings that held it to the door did. I split them off, along with a good chunk of wood, and kicked the door in. Smoke poured out, along with a wave of women, some of them elderly, some of them barely toddlers carried by their older sisters. They fled into the open air, dragging the wounded and unconscious fellow prisoners. The last to come out was a teenage girl and an older woman who were supporting a coughing, red-faced man who had to hop. His other leg was a bloody ruin, the arrow that had taken him in the thigh still protruding from his clothing.

"Kira!" The old man with the hoe helped them out, taking over from the old woman so that she could sit on the ground and cough. "Bernard! Thank the gods!"

Exhausted and more than a little stunned, I fell back as the heat of the burning granary beat against my face. The entire roof was on fire now, and it wasn't long until all the grain inside would be gone. A moan went up along some of the survivors as they watched the year's harvest go up in flames.

"Thank the Lord and Lady you came, stranger. Owen here tells me we'd be dead if not for you." Bernard, the old man with the arrow in his thigh, limped over to me and sat down. He was tall and stooped, with a scraggly beard and big ears. His eyes were very green.

"No worries. But we better fight these fires before shit burns down." I gave him a flippant salute. Owen the Hoe Guy gave a curt nod to me in reply.

Bernard waved a hand, sinking down against the nearest wall. "Aye to that. Go, Kira. Owen. Go put the fires out with the others. This wound of mine will have to wait."

"It can't, Alderman," Kira replied quickly. "A puncture wound like that will fester. Go with the adventurer, Dad – he'll do the work of two men."

"Ten men." I almost started flexing, but we didn't have time for shenanigans. "Come on!"

There was really no time to lose. The granary could not be saved, but several of the thatched houses were not burning as hard as that building. I joined the bucket line without question, hauling water as fast as my enhanced strength allowed for, passing it over. We managed to douse two of the four that were on fire, but the others were beyond hope. All we could do was watch as the roofs caved in and the contents of the houses went up in flames, while the families that had lived in them wept.

Quest updated: Assist the Soldiers at Lyrensgrove
You arrived at Lyrensgrove to find it under attack by unmarked assailants. After joining the villagers, you have repelled the marauders and spared most of the townspeople.
Reward: EXP, +200 renown, new friendly faction: Lyrensgrove (Bernalt, Alderman).

"Shit." I spat into the dirt, frustrated, and went to find Cutthroat before she killed somebody

Chapter 21

I found the huge black hookwing roaming loose. She was ripping apart one of the dead triceratops-looking herd animals, snarling at the corpse as she tore pieces off it. She'd pulled the tree down on top of herself and bitten through her reins to get free.

"Well, at least it's not one of the villagers." I sighed, pulling the broken rein straps off the trunk. "C'mere, girl."

Cutthroat eyed me balefully as I approached her, but food was enough of a distraction that I was able to tie the broken reins together without getting mauled. I slung them up on her neck and left her to finish off lunch, then walked back to loot the sacks left behind by the bandits.

The bandits carried no money, but they had decent gear. I frowned as I collected a bundle of ⟦Steel Swords⟧. They were all of similar make, stacking together in my Inventory, with the disclaimer that vendors would buy them for a fair price – 75 florints each. It was common for mobs assigned to a single area to have the same kind of trash so that you could grind the area and stack the items for selling, but in light of the Camp Guard's quest, I couldn't help but notice that these guys were uniformly and unusually well-equipped for bandits. Part of me wondered if these were the soldiers... but that didn't make much sense to me, either.

I looted swords and their [[Leather Armor]] components, which could be broken down for crafting. Once that was done, I equipped Cutthroat's muzzle back on her in her sub-menu. She squawked with indignation as the heavy iron materialized back on her face, shaking her head and prancing away from the remains of the herd beast.

"Hey! Cutthroat, watch ou- oh." I watched as my champion destrier hookwing, bred for battle for generations, rammed herself into the palisade, screeching as she attacked the village's protective wall in a brand new round of pointless rage.

Hour by hour, my fantasy of pulling awesome stunts on the back of a dinosaur seemed increasingly remote. I shook my head and rubbed the bridge of my nose as her shrieks and the *whump* of scaly feet hitting the fence rocked the air. "Well, okay. You just... you do you, girl."

I returned to find the rescue and repair in full swing. The surviving villagers were putting out smaller fires and laying out the corpses of their fellows in carts. A young priest was giving the fallen a final blessing, his eyes full of tears as he clumsily recited from a slim book of prayers. At a bit of a loss, I wandered off to find Kira and her father at the herbalist's hut – easily now the most crowded building in the village.

The house only had two rooms, and they were packed. People huddled with dressings pressed to their injuries, or lay stretched out on the floor, some hurt, others dying. Kira and Owen were treating those with the worst injuries with an array of herbs and potions. None of them seem to be having quite the same miraculous effect that my poultices and mint potions did for me.

"Ser! Can you go into the garden and get me lobelia?" Kira called to me. "As much as you can carry."

I felt a flash of panic. "I... have no idea what lobelia is?"

"It's a flower," Kira replied. She had her hands pressed over a cloth, leaning her weight down onto a semiconscious man's abdomen. "It's violet, with three large petals and two small ones and narrow, watery stems. It looks like a little rabbit with wings."

Her description caused my HUD to ping. *[[New Knowledge: Lobelia C]]*

"I'm on it." Flying rabbit flowers. Okay then. Armed with my newfound knowledge, I hopped over rows of moaning people and hurried for the garden behind the house.

The herbalist's garden was packed with plants. I frantically ran down the narrow garden path, searching the beds for the right plant. The HUD helpfully highlighted the few plants that I did know – mint, basil, parsley, daisies – and to my great relief, the lobelia. It was a big, round, bushy plant with pretty, deep blue-violet flowers like Kira had described. They really did look like purple bunnies with little bee wings. I slung my spear back over my shoulder and used my knife to hack and cut away as much of the lobelia as I could carry. I left the poor bush looking like the half-finished Death Star.

"Here!" I reached Kira's side and knelt down, handing her fistfuls of flowers and stems. She took them, threw them into a mortar with a dash of bright liquid and a pinch of powder, then ground them together. I watched curiously as the flowers transformed into a uniform blue paste, which she applied liberally to the man's open chest wound. Several seconds passed. Then his eyes opened and he drew a deep breath. He was still out of it, but the plant got him breathing, like some kind of herbal defibrillator.

"Is that what lobelia is used for?" I asked, taking the blood-soaked bandage when she passed it back. "A magical resuscitation herb?"

"Lobelia can restart a man's heart if he's close to death, but his heart must have only just stopped beating." Biting her lip with concentration, Kira reached for a bowl of wet poultices, brushing past me in a tumble of sweet smelling, dark wavy hair. She peeled off the covering the man's abdomen and took it off to reveal organs that were doing their best to be external rather than internal. She slapped down a poultice over that mess, and reapplied the cloth and pushed my hands over it. "Hold this."

"Yes ma'am." Nothing like bonding over some spilled guts, as my old Sergeant used to say.

For hours, we moved from person to person. While Owen mixed, Kira and I applied. Now and then, one of us had to run out to the rapidly-depleting garden, but one by one, lives were saved and sometimes lost. I had mixed feelings about the amount of skill XP I earned. It was a lot, leveling me to Foraging 3 and Survival 4, and giving me my first levels in new skills: Healing (Field Medicine) and Herbalism. By the time we were done, everyone who had assisted was exhausted. The volunteers drifted away, but I had nowhere to go, so I waited around and helped clean up until it was completely dark outside.

"Do you have an inn here?" Setting a wooden bucket down, I slumped to a crouch beside it. "Somewhere I could sleep and get something to eat?"

"Yes, but don't even think about it." Owen looked over at me, his eyes hawkish and piercing by candlelight. "You're an adventurer, is that right?"

"That I am," I replied.

"Not from here, are you?"

I shook my head. "Nope. I'm from Tungaant. A land from over the ocean."

Father and daughter both turned pale and drew an infinity symbol across their chests from shoulder to shoulder.

"The Hells," Owen muttered.

"You're joking! Did you fly here?" Keira exclaimed. "How do you get across the ocean?"

"On a dragon, actually." I grinned, and scratched the back of my head.

Kira's excitement grew, while her father looked disapprovingly at me. She threw down the rag she'd been using to clean the floor and came over to join me. Now that I actually had time to look at her, I could see she was very pretty. Her hair fell to her waist, and she had eyes that were still warm despite everything she'd done and seen tonight. Her skin was well-tanned, and she had a light smattering of freckles across her nose.

"Did you see any demons?" she asked eagerly. "What is the ocean like? They say you can hear the souls of the dead calling from the waves."

"Kira," Owen admonished. "Come now, this is not talk that should be bandied about after something like what happened tonight. You, sir, I didn't even have time to get your name."

"Dragozin Hector," I said, bowing from the neck. "Uhh... Hector's my first name."

"I can't help but notice that your wounds healed," Owen said. His voice had hardened. "Completely, and with hardly any attention. Are you a mage?"

"I'm way too dumb to be a mage," I replied, unable to keep from smiling. "I'm Starborn."

Owen's eyes bugged, but Kira nodded, satisfied. "That's how you made it over the ocean, then. There isn't any demon that could kill a Starborn."

"That's ridiculous." The older man's voice rose with disbelief. "Are you telling me that you're some kind of legend? That you can come back from the dead?"

"I can and I have." I rolled my shoulders and stretched my arms. They ached, like the rest of my body. "Doesn't mean it feels good, though. And I still feel pain, and still get tired. On that note, let me repeat: is there somewhere here that I could get something to eat and a place to sleep?"

Owen glanced between me and Kira, and I could see him sizing up whether or not it was safe for him to leave me alone with her. "Me and you can go over to May's tavern and set you up with food and beer, if that suits you. It's the least we could do for the help you gave us."

"I'll come too," Kira said. "I could use some ale after a night like this."

I could see that her father wanted to argue, but he was too tired. He sighed and grumbled, but nodded. "We'll go together. And you will be coming home tonight, girl. No dallying."

Kira laughed, and shook her head. "'Girl' he says. I just spent four hours putting people back together, and he calls me a girl? Do you think I'm some kind of blushing maiden, Father? That I faint at the sight of blood?"

"You'll always be a girl to me," Owen said, but there was humor underneath the grumpy old man front. "I remember when you used to dribble grain soup all down the front of your pinafore-"

"Dad!" Kira blushed.

I watched on with some amusement, and a little sadness. My father had never been that protective of me. "Don't worry, Mister...?"

"No Mister. Just Owen."

"Well, don't worry about a thing, either of you," I said. "I have no designs on anyone's virtue. Give me a beer and point me in the direction of the nearest horizontal surface, and I will pass the fuck out. Pardon my language."

Kira harrumphed, and crossed her arms.

"No need to pardon yourself. Gods know I curse when the mood strikes," Owen replied. And then something curious happened. His name – which I could see when I focused on him – went from gray to gold, and a small Skill icon appeared beside his ear. Kira had the same thing going on, but I hadn't seen it earlier. I must've been staring, because she cocked her head.

"Is something the matter?" she asked.

I startled back out of the HUD overlay, refocusing on the world around me. "No, nothing's wrong. But I was wondering... When either of you have some time, would you be willing to teach me more about medicine and herbs?"

"Sure," Kira said. "We have to do the rounds of the injured tomorrow morning. You can come with me and I'll teach you what I know."

"I think not," Owen scoffed. "I'll give him a tour of the garden while you work. You don't need any distractions."

"Dad-"

"You're still an apprentice, Kira. That's how we're doing it."

Kira huffed, slinging a cloak around her shoulders, eyeing me sidelong. "You never let me do anything fun."

Chapter 22

May's Tavern was surprisingly full. Those people who were now homeless were eating and sleeping here, while others had come to drink to their victory or drown their sorrow and terror. The big L-shaped building had a small singed hole in its roof, but as we stepped inside, the warmth and rich smells of liquor, ale, garlic, fresh bread, and savory meat washed over us. My stomach growled. Oh, right: I hadn't eaten anything for nearly ten hours.

A row of shuttered windows ran along the far wall of the inn. An open kitchen was behind a long oak bar, taking up the far quarter of the tavern room to my left. It faced double rows of tables and benches where people talked, played cards, and ate like starving wolves. Clean straw littered the floor, and stained-glass lamps illuminated shelves of bottles. The waitresses were busy, pulling tankards of dark, fragrant ale and cider from chrome taps. Despite the losses to Lyrensgrove, the tavern was nearly full. Eyes were sunken and faces careworn, but in the end, the village had won and everyone knew it was something to celebrate.

"I hope you can drink, adventurer. What do you want?" Owen asked me. "The first five are on me, if you can handle more than one."

"My bladder will give out before my liver does." With all the self-assurance of a soldier who had recently been on tour drinking his way around the world, I swaggered up to the bar slightly ahead of Kira and thumped my fists down on the top. "As for what I want, what do you recommend?"

" May's firebrew cider is the best this side of the Oerthe River!" Owen drew up beside me, and to my surprise, threw a friendly arm around my shoulder. "May! May, this is the adventurer who came in swinging for us today!"

May turned out to be one of the older-looking women working behind the bar. She was small-framed, with long blonde hair done up in braids, and a homely but open face. She smiled broadly at Owens words. "I wouldn't have known if you hadn't told me. Who'd have thought this long-haired, distinctly foreign gentlemen wasn't one of our boys come in from the field?"

"You have to forgive Dad," Kira replied, squinting her eyes like a smug cat. "He's getting a bit funny in his old age."

Owen puffed up a little. "Still strong enough to fight off the rabble!"

"Yes, Da." Kira held up three fingers to the tavern's owner. "Three of your best, May. To the brim."

"Just as well I like cider," I remarked.

"Of course it'll be to the brim, and don't you even *think* of giving me coin." The last was directed at me, and May's tone brooked no argument. "I was locked in the granary with Kira and Bertrand, and I don't doubt that I owe you my life." May briskly moved to the taps and set out three tankards still damp from being recently washed. "And let me guess: none of you have eaten, and you're more than long past due for something in your bellies other than ale." She turned her head as she poured, calling back to the cook. "Lyra! Three bowls!"

We took a table, followed by a barmaid who plunked down three big mugs of sweet-smelling, cold, frothy cider. My throat was dry. I lifted my tankard and had a swallow to take the foam off. I expected to be grossed out at how sugary it was, but it was nothing like the glorified fruit soda I was used to. It was rich with the taste of fresh apples and molasses, and hit my belly like a warm, spreading flame.

"So, where to from here?" Kira took a pull off her mug, and her face immediately flushed. "It's still a warzone in these parts."

I nodded. "I noticed. I'm headed-"

My words were cut off by a round of cheers at the bar. Three very drunk men gathered in a cluster had just received their drinks, and were shouting at the top of their lungs. "Long live the King!"

The King? As in, the 'Mad King'? I stopped talking, watching Kira's and Owen's moods shift from exhausted but relaxed to high-strung and scowling in an instant. They both looked at me as May began chewing the group out.

"Not in my place, you lot! Not after tonight! That's the last of this talk, you hear?" There was a note of panic in the woman's voice.

"Ugh." Kira shrunk onto her seat. Owen was tight-lipped.

"What?" I cocked my head. "What was that about?"

"Politics. Don't worry yourself." Owen grimaced, glancing over his shoulder at the racket. "Now, what was it you wanted to know about herbs?"

"Pretty much everything," I said. "I'm good at cooking, but I've got no experience with potions and herbs."

"If you want to stop from dying when someone sticks you, you can start with Bonebreak," Kira piped up. "Comfrey. It's good for cuts, that sort of thing. Garlic stops wounds from going bad, but you can't use too much of it or it will make someone sick. And there's balm and hyssop..."

By the time we left the tavern, my alchemy knowledge base had swelled to about twenty items, most of them herbs. Some of them were familiar, such as garlic, strawberries, garlic, and onions. Others were definitely fantasy plants, unique to Archemi. Moontears, a yellow drooping berry which was ground into a paste for burns; and starling, a stiff green shrub with spiny little fruits that could be boiled, mashed, and used to dull pain. There was no room in the tavern, so I went back with the healers to their home and slept on a rough mattress of straw and one of Owen's cloaks in front of the fire. It was surprisingly comfortable, and after a tankard and a half of the excellent cider, sleep came easily. I dreamt of flying on a beautiful white dragon like Talenth, the wind whipping my face and arms as we soared over an endless desert. In the distance, there was an oasis that we never seem to reach.

I stirred to the sound of bells: the deep, melodic tolling of church bells. The sound cascaded from somewhere outside of the hut, rolling through Lyrensgrove with the pale dawn light. The straw and wool cloak felt very real and very warm, as did the chilly air. I stretched and yawned, semi-consciously searching for the deviations from RL. There were a few changes that stood out. My joints didn't pop when I moved, for one thing. For another, a red envelope icon flashed in the corner of my eye.

I called the HUD, yawning again - deeper, this time - and went to the message center. There were two 'Unread' icons. The first message was from Temperance, while the other was a forwarded announcement from the Dev Team. Weird that they hadn't just sent it to me directly.

Temperance's message was titled: "Physical Body Status". My skin crawled with a nasty cold creep when I considered what the email was about, so I opened the Dev Team forward first.

Good Morning, Players!

We hope you're enjoying your time in Archemi, and if you're not, please start a ticket with us and we'll see what we can do!

We have rolled out some bugfixes and other features based on Beta feedback:

- Clipping and terrain physics issues are a W.I.P, but we have substantially decreased the likelihood of accidental dismemberment during teleports. Sorry about that!

- Better/more realistic weather in Oren, Zaunt and Lalanthir.

- Players reported mob spawns in the Hercynia region were scarce, a hangover from the alpha testing phase. We have implemented a large increase in spawns to assist with leveling.

- Pain duration during health recovery has been decreased 15% by popular demand.

- Soul shard/gear recovery points are now always accessible. If you died in an inaccessible position, the point will be moved to the closest accessible location. Don't give up!

- The Level 10 cap, decreased EXP, and the difficulty cap on NPC hostiles is still in place, and unlikely to be removed until the refugee migration is complete. We're sorry for this, but the risk of early testers surpassing new intake is a real one, and we want to make sure everyone starts on an equal footing.

Thanks for your patience and understanding. As you know, Archemi's development had to be rushed ahead of the pandemic and we're still catching up on everything. Several ill members of the Dev Team will be transferring to their virtual stations over the next couple of weeks so that they can continue working from the inside.

Have fun!

Your Friendly Neighborhood Devs

I nodded to myself as I read. More mobs would be nice – though I shuddered to think what it would be like trying to fight on Cutthroat's back.

The Devs had attached a list of known issues in my area. My fellow PCs had been busy - the only things in this part of the world I apparently had to worry about were some collision issues with a bridge in Liren that had trapped a couple of players, and the report of a homeless NPC following a player around while chirping the same phrase over and over. I guessed being a crazy bum in Archemi was 'just a bug'. IRL, we called that schizophrenia.

Temperance's letter was next. I opened it, stomach churning with formless anxiety. She was probably just checking in, but...

Good morning, Hector,

I am writing to let you know that your body expired at 4:02 a.m. on Thursday, the 12th of September 2059, due to complications of the HEX retrovirus. The rest of your transition team and I offer you our condolences and support in light of this difficult news.

We would like to encourage you to reach out to our [[Support Channel]] if you experience anxiety, depression, dissociation, or any other issues. Your remains are being treated as per your contract terms you signed with Ryuko, and will be stored in cryogenic containment as the world continues to search for a cure for HEX.

We thank you for your service and for being willing to face this great mental and existential challenge.

Temperance

I rubbed my arm, where the Mark of Matir tingled under the leather glove I'd worn to bed. For several minutes, I sat there in stunned silence.

"Your body expired." Those three words sounded so inane, so... anti-climactic.

"Hector?"

I nearly jumped out of my skin. I whipped my head around, but it was only Kira. She was dressed in a long nightshirt, her hair a tousle of dark curls. When she saw my expression, her eyes widened.

"What's the matter?" she asked, stepping closer.

I shrugged, numb, and looked down at my hands. Flexed them. They felt solid, real, alive. If I blocked my ears, I'd hear my virtual heartbeat. It was an illusion, like the sleep - eight virtual hours condensed into a couple of minutes as an AI somewhere tracked me and adjusted my perception to match the game world. Dead. Fuck. That meant we were all gone. My entire family had been wiped out.

"Hector? What's wrong?"

Her voice shook me out of my brief reverie. "It's... I can't explain."

"Did you have a bad dream?" She came to me and knelt down, tucking a strand of hair behind her ear.

"No, nothing like that." I took a deep, steadying breath. It didn't help much. I was dead - the meat bicycle I'd ridden my whole life was gone. So what was I now? A copy of the real Hector Park? A ghost? "It's... it's a Starborn thing. I don't know how to explain it without sounding really weird."

"Whatever it is, I'll do my best to accept." The girl's eyes were a dark amber-brown in the sunlight, and earnest. "Unless it's something really horrible, like... I don't know... like you have a peculiar interest in barnyard animals or something."

That made me snort. "It's like we live multiple lives. And I just died in one of them."

Kira frowned. "How strange. And you know for sure that... you died?"

I nodded.

"That must be terrible."

"Yeah. Not as bad as knowing everyone around me died, too." I rubbed my eyes, then the back of my neck, staring at the cold ash in the fireplace. When I'd read that line about contacting psych support, I'd smirked a little. Me - Army tough guy, motorcyclist, bursting with machismo - talk to a shrink? But as I made myself get up for the day, intrusive thoughts kept pushing their way in. I wondered which one of the main symptoms had... well... killed me. While I'd been flying on Talenth with Rutha and Skyr Arnaud, had I, the real flesh and blood me, been choking to death on my own lungs? Did I have a stroke? Bleed out from the liver?

"You know what helps me when I'm stressed?" Kira spoke up after a couple of minutes of silence. "Passionflower and catmint tea. Can I make some for you?"

"Sure." It couldn't hurt. I now knew both those herbs were for treating anxiety. In game situations, they gave +3% bonus Combat XP and protected against the Fear debuff for thirty seconds. "I need to go and... uhh... attend to some morning needs before I drink any tea, though."

"You could just say you're taking a piss. Dad uses the chamber pot outside," Kira said, pushing herself up onto her bare feet.

The prim, huffy tone of her voice cracked me up, and the black cloud lifted a little. "Thanks. Not just for the tea."

"Hmm? What? I didn't do anything." Kira already had her arms full of firewood, and looked back at me.

"You did. You helped shake me out of a dark place."

"Of course I did. You saved my life, and besides that, it's what we do here. The world is cruel, but we can always try to be decent people. That's what my mother always said." She turned back, stacking the timber into the hearth.

I considered Kira for a moment, and all at once, her circumstances clicked. NPC or not, she'd lost someone important to her, too.

"You don't have to answer me... but did the war get her?" I asked, taking a seat beside my pack. While we talked, I reorganized my inventory.

"Yes." That was all she said.

"I lost people to war, too," I ventured. "Not here. Somewhere far away."

"I know." Kira turned from the hearth with a mug of tea cupped in her hands.

I took it with a small smile. "Educated guess?"

"People who've been through grief have a look about them." She prepared a cup for herself, and sat down across from me. "Work as a healer during wartime for long enough, and you learn to spot it."

"Smart *and* beautiful," I said without thinking.

Kira blushed, bringing her freckles out in sharp relief. "Don't give me that. You're about to leave. And you've got a woman's scarf tied around that spear of yours. Where are you headed from here, anyway?"

Now that I had the chance to sit and watch someone in broad daylight without interruption, there were things that told me Kira wasn't a player. The way she handled her cup, for example. There was nuance in her speech and emotions, but the way she drank was identical each time.

"North," I said. "I want to join the Skyrdon and become a Dragon Knight."

The herbalist's face froze.

"I figure by the time I reach there, I... what?" I stopped mid-thought, and glanced up at her, puzzled. "What's the matter? Did I say something?"

She flushed and shook her head. "No. No, nothing. I just remembered something about what you said earlier. You were saying how you somehow live separate lives, and you know when you die in one of them. I often dream I'm someone else."

"Oh." I eased down, but was still confused. "Well, I figured. You want to go adventuring, right?"

"That's not what I mean." The woman's brow creased. "I mean, like... I dream of being somewhere else, as someone else. In those dreams, I'm dying in a place with people moaning all around me, or I'm locked in a room full of light, or running through the ruins of huge buildings. Sometimes I'm fighting. But when I wake up, I can't remember what I was fighting for. Dad says its nothing to worry about... he says everyone has dreams like that."

I finished off the last of my tea and stood up, shrugging into my pack. "Well, I guess. Everyone has bad dreams sometimes."

"No. He means that we all have dreams like mine." Kira's eyes were wide and guileless. "Everyone we know. War is a terrible thing, Dragozin Hector. It's ruined this land, and... when you head north to seek out the dragon knights..."

I frowned, confused. "What?"

She looked up at me. "Please remember why you helped us. And please, *please* don't mention what you overheard in the inn."

Book Two

Long Live the Queen

Chapter 23

Two days' ride out from Lyrensgrove, and the blasted farmland and crumbling battlefields gave way to dark, dense forest. Cutthroat and I always rode *up*, and the hills grew higher and wilder the further north we went. The road began to climb, and soon the wasted plains of Ilia were laid bare to my right, rolling off into the horizon. By the fifth day, the view had turned into mountains: black giants crouched in regal, frigid cloaks of snow and fir. The plains vanished, plunging us into primeval wood.

The road to Fort Palewing was deeply rutted, but lonely. The few people who made this trip, taking supplies to the Skyrdon, had no use for inns. We slept in rude waystops that were little more than caves dug into ancient ruins. Many of them were dug into enormous half-circles of stone and broken columns that jutted out everywhere on the ground. There was enough room in these shelters for me, Cutthroat, and a small fire. The hookwing was uncommonly calm inside these ruins, displaying none of her usual savagery. Like a cat, she preferred to sleep in a loaf shape – her hook-claws tucked against her chest, feet pulled up underneath her, tail stretched out. While I repaired my armor with a thick bone awl and catgut, she kept watch, growling every time the wind whipped the branches of nearby trees against the standing stones.

Level-wise, I was still running behind where I wanted to be. The EXP penalty turned combat into an incremental grind. I'd fought ghouls, crows, coyote-like creatures, and yes – bunnies. But these woods were not for characters of my level. The wolves howling outside were Level 8, and I'd glimpsed other, larger shadows in the forest with red skull icons flashing warningly in the upper right-hand corner of my HUD overlay. Skills levelled faster than overall level, which was nice – but the insight required to learn new things was out of reach until I could push to Level 5.

We arrived at the fortress gates on the evening of the eighth day. The land outside Fort Palewing had been cleared so that guards could watch anyone - or anything - coming up on them from the forest or the road toward the ancient cliffside that marked the entry to the dragon knights' stronghold. A hundred feet away at the top of a sharply steepening hill was a high stone wall. Three guards waited at the barred gate. They were grizzled, dark men with frost in their beards and spears and axes in their hands. They watched me curiously as I dismounted and led my tired, muzzled mount toward them.

"Who goes there?" The closest one called.

"An aspirant. Hector Dragozin," I replied, when I was close enough to be heard over the wind. It was howling today, driving gusts of snow off into the air from trees and hillsides. "I've come to try out for the Skyrdon."

"Someone refer you for the trials?" The same guard jerked his chin at me as he spoke.

I pulled the Writ out of my Inventory, and it materialized in my hand. No one so much as blinked an eye. "I have a Writ of Good Standing from Lady Rutha, Court Sorceress of Ilia."

"I'll get a squire to take it to the Novice Master. Go find a place to camp. It'll take a while." The guard nodded curtly and went to thump on the gate. One of the huge black oak doors swung open smoothly, allowing him to slip inside.

I took him at his word and built a small fire. It was down to hot coals by the time the guard returned with a young boy who couldn't have been older than twelve. The kid strode toward me, his cloak hood drawn up, a crossbow in one hand, Rutha's letter in the other.

"Welcome," the boy said. He was dark-eyed and serious as he handed the Writ back to me. The wax had been broken. "The Novice Master is drilling the current batch of recruits in the Old Hall. He says to come with all speed."

"Is there a stable for my hookwing?" I asked. "She's kind of a special needs animal."

The squire seemed to notice the muzzle for the first time, but didn't look especially taken aback. "Of course. Come this way, *missiure*. We must hurry."

I couldn't believe it had been this easy. Head ringing, I followed the boy at a quick walk into Fort Palewing, glancing at every shadow in case the knight commander jumped out to lecture me on why my filthy barbarian self wasn't allowed here. We stopped to hand Cutthroat over to the stable hands at the central stable, and then the squire led me through a maze of buildings and up a flight of stairs. At the top, I was able to get a look out a window - and drew a sharp breath at the sight on the horizon. A dark tower lanced up into the sky like a spear, framed against the huge yellow surface of the moon at the other end of a dense forest. I could see the way the cliffs curved around like a bowl from here. We weren't in a valley - the Fort, the gate, everything was built into the rim of an enormous dormant volcano, a caldera larger than most cities.

I was taken to a section of the fortress that was mounted in the cliff. We went into what looked like an old church, a room with a dome ceiling and scaffolding holding a crumbling wall together. At the far end, a row of nine young men and women faced a tall, impressive-looking older man in the silver and blue armor of the Skyrdon. He had a short, well-groomed beard, steel gray hair and – once I got close enough to see - intense, intelligent gray eyes. Like Arnaud, his irises and pupils were unnaturally large.

"Another aspiring Bondee? Just in time," he boomed over the heads of the other would-be postulants, who turned to look at me. "Join us, young... hmm."

I did join them, stopping a short distance away when I noticed the awkward silence. Oh, right. Barbarian. I was the only Tuun in the room. There were four other PCs – I could tell by the fine silvery rings hanging behind their heads in the AR interface - but both they and the NPCs all had the luxurious clothes and bearing of young Ilian nobility. By contrast, I looked like some kind of road-weary Mongolian pirate.

"I brought the Writ?" I held it up hopefully, like a shield.

"I've seen it. No need to see it again, Starborn." The man motioned to the curious recruits, then folded his hands behind his back. "I am Skyr Tymos, the Novice Master and Castellan of Fort Palewing. Fall in."

I took my place at the end of the line, ignoring the obvious stares from the others.

"It is time you learned what you're all getting yourselves into," the Novice Master said. His reedy voice carried well in the chamber where he'd assembled us. "Now, as I was saying. For three millennia, the Skyrdon of Saint Grigori have played a vital role in the defense of Ilia and the continuation of the seven kingdoms of Hercynia. To become a Skyr means undergoing the same Trials undergone by Saint Grigori himself. They will very likely kill you – the Trial is dangerous, the training is difficult, and you will be tested to the very limits of your body before you ever set a foot on the hatching grounds. I will not even learn your names until the last of you are left standing. Your name will be 'Aspirant' or 'Postulant' – nothing more."

He let that sink in for a second before resuming his speech.

"Alright... we have five Starborn here with us today." The old knight nodded to each of us in turn. "You lot may immediately note that you cannot assign Fort Palewing as your Reincarnation Point. Now that you have arrived, this is your only chance to secure the right to stand before the altar of Saint Grigori and join your soul to that of a dragon. There are no second chances. You may perish from weakness, in which case you are not fit to become a squire, or bad luck, in which case you should feel blessed to have your feet on the ground and not in the sky. There is no such thing as an unlucky dragonman. Am I understood?"

"Sir yes sir!" One of the other PCs and I both burst out at the top of our lungs at the same time out of habit, voices bouncing off the high domed chamber. We looked at each other with a moment of delighted recognition, while the non-military members in our ranks murmured their agreement.

Skyr Tymos chuckled. "Such enthusiasm. Until you have proven yourselves worthy, you are not even truly a postulant. You are nothing but a guest here. To become a postulant and take the Trial of Marantha, you must perform a deed worthy of a knight under the supervision of a trusted witness, who will report back to me, the Novice Master, of your prowess in battle. After that - assuming you survive - you will gain the right to Trial.

An alert popped up in my vision:

New Quest: Prove Your Mettle
To be accepted by the Skyrdon of St. Grigori, you must prove yourself capable of holding your own in honorable combat against the Stranged

monsters and bandits menacing Camp Prichard, a small prison camp under the jurisdiction of Fort Palewing.

WARNING: This quest will fail if you use dirty tactics such as sneaking, ambushing, backstabbing unwary opponents, pickpocketing, etc.

WARNING: If you die, you will respawn in the closest town and will not be able to take this quest again.

Difficulty: Very High

Reward: Experience and right to take the Trial of Saint Grigori.

A prison camp? Ugh. Even so, I accepted the quest without hesitation. Had to be in it to win it.

"Good," Skyr Tymos said as we all confirmed. "There's ten of you here, plus another twenty-two aspirants in the barracks. Thirty-two of you, and only three eggs in the Matriarch's last clutch."

Only three!? My heart sank and leapt at the same time.

"By the time the Trial is over, we normally end up with as many postulants as eggs," Tymos said. "It is a sobering thought to bear in mind. For now, however, you'll be assigned to Camp Prichard and working in teams to rid the area of threats. If you have not already begun the Path of the Knight, then you will need to start it as soon as possible. You cannot become a Dragon Knight without being a Knight first. Any questions?"

I was about to put my hand up to ask about the Knight path requirement, but wasn't fast enough. Skyr Tymos nodded to a sallow, sandy-haired man with strange red eyes. He was one of the PCs.

"What can we expect at the camp?" The player asked.

"Camp Prichard is a work camp for Royalist rebels. The village also still has some of the old inhabitants, who are freedmen. They run the place, while the prisoners are involved in cleanup and excavation activities, scavenging weapons and relics and the like," Skyr Tymos replied, studying the man down the bridge of his long nose. "That means the camp is attractive to bandits and other swine. They waylay caravans along the roads leading to and from Liren. You may be dealing with those bandits, or you may be sent to hunt one of the magic-tainted beasts that are known to prey on unwary villagers. We keep the population down, but there's always some new Stranged beast out there causing havoc."

"I see. And when will we be going?"

"Tonight, and then we start patrols at dawn."

"That's all, then. Thank you, Skyr," the aspirant said.

The other ex-soldier - a tall, handsome man with alabaster skin and a short, stiff crewcut of feathery white hair - was the next to raise his hand. "Do we have information on the operational capacity of these bandits? Are we talking about organized outlaw knights with mounts and decent arms, or poorly equipped rogue peasants bringing people to bay with farm tools? What about level?"

I nodded as murmurs went up around the group of aspirants. It was a solid question.

"I'm sure you, Master Hyland, are better acquainted with them than most. These troublemakers are rabble and deserters from the Kingsmen," Tymos replied gravely. "Rebels, the lot of them. Don't give them any quarter, or assume you'll have an easy time with them just because they're wielding clubs instead of swords. They'll bash your skull in as soon as lop your head off. Anyone else?"

Another one of the aspirants, a woman with a tense square jaw and large, deer-like eyes, spoke up next. "Can we learn anything about the Bonding ceremony now, or-?"

"No. If you gain the right to attend a Trial, you will learn about our dragons," Skyr Tymos didn't even let her finish.

When no one else spoke up, Skyr Tymos nodded and came to stand in front of us at ease. "Alright - enough talk. Go ready yourselves. You'll be meeting Sergeant Blackwin at the Southern Courtyard in half an hour. You may bow and leave."

The others all bowed the European way: knee bent, foot outstretched, a hand over the heart and a flourish out to the side. I caught myself as I started a Korean-style bow from the waist, and clumsily tried to mimic the gesture just as everyone else stood up and dispersed. Tymos' eyes twinkled, but he said nothing.

I wasn't surprised when the white-haired man pushed his way over to me, hand outstretched. I smiled and clapped forearms with him before shaking.

"How's it going, brother?" He had a deep, cheerful voice with a strong Kentucky twang. "I'm Baldr. Baldr Hyland. What's your name? You a soldier?"

"Hector P..." My tongue caught on my real-world surname. "Just Hector. And yeah, I was a soldier... in a galaxy far, far away."

Baldr flashed a broad grin. "Pleased to meet you. Where you from?"

I smiled back. "The 79th. I was just a conscript grunt, nothing fancy."

"Least you suited up and served your time. Same can't be said of everyone. I'm a Screaming Eagle, 21st PAD platoon," he said, and not without a little pride.

Damn. PAD were the Powered Armor Division. "You were a Tin Man?"

"Yup. I was probably clanking around on the Crescent Front around the same time the 79th was there."

That meant Baldr was a career soldier, not a conscript like me. I nodded. "Yeah, probably. I went to Crescent twice. My last tour ended in May."

"Fuck. I can't even remember what month is it is now." Baldr shrugged, grinning, and scratched his head. "What did you do?"

"Saw a lot of jungle and desert, shot at a lot of shadows, hit some of them. Managed not to get killed." It felt odd to be discussing the 'real world' again, especially after the journey to the Fort. I'd resigned myself to the loss of my body over the last week and, and Archemi now felt more real than 'real world' ever had. "It's almost the end of June."

"Right. Well, my last port was Syria. I'm lucky I made it out, too. Can't believe I managed to survive the Glass Lands and then get HEX when we were back on base," He sobered a little at talk of war. "You come down with the bug too, huh?"

I nodded. "I'd just hit Stage 3 when I was uploaded."

"I was on the second day of HEX," Baldr said. "Only reason I'm here is I drew the long straw. Were you in the lottery?"

There'd been a lottery? I vaguely recalled Temperance saying that Ryuko had been working with the 101st on some kind of research. The 21st PAD was part of that battalion. "Nope. Whatever lottery you were in was probably limited to your regiment.

"My brother worked for Ryuko..." I trailed off, silenced by the sudden pang of pain and guilt that constricted my throat. "We both had the virus." I finished weakly, not really able to continue the train of thought.

"Fair enough." Baldr grunted. "Well, it is what it is. Tell you what though - I love this place. Screw that level cap, though. I've just about maxed out already and there ain't nowhere to go after Level 12."

I arched an eyebrow. "You hit the cap already?"

"Just about," he replied. "Bugs the shit out of me, though. I'm used to being top dog at everything I play at. We're going to be fucking around in the kiddy pool for who knows how long."

"Take it you played games other than this, then?"

"I was top of the North American chart for TWFL."

TWFL was '*Total War: Fatherland*': a VR-FPS for gun nuts. I liked FPSs, but the Total War series had too much anti-Asia propaganda for me. "Damn. So *you* were *Archangel_Savage*?"

"Hell yeah I was." Baldr grinned. "But say, how'd you get that fancy spear of yours? I've been searching for good gear since I got here, and I ain't found squat."

"That's a long story involving a sorceress, a slave ship, and a guy named Bob. How about I tell you at the stable? Sounds like we need to move out."

"Yup." He jerked his head toward the door. "Either we move out or the Queen Bitch rips us a collection of new holes. She's the Sarge here. Good but tough."

"I literally just got to this damn fort, but yeah... my factory-issued asshole suits me just fine." I rubbed my face. There wasn't even going to be time to get a drink and rest for a few minutes. Ugh.

"I wouldn't try calling Lady Anya Blackwin 'Queen Bitch' to her face, if I were you," the red-eyed blond man said as he strode over to us. He had a strange accent – not American, but not quite British. His voice – and his build and mannerisms - were the kind I associated with expensive lawyers. "She's the officer who leads the ground forces here, you know."

"Hey, now, don't you go insulting Sergeant Queen Bitch like that," I said. "What's your name?"

He blinked owlishly at me, his expression flickering with confusion. He held out a hand. "Lucien?"

I caught his limp hand and shook it briefly. "Okay, Lucien. I was a conscript, and even *I* know this. If a man like Baldr calls this Blackwin a name like 'Queen Bitch', that means she earned it through hard work and dedication. You don't go telling sergeants they're officers, or she'll hand you your balls in a box. 'NCO' is fine. Sarge is better."

"You call her 'Sir' even when she's 'Ma'am'," Baldr added.

I nodded. "*Especially* when she's 'Ma'am'."

Lucien looked bewildered. "You're both ex-military then, I assume?"

"Naw. Hector was a sportsbar gigolo and I was a French maid. Little skirt and an apron and everythang." Baldr punched me in the arm, just hard enough to make it competitive as well as friendly.

"He worked for a fat drug cartel mobster with sweaty little hands," I said, wiggling my fingers.

Baldr sighed. "That fucker was always trying to grab my ass."

"I... see. Well, gentlemen – hadn't we better go and see the 'Sarge' then? Because everyone else appears to have left." Lucien nodded toward the door.

He had a point. The room had cleared out while we were talking shit. I narrowed my eyes and pointed at his chest. "In Soviet Ilia, Sarge sees you!"

Chapter 24

We left the briefing hall and headed for the Fort's courtyard to find it bustling. Hookwings snipped and snapped, brandishing their claws at each other. I doubted Cutthroat was going to be happy about being taken out again.

"Baldr! Lucien! About time your feathery milk-drinking asses showed up!" A black-haired woman in plate armor and a distinctive fox-fur capelet yelled at us as Baldr and I drew near and stood to attention. Lucien tried to copy us as the woman continued. "These bloody hooks are about ready to eat your poor squires. Go saddle up – and no, not you, Tuun. I've yet to get the measure of you."

One could assume this was Queen Bitch Blackwin. I fixed my best parade face onwhile Baldr saluted. He grimaced at me in sympathy, then turned and ran off into the forming rank.

"Huh. Well, what do you know?" The Sergeant was no taller than I was, but she radiated authority and confidence. Mid-thirties, plain, but strong. Her hair was razor straight, her mouth thin, and her eyes were a hawkish yellow-brown. "You're far from home, Tuun. Came here with a letter from the White Witch and everything, so I hear."

"Yes Ma'am. We went on a nice ocean voyage together," I said.

She snorted. "The kind of voyage that ends in Skyr Asslord scraping your ass off the coast of Zaunt, right? Well, don't think that writ gives you any special advantage here. My name is Anya Blackwin, and I'll be your gracious hostess for the duration of your stay at Fort Palewing. I command the Warden's peacekeeper units stationed here with the Skyrdon. You can call me Ma'am or Sir, but call me 'Lady' and I'll have you cleaning chamber pots until the smell of shit is burned into your soul. Are we clear?"

I saluted. "Crystal clear, Ma'am."

Blackwin nodded curtly. "Good. What part of the Tungaant are you from?"

That threw me for a second. She'd used the proper term for the plateau country? I thought for a moment, trying to keep the question out of my voice as the uploaded information filtered in from my memory. "Yetzin Langhuur. The south... near the Bulang Mountains."

"I fought in Bulang Kettu. Good people, and tougher than stone. May you do the Songmaster proud in battle," she said. "Now, that hookwing you brought in. What's her name?"

"Cutthroat, ma'am." I replied. "I was wondering if I could swap her-"

"Cutthroat? I like it." Blackwin clapped her hands together cheerfully. "You're going to take Cutthroat with us to the Ditch. You might want to get a whip and chair before you go into her stall, though – the squires just fed her. They get bitchy when they're eating."

"How wonderful," I said flatly.

The sarge grinned, her eyes glittering. "Every day's wonderful here with me. Dismissed!"

Resigned, I saluted smartly, then trudged my way into the long stable building.

Hookwing stables are not nice places. Chunks of tarry black dung lay among the straw and sawdust, and the building smelled of blood and offal. I didn't have to ask which stall Cutthroat was in. The door was hanging loose off its hinges, and a big chunk was missing. Cutthroat's long black tail swished out into the open corridor. Her muzzle was lying on the floor, but the stablehands hadn't been able to get her saddle off, so she was still wearing it – not that she cared. The raptor was stuffing her face from a trough of pig guts, throwing her head back to chug them down. When I caught her by her nose rings and yanked her head around, she screeched with rage and turned on me, bloody jaws gaping. The chomp missed me by inches.

"Nope." I dodged the waving claws, and gave up trying to control her with the reins. She was too strong. Instead, I just let them go and made a rude gesture at her. "Come at me, bro."

Like a drunk jock, Cutthroat puffed up and lunged at me as I backpedaled, throwing what remained of the door onto the floor. I ran down the aisle with my dinosaur in hot pursuit, and ducked sharply around the outside wall. Cutthroat came blundering out into the open, knocking a young squire to the ground, and it was then that I caught her again. I grabbed the reins under her chin and used them to hold her jaws closed while I equipped her muzzle. When it appeared on her face, she shrilled furiously, foam dripping from the corners of her mouth.

"Wow," the squire who'd fallen over said. "She really hates you."

I grunted, holding the hookwing's head in place as she spat and struck like a snake. A muzzled snake. "No. She just hates. She's like the physical embodiment of hatred."

"Okay! Fall out!" Blackwin called from the front of the rank. "All together now!"

"Can you clap your hands for me? Distract her?" I asked the squire.

He nodded, but backed up a respectable distance before doing so. Cutthroat's pupils turned huge at the motion and sound, which caught her attention long enough that I could let go of her jaws and scramble up onto her back. The sound made her forget about me. Instead, she lowered her head, stalking the clapping squire with the single-minded focus of a predator until I yanked her back by her cheek and nostril rings.

"Okay, psycho. Off we go." I nudged her in the ribs and turned her to join the rank.

Cutthroat seemed bewildered by the other hookwings, pulling her head back on her neck as we joined the back of the line. For a moment, she was fine... and then we started to move off. As soon as the line began walking, she lurched forward like a battering ram to shove past the recruit in front and barrel her way into their place. The startled rider hung on for dear life as their hookwing turned its head and snapped at mine, but Cutthroat smacked their jaws aside with casual strength and bulldozed her way into the smaller animal's place.

"Control your fucking bird!" the recruit yelled out from behind us.

"Sorry! She's got a gland problem!" I shouted back, as me and my trusty mount ploughed our way through the rank.

Camp Prichard was four hours southeast of the Fort: a village much less welcoming than Lyrensgrove. It was surrounded by a twenty-foot high log wall. The logs were lashed together with sinew and bound with pitch. Their tips had been sharpened; the wall supported by parapets and walkways crawling with guards. Like the soldiers at the Fort, they were nearly all rough-looking mountain men and women, but they were wearing the purple and white Ilian uniform.

Our arrival wasn't a triumphant band of brothers, 'knights in shining armor' arrival. When the peasants keeping watch in the commons outside of the walls saw us, they reacted like a horde of brigands had appeared. Men jumped up, women vanished behind trees and into barns, and children were given hurried messages and told to run for the village gate. By the time we reached it, people had come out of their houses to gawk. I saw a girl sneak out of her house, wait until she thought she was in the clear, and then run for the edge of the forest. The houses here – huts, really – were old and run down. The place smelled like rust and animal dung.

"Where's the lieutenant!" Blackwin shouted.

"He's coming!" Someone called from further back. The crowd was already parting, revealing an overweight man hitching his sword belt on as he hurried forward, an escort trailing behind him. Baldr pulled up by my side on his smaller, far more tractable hookwing.

"That's more like it. How fare you, Beold?" Sergeant Blackwin dropped down from her saddle and strode over, pulling her gauntlets off and hanging them from her belt.

"Oh, very well, *Maesuire* Blackwin. We're doing fine." The lieutenant wrung his hands. He was blubbery and unattractive, with a wisp of hair clinging to a doughy round head. "This is... something of a surprise. We welcome you here of course..."

"Of course you do. You're a loyal citizen of the Warden, and we're here to keep the Warden's peace." Blackwin stopped in front of him, but didn't offer to shake. "It's been a while since we garrisoned here. I've brought some thirty strapping young things to make sure everything's in order. Word around the Fort is that you've been having a monster problem."

"Yes, my L- Ma'am." We perhaps weren't expecting... haha, there's more young dragon riders at every turn, isn't there?" Lieutenant Beold flashed us a watery smile. The two young men with him were both trying not to scowl.

"Looks like we're the auditors," Baldr whispered to me, leaning in a little.

Beold continued. "Please, *maesuire*, you must be tired. We'll show you to your rooms. The barn's alright for your troops? There's not enough lodging..."

The Sarge nodded. "Absolutely. The survivors will work their way to a proper bed tomorrow eve. But I'd like a tour of your holding facilities. Just to see how the maintenance is holding up."

"As you say, *maesuire*." Lieutenant Beold looked over our ranks again, and this time, it was not anxiety written on his face: it was defeat.

The Fort troops and their senior servants were bunked indoors - us aspirant nobodies got the barn loft. I was a city boy, and the idea of sleeping on hay wasn't my idea of a good time, but I wasn't going to show any of that in front of the likes of Baldr and Lucien.

"What do you think that was all about?" Lucien whispered to us. He was using the HUD's messaging system.

"No idea," I replied.

"Then let me tell you," Baldr said. He was lying about twelve feet from me, his hands laced behind his head. "This village used to be a strategic location for Kingsmen. Rebels against the Warden's Council. The Palewing Garrison took it over, and that shitwipe – Beold – was put in to watch over it."

"Miserable fucking place," I said, thinking back to Lyrensgrove – and what Kira had said to me the day I'd left. I'd concluded that the men I'd slaughtered in the village were the soldiers I'd gone there to help. I was hoping that their behavior wasn't typical of Ilia's troops.

"Who or what are the Kingsmen, exactly? Who's the Warden? Did he overthrow the monarchy or something?"

"Warden Scandiva led a revolution that overthrew the Illandi Dynasty," Lucien explained. "This country is technically a representative democracy now. Like post-Revolution France."

"Yeah," Baldr said. "And just as batshit as post-revolutionary France, too."

So we were here to suppress revolt? Ugh, politics. "Why? What was the basis of the revolution?"

"Scandiva's a military man," Baldr said. "And he did what all great men do. He saw something he wanted, so he took it. The King was nuts, Scandiva didn't like the way the country was going... so he got tight with the court, found the King's weak spots, and moved in for the kill."

The casual way he relayed the story was just this side of creepy. "So, by 'revolution', you mean a military coup."

"Same thing, ain't it?" Baldr shrugged, and yawned.

"Right." I rubbed my eyes, grimacing. "Well, I'm done. I've got to sleep. Hector out."

"Sweet dreams." Lucien said wryly.

Once I found a comfortable position, sleep hit me like a ton of bricks: deep, dreamless, time-dilated sleep, the kind where you feel like you closed your eyes, counted to five, and open them again to find the sun shining. Game sleep.

We hustled out to find that the center of the village had been converted into an improvised ordinance line. The quartermaster was set up in his tent, banging some dents out of pieces of armor, while Blackwin and her men were getting ready around a map. There was a mage here, too. He was working at a table in heavy robes, his face concealed by a deep hood. We assembled in a loose rank. I watched the others, and assumed the same old-fashioned at-ease posture they did.

Blackwin strolled between the lines, correcting form, and once she was satisfied, she stopped in front of us and linked her hands behind her back.

"Good morning, would-be dragon riders! Today is the day! This is your only chance to qualify for the most-holy-and-arduous Trial of Saint Grigori! If you can't survive a couple of bandits on the road, you are certainly not going to survive crashing into someone at fifty miles an hour while ten thousand feet off the ground! And if you can't survive those bandits without a respawn, believe me when I say you *won't* enjoy the Bond Sickness." She paced in front of us in her blue and silver armor, scanning our faces with her hawkish amber eyes. "The faster you perform your feat, the faster we get to leave this sty and go home. You will be working in groups of four. The first order of the day is outfitting with basic weapons, armor, and supplies. Once you have obtained your share from the quartermaster, you will sort into teams and be assigned your task. Am I understood?"

Bond Sickness...? I glanced at Baldr as everyone - myself-included - shouted out in reply. "Yes Ma'am!"

"Salute! Dismissed!" The Sarge barked each word as we complied.

While we lined up, the quartermaster laid out chain shirts alongside basic, but non-rusty weapons. There were jerkins and leather and wool pants, armor and weapons, packs and belts, and I finally got to see what was going on at the other table. The mage behind it motioned with his gauntleted hands over a collection of small metallic spheres. Mana gas shot out like tiny lightning bolts from the crystal-sheathed gloves to each sphere, activating it and causing it to jump up and hover in the air.

Bursting with questions, I waited for my turn. When I reached the quartermaster, he already had a pack and a sheathed sword and shield ready on the table. The man had the build and clothing of a blacksmith.

"Do you mind if I compare the stats of this gear to what I have on?" I asked. "Or do we have to be in uniform?"

"No, but I'm sure the sergeant would prefer it." He heaved the armor and weapons to one side, and threw a bandoleer on top of the bag. "This might be useful."

"Thank you, sir." The ⟦Ilian Militia Armor Set⟧ was of identical quality to what I was wearing, with no special buffs – it weighed more, had one less point of Slashing defense but +1 resistance Bludgeoning Damage Reduction compared to the Jack of Plates. I decided to stick with what I had. The bandoleer was definitely useful, though: it took me to 40 item slots. I opened the inventory in the backpack he'd handed me, and transferred the contents over to my own. "Are you a blacksmith?"

"Weaponsmith, aye."

"Then I have a question for you." I lay the Spear of Nine Spheres on the table. "Do you know what metal this is?"

"Let me see..." he muttered, taking it in hand. "If I'm seeing this right, this is bluesteel. Steel forged in mana fire. Where'd you get something like this?"

"Long story. Is there anyone at the Fort that can repair it?"

"Gods, no." He shook his head and handed it back to me. "This is an Artifact, and Mana fire is deathly poisonous. It'd kill a man, or Strange him. The only ones who work bluesteel are the Mercurions. You'd have to visit them, I reckon."

I got an alert. *⟦New Glossary Entry: Bluesteel A⟧*

"Thank you, Sir. And one last question: how do you go about acquiring trade skills in this... uh... here?" I asked, glancing across as Baldr and one of the female PCs strolled up.

"Find a Craft Master. Or you can read Skill Manuals to get started, if you can find them," the quartermaster replied, watching the other aspirants browse the things on the table. "The cunning men in the guilds scribed their knowledge into books so they could send them off to frontiers and train people without the masters needing to travel. They're Stranged things, but they won't hurt you."

"Do you sell any?" I asked.

The man shook his head. "No, but you can find them in the library back at Fort Palewing. Survive the day, and you'll be able to learn all you like. Now, off you go - I have to see to the others."

I waited off to the side while Baldr and the woman – the hard-jawed girl with the large doe eyes – got their gear. While they were busy, I had a look through the few other things I'd gained with my new gear:

Awl
A thick bone needle used for sewing leather and hide. Used for crafting and repairs.

Needle
A slender steel needle used for sewing fabric. Used for crafting and repairs.

Hide Lace
Used to repair armor.

Catgut
Used to repair armor.

Pickaxe
Used to mine materials from the earth.

Damage: 6-7

Bonebreak Poultice x 5 (Alchemy Component)

A healing herb applied to injuries. Heals 50 health.

Pennyroyal x 5 (Alchemy Component)

Rubbed on skin, protects against disease-carrying insects for 1 hour. Poisonous if consumed.

Yarrow x 5 (Alchemy Component)

Reduces damage from [[Poison]].

Holy Basil x 5 (Alchemy Component, Cooking Component)

Protects against blood poisoning from cuts while [[Bleeding]].

I nodded thoughtfully. I knew all of those herbs thanks to Owen and Kira, but there was still a lot to learn about how to maximize the benefits of Alchemy. Poultices were the lowest-tier healing item besides food. You blanched herbs in boiling water, then dipped them in cold water and wrapped a gauze cloth around them before slapping them on an injury. Potions, tinctures, and decoctions were more effective, but required more ingredients and tools that the healers of Lyrensgrove couldn't afford. For some reason, this skill fascinated me. I'd always enjoyed life skills, especially cooking and smithing. Archemi's Alchemy system was so complex and nuanced that I wanted to dive right into it, but I hadn't had any time for life skilling because of the real-time demands of the game. I was contemplating my unused skill points when Baldr and his companion strolled over to join me.

"Hey there." I extended a hand to the girl. "Hector."

"Nethres." She had a husky, hollow voice that matched the hardness of her face. Like me, Baldr had stuck with his old gear, which was of much finer quality than anything anyone else here was wearing. Nethres was now wearing the issued heavy armor and carrying a sword and shield.

"Want to party up?" Baldr asked us both. "If we can pick up a DPS, we'll have our bases covered."

Nethres nodded curtly in acknowledgment. "Casper. He's DPS."

"Your buddy?" Baldr asked. "You know where he is?"

Even as Nethres shook her head, I saw the mage motion to us out of the corner of my eye and turned. "Hang on, we're being summoned."

We approached the table as a group, and the mage called one of the orbs to his hands, never actually touching it. It floated just above his fingers. Like Rutha, he wore a strange glove with channels and tubes for mana.

"Assspirants." His voice hissed out from under the hood. "These are Orbsss of the Watchersss. You will each be asssigned an orb for the duration of the day. It will follow you and observe your conduct, your successss and failuresss in combat, and it will report these things to your assessorsss. Once you have left the village, do not return until your objective is complete. If you perish, your orb will return here alone. You, Tuun, give me your hand."

Without hesitation, I stepped forward and extended an arm. The mage waved the orb into my palm and traced a sigil over it. The tracery flared a vivid crimson. I felt a warm jolt of energy through my hand, followed by a weird, hot smell, like a stone baking under the sun. The magical artifact rose and floated around, until it hung silently beside my ear.

"The orb isss now attuned to you," he said. "Lord Hyland?"

Baldr smirked and strode up, hand out. I couldn't help but snort at the title. How the hell had he wrangled his way into being a 'lord' anything? I'd been so taken with the whole Tuun concept that I hadn't really paid attention to the other Human starting options, but if you could choose to be aristocracy, then what was stopping everyone from being lords and ladies?

The mage repeated the small ritual for Baldr and Nethres. Once that was done, he dismissed us with a flick of his fingers, and the three of us went to search for Nethres' friend, Casper. He turned out to be a big, dark-skinned guy with a ponytail of tight cornrows that stuck out from under his helmet. We found him stringing the longbow he'd received from the quartermaster, bending the frame like a toy. In some stereotypical game world, he'd have been the heavily armored tank and Nethres the skimpily-dressed archer, but here, the reverse was definitely true. Admittedly, if I was built like Casper, I probably wouldn't want to wear a shirt either.

"Who've we got, kid?" He said to her as we walked over to him.

"Baldr and Hector," Nethres replied. "They're okay."

"That's a high compliment comin' from you." Chuckling, Casper hung his bow and settled his quiver across his lower back. "You ain't gettin' all verbose on me now, are you? Talkative and gregarious?"

Nethres' mouth drew across in a sloping grimace.

"You two know each other?" I was never good at this small-talk introduction shit. Obvious as it was, Nethres wasn't exactly giving me much to work with.

"Sure do. We knew each other in meatspace," Casper said.

"Military?" I asked.

"No. Construction." Nethres replied. "We were Shardbuilders."

"It's where I got my taste for the sky." Casper folded his arms over his broad chest. "And this was one of the options the union offered when we got HEX. We're stuck in here while President Powell is up in the Shard that *we* built."

"Hey now, I'd rather be here breathing the open air than being stuck inside a Shard," Baldr said. "Because sure, he ain't gonna get no

HEX, but Mr. President'll get real sick of his recycled water and 3D printed meals six months in, I tell you what."

I glanced over at the mage's table, and around at the other aspirants. We were all dolled up in leather and chainmail, with swords and bows. The wagons had wooden wheels. None of the thatched hovels had plumbing or running water. It was easy to forget about the real world in here. But all things considered... I had to agree. We'd gotten the better deal. "He's right. Think of it this way: those guys paid half a billion dollars each so they could live inside great big glass dildo with nothing but their own piss to drink."

That made Casper laugh, and Nethres smiled. The big archer clapped me between the shoulders, and I stumbled forward a step under the blow. "True enough, true enough. Hell, son – we're gonna be dragonriders!"

"There's only three eggs," Nethres said dourly. "And thirty-two of us."

"And? There's only six players. All that means is some of us have to wait a while until the next batch shoots out of momma dragon," Casper said. "Let's ace this thing!"

"Sure. Hold on, though – I think we have to form a team to get our orders." Brow furrowed, I queried ⟦Party Formation⟧ in my HUD, and then sent friend and party requests to the three of them. As each one accepted, I felt a warm pressure behind my eyes and was suddenly able to see more information about them. Their HP rings came to life with color and detail, showing their classes and their health, along with their level and EXP. Nethres was already a Level 8 Knight. Baldr was maxed out at Level 10 and seemed to have some kind of variant class 'Spirit Knight'. Casper was a Level 7 Warrior, and I was the lowest, at Level 4.

"Aww man, you're a baby," Casper said.

"Yeah." I hunched a little, feeling prickly. "I had a weird start to the game."

Nethres turned on Baldr. "I thought you said he matched our level."

"He does. Between me and him, we're Level 5 each." Unfazed, Baldr grinned. "Gotta learn somehow."

The woman was about to retort, but then our quest updated and all of us got the far-away look of people processing invisible information.

Quest Update: Prove Your Mettle

Now that you are at Camp Prichard, you and your team have been assigned to patrol the road leading to a recently cleared battlefield and supervise the soldiers and peasants working there. You must act in accordance with the Skyrdon's Code of Honor and report any sign of insubordination to an overseer.

Special: You may not die during this mission. If you die, you automatically fail the quest.

So you keep telling us, I thought, and dismissed the notification.

Chapter 25

Before we went out the village gate, I insisted we hang back and work on some drills to see how we functioned as a team. Baldr refused, overly confident in his - and our - abilities, but the other two were happy to participate. Just as well. Archemi was a weird game, in that magic couldn't be used to heal. There was no 'Cleric' or 'Priest' class tree. Food, herbs and potions filled the role, which meant that as a team, you were all responsible for healing one another. I had a feeling that there *had* been a Priest class, but that it had been snipped out of the game for some reason - maybe because the devs were predicting an influx of refugees.

The four of us rode out after that, and I was pleased to note that I was easily the best rider out of all of them. Nethres and Casper rode like nubs, bouncing around on the backs of their hookwings, while Baldr kind of faked it. I'd learned to keep Cutthroat on a short rein and ride her almost standing up in the stirrups. She worked best under tension, when she felt me alert and ready. If I slacked off or stopped paying attention, she got uppity. Riding a beast was nothing like riding a motorcycle, but also everything like riding a motorcycle. You had to pay constant attention.

"I h-hate th-these d-damn th-things," Casper said once we were out on the road. The hookwing's trot was nearly bouncing him off the saddle, causing him to stammer.

"Just remember you can only pull with the reins," I said. "You can't push, so don't lean forward. And hold on with your legs."

"And shut the hell up already," Baldr quipped from the front. "Every mob in a three-mile radius can hear your fat ass jingling up and down."

Hookwings weren't as smart as dragons, but they were good practice for the real thing. I'd gotten used to Cutthroat's antics after weeks of riding her, and even with EXP being hard to come by, I'd gotten a lot better – though nowhere as good as I'd been on a machine. It was humbling to have to relearn how to ride well again, but I was determined to master this new variation of the skills I'd learned as a teenager. It was already paying off: at Level 4, I looked a thousand times more comfortable on Cutthroat's back than anyone else in the group did on their nice, tame hookwings.

"What do you think 'bond sickness' is?" I pulled my mount up beside Baldr's. "I don't know about you, but I really don't want to get sick."

"Sir Tim said it's something to do with the dragons," Casper replied from behind. "Like, when you impress a hatchling, you get sick for a while. Then you get over it and move on. He said not everyone's tough enough to survive it."

"It's Skyr Tymos," Nethres grunted.

Baldr grimaced and shook his head. "Maybe that's what the Trial of Saint Grigori is? You have to be badass enough to survive bond sickness?"

"Maybe." Call me crazy, but I was kind of phobic of getting sick with anything after HEX - especially now that I knew my body was dead. The thought made me nauseous. Somewhere, the *real* Hector Park was bobbing around in a cryotank, dead as a doornail, veins being pumped with preservative solution while scientists took core samples out of his brain while I – his ghost – gallivanted around this make-believe world. My stomach shuddered, and that was an odd consolation of its own. Make-believe or not, I could still feel ill.

The land around Camp Prichard was grim. The forest had been cut down or blown up, and it was a steep, muddy wasteland of burnt tree stumps, overgrown ditches, and tumbled stone walls. The cold north wind whipped across the dirt and rustled the tall grass that had died at the side of the road. Crows picked at bodies left to rot and rust out in the sun. It didn't look like there was much meat left on any of the remaining corpses.

As we slowed, Nethres surveyed it with level eyes. "Lovely."

"That's war for you." Baldr's nose wrinkled. "Our patrol takes us around the field here."

"The Lieutenant didn't seem really pleased to see us," I remarked, reining Cutthroat so I could check my map. Our patrol route was marked. The region was low, marshy terrain, wetlands and scrub forest. There were some unlabeled huts here and there. I could assume that the valor requirements of our mission meant random looting wasn't on today's agenda.

"Course not. He's a peasant dipshit. Probably a militiaman who was pulled off the battlefield when they ran out of people who actually knew what they were doing." Baldr squinted, peering across the churned up field toward the edge of the living forest. "Some of those villagers are still Royalist scum, I bet. Nothing scares the rabble like dragons."

"Uh huh." I kept a wary eye on the dead battlefield as we moved off. Something wasn't kosher about this place. "That's what set off the Civil War? Crazy king?"

"Crazy as a cut snake," Baldr said.

Ugh, more politics. Not anything I was really interested in, but at least I had a basic idea what was going on now. "You sound like you've picked your side."

Baldr shrugged, keeping an eye on the road. "The family I... my character was born into is kind of a big deal in the Council. So are the Skyrdon, for that matter."

"How the hell'd you get into a noble house when you signed up to the game?" Casper called out from behind us.

Baldr chuckled. "Funny story, actually. Ryuko wanted soldiers for their emergency beta testing, right? So one day, every sick bastard from the 101st is pulled into a big meeting, and we're told that there's a lottery to join up with the beta. They couldn't take everyone right away – they were refining that GNOSIS thing of theirs. About ten of us won. They said they wanted to test out a range of starting positions. They assigned us roles, and some of us got test roles that aren't typical for new players in the game. I got 'Nobleman'. Can't say I'm complaining."

Cutthroat was getting more and more agitated as the seconds went by. She sniffed the air, and so did I: a weird, oily smell stung my nose. It smelled like pus, like the gross white shit that collected in the back of your throat sometimes. I unequipped her muzzle so that she had full use of her jaws. "Hey. Can you smell that?"

"Smell what?" Casper reined his hookwing in, looking around.

Nethres drew her sword, nose wrinkling.

"I smell a whole lot of dead... hey, yeah." Baldr's pale brows furrowed. "Now you mention it. Probably just swamp gas."

I saw some of the grass stir against the wind, and that's when it hit me. "No. Ambush!"

Half a dozen creatures that looked like giant skinned wolves bounded from the grass in deadly silence. The rotted things had no lips, only bare jagged teeth that oozed with violet ichor. Their health bars swam into view. Each red bar had a skull smoldering beside it, and their name: Barghest. Six high-level barghests, too high a level for the four of us.

Cutthroat shrieked her warning the same time I did. Baldr's hookwing trilled in terror and threw him, sending him flying. I heard someone else hit the ground behind me. My mount wasn't the kind of gal to run away, though. I'd barely got my spear lined up for a charge when Cutthroat flared her crests, banged her hook claws together, and sprinted at the pack of undead hounds with a banshee scream.

"I GUESS WE'RE DOING THIS!" It was the closest I got to a battle cry in the seconds before impact.

The creatures leaped at us, claws-first, and we collided like a line of quarterbacks. I drove my glaive through the shoulder of one. Cutthroat seized another snarling barghest in her jaws, and brought up a leg to rake a third, kicking its guts to the dusty ground. The other three bounded forward, clawing and biting, trying to pull me off the saddle to the dirt. It was so fast, so dirty, that I couldn't keep track of the alerts - but the rapid scroll, blood, pain, and the lightning drain on my HP told me all I needed to know.

"Get off! Get off, you motherfuckers!" Nethres rode up first, sword swinging. She struck one barghest off Cutthroat, who was prancing and bucking as she tried to get the savage creatures off her back and flanks.

I couldn't pull my spear out of the barghest's chest. It screamed and bled and thrashed, stuck on the blade. Desperate, I let go of the haft, holding on for dear life, and punched the one gnawing on my shoulder with all my strength. The blows didn't seem to faze it until my knuckle caught it right in the eye. The rotting eyeball exploded; the creature howled and fell back, and as it did, I saw it was studded with arrows: Casper's arrows.

Cutthroat dug her hooks into the body of the barghest in her mouth, and pulled down as she tossed her head *up*. Her claws ripped through its soggy flesh, and the barghest made a wet warbling sound as my hookwing tore its head off and flung the corpse away. She charged forward, head lowered, and I saw the chance to recapture my weapon as the injured barghest reared up to swipe and smack at her head, turning Cutthroat's jaws. Holding down with my thighs, I leaned forward and grabbed the very end of the polearm as it swung from side to side.

"Heal! Heal! I need a heal!" Baldr roared from behind.

Nethres cried back. "I'm trying!"

"Move left, Hector!" Casper yelled.

I jerked Cutthroat's reins to the left, wrapping my other hand around the Spear, and the hookwing dodged as a volley of arrows flew by her and thudded into the barghest's body. Even with the direct hits, its HP was still at 50 percent. And there were four more of them.

"We need to team up on one!" I shouted, carrying the spin all the way. I kicked Cutthroat in the ribs, making her charge away from the barghest in front of me as it ran and slashed with its front claws. "Gang up! Gang up!"

To my surprise, they seemed to hear me. Go Go Leadership Skill. Baldr backed toward Nethres, holding off a pair of slavering barghests. The howling creatures followed him, raining blows on his shield. They were slowly draining his health despite the barrier. They were so focused on him and Nethres that they didn't seem to see me.

We weren't supposed to use rogue tactics, but I either acted, or we died. I dismounted from Cutthroat's back and dropped to the ground, and then I used Power Attack while we were still flanking.

My glaive took the barghest in the back, dealing critical damage. It spun with a screech, barbed tongue lashing, and Nethres hit it from the other side. Casper got the hint: while we encircled the barghest, hacking and chopping, he ran a ring around us, peppering the others with arrows to stop them from ripping into our backs. The spooked hookwings were emboldened by Cutthroat's aggression, and rejoined her to fight one of the barghests as a pack.

"I'm out of herbs!" Baldr cried out hoarsely. His white hair was red with blood.

I healed him for twenty between blows, and saw his HP jump another percentage as Nethres spent an herb on him. We chopped the barghest until it stopped moving, and then the three of us turned as a unit to find the next. I was at half health; Nethres was just over half, thanks to her heavy armor. Casper was at about seventy-five. Baldr, the highest-leveled, was still only at half after the healing we did on him... and there were still four monsters to go. Three of them were descending on us in a gang.

I hardened my resolve in the few seconds it took for them to come into range. In my mind's eye, I saw myself on the back of a dragon like Skyr Arnaud's. I imagined flying on a creature like Talenth, of being able to touch something that size that trusted me completely... of having that bond, that companionship, for the rest of my life.

I activated the Mark of Matir, draining adrenaline points into the cold fire that spread up my arms, swung the glaive around... and dodged.

The barghests slammed into Baldr and Nethres, and I was right behind them, flanking the one furthest to the right. The Mark sucked greedily at the barghest's HP with every successful critical hit - every one out of ten to fifteen so blows critted as I triggered Bluster and Doubletapped, which was enough for me to charge my adrenaline and spam the HP recovery ability. It was only five points here, seven points there, but it kept me hovering around the halfway mark. With every activation, I felt a boost of dark power flush through me. Cold energy wriggled up my arms and through my chest, like a cold finger being drawn through my flesh.

Ting! ⟦You have reached Level 5!⟧

My HP jumped. If you leveled up in battle, you gained base HP and your health rose to match.

The hookwings tore one yelping barghest away from the fray, while Nethres went down under another. Baldr was hanging on by the skin of his teeth. I joined him on ganking the one that was mauling Nethres. She was screaming. The monster was up in her face and too close for her sword to be of any use. I spent my third-last herb on her to give her a second wind, but it was too late. Nethres gurgled and went still just as we hauled the screeching, struggling monster off her. The girl's toon vanished and turned to dust. Only her pack was left behind.

"We need to retreat! We can't do this!" Casper called out from the fringe of the battle.

"Fuck retreat!" I roared as I plunged my spear into the barghest's neck and twisted hard. The same rage that had surged through me when I'd been fighting the harpies was back. "We've only got two left!"

"Hold the line! We can do it!" Baldr bellowed, slamming the edge of his shield into the next wolf-like thing as it tried to pounce onto him.

This was where Baldr and I had the advantage. Even if Nethres and Casper were gamers, our training and real-world battle experience showed. VR gaming in a headset was one thing, but full-immersion, 'blood-and-guts and having your eyes clawed out' combat was quite another. Baldr and I could fight through our adrenaline rushes, while

Casper was caving now that his IRL friend was down and not respawning. The arrows were still coming - but they were now covering his retreat as he ran away like a yellow-bellied coward.

My blood boiled. I'd been a conscript. I hadn't learned how to fight because I wanted to. But when the draft had come around, I didn't crash my bike and break a leg to get out of going to war. I hadn't enrolled into college or gone overseas. I'd served.

"Piece of-!" My swearing was cut short as one of the last of the creatures broke through my guard and raked its claws across my chest, pitching me back and shaving fifty points off my health with one blow. I picked back at it - ten, eleven damage at a time.

"We can do it!" Baldr rushed forward as his health jumped, smashing the hilt of his sword into the side of the barghest's deformed head. "You'll hit Level 6 so fast your head'll spin, dude!"

"HurrrrrAHH!" I fought with the haft and blade, pummeling the barghest as Baldr pinned it with his shield and stabbed the damn thing. There were no more arrows covering us, but the four hookwings were fighting as well, attacking the other barghest one at a time like a pack of feathered lions. I was beginning to understand the rhythm of the monsters' attacks, the way they relied so heavily on their defense and telegraphed their bites and swipes. When I saw the monster open its mouth to bite Baldr, I jammed the head of my glaive into its face and yanked on it, splitting its head into a shower of blood, then dust.

The last barghest looked worried, its skinless brow furrowed. Its overpowering enemy red skull icon had vanished now that it was alone and facing multiple opponents, and it cowered back from Baldr and me as we charged. Neither of us intended to let it get away - we chased it as it tore off toward the battlefield. The hookwings, taking their cues from us, ran after it in a hissing, screeching pack. The creature found itself surrounded by a collective three tons of angry dinosaur on one side, and pinned by two equally pissed-off future dragon riders on the other.

When the dust cleared, we were left with blood-spattered weapons, armor twisted by claws, and injured, limping hookwings. But we'd won. And our golden orbs were still following us, recording everything. Nethres' and Casper's were nowhere to be seen.

"Shit." Baldr wiped his forehead. "Welp. That was fun."

"Nethres fought to the end," I said, leaning on my spear. I was out of herbs, and my health bar - and everything else - was throbbing. "If I see Casper, I'm knocking that fucking coward out."

"That all? We'll hang his ass. There's laws for deserters," Baldr said darkly. "Especially deserters in battle."

"I get why he ran," I replied. "I don't agree with it, but I get it. He's a civilian IRL. This game's combat is too realistic for a squish like him."

Baldr sneered in irritation. "He's fucking immortal, and he needs to grow a pair of balls. He'd respawn if he died." He sighed. "It's no excuse. I'll kill him if I see him."

"Just like that?"

"Just like that."

I shuddered with the effort to limp over to Cutthroat, who was busy tugging at the loot bag left by the last barghest. "I won't stop you. So... how do we divide this up? Fifty-fifty? Free for all?"

"Grab what you can." Baldr nodded grimly. He crouched down and pawed through the loot. "Cash and... eww, gross. What the hell is this shit?"

I looked over. He was holding up a [[Barghest Eye]] on a long stringy bit of flesh, his face a mask of disgust.

I grinned. "That, my good sir, appears to be an eyeball."

"Monster blood, monster skin, barghest bone, barghest eye... what the *fuck*?" He threw the eyeball away from him, wiping his hands on his surcoat. "Fucking gross, man."

"I'm more grossed out by the silver coins," I replied, happily looting all of the body parts along with ⟦7 x Ilian Florins⟧, ⟦Thread⟧, and ⟦Mana-Cured Leather⟧.

"What? Why?"

"It's not like the things have pockets. Where the fuck do you think they were keeping the coins?"

"On second thoughts, you can help yourself to all this shit." Baldr clapped his hands on his thighs and stood up. "I don't want no eyeballs and I definitely don't want no goddamn zombie ass coins."

"Never said anything about them being in their ass. I'm pretty sure they settle in their stomachs." I pointed at the sack. "You don't want the components for alchemy or anything?"

"Hell, no. I leave nerd shit to smart people. I'm just a jarhead. A rich jarhead. If I need potions, I'll buy 'em."

No skin off my back. I knew that the value of these items was something I'd unearth in the future, even if they were kind of gross in the present. I uploaded the first lot to my inventory, and went around the bodies until I found Nethres' gear. It was just the Skyrdon's armor and weapons. Anything else she'd been carrying had gone off with her to respawn. With a sigh, I loaded them into my inventory and took her pack. Casper had been a coward, but if any of the three of us deserved to go on, it was her.

Chapter 26

We still had to finish our patrol, despite everything. Baldr was nearly always in the lead, because I kept stopping to dig up a range of medicinal plants highlighted by my HUD. In the time-honored tradition of RPGs everywhere, I began eating them to see what effects they had.

"Blech!" I spat out a wad of purple flowers as a debuff icon flashed.

"Dang it, Hector, do you have to put every damn thing you find in your goddamn mouth?" Exasperated, Baldr looked back over his shoulder. "How many times have you poisoned yourself?"

"Urrr.... Sevnn? But mah Foragin skrrrl is luuk FVE now!" My mouth was numb from that poisonous herb, ⟦Henbane⟧, and my tongue wouldn't work properly. But what the hell: Foraging 5!

"Hey, look, there's a rock. You gonna stick that in your mouth too?" He jabbed his finger toward a stone by the road.

"Drrty. Nn no skrrrl imprrvment," I mumbled.

"How 'bout this moss? Or that bird shit over there?"

Rolling my eyes, I pulled Cutthroat over and collected the moss. And ate it. It conferred a small health buff that cancelled out the poison. "Woo! Antrrdote!"

"Bless your heart." Baldr growled, and turned back to watch the road.

The pauses I took to forage annoyed Baldr, but he didn't ever actually stop me. We'd nearly lost the battle with the barghests because we lacked Bonebreak Poultices and potions, and I'd set myself a goal of learning how to make something that healed at least 75HP. To that end, I collected all of the Bonebreak I could. It was a fuzzy, olive-green plant with feathery purple flowers. After I'd picked about ten of them, I got an alert. The herb's detailed description had been added to my glossary.

Bonebreak (Knowledge B)
Also known as Comfrey. An herb renowned for its ability to speed the healing of broken bones, mend wounds, and staunch bleeding. Poisonous if eaten without distillation. It is made into poultices by peasant herbalists and army field medics. Skilled alchemists can remove the toxins to make powerful healing potions.

I found other herbs, too: more henbane, green moss, lily of the valley, snowbells, onion grass, chamomile and droptick flowers, nightshade, and raspberries. I shared the raspberries with Baldr – they gave a small HP regen – and we both looked a lot better by the time we reached the edge of our patrol route. It took everything I had to not growl.

A chaingang was toiling in a bad-smelling muddy field, watched by guards on the backs of hookwings. The guards weren't wearing Skyrdon colors, and my HUD identified them as [Ilian Soldiers] and [Mercenary Guards]. The prisoners looked thin, frightened, and sickly. They were digging out everything from rusty weapons to old skeletons. The latter were being burned in a pyre overseen by a priest in red robes and a priestess in yellow and gray, who were working as a pair to administer last rites. All of the salvageable metal was being piled onto a wagon.

"All in order?" Baldr called out as we drew up.

"Aye, that it is!" One of the guards called back to us. He was an ugly man: dark-haired, pockmarked, unshaven, and jowly. "Got them bargies and geists on the road though. You run into any?"

I reined Cutthroat beside Baldr's hookwing. My armor was bloody and torn in places. "Sure did."

"Nasty bastards. Priests says they're the bodies of dead war hounds, Stranged up and wrecked by magic." The guard drew an infinity symbol over his chest from shoulder to shoulder.

I frowned, watching the laborers toiling in the mud. "This battlefield is contaminated with magic?"

"What? Do I look like some kind of wizard to you?" The guard hawked and spat. "I dunno. Prolly. We got them priests here, though – ain't nothing it can do to anyone."

I highly doubted that. Rutha and others had made it clear that mana was toxic as hell. "Time to head back, then. We killed half a dozen barghests on the way here. Lost two of our team."

"Right common around these parts," the guard replied. "You know them dragonmen thin your herd with them bargies and whatnot, don't you? Every time they bring recruits around, most of them end up on fires like that one o'er there."

Baldr and I both glanced at the roaring pyre.

"Noted. Anything you need?" Baldr asked, scratching under his helmet.

"You could call in one of your dragons to burn one of these louts and put the fear of the Gods in 'em," the guard grumbled. "Lazy mongrels. Warden should have 'em all strung from the gibbets."

"I don't think we'll be burninating anyone today." I tried to sound cheerful. "Or ever. On that note, we should get back to base."

The guard jerked his head toward the line of workers. "Don't feel sorry for 'em. This was the Mad King's country not a year ago. They picked the wrong side. It's their own fault they're here muckin' out this wallow."

We were the first to arrive back at Camp Prichard. When we reached the shanty tavern near the center of 'town', it was easy to see why the peasants had hidden their female constituents. Most of our supervisors were partying it up, drinking ale and shooting darts, playing knife and card games, and making the most of their downtime. The Order's men-at-arms were sleazing all over the matronly barkeep, who was continually swatting away hands from her ass and bosom as she delivered trays to tables. Sergeant Blackwin was keeping a close eye on them, like a stern aunt, but she wasn't stopping anything but the most outrageous behavior. Our presence here was not only a reminder of who was winning the war for Ilia's heart, but also a punishment.

I was less and less happy about what I was seeing, fuming silently while we hitched our hookwings and led the two spare mounts to the stables before going back to greet the Sergeant. She was leaning back against the wall, arms folded over her chest. She nodded to us, and as she did, our observation orbs zipped around our heads and flew to the masked and hooded mage. He was the only other person besides Sarge who wasn't drunk off his ass.

"Welcome back, men," Blackwin said as we closed in and assumed parade rest. "Two down, I see. Not bad. Report?"

"Six barghests, ma'am. We fought them to the death. Nethres perished in combat," I said. "Casper deserted."

"Better now than later. There's no place to run in the sky," Blackwin said. She glanced at the mage, who was writing something into a ledger at his table. "Did you take trophies? Proof of the kills?"

"*He* did. I didn't want barghest eyeballs in my pack." Baldr's nose wrinkled.

I squished my face up between my hands. "'Eeew, Sarge! I dun wun squishy eyeballs in my backpack! Eeeew!"

Baldr barked a short laugh. "Says the guy who was eating bird shit off the road."

"That's enough, kids." Grinning broadly, the sergeant pushed off the wall and stood. "The quartermaster will pay you for every monster you slew, assuming you don't start slap-fighting like a pair of catty handmaidens. Come with me. I'll review your performance and issue your next directive."

I swallowed, thinking back over my conduct during the fight with the barghests. What counted as 'dishonorable combat', really? We'd had to flank the monsters to be able to defeat them - not exactly the picture of chivalry. Neither was relying on our mounts for help. Baldr was clearly wondering the same thing. He had his game face on, but his jaw was clenched as we followed the Sarge.

"Missiure Jasper? How goes the report?" Blackwin stopped in front of him, arms crossed.

"I am done with the ssspheres." Jasper the Mage motioned to the two golden orbs on the table.

Blackwin held out her hands expectantly.

Jasper nodded, then dropped the pair of golden spheres into her gloved palms. He paused for a second to gather his wits and reached out with his gauntleted hand. "*Allum barathi.*"

As he spoke and gestured, the first golden sphere - and his witchglove - burned with a deep purple light. Blackwin closed her eyes and drew a deep breath. She was silent for several tense minutes.

Then, all of a sudden, she laughed.

"Baldr! My goodness, boy. You should know how to handle a bird better than that!" She chuckled. "Lord and Lady... the Tuun managed to stay on *Cutthroat's* back, and you bounced off our lovely Sweetroll, head over ass!"

"Uhh..." Baldr's face set into stony lines. "Well, uh, 'Sweetroll' might need some more training around corpse-eaters. She lost her shit and threw me. Didn't know what to make of them."

"Of course she knows what to make of them: minced meat. And that's exactly what she's doing in this recording." The woman still had her eyes closed, flickering under her lids. "You worked out they like to fight in pack formation. So do dragons. There's a lot to be learned about dragonkind from the hookwings, boys."

My chest swelled a little. I'd picked that right after all, then.

After a couple more minutes, she grunted. "Alright. Well, looks like a tough fight. All things considered, you're lucky you only lost two. All seems in order, bearing closer examination."

Both Baldr and I let out breaths we hadn't realized we'd been holding. "Yes Ma'am!"

"Listen to you, so full of energy." Blackwin opened her green eyes, blinking rapidly to clear them. "Must be a Starborn thing. Well, no need for bowing and scraping quite yet. We'll review this properly at the Fort, but for now, you can relax. Make yourselves comfortable. Get a drink, explore the village. I'll throw in some beer money, seeing as you're the first two to return."

As she spoke, a notification popped up:

Quest Update: Prove Your Mettle

You have passed the first - and the least - of the trials of the Skyrdon, proving your courage, skill, and luck in battle. Have a beer and wait for Round #2!

Reward: 200 EXP + 20 Renown + 50 silver pieces

Special: You may attempt the Trial of Saint Grigori.

⟦Reminder: Now that you are Level 5, you can take your first level in an advanced Path!⟧

Level 5? I blinked. Oh, shit! I'd leveled up during the last fight. I grinned as I dismissed the alert, but then I remembered that my first Path level was supposed to be the Knight class and my joy faded. Sword and board, ugh.

"Yes, ma'am. And I'll take you up on that drink, even if it's just peasant swill." Baldr saluted.

I didn't mind a drink now and then, but I just wasn't feeling it. Not after watching people being used as slaves in the old battlefield. Instead, I squared my shoulders. "Ma'am, mind if I ask you a few questions?"

Blackwin arched her eyebrows. "Of course."

"Are there good craftsmen here?" I asked. "Anyone I could learn from?"

"Not of any real worth," she replied, shrugging. "You're better off waiting until we get home. Talk to our smith if you want to bang on some metal, though the peasants know a lot about the plants and animals in the area. You can hit up Ethan, at the general store. He's probably more knowledgeable than most here."

I nodded. "Everyone has something to teach. Want to come with me, Baldr?"

Baldr rolled his eyes. "Yeah, sure, I want to go talk to a bunch of hicks about cows. No thanks - I'll stay here. I've got to dish out a stack of points and work on my combat skills."

"Baldr, you get one mug of ale, then tend to your mount before you settle in to any serious drinking," Blackwin said, shooing Baldr off with her hands. He rolled his eyes and smirked, but went without complaint.

Once Baldr had swaggered off, I refocused on the Sarge.

"Anything else?" she asked.

"Yeah, there is," I said. "I was wondering what this bond sickness is about. I have my reasons, but deadly illness is... Let's say I'm not keen on being sick."

"I can't tell you." Blackwin's easy humor vanished, replaced by sober intensity. "The nature of the Trials is secret, and for good reason. There's no harm in your asking, but now you've asked, you know what the answer will be. You a plague survivor?"

I cleared my throat. "Of a sort."

"You just faced down half a dozen corpse-eaters in dual combat, and you're afraid of a little cough?" She planted her hands on her hips. "If you've survived the plague with one foot in the grave, you can do it again. And that's all I'm saying 'til -- oh, look what the cat dragged in."

I turned to see what she was staring at, and saw four hookwings gallop in through the gate. Riderless, bloodied hookwings, their saddles torn by claws and fangs. The raptorine dinosaurs bolted for the stables, shrilling cries that were returned by Cutthroat, Sweetroll, and the other mounts. Golden orbs floated by their heads. All that remained of their riders.

"Excuse me." The sergeant broke away from her place, waving at her tipsy men. "Oi! You louts! Get off your bottoms and go help the stable boys with those birds! They're wound up fit to bite someone's head off!"

Well, this pre-Trial test was certainly showing signs of cutting down the competition. At a loss for words, I found myself drifting over to Baldr. He had a mug of ale in hand, his other hand braced on his thigh.

"Four more down," he said, a mirror of my own thoughts. "Want a mug?"

"Not yet. I need to do that Life Skilling with the locals," I replied, leaning on the table.

"No point." He waved his mug in the direction of the village. "They're peasants. They don't know shit."

"That's not true." I frowned, thinking of Kira and Owen working on their injured fellows with care and speed.

He gave me a look of sly disbelief. "Have you tried talking to any of them? The NPCs?"

"Here? Not yet."

"Watch this." He set his mug down and groaned as he got to his feet, pushing ahead of me toward the inn yard's fence. He leaned out over it, and waved a hand. "Hey! Hey, you, with the white cap!"

"Me, *Missiure*?" A man with pockmarked skin, muddy green eyes, and a faded green tunic - and a white cap - gestured at himself. He froze, like a mouse in front of a snake.

"Yeah, you. What's your name?"

"Garen, *Missiure*." He swallowed nervously.

Baldr leaned his elbows on the fence, and propped his chin on his hands. "What's your story, Garen?"

"Story?" Garen's expression widened with confusion. He was clearly terrified, his body tense with the need to flee. "Uhh... what do you mean by me story, *Missiure*?"

"Like, your history. Where are you from, what do you do?" Baldr said impatiently.

"I'm a swineherd, *Missiure,*" Garen said, eyes darting between me and Baldr. "J-Just a simple, godly man. I was borned here, and survived the War by Kyrie and Liric's sweet grace."

"What do you like to do?" Baldr asked.

"Uhh... I like my time out in the commons," Garen said. "G-Gives a man time to think, away from his wife."

"What kind of stuff do you like to think about?"

Garen seemed to draw a blank for a moment. "Uh... well, to be honest with you, Lord...""

Baldr waved him on.

"Food, a lot of the time." Garen's face suddenly relaxed into a momentary bashful smile. "After the war and all. The herds are just startin' to recover, so I'm thinking about what pies I'll be trying come High Spring, but also... I don't know... normal wonderin' things, I guess."

"Alright. Thanks, Garen. That's all I wanted to know." Baldr's mouth sloped to one side in a wry smile. "Enjoy your pie. That'll be all."

"Well, it's not 'til High Spring until we... am I free to go?" The man regarded us hopefully.

"Yup. Scoot." Baldr made a little shooing motion with his hand, and Garen clumsily bowed before rushing off at polite speed down the road.

"There," he said to me. "See what I mean? Dumb as shit. My barracks had a toilet-cleaning AI that was more interesting than these retards."

Maybe it was his comparison of a person to a bathroom robot, but I felt a twinge of something like irritation. I started walking toward the stables, and to my surprise, he followed.

"You and I are about as real as these NPCs now. And he wasn't being stupid, he was talking safe to you," I muttered.

He scoffed. "What do you mean 'talking safe'?"

"He's basically a prisoner in what was once his village, and you're a Starborn nobleman, Baldr. He was scared witless of you, because you could walk into his house, ransack it, rape his wife, walk out and not a single goddamn person besides our Sarge would call you on it. Like he said, he's simple, and he and his family are the ones who put the bacon on our tables."

"After he's had a couple of rounds with the pigs." Baldr chuckled.

"Whoa there, Houston, we just went from zero to HOLY SHIT BESTIALITY in less than five seconds," I stalked ahead of him into the barn. Some of the hookwings were eating offal that buzzed with flies. Others were preening or drinking out of wooden troughs, dipping their muzzles and then throwing their heads back to drain it down their long s-curved throats. Cutthroat was eating, and gave me the hairy eyeball as I approached. "Really? I mean... really? *That's* where your head goes?"

"You grew up in the city, didn't you?"

"So?" I went to the tack bench and took down a grooming kit: feather brushes, chalk dust for powdering said feathers, a wide-bristled brush for their scaled legs.

"I grew up in deep hill country. Little hill town in Assfuck-Nowhere, Kentucky," Baldr replied. "We had about a thousand people give or take, about half of them related. One diner, one cemetery, five churches, and a mob that ran out the census takers every year. The nearest grocery store was twenty miles away. There wasn't nothin' to do except hogs, hunting, and crushed up painkillers 'til the war started."

"Well, good for you. You should be proud."

"Yeah, good for me. Damned if I ain't proof that anyone can make it if they try." He gestured to the village. "These people could make something of themselves, if they wanted to. I'm guessing the Archemi A.I. lets NPCs have their own thoughts and motivations, right? But what do they dream about? Pies and pigs. Believe me, when the pond is that shallow, you get a crowd of folks what drink themselves to sleep, fuck their critters and marry their sisters. If I want to learn shit, I'll learn from people who actually know what they're talking about. I had my fill of moonshine and garlic cures growing up."

"Fair enough." I shrugged. Personal achievement, that was admirable. I could get behind it. But for the NPCs? That wasn't how the feudal system really worked. These people were bound to their land and circumstances. Still... I could see he didn't care.

"You ain't nothing if you haven't fought for it." He shook his head and scowled.

"Well, I know that."

"Do you?"

"I got called 'gook' and 'chink' every day of my life growing up," I said. "But you're right – I was born and raised in the city. My mom and dad were on the alien watchlist. We could barely afford to live there because of the asset limits..."

"Wait." Baldr's eyes narrowed. "You were on a *watchlist*? Why?"

"Dad was born in Korea." I shrugged. "North Korea, South Korea, the government doesn't care anymore. The party line is that the Pacific Alliance started the Total War and Korea is now part of the Pacific Alliance. We were in a camp when my brother was about four and I was just a baby. We were released, but we never shook off the stigma. We made the best of it. Mom grew and sold meat on the black market. Dad was fucking crazy, but he was a dentist like his father, and he worked hard and took care of a lot of people. Me and my brother were born here, so we were clean slates provided we jumped through all the hoops. No laws broken, all taxes paid, on time. College, no draft dodging... so on and so forth. We had the government come around to interview us sometimes. I would have been able to clear my name once my service was finished."

"Oh." Baldr looked down. "Well, it still ain't rural Kentucky, believe me."

I did. But in my own way, I'd started from the bottom and dug my way up, working shitty jobs and training with my bike every day. Steve had broken out of the poverty loop by being smart. I'd been about to break out of the same cycle through sheer determination, but then the draft happened – and that was all she wrote.

Baldr didn't seem to know what to say after that. We fell silent as we worked. Cutthroat snapped and snipped the entire time I groomed her, and even got me once - ten HP down the drain. I left my hookwing preening in her stall as soon as her claws and muzzle were clean. Baldr peeled off in the other direction once we reached the inn yard. No apology, no acknowledgement, but I didn't need any. I was used to working with guys I didn't necessarily see eye-to-eye with on a personal level, and so I brushed off my discomfort at his prejudice and went to level up my Alchemy skill.

Chapter 27

My first stop was the general goods store. It was one of the few wooden buildings in the camp, a long, narrow one-room warehouse filled with rows of rickety wooden shelves carrying supplies. It was manned by a crusty guy who looked like he'd seen it all and done it all. He was tall, stooped and craggy, with huge hands and maybe a bit of troll blood in his veins. When he saw me, his face set into hard lines.

"Good afternoon." I decided to go with 'friendly' rather than 'chirpy' with this one. "I was wondering what Alchemy tools you have, if any?"

He scowled. "I don't do trade with the False Crown."

This man was clearly out of fucks to give when it came to the Royalist talk. I shrugged. "I'm a foreigner, sir, and I haven't sworn fealty to anyone here. I want to support the village, though."

⟦Negotiation check success!⟧

"Adventurers always try to pawn off their bits of string and empty bottles onto men like me," the man said bitterly. "Can't be bothered carrying it all around. Tinkers! Pah."

I'd be lying if I said I hadn't done that in other games I'd played. But that reminded me: I didn't have any string, but I did have a stack of swords that I needed to get rid of. "I've got some stuff to sell, but it's better than empty bottles."

Some sort of NPC merchant imperative seemed to kick in, and the guy sighed. "Fine. Let's see it."

I pulled the mob trash from my Inventory, adding sword after sword to the counter, and the man's eyes widened. There were fifteen in total, plus some other cheaper drops.

"Steel," he said, picking one up. "I'll give you seventy-five florins apiece for these. You want Alchemy tools, eh? I can set you up with some basics, but this is a prison camp. You want good materials and tools, you have to go to Liren."

"I figured." I watched him, slightly unnerved by his suppressed excitement. And I had to wonder: had I just sold a King's rebel a bunch of sharp black-market swords?

Before I had the chance to say anything further, the shopkeep folded the swords into his own personal pocket of hyperspace and came around the end of the counter. "What do you want from us, then?"

"Uhh..." I recalled all of the tools Kira and Owen had told me about. "Mortar, pestle, muslin rags, grain alcohol, a pot, bottles-"

We went around, gathering items off shelves. When I was done shopping, we carried them back to the counter and he rang them up. I'd made 1125 Florins off the swords, and the Alchemy setup cost 50 of that – chump change, really. Money and swords definitely seemed to improve the shopkeep's opinion of me.

"Not from this land, are you?" He asked, as he bagged up dried herbs.

"No sir," I said. "I'm from a place about as far away from here as you can get."

"If I were you, I'd run straight back there with me tail 'tween me legs," the old man said. "What makes you want to join this pack of traitors?"

"I want to imprint a dragon more than anything," I said. "And be careful who you say that to. You'll end up hanged, or worse."

"Bah. I've seen sixty-nine summers, and the last three 'ave been the worst of my life. They can bloody well hang me already." The man spat onto the floor beside him. "You know what this little visit of yours will cost this village? The granary's barely a quarter full after last year's harvest. Witchcraft turned the farmland sour. We grew poisonous wheat in places last year, the kind that turned people's guts inside out or drove them mad. And why? Because we dared ask questions, is why. We wanted to know why our rightful liege had been murdered in his own bed. That's all. No rebellion. No mobs. The old Alderman asked a question. He was hung for that, and the 'knights' put in Lieutenant Fatso to babysit us."

I blinked, stunned into silence.

"Aye, didn't know, did ye?" His eyes flashed darkly. "Nor do you know how your lovely dragons came to burn our fields, eat our cattle, and take young men into the sky in their claws and drop them. That happened to the alderman's son."

"I wasn't here for the civil war," I said, carefully. "I'm working with the Skyrdon, not for them."

He snorted. "Well, now you know. As for me, I have to die of somethin', and I'll die on me feet or off the ground, but not on bended knee."

"I won't tell them about you, if that's anything." I couldn't help but feel sympathy. "On my word."

"Huh." The old man stared at me for a long moment, as if deciding whether or not I was full of shit. It was weird as hell to see an NPC do something like that. He wasn't just selecting from a variable: he was making a *decision.* "Well, get your dragon and get out of Ilia, I say. Nothin' to be found here but war and bad blood."

"I'll take it to heart," I said uncertainly.

There are times during some video games where you wonder what side you're really on. I was having one of those moments, dwelling on what I'd seen and what Owen had told me versus what the people in my faction believed and said. I didn't really have a personal stake in the politics of Ilia yet, but I didn't like what I was seeing here. War was one thing: poisoning the land and punishing the people for asking questions of their new government was quite another. I went back outside to find Camp Prichard foggy and damp, the air clinging to any exposed skin like cold hands. More recruits were returning – and more riderless hookwings.

One of the other player characters - a pretty blonde sorceress – sobbed with pain as she was helped down by the two others from her party. Her robes had been torn down the front, baring her body like a bathrobe. It was far from titillating: the girl was trying to hold her guts in with both hands as the others got her down and medics swarmed across to help her.

Chilled, I scuttled by and went to find a quiet place to build a fire and get started on making medicines. We were going to need them.

Making a fire in Archemi was just like making one in the Outer World, as I was starting to think of it. You set up the firepit, collected tinder and kindling, and set aside two sticks - one harder, one softer. Once the kindling was ready, you carved a little hole in the softer stick, set it over the tinder, and used the harder one to drill by rubbing it briskly between your palms. After a couple of minutes, hot ash and embers fell out onto the tinder and caused it to smoke. When it caught alight, you fed it onto the fire, and coaxed it to life. Amazing what you learned at boot camp.

My 'stove' was a flat stone set on other stones and placed over the fire. Once I had a pot of water going, I brought up my crafting menus to see what I was able to make. There were enough herbs and other ingredients to be able to attempt several potions. After sorting them into separate piles, I cracked my knuckles and got to work.

The first couple of potions were foul, as expected, really little more than brown sludge that didn't help anyone or anything. I went back to making poultices for a while before reattempting the decoctions. It wasn't until I hit Alchemy 3 that I produced anything useful from the pot, but eventually, I was able to create my first ⟦Moss Tincture⟧, which healed 70 HP over 60 seconds. That single success inspired me to keep mashing, boiling, straining, and brewing. One after the other, I was able to fill bottles with brightly colored solutions.

⟦Your Herbalism skill has reached level 5!⟧

⟦Your Alchemy skill has reached level 4! This is the maximum rank you can attain with your current tools and tuition.⟧

"Bummer." Annoyed but resigned, I sat back from my improvised laboratory and beheld the fruits of my labor. I'd managed to make five different potions, some more useful than others:

Barghest Serum (Poison, FATAL)
A deadly poison that allows you to see in the dark for 60 seconds.

Lightning Strike Potion (Poison, FATAL)
A deadly poison that recovers 10 Adrenaline Points.

Strong Insect Repellant
Repels all normal insects for 120 minutes when drunk. Also kills parasites.

Moss Tincture
Heal 70 HP over 60 seconds.

Berry Sauce

Good over ice cream. Prevents starvation.

The 'fatal' potions didn't make a huge amount of sense to me. I could guess why they were toxic – these were the brews that contained poisonous herbs, mana-infused monster parts, or both. Magic wasn't for drinking in Archemi. Still, that they listed effects – other than death – was weird. There was possibly some way to get used to the poisons and withstand their effects to get the benefits of the potion.

I was out of herbs, so I put out the fire and went into the barn to repair my weapons and armor before returning to the inn. Trial and error taught me that the awl, wire and catgut was for repairing the metal and leather parts, while needle and thread was for clothes. It seemed a little pedantic for a game, but the task calmed me down and let my mind relax. There were a lot of injured, riderless hookwings in the yard now. Nine more people had returned. Thirty-two had gone out, and there were only eleven left.

I hadn't taken my first level in Knight yet. Every time I wandered to the Character screen, I found myself feeling gun-shy. When I'd seen the Tuun during character creation, I'd felt the pull immediately. With the Knight class, I was having cold feet. There was no genuine imperative for me to take the Path now. However, I noticed all the other melee characters who'd survived the quest had acquired an opalescent corona and a deepened sense of presence. The magic players had taken their own relevant Paths, I assumed. I was the only one who still had the basic green corona when I emerged from my hidey-hole and joined rank. My hope had been that no one would notice.

"Still green, Tuun?" Blackwin brayed, hands on hips. "Saving yourself for the right woman, are you?"

There was only one way to respond when your sarge trolled you like that. I stiffened and saluted. "Saving myself for Cutthroat, Ma'am! She doesn't like it when I cat around!"

"Ma'am! Requesting to be the bridesmaid at the service!" Baldr barked, standing to attention.

The others - the non-soldiers at least - started laughing.

"Alright, alright. Nice to see you're all in good spirits," Blackwin said. "You lot are the last aspirants standing. Get on your damn birds and let's get out of this hovel. You've a meeting with the captain. And then the Trial starts."

"You mean this wasn't the Trial? Ma'am?" The young, blonde sorceress who'd been disemboweled earlier was back on her feet. She spoke up nervously.

Blackwin scoffed. "Of course it wasn't the bloody Trial. If slapping bandits and corpse-eaters around was all it took to join the Order, we'd *all* be flying dragonback, wouldn't we?"

The sorceress blushed. "Yes ma'am."

"This was just to weed out the sap-lickers that didn't stand a chance of making it," Blackwin continued. "But remember what you did today. You'll talk about it with the Matriarch of the Eyrie when you visit her to view the eggs."

The eggs! My breathing sped a little. *Will they let us touch them?*

"Fall out! Get moving!" The sergeant's voice broke my thoughts - and those of the other candidates. "Go!"

All of the surviving riderless hookwings 'packed up', nipping and squawking at each other as they found their natural pecking order and trailed after the rank. I couldn't say the same for Cutthroat.

"Why are you such a fucking hose-beast!" I yelled, as she twisted her long neck and bit me hard on my upper arm. When she started to shake me like a dog, I punched her square in the side of her head. The creature let go with an irritated hiss, whistling with fury when I grabbed a nose rein and yanked it. "You want a piece of me?"

Hauling on that one rein made her spin in place, turning her around in the rank and sending the beasts behind me into conniptions. Cutthroat drooled, bucked, and then bolted forward as I regained control of all four reins, trying to skittle me off her back and into the hookwings ahead of me. They sensed her barreling toward them, and leaped out of the way with screechy cries of alarm.

"You cock-sucking- AARGH! I'm going to turn you into a feather duster!" I roared as we thundered past Sergeant Blackwin and the startled mage that accompanied her.

Chapter 28

We arrived back at the Fort at night. It was raining, torchlight and moonlight both gleaming off cobblestone and mud in the stableyard. Even with the rain, you could see the moon, Erruku. It was so enormous and so bright that it lit the sky with a weird yellow-gray light. Bright seams of it were visible through the breaks in the clouds. Sargent Blackwin had run ahead, and when we reached the stables, she was waiting for us.

"Hop to it! Get those animals cleaned up!" She yelled at us as we dismounted, stiff in the legs and back. "Chop chop!"

As soon as I was on the ground, Cutthroat tried to bite me. Her teeth narrowly missed the back of my neck, but they did miss. I was ready for it, this time.

"Cut it out." I grabbed her by the muzzle, and half-led, half-dragged her into the stable as she squawked in indignation.

Cutthroat settled down once I led her to her stall. The daily delivery of entrails had been deposited there, and it was apparently in a state of perfect ripeness, because she bounced over to the buzzing mess and began snarfing it down. Thoroughly grossed out, I left her to her feast. I wiped down her saddle outside, hung it to dry, and rejoined the others. As I exited the stable door, twin shadows passed overhead, the wind thundering in their wake. Winged shadows.

I ducked back under shelter and looked up, eyes widening as the pair of dragons curved around a tight spin and backwinged to land behind the row of buildings that separated the stable from the main courtyard. When everyone was out, I hustled there at a jog, arriving to find the two dragonriders already dismounted. I recognized Talenth right away. The huge, graceful white dragon had his head dipped down to Skyr Arnaud's armored shoulder, sniffing over it delicately as Arnaud absently scratched his chin. The other, smaller silver dragon belonged to Skyr Tymos. Like his rider, the dragon looked old and wiry. As everyone drew closer, we could see the patina on his scales, the chips in his horns, the faint misty glow of his eyes. Both men had pulled out the stops today and were dressed in full ceremonial platemail. The steel was intricately engraved, their white surcoats were spotless, their blue cloaks immaculate. They looked exactly the way that dragon knights should.

The other recruits gaped at them, men and dragons, and it occurred to me that most of them had never seen a dragon before, let alone ridden one. I was probably the only one to have ever done so.

"Hail, aspirants." Skyr Arnaud was every bit as impressive as I remembered. The expression of tenderness left his eyes we clustered together in rank. "Let's see... ten, eleven of you. Not bad. We've had fewer return than that..."

He trailed off as he spotted me.

"Skyr Tymos." The warmth had left his voice. "When did you admit this Tuun?"

"Only yesterday, Commander." Tymos replied. "He came with a personal missive from Lady Ru-"

"Rutha of Vasteau, yes. I'm sure he did. So you admitted him on the word of a knife-ear witch?"

Now everyone was staring at me, including the dragons. I squared my shoulders, hands folded behind my back.

"On the word of Warden Scandiva's court sorceress, Sir," Tymos replied crisply. "He passed the screening with flying colors. As did everyone else here."

"I see. Well. Perhaps we need to review our screening requirements." The knight commander sneered, and then he turned his icy glare back onto all of us.

"You have all passed the basic screening, which means you are ready to take the Trial of Marantha, if you dare." Arnaud began to stroll along our line. His armor barely made a sound as he walked: no clanking, just the whisper of metal against leather. "I will be both blunt and brief. Most of you will die in the Trial, if you choose to undertake it. The road to becoming a dragonman - or woman - is long, painful, and exceedingly dangerous. We do not administer the Trials lightly. We do not do so in vain. The fact remains that of every twenty candidates we submit, perhaps five make it out alive and hale, without disability or death."

No one moved a muscle or said a word as his words faded into the still air.

"Saint Grigori was the first king of Ilia, and the Emperor of Hercynia some two thousand years ago." Tymos spoke up, his reedy voice cutting through the cool, damp night air. "Like all humans of that era, he was born a slave. The Aesari enslaved all humans, dragons, Mercurions, and Catfolk under a vast empire that spanned the world. To control us, they commanded great Artifacts, machines fused with magic that cowed the other races into submission. But Grigori was Starborn, and he knew he would rise to a different fate."

"When the humans and Catfolk rebelled in the desert lands of the South, Grigori was sent by his Aesari masters to fight the self-appointed

Queen of Heaven and Earth, the Starborn Sachara." Sergeant Blackwin spoke from behind us, her voice keeping the same ritual cadence as the others. The less disciplined among us turned their heads to look back at her, but the other soldiers and I did not. "But instead, he fell in love with her. Sachara inspired Grigori to fight for the freedom of his own people. Rather than oppress his own kind, he turned on the Aesari and led a rebellion that freed him and his followers, including the sorceress Marantha, from the shackles of the Aesari. In the wilds of what is now Ilia, Grigori and Marantha hit upon a plan: convince the dragons to help them in their fight for freedom, and fly with them into battle against the Aesari's machines."

Arnaud took up the story without missing a beat. "But to fly the dragons was suicide. The *Solonkratsu* are our world's most ancient people. Their blood is the very stuff of magic, which Stranges human flesh, sickening us and turning us into monsters. Grigori was able to forge a secret alliance with the Great Matriarch, but to ride her children, he had to transform. With Marantha's help, Grigori obtained the ingredients for a series of potions and underwent the first Trial."

"He came through three days and three nights of sickness, but at the end, he had received the Gifts of the Ordeal," Tymos said. "The senses of an eagle, lungs capable of breathing thin air, a body strong enough to endure the speed of flight and the mana in a dragon's blood, a lifespan to match a wyrm's. Grigori became the first Skyr, bonding with the Diamond Queen, Lirenian. The Trial was dangerous, but Saint Grigori inspired others to dare. Many of our heroes died or were crippled, but when the bond between man and dragon was forged, it was nearly undefeatable. Our dragonriders slew the Aesari in great numbers, cutting through them like a scythe and bringing down their Artifacts and weapons. Grigori eventually joined with Sachara's force, and together, we liberated humankind from bondage."

We were all now regarding the Skyrdon with renewed understanding. Their weird eyes, aura of power, and impressive agelessness – even Tymos, who looked 'old', could have been anywhere between fifty and five hundred years old... they were mutations caused by the Trial.

"There are fewer of us today, but the Trial remains the same." Arnaud gestured to the distant beacon shining at the top of the Eyrie. "Dragons are the most powerful allies of humanity, but the sacrifice is a greater price than most are willing to pay. Between now and the actual time of the Trial, you may leave with no loss of honor to you or your families. You can leave entirely, or join the ranks of our soldiers, which means you will continue your training with Blackwin in Fort Grigori. If you wish to continue, step forward."

There was a ripple of hesitation along the line. Baldr and I stepped forward nearly at the same time: him with his jaw set, his head held high, me with my stomach quaking and my hands fisted by my sides. Lucien joined us, as did the blonde sorceress. The others looked down, unmoving.

Is this the right decision? It was the thought on everyone's mind as the knight commander and Skyr Tymos waited patiently for several long minutes. Arnaud moved, as if to speak, and at the last moment, the tall, dark-haired boy who had ridden with the sorceress stepped forward.

"So be it," Arnaud said, his gaze briefly flicking to me. "The rest of you will leave with Sergeant Blackwin. Feel no shame and do not fear dishonor. You have done well to reach this point, and you have done Ilia service with your first test. I have no doubt you will do well here."

A murmur of thanks rippled out from behind and around us, and the other five candidates withdrew. Six of us stood unevenly spaced in front of the Skyrdon and their dragons. I glanced up at Skyr Tymos' beast, who regarded us with inhumanly patient, luminous eyes. There was something in them - and in the expression of his human rider - that was bittersweet.

When the others had left, Skyr Arnaud regarded us with cool consideration. "The first part of the Trial is to gather the ingredients for the Trial of Marantha, the transmutation you will undergo. You have three days to prepare yourself and gather the ingredients from the ruins of Cham Garai, the ancient city that surrounds the base of the Eyrie."

The quest alert I was expecting arrived, and I reviewed it carefully:

The Trial of Marantha

You have accepted the dangerous Trial of Marantha, an ordeal which gives humans immunity to mana poisoning, extended lifespan, the ability to withstand great heights and great speeds, along with many other advantages... assuming you survive.

To attend the Trial, you must go into the ruins of Cham Garai and collect the following ingredients:

- *Crowned Eagle Eggs from the nests that pocket the old buildings*
- *King's Sorrow, which grows in stagnant water*
- *Catseye Mushrooms, which grow in warm places underground*
- *Red Rashovik, a Stranged herb found on the ancient battlefield beyond the swamps.*

Once you have the ingredients, you will take them to the Temple of Kyrie at the base of the Eyrie, where the Trial of Marantha will commence.

Difficulty: Level 10

Reward: EXP

Special: Timed quest: must be completed within 72 hours of acceptance.

Special: Undergoing the Trial of Marantha may result in permanent stat or ability loss, or a physical penalty. If you die during the Trial, you will respawn in a neutral location, but will not be able to take the Trial again.

"If you accept, know this." Arnaud reached up as Talenth dipped his muzzle down, caressing the dragon's jaw without needing to look back. "We will hold you to the highest standards of loyalty, discretion, and honor. Loyalty to us, the Skyrdon, and to Ilia: her government and her people. You will fall into line and subject yourself to the authority of your commanders. There is no room in our ranks for rebellion or cowardice. Am I understood?"

"Yes, sir!" The five of us shouted. I answered more out of reflex than anything. I'd heard the honor and loyalty talk before, from different lips in a different world, and it still sounded like a load of horse shit.

"Then accept your quest, and I hope to learn your names soon, once you have passed the Trial of Marantha," the commander said. He looked at me, though he continued speaking to us all. "Be sure to take your first level in the Knight Path before you attempt the Trial."

Oh. I'd almost forgotten about that, but joined the chorus anyway. "Yes, sir!"

He nodded. "For now, you will salute to me as dragonmen, even though you are yet to endure the Trial. Right fist to left breast, then out, then back to your side."

With a deep breath, I saluted with the others. My HUD flashed, and that was that.

Quest accepted.

Chapter 29

We left the yard and followed Skyr Tymos back to our dorm. The room had enough beds for ten people, but there were only six of us left out of the original thirty-two. The Novice Master lingered while we set our weapons and packs down and shucked our damaged, dirty clothes.

The misery of Camp Prichard was on my mind, and Kira's solemn warning echoed in my ears as I undressed, absent-mindedly pulling off my gloves. The Mark of Matir prickled as Tymos glanced at me sharply. I scrambled to cover it back up, but there was no way he hadn't seen it. *Shit.*

"You, Tuun. Put those back on. I have a job for you," he said. "There's a sack of soap out by the kitchen doors, along with a large pail. The chamberlain only set out enough soap for three, so we will fetch more."

"Yes, sir." Flustered, I turned to conceal my hand from the others as I pulled my glove back on.

"I love good service," Baldr sighed happily. He hadn't seen the Mark.

My fatigue vanished with a fresh wave of anxiety as Tymos fell in beside me. We headed for the kitchens together, tensely silent. I was not at all surprised when he hung back, and closed the door with a thump behind us.

"Hector," he said. "That's your name, isn't it?"

"Yes, sir." I turned to face him, arms crossed over my chest. "Is this about-?"

"Your glove." He nodded to my right hand. "Take it off."

Watching him warily, I pulled it off again. He sucked in a tense breath through his nose, chin lifting.

"By the Nine." Tymos' eyes were intense as he took my hand in his. My discomfort was increasing by the minute as he pushed my sleeve up, examining the design and shaking his head. "Halcyon spoke the truth."

"Who?" I fought the urge to shrink away. "Your dragon?"

"Yes." He released my arm. His face was drawn into grim, hard lines. "You will be the death of the Skyrdon, boy. But it's right and proper you are here."

I took a step away from him. "What? I don't know what you're talking about, but I'm not here to do anything to anyone. I didn't ask to get this tattoo... it just happened."

"No doubt," Skyr Tymos said heavily. "Few people ever ask for Matir's blessing."

Then it dawned on me. Tymos wasn't angry. He sounded... reverent. Some of my concern was replaced by hope. "Wait, do you know what he is? Why I have this?"

"I know Halcyon's stories, and the myths of my ancestors." Tymos said. "Come, put that glove back on. I wish to move to a place where I know the walls do not have ears."

I followed him through the kitchen and outside into the herb garden behind the Old Hall wing of the Fort. The old knight strode over to a low stone bench, and gestured to the space beside him as he sat down with a resigned thud. I joined him, surprised at how alert I still felt after a full day of riding and fighting.

"There are wild tribes who live in these mountains," Tymos said, eyes lifted to look at the blue-and-white dragon flag fluttering from the rampart high above our heads. "The Aedui, they're called. They answer to no king or warden, and they still keep to the old gods. The Nine were worshipped by humans and dragons – and the Aesari. Matir is one of those old gods, the god of darkness. In my tribe, he was known as the Lord of Wolves. He is the most deeply revered of the Nine.

I blinked a couple of times. "Matir is... what? The dragons worship a god of darkness over anything else?"

"Darkness is the beginning of life, boy," Tymos said. "Life begins in the dark soil, the dark womb, the darkness of the mind. It begins with urges, hidden thoughts and desires. Artists and scribes work best at night. It is a place of obsession, creativity. Matir is all of these things, as well as the assassin's blade, the trade deal made in secret, the dark oil that greases the wheels of society. The dragons as we know them today... are not the dragons of old."

Mystified, I listened as the icy night wind rustled the rows of plants around us.

"The Nine would choose champions from time to time," Tymos continued. "Their avatars in the flesh. The dragons have a prophecy about the champion of Matir, the 'Herald of the Hidden Seed'. But I can't tell you about it."

"Why not?"

"Because I cannot." He shrugged, not looking at me. Tymos' eyes were dilated in fear, the cold rivulets of sweat running down his face. "I *cannot* tell you, just as I *cannot* tell you anything more about The Nine.

But you bear their mark. I *can* tell you what I observe. Do I have your confidence?"

"Of course, sir," I blurted.

He nodded briefly. "We have had a spate of disappearances since the close of the revolution. Soldiers vanishing. Three knights had fatal accidents during training or patrol. If a dragon-bonded Skyrdon dies, his dragon commits suicide... The magnitude of the loss is terrible. They were good people, Hector. They were good knights and good fliers."

I hunched in, arms crossed against the cold. "You think they were...?"

"Aye. And I know who did it, too." The old man looked up at the same banner he had before. "The Mata Argis. The Warden's eyes and ears, the faith militant of the Church of Kyrie. Three years ago, after the war, a contingent of six came to board here."

I couldn't help myself. "No one expects the Mata Argis."

Tymos snorted. Somehow, he got the joke. "The commander didn't want them here. But the Skyrdon are deeply in debt to the same merchant lords who backed Scandiva's revolution. Our years of grandeur are long past... and I think you will come to understand why when you meet the Matriarch and view her eggs. If you *do* meet her. The Mark is no guarantee you will survive... but I hope you do. For her sake."

"The Matriarch is the Queen dragon who lays all of the eggs, right?"

He nodded.

I frowned. "And she's supposed to lay more than three at a time?"

"Yes." Tymos stood and walked stiffly back toward the kitchen door. I trailed after him, brain buzzing with unanswered questions.

When we were inside, he drew two buckets of hot water from a huge cauldron bubbling over the hearth, and passed one of them to me.

"Sir, I have a question," I began, taking the bucket out of his hands. "I'm ready to take my first Path. To become a Skyr... do you *have* to take the Path of the Knight? Or can I take another Path?"

"The only Path worth taking is the one you forge yourself," the old Skyr said heavily. "Don't learn that lesson the same way I did."

What was that supposed to mean? I scowled at his obvious depression and regret. "You don't believe in the Order, or their saints and gods, do you? Why are you here?"

Tymos glared at me with his strange blue eyes, pupils huge in the dark. "I can't tell you. But as I said, it's right and proper that you're here. Now... never speak to me of this again, and assume everyone is watching you. You and your dragon will be safer for it."

And with that, we went back to the dormitory. The others were already in their sleeping clothes, sitting around the hearth or lying on their beds. We set the buckets down beside the single round wooden tub we were to share.

"No wallowing," Tymos said to the assembled. "You clean yourself standing, rinse off in the tub, and then leave it for the next. Dirtiest goes last."

"Thanks, Gramps." Baldr looked over his shoulder from his place by the fire, where he was sitting almost knee-to-knee with Lucien, the light-haired man with the waspish face and red eyes, the one with the posh lawyer voice.

"Then I guess the Tuun is going last," Lucien said.

Baldr laughed it off. "Hey now, Luci – don't you be ragging on Hector. He's my main man. You want to join us for a hand, Hec?"

"Sure." I didn't, really. What I wanted to do was lie down, level up, review my character build, and choose my Path. I knew what I was going to pick, but I wanted to make sure my skills complemented my decision. Even so, there was nothing to be gained from socially isolating myself from the guys who would be my wingmates someday.

Tymos' words were hanging on me, running through my mind as I sat down across from 'Luci' and accepted cards Baldr dealt to me. It was plain old 'Go Fish', but with cards that had lurid pictures of topless women on them.

"So, you were both soldiers," Lucien said as I sat down. "I've been meaning to ask-"

"If you want to know what it's like to kill someone, the answer is 'no'." I cut him off as Baldr just stared..

By the way he deflated, I knew he *had* been about to ask that question, but he was too proud to back down. "I wasn't going to *quite* ask that, actually. What I was going to ask is whether or not this game world is very realistic or not. I figured one or either of you might be able to compare the battlefields of Archemi with those of the real world."

His oh-so-casual tone on the subject turned my stomach. Killing the bandits raiding Lyrensgrove hadn't hit me the way that the shipwreck had, but I wasn't inclined to dwell on any of those experiences. I sure as hell wasn't about to willingly 'compare' them to my experiences in the field. I slapped a card down. "It's a fantasy world with fantasy physics."

"Violetta was terribly injured. It made me sick to look at." Lucien said, leaning in over his hand. He was taking extraordinary pains to hide his cards from us. "She got ripped open by her own hookwing, you know."

"They're big critters." Baldr shrugged nonchalantly, his face an unreadable mask.

"It definitely seems to me that it's more realistic than any game I ever played," Lucien said. "I mean, there's not even a defined PVP system, as such. In most games, you can't flag a player under level 10, but that isn't true here. You can flag *anyone.*"

I glanced up from my hand at him. Lucien was as green as spring grass, but there was the seed of something nasty in him. I'd seen the same glint in the eye in some of my fellow conscripts during Basic Training. Cowards with dreams of conquest. They went crazy on the front lines, gutting enemy soldiers for kicks, trying to instigate the abuse of prisoners. When their sergeant yelled at them, they turned into bleating lambs, but give them a bayonet...

"They have another name for griefing here," I said, laying down the next card. "Murder."

Baldr chuffed. "I asked about PVP when I was being loaded in, actually. They told me a little bit about how it works."

"Oh yeah?" Lucien perked up.

"Yeah. If you grief someone who's got a lower gear score and level combo than you, you get a mark, like the Mark of Cain," Baldr said, leaning back in his seat. "Soldiers will chase you out of town. You won't be allowed anywhere. NPCs shun you. And you keep that mark until the player reaches the same level as you."

Lucien pulled his head back, the same kind of striking snake motion that Cutthroat did when she was irritated. "That's obnoxious."

"About as obnoxious as murder," I snapped. "Which is what it is, in a game where people feel pain and die."

He scoffed. "Like you have a leg to stand on."

I stood back up, and threw my cards on the table. "I've changed my mind, Baldr. Have fun with Luci here."

Exasperated, Baldr turned on Lucien as I left. "Not another word that ain't 'I'm sorry, boss' out of your damn mouth, you hear?"

"My entire family was-"

"I don't give a fuck. I was out slogging through the motherfucking jungle to defend your lily-white draft-dodging ass, so you either apologize, or you get the fuck out of my sight."

I paused, back to them, and waited.

"Well, when you put it like that." Lucien still sounded snotty, but chastened. "I *am* sorry, Hector. I lost my family to the War very shortly before starting these trials, and it's made me a bit morbid."

"So did I," I replied, half-turning back. "Just after I came back to San Francisco, after my second tour fighting on the Crescent Line."

"Ground fighting, at that," Baldr affirmed.

Lucien held a hand out. "It never occurred to me that it would be anything other than..."

"Cool?" I arched an eyebrow.

"Something you'd be proud of, actually."

If you're proud of killing someone, anyone, there's something fucking wrong with you. That was what I wanted to say, but just as I had made peace with the psychos in my regiment, I had to make peace with this asshole. For all I knew, he'd survive the Trials, Baldr would die, and we'd be stuck together as teammates. At least I'd have a dragon to keep me company.

I jerked my shoulders, trying to relax them, and turned back. "Did you lose your family to HEX?"

"No. They were killed in the invasion of Hawaii. I'm part of the beta development team who migrated with Ryuko to Aurora Shard." Lucien set his cards down, game forgotten in the thick tension that had overtaken our corner of the room. "I log in for ten hours at a time to test the game, go back to report, then come back. I'm helping them test certain things."

So that was why I didn't remember seeing Lucien when we were all bedded down in the stable. For some reason, that pissed me off even more, knowing that this guy could just merrily hop back into his body. He actually *was* playing a game, but this was the only life Baldr and I had left.

"Shit, really?" Baldr chuckled darkly, and leaned back. "Like what?"

"This is still sort of secret, so don't go telling anyone." Lucien dropped his voice, leaning in as I rejoined them. "But some people don't make the 'jump' very well. They start going crazy, lose their minds, and unravel. The system can't keep them together. About a dozen of us are in here doing reality testing. We log in for ten hours, out for ten hours, and the whitecoats compare our waking brain data with our in-game brain activity. They want to make sure that the system can really sustain a human consciousness."

Baldr and I exchanged glances.

"No one told us that," Baldr said, flatly. "I thought-"

"That they had that all sorted out? They weren't even halfway through testing OUROS when the CEO forced this 'refugee program' through." Lucien linked his hands between his knees, his expression not unlike that of a smug cat. "I hear that the first test subjects were prisoners of war."

While they talked, I went back over my ⟦Terms and Conditions⟧, searching mentally for keywords. Surprise surprise, there was nothing about this particular information - just the usual *cavaet emptor*-style disclaimer about unspecified 'risks'.

"And I can tell you something else. They really wanted soldiers for the beta," Lucien admitted. "Management, that is. They wanted to know if the, uh, 'conditioning' you guys get makes you more resilient. I heard that one of the major A.I developers went nuts in here and had to be banned from his own game."

"Jesus." Baldr shook his head. "We really are guinea pigs then, aren't we? Can they hear us talking about this?"

Lucien shook his head. His sharp features were intense now, and he gestured with his hands as he spoke. "Aurora Shard is in Alaska, and Ryuko is running a skeleton crew. So honestly, I don't know, but I'm willing to bet they can't. They have recording functionality here, but all the available memory is being used to load people in. Even if they *are* logging us, there's not enough people on the ground to review every minute of footage."

I still didn't like Lucien, but he was trying to make up for being a creep by being a useful creep, so I sat my ass back down. "What's the story about the Dev?"

"It's more of a rumor than anything," Lucien said. "That he was one of the guys who coded OUROS, and he was an early entry into the game."

"My brother probably knew him, then," I remarked.

"Dead? Alive?" Baldr pressed him anyway.

"Dead. I don't know if it was from HEX or not, but given he was in the Shard, I doubt it. For whatever reason, he was one of the first to try to hop over permanently. He made it, but he went nuts."

With a repressed shudder, I couldn't help but wonder if Crazy Dev's upload had been glitched, like mine. I still wondered if Steve was here, too... or part of Steve.

"Well, shit." Baldr shook his head. "Here I was all worried about the Trials, when maybe I should have been worried about waking up in the morning. Speaking of that, though, time for bed. We got a busy day tomorrow digging up magic weeds."

"I'm not worried." Lucien was the first to stand, tense with suppressed discomfort. "We're player characters, so even if we don't pass, we'll respawn in our original spawn points. We won't be able to ride a dragon, but there's something to be said for the city."

"I won't lose," Baldr said.

"I can't afford to," I said. "My original spawn point was several miles over the open ocean."

Baldr chuckled. "Guess you're going for a long swim if you die."

"Thanks, Captain Sympathy." I rolled my eyes.

Lucien snorted. "Don't worry. We're not going to encounter anything over CR 10 in the ruins. The high-level monsters are all turned off. We're lucky to be trying out for the dragons now, actually - it'll be harder when they re-enable all the features."

"But there's still only three eggs," I said, watching him steadily.

"Indeed." He smiled thinly. "And six of us."

Chapter 30

"We really have to go by ourselves?" Violetta, the sorceress, asked nervously at the breakfast table.

"Yes. Alone." the sullen, dark-haired man replied. His name was Pravoslav, and he had the accent to match his name. "We go into ruins alone."

Baldr and I ate in studied silence, both of us preparing in our own ways for the challenge ahead. Lucien wasn't here yet. Presumably he was logged out, eating real food in his fancy Shard quarters, looking out over a dying world from a tower nearly two miles high. It was almost enough to make me regret not punching him when I had the chance.

"Ugh. I wish I hadn't taken Mage now." Violetta slathered a biscuit in butter, lips pursed. "They nerfed this class. Mage is usually the best for DPS, but this whole thing has been nothing but a grind for mana. I need to travel with a tank. A *rich* tank."

"Why you try to become dragon knight, then?" Pravoslav asked. "Not good class for mages."

"I was going to say," Baldr added wryly. "You got your work cut out for you, squish."

"Why do you think?" Violetta jabbed her butter knife vaguely in the direction of the Eyrie. "We're all here for the same thing. And being a mage *does* have some advantages. I'm already partly immune to mana toxicity, for one thing, so the Trial should be a breeze, assuming I don't die in the ruins and lose all of my EXP because we're not allowed to work together. It's ridiculous, if you ask me."

"Bless your heart." Baldr chuckled between forkfuls of bacon.

"We compete for eggs," Pravoslav grumbled. "Maybe three of us survive, maybe four."

"Or maybe we'll *all* survive, and the quest is made out to be a bigger deal than it is," Violetta replied primly. "I mean, we're some of the first players here, if not *the* first players. I doubt they'll actually kill us off."

Only one end of the long table held food. The rushes on the floor were clean and untrampled, and there was no fire in the hearth. The room was frosty, and felt and sounded empty. The sound of a chair scraping on the floor or a boot kicking a leg of the table echoed like gunshot.

"What you going to do?" Pravoslav asked everyone. "Going today? Or training a day, go tomorrow?"

"I'm out and away as soon as I've filled the tank," Baldr said, and patting his stomach. "Got my Path, got my gear. I want to find my mushrooms and McGuffins and get this shit over with. We get to see the eggs and their mom before they hatch. Want to make a good impression."

"Hah. Such confidence." Pravoslav seemed impressed, rather than irritated. Baldr had that good ol' boy thing down. "What about you?"

He was speaking to me. My plan was to go to the library and ask about Skill Tomes and the locations of the herbs, eggs, and mushrooms we had to find in more detail. I wanted to see if I could head off a wild goose-chase through dangerous ruins. "I'll be staying around here for a bit. Thought I'd head out in the afternoon."

"I have to study more," Violetta sighed. "There's so much to learn about this game. I'm hoping to master at least two more Words of Power before going out into Cham Garai. It's an Aesari city, you know - so I reckon there's some deeper connection between the Skyrdon, the Aesari, and the dragons."

"What do you know about them?" I asked, genuinely curious. There was still next to nothing in my Glossary about the Aesari, other than what Rutha had told me.

"They were an avian-angelic race, I guess you could say," the sorceress said. "One of the three Elder Races: the Aesari, the Prrupt'meew - the Meewfolk, - and the dragons. The Elder Races are the native sentient species of Archemi."

"Humans aren't native?" I tilted my head. "What about the Lysidians? The elves?"

She shook her head. "Nope. We're an introduced species. We came with the first Cataclysm, when the Drachan invaded Archemi. The Elder Races drove off the evil dragons, and the Aesari just sort of took over everything after that."

My index updated with that information. Satisfied, I nodded. "You think there's some link between the Skyrdon and the Aesari?"

"Well, Captain Arnaud told us that story last night." The sorceress flushed prettily as she spoke his name. "But he left parts of it out. First, Saint Grigori was a Starborn, but he died somehow. Perma-died, that is."

"Not a player character, though," Baldr grunted around his toast.

"No. Just a mythological figure. Then there's the fact that Fort Grigori is built on Cham Garai. Liren has facilities for dragons in the cliffs, but the dragons don't live there - they live *here*, leagues away from civilization in the Eyrie. Which doesn't make sense to me, because

Liren is so convenient and is so much closer to the King... well, the Warden and the Council now, I guess."

"Yeah, don't go talking about the royals around here," Baldr said. "'Round these parts, they'll pull your fingernails out for saying nice things about the old king."

Violetta shrugged. "My point is that the Skyrdon would be of more use living closer to the biggest city in the land, don't you think? To defend it?"

"Depends," Pravoslav said. "Depends on whether they want to defend city or borders, farmlands or buildings. Dragons flying over a city... they bleed, turn citizens into mutants who slaughter everyone. Who knows?"

I mulled over what Tymos had said to me. The old man had seemed to know something about his Order, something that upset him, but what? Suddenly, I wasn't hungry - I was itching to get to work. I pushed my wooden plate away and rose, stretching.

"Good man. Had the exact same thought." Baldr did the same thing. "See you guys at the Eyrie, right?"

Lucien barked a short, bitter laugh.

Baldr and I walked out together. I stayed quiet until we were out of earshot.

"I'm hitting the library to get more info on the locations of the herbs," I said, keeping my voice low. "The quest only gives two specific coordinates: the eggs, and the Red Rashovik. If I learn anything, I'll PM you."

He nodded. "I'm going to do a bit of training myself. Heads up - the Bulwark combat skill is really good if you pair it with Active Defense. If you haven't taken it already..."

He was talking about the Knight Path. I shook my head. "Thanks, but I'm not taking Knight."

"What?" His eyebrows arched.

"No. I can't." I'd spent a couple of hours poring through the information available through my HUD, matching combat skills with the Lancer Path progression. The only reason I hadn't leveled up yet was because I wanted to see if the library had any of the Skill Tomes that the Quartermaster had told me about. "I'm not built to tank. I'm taking Lancer."

To my surprise, Baldr frowned. "That's not how you reach the Dragon Knight Advanced Path."

"No, but it might open up another AP," I replied. "If Violetta can go into this as a Mage, I can go in as a Lancer."

"You know as well as I do that she's going to bite it during the Trial. She's got a bad attitude." Baldr stopped dead in the hall, and I stopped short, turning back to face him. "We were given an order by the Commander. Sure, this is a game and all, but by God it's the only world we have now. We're joining a military organization that has, for all intents and purposes, been one of the best fighting forces Archemi has ever known. They got their way of doing things, and they have their reasons for why they do it that way."

"Well, sure-"

"The nail that sticks out *will* be hammered down, is what I'm saying." Baldr regarded me steadily, his eyes piercing blue in the early morning light. "You know what the Commander wants, and you know what he's going to say when he hears you've taken Lancer instead of the class that you're meant to take. How the hell is a Lancer going to work inside of a unit? You gonna jump from dragon to dragon?"

I was beginning to feel prickly now. "I'm sure there's other Lancers among the Skyrdon. It's *my* life. My life, my choice."

"Not if you swear the vows and take the Trials it isn't." The big man's brows furrowed. "And this here's the problem with conscripts. You were drafted and didn't have a choice then, but you're *here* of your own free will, Hector. Because you want something they got and they want something you have. Fall into line, like he said, and don't fuck this up. He hates your guts already, that's plain to see. I like you, but if he makes an example of you, there ain't shit I can do to help."

We split up at the door. I didn't really have anything to say to his lecture - nothing polite, anyway - so I kept my mouth shut and nodded stiffly to him as we went our separate ways. I'd lost some points with Baldr, but I'd had a bellyful of blind loyalty in the military. The Skyrdon *claimed* to be an ancient fighting force. They could claim anything they liked, but Tymos had implied that they weren't necessarily what they seemed, and I couldn't shake his conviction. *The only Path worth taking is the one you forge yourself.*

My first stop, the library, was located in one of the old stone towers of the castle at the center of the fort. Fort Grigori had three main sections within the confines of the outer walls: the main courtyard and its two attached buildings, which had a ramp that led to the castle. The castle had a main corridor that ran all the way through it to the back, where the bulk of the units' soldiers were camped. The library was in the tower that overlooked the encampment.

The castle was chilly, but the library was warm. Heat washed over me as I let myself in through the black walnut doors. The interior was old, worn, but cozy. The ceiling vaulted high overhead, and a single chandelier hung where the designs met in the center. A stone walkway spiraled up the inside of the tower, and hundreds of books filled the shelves built into the walls. It smelled like old paper and leather.

There was only one person in here, and he was a Siamese cat. The Meewfolk librarian had silver rings clamped at different lengths along his long, twitching tail. He wore a long linen kilt, like the kind I'd seen in Egyptian pyramid drawings of priests, and no shirt. His fur was cream, except for his points – his nose, ears, feet, hands, and tail were a dark chocolate brown - and his ears were heavily pierced. He was carefully paging through a very old, fragile book on a wooden lectern with one hand, a brush held in the other. When the door closed, his ears twitched, and his head lifted slightly.

"Ahh. I remember you. The Assspirant from Tungaant." He didn't look up, but with senses as keen as a cat's, he didn't have to.

There was no mistaking that voice. This had been the mage who'd accompanied us to Lyrensgrove.

"Good morning, sir." I resisted the urge to salute. "I hope I'm not interrupting."

"You are, but it is of little consequence. The book has waited three hundred years for new glue - it shall wait ten minutesss more."

"Hopefully I'm memorable for the right reasons, sir." I tried not to stare. Meewfolk really did look like giant walking cats. "I came here to research some stuff before the Trial."

"'Sssome stufff," he echoed, dabbing carefully at a yellowed page with the brush. His voice was light and melodic, with an accent that was hard to pin down. Something from Asia, not Europe. "Please define 'sssome stuff'."

I drew myself up. "First, I'd like a map of the region. Second, some books describing the herbs we're meant to be looking for. I was also going to ask about Skill Tomes, if you have them. How should I address you, sir?"

"You may call me 'Jasssper'. No 'sssir'." he replied, still looking down at the book. His tail was now curled like a question mark. "And yes, you were memorable for the correct reasons. I *do* have Skill Tomes here. What are you looking for?"

"Herbalism. Cooking. Armor and weapon repair. Any healing or self-surgery stuff. Anything to do with the Lancer class," I replied. I'd been rehearsing my demands all morning.

Jasper raised an eyebrow, an odd expression on his pointed Siamese-cat muzzle. "I hear you, though I am curiousss. Why are you not out, stretching your sword arm like the othersss?"

"I don't want to run off blindly into the dark," I replied, crossing my arms. "But I don't know if these books will work. I can barely read."

"That is no problem with Skill Tomesss." Jasper set the brush down in a small pot of clear, thick liquid that smelled more like oil than glue. "Their magic operates regardlesss of your ability to read them. The othersss... hmm. Well, you may try to read them, but you could just as readily put them in your Inventory, ssscan them, and then return the books to the shelves."

I wasn't sure which was stranger: a giant talking cat telling me how magic worked, or Jasper talking about Inventories as if they were a normal part of life. The librarian left his work and drifted to one of the shelves. He unlocked the wooden cover and lifted it.

"Let me sssee... herbalism, armor repair, the elements of sssmithing, and recipes for the road?"

"Great!" I came closer, glancing over at the book he'd been working on. The pages crawled with black writing that left me dizzy. "How much?"

"Each book is worth one gold guilder to use, but I do not imagine you have that kind of coin," he replied, taking them to a larger table. "However, I am willing to trade these and one other Skill Tome for a boon. The other Tome contains Jump, one of the mossst useful martial skills for the Lancer path, and a martial legacy of my people."

I *did* have the money – barely – but if I could save my Florins and Guilders for a rainy day in exchange for a quest... "Your people favor Lancer?"

"The men do." He inclined his head gracefully. "We live separate lives from our womenfolk."

"What do you need?" I walked over to him. Jasper was nearly seven feet tall, when he stood up on his feet. Well... paws.

"You are going to Cham Garai for your herbsss and fungi," he said, laying a clawed hand on top of the stack of books. He left them there and walked toward a shelf of parchment scrolls. "In the swamp that surrounds the ruins, there are six plants I require for the creation of inksss. Sunwort, blackweed, green algae, widowberry and crimson lily, plus a rarer plant, ghostbell. You are in luck, as ghostbell is often found alongsside king's sorrow, which you require for the Trialsss. If you bring me these plants, you may read a Skill Tome for each lot."

New Side-Quest: Ink, Glorious Ink

Jasper the Librarian has need of some special plants to make ink for his work. Cats are notorious for their dislike of water, and the Meewfolk are no exception... so he is willing to pay for you to wade around in the swamp to avoid getting his fur wet.

Reward: Skill tomes + 10 EXP

Difficulty: Level 4

A quest that was a lower level than me didn't pay much in EXP, but I wasn't doing it for the experience. The Jump skill alone was worth a lot, as it would allow me to select a different combat ability when I took my first Path level. But even so... "That's six herbs, and only five Skill Tomes. This will take up some the time for the Trials-"

"But I will give you some aid in locating the herbsss for Marantha's Trial," Jasper finished. "And that is worth the collection of ghostbell. You would be surprised how few aspirants come here first, so bedazzled are they by the dragonsss and the terror of the Trial. Now, look at this map."

I stood beside the librarian as he opened the map out on the table, searching over it. It was a map of the local lands: the fort, the road that led into the forest behind it, and then the marshes where the road ended. There was a ghostly red outline of a broken city extending through the marshy forest, all the way across the land dividing the swamps from the old battlefield and what I assumed were surface ruins, and then the base of the Eyrie. As I took it in, an alert informed me that the Map of Palewing Crater had been added to my Inventory.

"You will search the shores for widowberry, which grows on small bushes with dark leaves, and green algae, which is plentiful where the water laps the mud. Look around here for king'sss sorrow." Jasper indicated the deeper area of the swamp. "And with it, you will find ghostbell. Blackweed is found under deeper water, growing in the silt below the surface, and is plentiful. Crimson lily grows in shade, sunwort in bright light, and you will see those areasss when you enter and move forward..."

As we worked through the map, highlights appeared on my virtual copy, indicating areas of potential search. I could flip through them, bringing up a circular 'zone' that was shaded in, showing me where I was likely to find the various herbs. When we were done, I nodded. "Mind if I use the Herbalism Tome before I go? I'll be taking a hookwing, so I can come back once I've found your herbs, learn my skills, and go back into the swamp."

"Of course. And do not worry, it does not take an aspirant three daysss to reach the temple with their ingredientsss, unless they are very unlucky inside the ruinsss - or do not have the foresight to visit me."

Jasper rolled the map up, and handed me one of the books. "Open this to the first page."

I took it - it was lighter than I expected - and did as he'd said. A brilliant green sigil crawled on the page, and I got a telepathic prompt: *"Do you wish to use Skill Tome: Herbalism (Beginner)?"*

"*Yes,* "I thought back.

The sigil flared, and the book discharged a pulse into my hands. The influx of information was like warm water poured between my ears. My temples grew hot, and my head pounded painlessly - but as soon as it began, it was over.

[Your Herbalism skill has reached level 6!]

[Your Herbalism skill has reached level 7!]

[Your Herbalism skill has reached level 8!]

Suddenly, I knew exactly what Jasper wanted, and why. All the plants were used for making different colored inks, except for the ghostbell. That one was made into an invisible ink that dissolved other colors on parchment and vellum and made them easy to sponge off.

"Alright. That helps." I shook my head, clearing the last of the magic fog out of it. The sigil inside the book was no longer glowing. "This kind of magic isn't toxic, is it?"

"Greencrystal is a ssstable form of mana," Jasper said. "It is only slightly toxic... as much as breathing in the smoke of the city for a minute, or less."

"Huh. Well, thanks." I rolled my shoulders, and was about to leave when a final question occurred to me. "By the way... is the Trial of Marantha as terrible as it's made out to be?"

The Meewfolk blinked his huge, luminous blue eyes, pacing back to the ancient book he had been working on. "It is worse than you expect. Remember to wear gloves and washhh them thoroughly when you collect king'sss sorrow. The juice is poisonous enough to stop a man's heart if it splashes hisss skin."

Chapter 31

After the library, I went back to the fortress courtyard and the stables, and found Lucien saddling his gold-and-brown hookwing with saddlebags, a camp roll, and other useful gear. He smirked when I pulled Cutthroat out into the open, hauling on her bridle reins. She hissed continuously and shrilly and tried to drag her feet on the ground.

"Why do you keep her?" he asked, watching as I hitched the spitting, stamping hookwing to a post. "They have better mounts here, you know."

"She's good practice," I said, and started back for her gear. "Cutthroat might as well be flying half the time. I always liked temperamental rides."

"Redheads?" he snickered.

"Bikes with too much torque and a lot of snarl," I replied. "I was a motorcycle stunt rider."

"I see. So, what now? Heading for the swamp?"

"That's the plan." When I came closer to Cutthroat, I made sure to do it from the side. She bristled as I approached, but let me equip the saddle blanket, saddle, breastplate, crupper, and bags. The two saddlebags didn't match, but I hardly cared. They raised my inventory capacity from 30 to 80. "How's the real world?"

"Very bad," Lucien replied. "Los Angeles is gone."

"Gone?" I chuckled, not even sure why I was laughing. "What do you mean, 'gone'?"

Lucien wasn't laughing, not even nervously. "They just declared it. The entire civilian population is wiped out. Dead. The only survivors are the ones in Beverley and Golden Point Shards."

"Well, at least we'll still have celebrities, Hollywood producers, and investment bankers to rebuild the world for us," I joked, half-heartedly.

"It's not funny," Lucien replied tersely.

"You seemed to think killing people sounded like a whole lot of fun yesterday." I stashed everything I didn't need to carry on Cutthroat's back, to her great displeasure. "To you, this is just a game. I'm one of those people who were wiped out. You're not."

Lucien regarded me aloofly. "Not yet. But there's talk of the Pacific Alliance calling for a nuclear strike on my Shard."

"Then be glad the backup servers for Archemi are in space."

The other man's eyes narrowed. "You really don't care, do you?"

"I care a lot. I cared about the people on the ground, but they're all dead now." I turned to face him again. "I don't care about the people who started the war. And why should I? They made it into the tower on time."

"The Alliance started the war-"

I snorted and rolled my eyes. "That's propaganda, and you know it."

Lucien flinched as he cleared his throat. "Anyway, my parents worked for the UN right until the end. I was overseas when they called the draft."

Of course you were. "And you came back just in time for Shard intake and exemption, right?" I said, going around Cutthroat. Being careful to avoid her claws, I pushed her hook-arm up and reached for the swinging end of the cinch. "You want to know why I sound like I don't care? I'm exhausted by how much shit I saw out there. All my buddies died. My house smelled like a rotting corpse when I went to go find my brother. *This* is the only world that matters now."

"I see." But he didn't look like he 'saw' much of anything.

I came back around, and was reaching to unhitch Cutthroat from the post when she suddenly twisted her head and clamped her jaws on my arm. Her teeth dug into the leather, and I jerked my arm back reflexively. The glove slipped off, and instead of my arm, her powerful jaws crushed the empty gauntlet.

"Fucking hell, Cutthroat!" I whapped her neck, and she dropped the gauntlet with an indignant squawk. Annoyed, I picked it up, and stood to see Lucien staring at my bare hand - and the Mark of Matir.

"What's that?" he asked. "Some kind of tribal tattoo?"

"Yeah." Quickly, I pulled the gauntlet back on. "Lots of tattoos in Tungaant. Lots of body modification in general."

"Oh... well, that doesn't surprise me. Nomadic plainsmen, and all." Lucien nodded, eyebrows arched, and used the fence to mount his hookwing. "Well, I'm going ahead. Perhaps we'll see each other before the Trials. If not, good luck. You're going to need it, with *that* hookwing."

"Sure. Good luck." I grunted without looking at him. I told myself it was mostly because I was busy trying to stop Cutthroat from disemboweling me while I prepared to get on her back.

Once I was mounted, the big hookwing settled down. When I urged her to a walk, she flicked her tail and started off obediently, but sullenly. We were getting better.

I rode her through the castle grounds and around, heading for the rear gate that was marked on Jasper's map. Six guards were stationed there: two by the door inside, and four outside. One of the interior guards nodded to me and pulled a lever to raise the gate, admitting us out into the wilds beyond the fort.

Like the front of the fort, the back had an area of cleared foliage and cut trees, but the lush forest began barely a hundred feet from the walls. It only grew thicker as we plunged down the narrow trail that led into the wilderness. I'd expected to feel nervous, or even to have flashbacks of the jungle battlefields I'd fought in, but there was only a dizzying, growing sense of freedom as we plunged down the trail. It was only a matter of time before these wild places were colonized by the waves of refugees that were sure to pour into the game soon, but for now, the forest that separated Fort Palewing from the Eyrie was a wild place, dark and green and damp and without another human soul in sight. There were no tattered flags or broken spears... just me and Cutthroat.

"Yah!" I urged Cutthroat to a lope, rising from the saddle as she picked up speed.

The hookwing barked a high, raspy cry and began to sprint down the trail. I grinned, half-standing in the saddle like a jockey. The wind rushed by, and for the first time since I'd arrived in Archemi, I felt *it*: the thing that had made me a rider and a stunter. *The Edge.* The point where you were doing something dangerous, where excitement and fear became indistinguishable and there was nothing but the rush of the wind and the pounding in your temples, and the madness... the mad joy that caused me to shake off one of the stirrups and bring my foot up on the base of Cutthroat's neck.

"Steady... steady..." I measured the rhythm of her gait with my foot, gained my balance, and stood. My spirits lifted. I was surfing her the way I'd surfed my bike a thousand times. It was wobbly at first, but I got the hang of it... all the way to the point where the trail softened, and my hookwing sharply skidded to a halt in front of the mud and sent me flying.

"OH YOU FUC-!" Whatever other colorful names I had for Cutthroat were cut short when my face met the trunk of a tree just off to the side of the path.

That was why they called it the edge. Sometimes, you went over it.

There was no birdsong out here, no other sounds except the croaking of frogs and the wind whispering through cattails as I rolled over, sat up, and waited for my head to clear. Cutthroat snuffled over the mud, uncaring as I got back in the saddle and urged her forward. The ground was getting wetter and muddier, and as we pushed down an even smaller trail, I thought I heard a distant humming sound... like a hornet's hum, if the hornet was the size of a cat.

Cutthroat put her head down and began to slink as we broke out near the edge of the swamp, walking with a quiet predator's step. Beyond the treeline and the wall of reeds that fringed the area, a couple of huge, two-foot long dragonflies flitted and battled one another in the air. I braced my spear, studying their movements. The ⟦Giant Dragonflies⟧ had health meters, but dragonflies weren't normally aggressive insects. No stingers, weak jaws.

Cutthroat weaved her head from side to side, staring fixedly at the dragonflies. I was about to urge her to leap out when a small shape cut through the reeds at the water's edge - a fox. In a split second, the dragonflies stopped fighting each other and turned on the newcomer. The fox had turned and was starting to run when they hit it, ejecting huge, dripping spines from the end of their tails into the animal's back as it tried to hide. The fox yelped piteously as it went rigid and tumbled into the water, dead.

Oh. Okay. Right. So this was basically Australia. Everything here was horribly poisonous and out to kill me.

I made sure I had a tight grip on the saddle, and when the [[Giant Dragonflies]] swooped down to start eating, I kicked Cutthroat in the ribs and urged her into a charge.

The raptorine hookwing darted out, head flattened, her tail held rigidly behind her. The dragonflies noticed us and buzzed upward when her feet splashed into the muck. I slashed with my spear and struck one out of the air. My mount nearly threw me off her back as she sprung up and forward. With a hiss, she took the second one down with her long claws. The one I'd knocked to the water had its wings stuck, but it arched its long abdomen and jabbed at my leg, scraping off the metal greave protecting my skin and ripping through the fabric beneath.

"DIE!" As Cutthroat spun, I plunged my spear down into the dragonfly's underbelly. Its carapace cracked with a satisfying crunch, and the insect thrashed wildly before expiring. My mount, grappling with the other one, tore its head off with her jaws and spat it into the water. She'd been stung once, but hardly seemed to care as she messily devoured the twitching remains of the insect skewered on her claw.

"Gods, that stinks." Wrinkling my nose, I slid out of the saddle and dropped down into the ankle-deep water. It was warm and fetid. I looted the dragonfly for some [[Blue Chitin]] and [[Dragonfly Ichor]] - potion ingredients, most likely - and the body of the unfortunate fox for a [[Raw Pelt]] and [[Fox Meat]]. "Into the Inventory you go."

Once that was put away, I looked around, and was pleased to see that two of my quest objectives were right here. Green algae floated in the stagnant water, and collecting five was as easy as dipping a wide-mouthed flask into the muck. There were crimson lilies here, too, growing in a cluster among the reeds. I picked more than I needed, and watched with satisfaction as the accompanying advanced Knowledge updated in my Glossary.

Behind me, a raven called: a low, throaty rattle, loud enough and close enough that I turned to look.

Everything went black.

It was like the void before character creation. I was breathless, bodiless, yet somehow still present. The world flooded back after a second of nothingness. I was on my knees, about to stand up when everything blanked again.

What the fuck is going on?! The darkness lasted longer this time. When virtual reality returned, I was flat on my back, lying on top of the glassy surface of the water. Cutthroat was sitting in the muck, resting on her tail, staring vacantly through me. The swamp was utterly silent.

My skin crawled as I sat up. The surface tension suddenly gave way, and I yelped as it dumped me into the water. It splashed normally as I pulled myself back out. I could feel the skin of my arms when I rubbed them, and breathe in the earthy aroma of the marsh. "Cutthroat!"

At her name, the light returned to the hookwing's eyes. She shook her head, as if dazed, and wandered over to me. She ducked her head and pressed it against my hand, and that scared me as much as her blank stare had. It was completely out of character for her to seek affection.

Suddenly, the sounds of the environment returned. Croaking frogs, rustling reeds, the slosh and gurgle of water lapping on mud. Heart hammering, I turned, searching for anything out of place. Then I went into my HUD again. It was possible I'd triggered some kind of glitch by sorting my Inventory, but everything in there looked normal. I checked my stats, character sheet, message center. No creepy messages. No messages at all, actually.

Chewing my lip, I lay a hand on my hookwing's black feathered neck, wary of her personality flipping back to being aggressive and bitey, and fired off a quick report to the Devs about what had happened. Then, with the unpleasant sensation of eyes lingering on the back of my neck, I resumed my search for plants.

It might have been my imagination, but the swamp sounded subtly different than it had before. Cutthroat followed me, but as the minutes passed, her normal personality resumed itself. She snapped irritably at flies and at my hand when I went to stow [[Cattails x 10]] and [[Kudzu Fiber x 20]] for eating and making baskets. I quickly found the blackweed, sunwort and widowberries for Jasper - widowberries, a kind of nightshade plant with poisonous fruit, were everywhere around here. As I was gathering some spare berries into a sack for Alchemical experimentation, I got a PM from Baldr. He was still in my party, though we were out of range for any EXP sharing or bonuses. All it said was: "WTF?"

"I know, right?" I replied, sloshing through the muck. We were deep in the marshes now, and I was in one of the highlighted areas supposed to contain king's sorrow, the virulently poisonous plant we needed for the Trial. "You felt that too?"

"I blacked out. Well, the world blacked out. Just woke up. What time is it?"

Only *just* woke up? I checked my HUD. 'Just going on eleven hundred hours, local time."

"Shit. I was out for an hour." Then it hadn't just been me - but the event might have affected us all differently. "Some kind of fuckup on the outside, maybe? Do you feel okay?"

"Maybe. And yeah, I think I'm fine." But Baldr seemed vague and out of sorts.

"I logged a report with the Devs," I messaged, pushing aside a waving forest of cattails. Then I froze. "And I... I'm going to have to get back to you."

"What? Everything alright?"

Behind the curtain of reeds was an open space of shallow, brackish water. A small stone hexagon pillar rose from the middle of the pond, pitted and cracked with age. Matir leaned against it, arms folded, his cloak thrown back. The avatar of the Black God looked taller and thinner than I recalled.

"I hope so. BRB." I closed the chat with Baldr, and waded forward to greet him.

Chapter 32

"Hello, Hector." Matir was toying with a very dark red stem of leaves and berries in his long hands. I recognized the spindly branches and the soft blood-red fruit immediately. It was a stem of king's sorrow.

"Wasn't expecting to see you until Myszno," I said cautiously.

"Nor was I," he replied. His voice was light, crisp, but there was no trace of dark humor this time around. "But you are my Herald, and so I come to you with grievous news... and a warning."

"News?" I let go of Cutthroat, curious to see what she'd do. The big dinosaur hissed through her teeth, and hung back near the reeds. I advanced a couple of steps.

"The Architects have fallen silent," he said.

It took me a second to realize what he was talking about. The Devs. "The blackout? You know what happened?"

"It rippled through all Creation." The point of light in the void that passed for Matir's face spun like a small galaxy. "And the Architects have always whispered in the ears of the Gods, until now."

There could only be one reason why the Devs and Temperance had gone silent. I rubbed my face, rubbed my eyes, heedless of the dirt, my imagination consumed by the image of the Pacific Alliance raining nuclear fire down on Aurora Shard and the other Shards on the West

Coast. But that couldn't be right. We had missile defense systems, we had...

A population wiped out by disease, and no one to man the stations. Battleships empty of soldiers. Our cities were now a graveyard for hundreds of millions of people. And above them all, a desperate elite on both sides of the war who preferred false victory to a real defeat.

Fuck.

"They nuked us," I said, hollowly. "They fucking nuked us. The game reset. We blacked out... because it had to reboot. From the orbital servers."

Matir watched me in grim silence.

"They fucking nuked us." I couldn't believe it, but at the same time, I couldn't believe anything else.

While Matir waited, I tried PMing Lucien. He was online, but the message bounced. The asshole had me blocked. I swallowed, steeled myself, and looked up at Matir.

"What does that mean for us?" I said. "Players? The Starborn?"

"There are some two thousand of you here already," Matir replied. "And I assume no more will arrive. That is where my warning comes in. A great evil lairs within these ruins, Hector. I suspected you would come here, given your association with the White Witch, Rutha, and so I waited... because you would have seen the trap laid here, and reported it to the Architects. Now the Architects cannot be reached, save for those few who have incarnated here as Starborn," he twirled the deadly flower, "and they are now as powerless to remove evil from this world as all other mortals."

Two thousand? How long have I been in here? There were only a couple hundred when I arrived, and that was... what? Three days ago? Four? And it seemed Matir had some awareness of the nature of his reality after all. "I don't know how I feel about the God of Actual Fucking Darkness talking about 'removing evil' from the world."

Matir dropped his chin down, and the darkness of his face shimmered and danced. "When a babe is born, it screams in pain and terror as it emerges from the darkness into the light. Yet this passage marks the first moment that the child is truly human. Darkness is not the same as Nothing, Hector. As you know very well."

Memories of a dark jungle at night, the smell of blasted earth and atomized rubble and burning trees, the sounds of rifles rattling and men screaming... they flooded back, and with it came the old combat surge: the pounding temples, the tunnel vision, the sudden reptilian focus. I fisted my hands. "Then why don't you do something? Why are you trying to manipulate me into doing this shit for you?"

"Because I am still imprisoned. My power, and that of my brothers and sisters, is used to maintain the Caul of Souls," he said simply.

I blinked a few times. "Well, fuck. Why?"

"That is a long story," Matir replied. "The important fact is that my prison has weakened enough that I awoke and discovered that I could project my image and voice to a chosen few."

"Why just you? What about the other Gods?"

"Solnetsi and Khors also stir," Matir said. "But I am the first target for those who seek to bring ruin to this world. There are... cultists... who expect that I am some Dark Lord who will lead them into the transcendental apocalypse they desire. Needless to say, their expectations are exaggerated, but the fact remains that those who sabotage the Dragon Gates, the portals which sustain the Caul, have focused their efforts on liberating me. And there lies a story, one which I must tell you now that the Architects have fallen silent."

"I'm all ears."

Matir straightened, and stepped away from the pillar. Shadows seemed to cling to him, trailing in his wake.

"Once, an Architect fell to Archemi. His name was Ororgael. Like you, his spirit did not incarnate correctly. Unlike you, he was not rescued from purgatory by one of The Nine, nor by any of the Young Gods of humankind... he was rescued by the Drachan."

My eyes widened. "The Void Dragons? The ones that invaded Archemi-"

"Some five thousand years ago, yes." Matir finished. "Meshtaroth, the most powerful of the Drachan, is contained by the Caul of Souls, but he does not sleep. He is practically a god unto himself, and he saw in Ororgael the potential for an avatar. He was a bitter, brilliant, twisted being... a true Architect, but a loathsome one. He hated his own kind. He hated other Starborn, and the fact that he had to share what he saw as *his* world with them. He found a position of power here, in Ilia, and became a master of time and space... abilities he abused to shape the world to his liking. He found a way to exclude Starborn from being incarnated, and with that, the other Architects were forced to intervene."

I frowned. This sounded like the 'crazy Dev' that Lucien had told me about.

"They pulled him out of Archemi like a tumor," Matir continued, passing the stem of king's sorrow from hand to hand. "They even attempted to rewrite history to erase him. But cancer has a way of hanging onto the body, doesn't it?"

"You're saying he's still here?"

Matir shook his head. "That, I do not know. But I think it is no accident that my Herald is here, in Ilia - the very seat of Ororgael's power. I do not think it an accident that you consorted with Rutha of Vasteau, the White Witch... Ororgael's finest apprentice, and his lover."

The revelation hit me like a hammer to the gut. "Rutha? Rutha was-?"

"Aye," Matir agreed.

I held up the Spear. "But she gave me this. She told me I had to restore the Gates with it."

"Gates that would have remained stable, had her master not interfered with them." If Matir had a mouth, the words would have been accompanied by a wry smile. "But take heart, my Herald. She currently acts in innocence. As I told you, the Architects rewrote history to erase her master... and I doubt she even properly remembers him or his agenda. Perhaps this is something he anticipated... something he prepared for."

"Does that mean Rutha is in danger? Could he could still execute his plans if he was deleted?"

"Anything is possible."

"Then Rutha giving me this spear, this quest... was it like a... what's the word?" I struggled for a moment. "A contingency? Ororgael's contingency?"

The god bowed his head.

Puzzled, I called up the 'Restore the Spear of Nine Spheres' quest, and had the HUD read it to me aloud

New Quest: Restore the Spear of Nine Spheres
The Spear of Nine Spheres, an ancient Aesari relic, was used to create the Caul of Souls - the great magical seal that protects all of Archemi from the Drachan. The Court Sorceress of Ilia, Rutha, believes you can become a hero worthy of wilding the spear and revitilizing the Caul.
Reward: ??? (Varies)
Difficulty: Epic

Special: This is a unique quest.
Special: This quest relates to a world event.
Special: This is an evolving quest. Updates will appear in your log.

Now that I thought about it, this was a weirdly advanced, epic quest for a random noob like me to receive. I hadn't imagined the misspellings, either. It was just believable enough to really stroke your ego, but vague enough that it could lead to anything. "This quest is some kind of a trap. It has to be. It's not part of the game... or, it uses like... end-game content, repurposed. But why?"

"I can only guess," Matir replied. "The Architects are terrifying, Hector. Not even a god can fathom their designs and motives. They created my reality as surely as they created yours."

He extended the poisonous branch to me. Numbly, I bought out the leather sack I'd gotten specially for carrying this plant. I turned it inside out, wearing it like a mitt, carefully took the king's sorrow, and then folded the sack over it.

"I'll go back to Liren and dig into it when I can," I said, filing all the information away. "If it's true... if the Devs – the Architects – are dead, then we're on our own here. Bugs and all. The last thing we need is some crazy admin fucking it up from the inside."

"Indeed, my Herald." Matir returned to the hexagonal pillar, wisps of his robe winding around it. "This quest is a burden that requires one willing to dig in the dark."

"Someone like me?" I added the herb to my Inventory. It left a bitter smell in the air. "Why did you choose me, anyway?"

Matir spread his long hands, stained red with berry sap. "Among other things, I am known as the Lord of the Hidden Seed. It is my nature to notice that which has unmanifested potential and bring it into being."

"You could have asked me."

"You would have refused." The dark wryness returned to Matir's voice. "Because you have always chosen to avoid the suffering that accompanies true growth."

I blinked, mouth open to retort, but in the moment between when my eyes closed and opened, Matir had vanished.

"Jerk." I crouched down, and rinsed my hands off nervously in the water. As I did, I saw a shadow nodding across the surface of the marsh. When I went around the pillar, I found the remains of the wiry king's sorrow plant, along with a cluster of eerie, near-translucent flowers with silvery stems. Ghostbell. I reached for it mechanically.

Quest Partially Complete: Ink, Glorious Ink
Return to Jasper with the plants required for making ink.

I stared at the quest notification for a couple of minutes, listening to the distant drone of dragonflies and other low-level creatures, and it finally hit me that this was it. This was my life now. There was no way to know how long it would last, how many days had passed outside of the game, or whether everything would just turn black and disappear. The Spear felt like it weighed a hundred pounds in my hand. Whatever I'd stumbled into, I couldn't do it alone. I needed help... I needed a party. Allies. And I needed a dragon.

Chapter 33

Me and Cutthroat rode back to the fort to find it bustling. If any of the NPCs knew anything had happened, they weren't showing it. I delivered Jasper's plants, and he gave me the other skill tomes I needed: The Jump skill, basic smithing, intermediate sewing and armor repair, and cooking. I knew the basics of campfire cooking out of game, but there weren't any MREs or ramen noodles here, and I wanted to make sure the things I made gave me buffs or enhanced health regen.

I had to take a couple of deep breaths before I found a place near the gate and brought up my Advanced Path menu.

All the areas that were grayed out were now in color. The first thing I got was a pop-up:

[[Congratulations! Now that you are Level 5, you can select your first Advanced Path!]]

[[You have unlocked a Secret Path: Dark Lancer]]

[[You have unlocked new Combat Skills: Herald of the Hidden Seed]]

My eyes widened. As the Mark of Matir tingled and itched, I navigated to the Path description and read.

Dark Lancer

Wielders of the almost limitless power of Darkness, Dark Lancers are warriors who channel the power of shadow into strong energy-draining attacks and dizzying evasive maneuvers. Naturally resilient to magic, poisons, and diseases, they can clear even the most chaotic battlefields with ease.

"Huh." Being resistant to disease sounded good. Too good. In fact, the class sounded like it had been tailor-made for my particular set of circumstances. *Hmm.*

I opened the Paths menu and had a look at the skill trees.

Jump still formed the basis of the class, but all of the other skills were different from the typical Lancer. For one thing, they punched a lot harder – *a lot* harder. Damage was up, but the skills consumed large quantities of Adrenaline Points per activation:

Jump I

You spring into the air, making a powerful attack on landing.

Required AP: 8

Damage: 300%

Flow combinations possible

10ft vertical Jump. Leaves you vulnerable to being knocked from the air

Inflicts Stun debuff (15s)

Jump distance can be improved with the Acrobatics Skill

Shadow Dance I

Become immaterial and evade attacks with supernatural speed while draining health.

Cost: 25 AP

Cooldown: 3 sec

Invincible during Dash. Effect nullified during cooldown

Dictum I

Push your opponents forward with a powerful whirling strike, draining their health and energy.

Required Level: Dark Lancer 1

Required AP: 10

Damage: 200% x 2

Max 6 targets

Pushes enemy forward

2% of max HP recovered on every good hit

2% of max AP recovered on every good hit

Mantle of Night

Boost Movement Speed and Special Attack Power 20%

Drains 5 AP every 3 sec

Whirlwind Butcher I

Dash toward enemies and cut them down with the power of shadow.

Required AP: 20

Cooldown: 5 sec

Push Damage: 150% x 2

Extra Hit Damage: 150% x 3

Max 6 Targets

AP recovery +10 on every good hit

Invincible while moving

Knocks targets into the air

Knocks targets down

Extra Hit activated on good hits

Blood Sprint I

Cooldown: 3 sec

Forward push damage: 125% x 2

Extra damage: 125% x 2

Max 3 Targets

Attack speed: +10 for 5 sec

+30 Bleeding Damage every 2 sec for 10 sec

Stun on good hits

Chain: Blood Storm 1

After using Blood Sprint

Damage: 220% x 2

Max 5 targets

Stun on good hits

+ 10 HP recovered on good hits

Mark created on target after Master of Blades is learned

As the individual skill trees grew, so did the damage and effects. In my head, I put together the available skills in chains and combos, and realized I was actually intrigued. The attacks were fairly basic at Tier I, but from Level 20 onwards, things got really interesting. Everything was acrobatic AoE, focused on evasion instead of defense. The last tier of the Blood Strike to Blood Storm chain boosted damage up to an impressive 650% per hit, with a base +100% critical hit rate, improved accuracy and movement speed on top of a +50 HP regen, and you could hit up to 6 targets at once. There were ranged, explosive energy attacks that could be useful from dragon back later on, too. Long cooldowns and

AP gluttony wouldn't be a problem, as long as I had lots of combos to cycle through, and kept a good supply of Adrenaline pots...

I had a look at the Mark of Matir information next:

Herald of the Hidden Seed

As the chosen avatar of Matir, the primordial elemental god of Darkness, you can gain the use of certain powers within the domains of Shadow, Knowledge, Life, and Death. You may pick one Herald power per 4 levels. New powers will become available at level 12.

Life for Life

Channel a blast of damaging dark energy into your enemy and drain their lifeforce to replenish your own.

Damage: 128% + 50% max HP regen

Double damage on surprise attack or backstab

Cost: 5AP per second

Touch Attack 1 Target

Stuns Target

Inflicts Corruption debuff 15m (Player and Target)

Special: Using this ability on Undead negates HP regen and causes HP damage instead

Close the Wound

You draw on your own raw lifeforce to heal another's injuries.

Heal other player/NPC 50 HP per sec while ability is active

Cost: -30HP and -10AP per sec

Suppurate

You channel dark power into a person's wounds, destroying the body's ability to heal and causing their injuries to fester.

Cost: 20 AP + 10 HP

Damage: 120% + 5% max HP per hour until enemy receives treatment for infection

1% chance to cause Blood Poisoning per 5 Levels

Inflicts Corruption debuff 15m (Target)

Blessing of the Raven I

You call on your power and gain increased insight into knowledge and skills

+10% Skill EXP for 45 min.

30 Min cooldown

Tempting. But tempting mortals was what Darkness did, didn't it? I had a feeling that if I took this class or these new and admittedly awesome abilities, I was somehow signing my soul away to Matir. I flexed my branded hand, flipping to the normal Lancer path, then back to Dark Lancer. Old stories about signing contracts with the Devil whispered in my ear as I brought up the confirm box and accepted my first level of Dark Lancer.

A bubbling violet nimbus surrounded me, and I sucked in a deep breath as a flood of knowledge and context flashed through my mind. With it came a mix of feelings – relief that the game was still working despite some cataclysm happening on the outside. Fear, because the information was alien, but only for a minute... then it naturalized in my body, as if I'd always known how to properly handle a spear... and push energy through it. Experimentally, I focused that energy on the haft of the Spear of Nine Spheres.

The air around me darkened slightly as the Mark of Matir surged. I felt the tug of energy that began low in my gut, rippling up through my body and then along my weapon. Ebon flames briefly flickered over the bluesteel blade, then vanished. It didn't feel bad. To the contrary. I felt... stronger. Fiercer. I felt the way I felt on the stunt track, when the bike I was riding did exactly what I made it do, no matter how improbable the maneuver seemed. I had *command.*

I got Jump by default thanks to Jasper's quest, so I didn't have to spend anything on that. I had enough points to select four skills, and after reviewing them and matching up the various potential combos, I took Shadow Dance, Whirlwind Butcher, Blood Sprint, and Blood Storm. Dictum and Whirlwind Butcher were nearly matched for damage, but extra AP meant more special attacks, which meant more damage in the long run. 2% regen on a hit was so-so, and the maneuver didn't have as much mobility as Butcher. I was better off healing with pots.

Of the Herald skills, I decided fairly quickly on the first and last: *Life for Life* and *Blessing of the Raven.* Healing others would be good, but there were items that could do that – items I could craft if I was better at Alchemy, which Blessing of the Raven would facilitate. I was pretty sure it was stackable, and a 10% EXP buff that stacked with other items was going to be awesome at all levels. In the games I'd played, you could usually craft profession outfits that gave you a 5-10% bonus on certain skills, plus consumable life skill buffs. Plus 30% skill experience to crafting? Yeah. Hell yeah.

I gathered my wits and closed the window. I was preparing to walk back to Cutthroat's hitching post when a great winged shadow passed overhead, kicking up gravel and dirt and making the awnings and flags flap. I shaded my eyes, ribs vibrating with the power in Talenth's wings as he turned on a wingtip and landed in a cloud of dust. The huge dragon made his descent look effortless, even if he couldn't disguise the booming rumble of his weight settling on the ground.

Skyr Arnaud vaulted down, and to my surprise, Sergeant Blackwin followed. They both looked mildly surprised to see me.

"Why aren't you out foraging, Tuun?" the knight-commander demanded.

"I went on a recon pass, came back to prepare properly, and am about to go out again, sir." I saluted the way he'd told us to, right fist over left breast, and stood to attention. "Did a short quest for the librarian to gain some necessary skills before the Trials."

"Hmm. A more tactical approach than what I expected of you," he said.

I remained at attention, looking through him. "We barbarians love tactics, sir."

His eyes narrowed.

"The Tuun make for good soldiers," Blackwin spoke up, and winked at me from behind Arnaud's shoulder. "We fought alongside them in Bulang Kettu. Tough as nails and as fearless as the cold iron they're made of."

"Though surely lacking the discipline and stature of our knights," Arnaud added crisply. "Which reminds me. I needed to talk to you about your assessment and the exercise at Camp Prichard."

"My assessment?" I asked.

"Yes," he replied. "Come, I will walk you to the gate. Alone, if you please, Maesuire Blackwin."

"Yes, sir." Even *she* sounded confused.

Arnaud jerked his head, and I followed, leading Cutthroat by her nose on the other side.

"You have been judged worthy of taking the Trial by the council of assessors," the commander said, once we were out of earshot. "But I have some lingering concerns. First, your fighting style is unorthodox. Second, Baldr Hyland mentioned that you went to fraternize with the locals at Camp Prichard. Why?"

I wasn't sure what I thought of Baldr tattling on me to the K.C. Nothing good. "I didn't know going to the general store counted as fraternizing, sir. I went to buy supplies for alchemy and potion making."

Skyr Arnaud nodded. "And what did he say? The shopkeeper?"

I sensed a trap in his words. "He was grumpy... he didn't want much to do with me."

"And why was that?"

"Because I'm foreign," I lied.

"Hmm." Arnaud's fine brows creased. "Ethan – the merchant – fought in the Civil War on the wrong side. He was imprisoned, reformed, and then released back to Camp Prichard after he confessed valuable information. There are still Royalists everywhere. You know that the Skyrdon used to be the Crown's elite force, don't you?"

"I suspected, sir," I replied. "Because the Skyrdon would have served their country regardless of the individuals ruling it, and if a monarchy was in power, they'd have served the King or Queen then as loyally as they serve the Warden now."

"Indeed," he said. "We were a decisive force in the revolution. Did Ethan voice anything suspicious?"

Other than his abiding hatred for the new regime that had tortured him? "No, sir. But I don't know enough about the Revolution to really be able to look for particulars. There may be cultural terms I missed..."

"The Revolution was instigated by the mage who advised - or one might say, wrangled, the last King of Ilia, Rovsin Illandi the Fifth."

"Okay." We were within sight of the gate now.

"Rovsin was insane," the commander said sternly. "Consumed by strange crazes, convinced he could predict the future, prone to fits of delirium and lethargy. His heir, Johannen, was not much better. He made decisions which turned the populace against him, and then decisions that turned the nobility against his family. His own court wizard denounced him and secretly gathered a force for the coup, which was successful. Johannen managed to escape - though we do not know if he managed to get far, or whether or not he is now dead. Pritchard is still a hotbed of hidden Royalist sympathy, which is why we do our exercises there, and at other towns that survived the war. Nothing to quash thoughts of rebellion like boots on the ground and dragons in the sky."

The thought of the dragons being used to oppress people like Owen and Kira made me distinctly uncomfortable. They were the nuclear missiles of this world's military... weapons so powerful that they instilled compliance through their very existence. I thought of Talenth and the others laying waste to a village, the people dying of burns or turning into monsters, and my thoughts drifted naturally to the sights I had seen during wartime in the real world.

"If you remember anything, report to me," the knight-commander said, as we neared the gate. "Preferably before the Trial. I suspect the Mata Argis will want to talk to you as well."

I decided to keep on playing dumb. I glanced at my quest timer. It was close to three p.m. "The who?"

"The Mata Argis are the eyes and ears of the Council." Skyr Arnaud watched with some amusement as I tried to mount Cutthroat. I got my foot in the stirrup, but as I moved to pull myself up, she stepped to the side and forced me to hop after her. "Hunters of heretics and investigators of treason."

Secret police, in other words. Skyr Tymos hadn't been exaggerating. "Ah."

"Yes, 'ah'." He inclined his head slightly to the guards as they saluted. "But that may not be of concern for you much longer."

"Thank you, sir." I finally managed to get onto my hookwing as she pranced and fluttered, and pulled her head up into a short rein. "Before I leave, may I ask you something?"

The knight-commander regarded me peevishly. "If you must."

"Did you notice anything weird about an hour ago?" I asked. "Like... a brief blackout? Loss of time?"

His brow furrowed. "No. Why?"

"Then it must have been when I picked the king's sorrow." I grinned sheepishly.

"I doubt it. If you touched that plant with your bare hands, I doubt we'd ever see you at the Eyrie again." He sounded almost regretful.

"Thank you, sir." I saluted again, and watched from the saddle as Skyr Arnaud swept his gold-trimmed cloak and stalked back down the path to where his dragon waited.

Chapter 34

The monsters of Archemi had been underwhelming so far, except for the barghests at Camp Prichard. They'd really been nerfed, and most of the creatures I found in the swamp – the dragonflies, bugs, foxes, even frogs - were nothing but target practice for my new Dark Lancer skills.

I Blood Sprinted and Whirlwind Butchered my way through the mobs like a scythe through wheat. A violet-and-black fire scythe. In some ways, it was just as well that the mobs were easy, because it wasn't just enough to take the combat abilities and the Path. The knowledge and basic body memory had been drilled into my head, but putting the Dark Lancer moves into practice, tactically, was a whole other ballgame. I drew out fights with the weak but extremely nimble dragonflies, letting my adrenaline points build. Then I practiced Jump and Shadow Dance to dodge and flank as well as attack. Jump let me spring into the air; Shadow Dance practically teleported me along the ground in any direction, and my first few tries using it were hopelessly disorientating. It was an extremely useful skill, though: the fraction of energy it took to scoot around was easily made up by smashing my spear into an enemy's back. It was fast, it was brutal, it was flashy, and I loved every minute of it.

There was only one problem.

I was a Dark Lancer, and I'd probably screwed the pooch where the Skyrdon were concerned. There was a very good chance these Mata Argis people would throw me in the brig as some kind of heretic... but that was a problem for another day.

A couple of hours of killing bugs later, the sun was sinking toward the horizon, and Cutthroat and I retraced our steps to the hexagonal pillar where I'd spoken to Matir. Not far from there, we found our first Aesari ruin - a crooked stone archway, half-sunk into the bog, but otherwise surprisingly intact. As we pressed on, more half-sunken stone emerged from the shadows. There were broken walls, columns, and spires, all of them elegant and coldly beautiful under layers of moss and hanging vines.

There was a large, round, empty patch on my map surrounded by tiny debris marks flagging the remains of buildings. We traveled along what might have once been a busy city road. Most of the structures had sunk so far down that only cornices remained. I had a quest location marker up, and it highlighted the remains of an enormous, round, white stone hall.

Wide-eyed, I reined Cutthroat some distance away and looked it over. This building would have soared up hundreds of feet if it hadn't sunk. Only the very top of it was visible, the rest submerged into the bowels of the earth. The swooping arches and upper level of the temple - I was pretty sure it was a temple - jutted through the knee-high mist that had risen from the swamp as night fell. The top doorjamb of the main entry to the building was visible, half buried in the muck. The doors were sealed. I would have to find another way in.

I dropped from Cutthroat's back, landing in the stinking water. It was warm and thick from all the decaying organic matter in the swamp. The splash had barely passed when a bird launched itself from the roof into the air, startled by the noise. A big bird... and a named enemy. It was an eagle. A ⟦Crowned Eagle⟧!

Excited, I slogged as quickly as I could to the edge of the building. I began to search around it, looking for a way up. It was too high for a normal jump in most areas, but I could jump higher than the average noob. When I found the lowest part of the roof, I tensed my body and bunched my legs, resisted the urge to wiggle my butt like a cat, and sprung lightly up into the air like I'd been slingshot. My adrenaline points burned down as I Jumped to my maximum height limit and landed on the slippery roof like a ninja. There wasn't a single damn knight who could have pulled *that* off.

Feeling pleased with myself, I advanced carefully over the slimy tiles, half-crawling my way over toward the spot the eagle had startled up from. As I reached the apex of the roof, I saw a ragged hole, a place where the tiles had been smashed and the underlying timbers had rotted away inside of the stone shell. More surprising was the light I saw burning inside the building. A glowing sphere hovered over an altar of some kind. The familiar smell of ozone hit my nose a moment later, soon followed by a flashing blue warning. *Magic.*

Slowly, I worked my way around the hole toward the nest. It was big, and occupied. A Crowned Eagle waited there, the second of the mated pair. That meant it was sitting on eggs, and it didn't look pleased to see me.

"Here, chicky chicky," I crooned, sidling over the tiles. One of them slipped under my boot, but I kept my balance.

The eagle flared her - or his - crest feathers. "Crowned Eagle" was an apt name for this bird, a beautiful brown and gold-flecked creature with brilliant gem-like eyes. It probably weighed at least twenty pounds and a wingspan of ten feet or more, and as I got closer, I saw it had a health bar with a red skull. It was just an ordinary beast, not a monster, but...

I wedged my feet against some of the more stable tiles and greenery, and turned my spear around so that the blade was pointing away from the bird. I didn't want to hurt it if I didn't have to. Experimentally, I jabbed the butt of my weapon at it.

I didn't even get in one poke before the first eagle struck, falling out of the sky like a sledgehammer. It raked me across the head with its claws - an incredibly powerful blow that threw me onto my back. I slid across the roof, trying to break my momentum as my vision blurred with messages.

[[Crowned Eagle King lands a critical hit! 56 damage!]]

[[You are stunned!]]

[[You are bleeding!]]

"Oh you ass-blowing piece of-!" I had barely gotten over the hit when it dove again: this time, with a piercing shriek. Claws raked me again, taking another 50-ish damage off my HP, and was followed up by a blow from the second eagle. Mama had joined the fight. Three hits took me down to below half HP. Something was wrong.

"What the fuck?" I dodged claws and beaks, trying to get a bead on them. Now that I was in combat, I could see the monster's levels. Both eagles were Level 20.

Wait. What? There *were* no Level 20 mobs in Archemi!

Cursing, I spun my spear around and swung it like a baseball bat in desperation. The weighty haft knocked one of the huge eagles out of the air, sending it spinning away with a squawk. I found a fighting stance just in time to block another set of vicious talons with my spear. The bird was so strong that he nearly pulled it from my hands.

These weren't like the barghests. There was no way to cross the level imbalance, not with creatures nearly three times my level. I was just getting ready to run when the eagle closest to me screamed, a sound that drilled behind my eyes and wiped my vision.

[[Crowned Eagle uses Fury Scream! You are blind!]]

"Can you not!?" I wasn't sure if I was chewing out the HUD or the psycho bird that was bashing into my head and face. I instinctively blocked the next slash as its wings beat around my head. I triggered Blood Sprint and hit, sending dark fire splashing over the eagle's feathers. It squalled, knocked back, and screeched as I followed up with the Blood Storm combo. Its health ring didn't budge. I Shadow Stepped away from the next aerial strike, shooting past the bird as it dived... and then I realized something. They were both focused on me. Fighting these things was for suckers.

"Thanks!" Before either of them could react, I turned back and sprinted for the nest.

The eagles shrilled as I dove for the untidy mess of twigs and bones. There were three spotted brown eggs in there, each one the size of my clenched fist. I only needed one. I ducked and rolled under the sharp talons of the enraged parent bird, and victoriously clamped a hand on the nearest egg.

[[Quest Updated! The Trial of Marantha. 2/4 Ingredients Obtained!]]

I irritably brushed the HUD closed, and in the moment of distraction, one of the eagles bodily tackled me from behind and knocked me face-first into the roof. My face slammed onto tile, and pain - and blood - blossomed as my nose burst like an overripe berry. Bleeding everywhere, I scrambled up and away with the egg clutched to my chest, dodging and weaving away from the swooping eagles to the edge of the roof. I was just about to reach it when I took two blows to the head and shoulders, one after the other. They were only glancing blows, but they pushed my already-unsteady ass forward. Before I knew what was happening, I'd slipped. With the spear in one hand and the egg in the other, I fell down the hole and right on top of the glowing orb of light.

I crashed onto the altar on my back – there went another 20 HP - and as soon as I touched the orb, a tall cage sprung up from the floor around the altar and a piercing alarm screamed to life around me. It drowned out my moans as I picked myself up, clutching my back with one hand and the egg to my chest with the other.

"Okay! I suck! I get it!" I shouted aloud in frustration, trying to get my bearings. My eyes were running, my nose was spouting blood, and I was fairly sure I'd broken my spine if the pain was anything to go by. "For fuck's sake, stop already!"

To my surprise, it did. The orb sunk toward the floor and disappeared - but the cage remained. It was high - about twelve feet tall - but if I Jumped from the altar I could make it.

I was just getting my bearings to make the leap when a loud 'clunk' reverberated through the ruin. An entire section of the floor broke away and tipped down, revealing nothing but yawning black space.

"You have to be fucking kidding MEEEEEE!" I scrabbled with my heels, trying to leap for the edge, but to no avail. The trap spun all the way over, and I slid and then tumbled helplessly into the abyss.

Chapter 35

The wind tore at me as I plummeted down with extreme realism, spinning head over ass in an uncontrollable, fatal dive. I fell past ledges and bridges, howling cave mouths, and then joined a thin waterfall that tumbled down into a hole that seemingly went forever. I spammed health items, but it was the water that shocked me out of panic. Waterfall meant water. *Water landing? Water landing!*

I managed to straighten out in the loose cascade of water. It wasn't enough to break my fall, but it was enough to guide me in the darkness as I unexpectedly dived into a huge cavern, headfirst, and crashed into the shallow, icy underground lake.

⟦You have taken 144 points of impact damage! HP 70/320.⟧

My heath drained to less than one-fourth of my HP as I came up in agony, gasping for air. For several minutes, I flopped around as my vision pulsed and throbbed, also very realistically, and then flailed for the nearest patch of land. I was almost within reach when something wound around my ankle and tried to haul me back under the surface.

I was lucky to get one gasp of air before vanishing under the water a second time. I squirmed in the grip of the monster trapping me, trying to make out what it was even as I thrust my spear blindly. It was so dark I couldn't see much: a gaping maw about to engulf my leg; a tongue that lashed; blood spreading through the water as I sunk the point of the blade into flesh and twisted it. The shock of pain made the huge creature pull back and dart away, inhumanly fast. Even though I couldn't see it clearly, the HUD identified the creature for me: a ⟦Stranged Giant Frog⟧.

'Giant' was correct. On land, frogs were ridiculous croaking sacks of air. In water, they were slippery, fast, and terrifying. The ones in this underground lake were big enough to swallow me whole, and now that blood had been spilled, dozens of them were heading for me, their life meters gleaming in the darkness. Each mob ranged in size and level, from five to seven.

I burbled whatever swearwords came to mind as I powered through the water back toward the shore. My Adrenaline Points surged as I reached the rocks, kicking a slimy shadow as it rammed into me. My boot hit a rubbery snout, and I pulled myself onto land belly-first, like a seal. Not graceful - not with armor weighing me down - but effective.

"Fuck this goat-sucking bullshit piece of crap-!" Drenched, my HP throbbing down in the red, I turned to face the pool with my spear leveled, but the frogs in the water weren't interested in following me out.

"Yeah! Stay there!" I made a rude gesture at them, still catching my breath. I was about to straighten up when a thunderous croak rumbled the air of the cavern, and I realized why the frogs were so willing to let me go.

Slowly, I turned. A bus-sized figure squatted in the shadows. Black slime covered a tank covered with rough green skin. Glowing crimson eyes with hourglass-shaped pupils gleamed in the light cast by the luminescent fungi on the walls. Each one of the creature's eyes was larger than my head. But worst of all were the tentacles. Four barbed, black tentacles writhed behind and above the ⟦Behemoth Aberration⟧'s warty back, hanging over its head like scorpion tails.

It was Level 12. I was level 5 and at 21% HP, so I did what any experienced fighter would do.

I ran like a little bitch.

"Nope nope nope! That's a *nope*!" The tentacles smashed down on the ground behind me. Pure instinct forced me to roll and dive just as a spew of slime streaked through the air just where I'd been. "Noooope!"

I dashed for the first cave entry I could find in the gloom, diving forward as the mutant frog's barbed, acid-coated tongue smashed into the wall beside the open door and sent chips of rock and moss flying. I scrambled in and down, running, skidding, and sliding over the rough ground as the beast hopped after me. It wasn't particularly fast, but its legs could propel it in a leap that closed the gap between us and shook the ground when it landed, nearly throwing me off my feet.

"Death by giant hentai frog is NOT my kink, okay!?" I shouted at no one in particular as the beast squeezed itself into the cave mouth after me, its flexible, squishy body sliding through the narrow space behind me.

The tunnel narrowed. I folded my spear into my Inventory and kept running, but that second of slowing down put me within AoE range. A tentacle lashed out, and the tip sliced across my calf, sending me stumbling. The green Poison status alert flared to life.

[[You have taken 5 Slashing damage!]]

[[You are poisoned!]]

Cursing and limp-running through the dark caves, I followed the blasts of cold, stale air coming from deep within the ruins. At any point, I *knew* I'd run into a dead end, and then I was going to get the full virtual reality immersion experience of being eaten alive by Frogger. Panting, I rounded a corner and found myself facing a wall of black... but a wall of space, not of stone.

My salvation was a hole about four feet tall and barely a foot wide. It looked out over an ancient hall that was dimly lit by rows and rows of flickering, tired-looking mage lights. It was cavernous, hundreds of feet long, with marching rows of moss-covered columns receding into the darkness.

Frantic, I squeezed myself through the gap, sending chunks of stone tumbling to the floor below. The limestone was soft, weakened by thousands of years of erosion and damp air. Once I was outside and able to find my footing on the rough surface of the wall, I threw myself from the precipice into a forward roll. It was a move I'd practiced over and over again during martial arts training, but not from a height like this... but it was surprisingly effective and carried me through to my feet so fast that I nearly fell onto my knees.

The Aberration was apparently hungry, because he was right behind me. He squeezed through the gap, raining chunks of stone into the hall, and slithered to the floor with enough weight that the floor around it cracked and sunk. This was a boss-tier monster, well and truly aggro'd, and it wasn't going away. I would have to fight.

In the true spirit of RPG adventure, I stuffed a piece of beef jerky in my mouth, slapped two poultices on to lift my HP back into the yellow and yelled a garbled warcry. But then I dodged around a pillar with a short girly scream as the Aberration Frog went berserk, slamming its tongue around like a bullwhip. It hit the pillar and sent cracks running through the ancient stone.

"You guys are meant to be on easy mode! Why do I have a goddamn XP penalty and a level cap and you don't!?" Frustrated, I dodged and ran ahead as the ponderous frog hopped and wobbled its way toward me. Every time it landed, gravel and dirt rained down on us from above.

A single solid hit from that tongue or those tentacles risked killing me. The food and poultices were regenerating my health, but not fast enough. It was only up to half, and I was going to be able to take one blow - no more than that. At least my AP were going to fill up quickly.

Frogger wasn't going to give me any time to think of a plan. It bounded forward, almost landing on top of me. On reflex, I stabbed it in the leg. The spear blade went all the way into its rubbery flesh. Take that, fucking frog!

[[You hit Aberration for 12 piercing damage! (HP 2478/2490)]]

"TWO AND A HALF *THOUSAND*?!" My shriek of rage bounced off the walls.

All I had going for me at the moment was my speed - Frogger was slow and I was relatively quick. Panting, I zoomed to the side in a puff of shadow, turning invisible and invincible around the next tentacle smash. In another moment, I lunged forward with Whirlwind Butcher, striking as I spun past the mutated frog's slimy bulk.

[[Critical hit! You hit Aberration for 34 damage! (HP 2444/2490)]]

That powerful attack still barely clipped its HP. I turned too slowly at the end of the sprint, and the tongue struck me a glancing blow that knocked me tumbling across the floor toward the far end of the giant room.

[[Aberration hits you for 103 damage!]]

That shitty little love-tap took me from 179 HP to 76, just like that. This monster was too OP for me to have a hope in hell in face-to-face combat.

While the jerky regenerated hit points, I ran for the front of the room, where the pillars converged around a dais. It was overgrown with mutated plants that concealed a huge bronze door. That door didn't look like it was going to open any time soon, but there was something to be said for the arrangement of pillars. The space between the crumbling supports was much narrower here. Even as I began to put my strategy together, the enormous frog tried to leap after me. Instead, it crashed clumsily into one of the pillars, shattering it and toppling the rubble all over itself. The giant frog half-croaked, half-roared as it slashed at the remaining stone with its tentacles... and then shoveled the broken chunks of rock into its mouth. Jeez. Whatever magic steroids it had eaten to reach this size hadn't made it any smarter than a normal frog.

While it was distracted, I squinted up at the ceiling. Seams of luminescent moss glowed above the sputtering mage lights, shining off wet earth. Stalactites of varying sizes hung down like spears. Most of them were small, but a few of them weren't. Bringing down the house on the frog meant bringing it down on me as well, but if I had to pick a way to die, being squashed like a bug was preferable to being eaten alive like one.

I steeled myself, puffing and rolling my shoulders, then ran back out toward the boss monster. "Come on, fatso! Let's dance!"

The Aberration spat out the rocks it was trying to eat as it screeched, disturbed by my movements. It surged toward me with all four tentacles and its tongue. I triggered my Jump ability. A surge of power gathered in my legs, a thrill of raw energy that allowed me to spring off the ground like a cricket. I landed on Frogger's back, bouncing off and rolling ungracefully to the ground behind it.

The creature whirled around in place and stormed toward me, tentacles smashing the ground to help propel it forward. It blasted through another sandstone pillar like a bowling ball. Rock exploded in all directions, and a piece of shrapnel clipped me over the head. The world spun as I staggered behind the next pillar. There was no time to rest before it rumbled toward me, lashing out with its boneless tentacles in all directions.

"You want my ass?! Come get it!" I wasn't feeling the bravado any more. Dizzy and bordering on hysteria, I lurched out of way as the tongue swung wildly toward me, and clumsily led the frog around in a rough circle around one of the biggest stalactites in the room.

The mutant creature charged tirelessly, but without cunning or strategy. It bust right through the crumbling stone in its efforts to reach me. My vision pulsed red as the frog, sensing victory, slapped the final pillar aside and opened its mouth wide to pull me in. Its mouth was still open as the ceiling collapsed on us both.

Chapter 36

The huge stalactite – and a good amount of the surrounding ceiling - plummeted straight down through the top of the mutated creature's head. I watched the frog's HP plummet into the red zone.

"HEEEEEEEEEE!" the frog wailed, lashing out spasmodically at everything within reach. I ran around it, narrowly avoiding being brained by falling stone as I readied Jump and leaped up like a cat. I drove my rusty Spear through one of the Aberration's red glowing eyes, causing it to scream again. "REEEEEEHH!"

[[Critical hit! You hit Aberration for 51 piercing damage!]]

"AHHH!" I roared back at it, twisting the weapon viciously.

[[You hit Aberration for 34 piercing damage!]]

The eyeball burst, and tentacles fell limp, as did the tongue. I viciously stabbed the spear in again, up and down, reducing the frog's eye socket to bloody jelly as it struggled to free itself from the lance of stone pinning it to the ground. With every thrust and twist, it grew weaker. I ignored the blow from a fist-sized rock that bounced off my shoulder, and kept going until the monster stopped kicking its webbed, clawed feet across the floor and went still.

[[You have defeated Behemoth Aberration!]]

[[You have gained 126 Combat EXP!]]

[[You have gained an Achievement: David and Goliath (+150 Fame with Trophy, +100 Bonus Combat EXP)]]

[[Congratulations! You are level 6!]]

"Fuck." Teeth clenched, I stumbled off the corpse's back and wobbled away to look back at it. Thick blood and slime pooled on the floor. It stank like rotten milk.

The only explanation I had for the frog was that the game reset had screwed up the limitations the Devs had put on Archemi. Fortunately, that also seemed to have removed the EXP penalty - and in theory, my level cap. That was good and bad. On the one hand, I was no longer condemned to a life of noobery. Great. On the other, this game was about to turn into Lord of the Flies. I had to level, and I had to do it quickly. Not so great.

Resigned to the stench, I searched the smelly body for loot and got a list of items. The trophy was good, but probably disgusting. I doubted that a Behemoth Aberration trophy was a gold cup with 'Number 1 Frog Murderer' inscribed on it.

[[Raw Meat x 5]]

[[Infused Monster Hide x 4]]

[[Behemoth Aberration Trophy x 1]]

[[Venom Sac x 2]]

[[Giant Frog Eggs x 4]]

[[Frog Fat x 4]]

[[Bluecrystal Shards x 3]]

[[Greencrystal Shards x 5]]

[[Strange Crystal x 1]]

When I stashed the loot in my inventory, it automatically sorted into different sub-menus. The raw meat was food – I wasn't convinced I really wanted to eat it, given how the monster smelled, but it apparently regenerated 35 HP over 35 seconds – and nearly everything else went into 'Crafting' or 'Alchemy', except for the Strange Crystal. That was a Quest Item. Interesting.

In a lot of games, cooking edibles listed as 'raw' tended to improve the regen rate, so I left the frog carcass and headed toward the big door I'd seen earlier. A lot of the plants covering the door and the dias were dead and dry, so I pulled them down, using a dagger to hack at the woody vines further back. After a few minutes of work, I had an armful of kindling and firewood, which I took out to the middle of the dias. After gathering some stones, I had a firepit, and shortly after that, a campfire. I threaded the raw meat on some skewers, and set them aside. The flames needed to die down so I could set them to cook over the hot embers. I knew enough about cooking – IRL and in-game – to know that if you stuck meat directly into flames, you ended up with charcoal on the outside and raw meat in the middle. You let the embers and hot stones do the cooking.

While I was waiting for the flames to reduce, I went over to the door. The bronze was streaked with long green tongues of corrosion, but it was still strong. I pulled away more vines to examine the intricate reliefs on the surface. The images looked kind of Egyptian, except that the largest people had wings and were interacting with dragons and smaller, less important-looking humans had long, pointed ears. I was surprised to find that there was a seam down the middle of the door, which ended in a diamond-shaped depression at waist-height. A ⟦Strange Crystal⟧-shaped depression.

"Huh." Curious, I pulled the crystal from my Inventory and tried it in the slot. It was a perfect fit.

For a few seconds, nothing happened. I was about to remove the crystal and turn back to the fire when a low rumble froze me in place: the sound of gears grinding from deep inside the walls. I took a step back as the door cracked down the middle, showering me with dirt, and then slowly pulled back into the doorway on either side, revealing one of the most beautiful rooms I'd ever seen.

It was a giant geode, an egg-shaped, uneven dome of pure crystal that arched like a cathedral overhead. The crystal spars were a brilliant, opalescent blue, the surfaces crazed with slick rainbows of color that shifted with the flickering of the fire behind me. It was warm in here, and I didn't have to be a mage to know this place was lousy with magic. I felt it in my bones, thrumming, and smelled it in the eerie, earthy odor of electrically charged dust that hung in the air... and saw it in the girl frozen in the immense crystal at the end of the chamber.

She hung as if suspended in water, her brilliant white hair floating weightlessly behind her. She was golden-skinned and painfully beautiful; slim and graceful and almost translucent by torchlight. She had wings, each feather perfectly sealed into the stone, and instead of ears, winglets that swept back from the sides of her head. All she wore was a sleeveless, thigh-length shift that clung to the slender curves of her body. The fabric had frozen in ripples, blowing out behind her.

Fascinated, I stole closer, looking for the source of the power that had blown through the crystal. A gleaming pearl was imbedded in the stone. The girl's hands were poised in front of where the pearl had been stopped, lips parted, as if she'd been casting a spell just as her mineral prison closed around them. As I drew near it, the Spear began to throb against my palm. I looked down at it. It was glowing faintly, resonating with the frozen woman.

Quest Updated: Restore the Spear of Nine Spheres

Investigate the Ancient Shrine of Light (Part 1 of 3).

Reward: EXP, Mental Skill EXP, Ancient Treasure

I almost accepted on reflex, but then recalled what Matir had told me and held off, letting the window hang. This Spear quest... I really did think there was something weird about it. I called up the Glossary and looked up 'Ancient Treasure':

Ancient Treasure

An ancient jewelry box. Contains Gold Grade accessories.

Market Price: 5,000,000 guilder (Ilia)

My eyes bugged. Five MILLION guilders? This game didn't have the crazy inflation that some games did. Five million was a lot of money. Too much money.

I tried consulting the Glossary for the pearl imbedded in the crystal, but found nothing in there about it. I settled for walking around the room instead. Eventually, I found a golden plaque buried under a thin layer of crystal that was easily chipped off with my Spear. The surface of the plaque crawled with magical runes that blurred and leapt at me when I tried to look at them. They seemed to lift off the metal, like a 3D illusion. Even as I stepped back, the room around me warped, fading to blue, then white.

...A rumbling round gate closes over a pit of boiling white mana, the doors sealing into a nearly perfect circle. Around it, a circle of robed, winged people: Aesari, chanting even as the radiating magic melts the flesh from their bones. Their feathers catch fire, and their singing turns to screams. New magi take the place of the fallen, sustaining the chant. Inch by inch, the gate closes... until finally, it is closed.

A man steps forward, the Spear in his hands. He is the Paragon of the Nine, and the Spear is whole. The bluesteel is polished to a brilliant metal finish, crawling with a constant bloom of spirals and sigils. All nine holes are full, and as the Paragon brings his Spear down the seal the Gate of Light, one stone flashes brighter than the others. It is Taath

La'Hah. The Pearl of Glorious Dawn. The key to the Dragon Gate of Light, tomb of the goddess Solnetsi...

I shook my head as I stumbled away, teeth ringing. The magic pumped information into my brain, so much of it so fast that I clawed at my scalp in an effort to contain it.

...A thunderous veil of light pours from the spear, over the gate, swallowing the magi who have been holding the power of the Goddess contained. The pearl falls from its setting, its power spent...

The vision faded as quickly as it had come, leaving me alone in the cold. I turned to look back at the frozen Aesari. She was glowing softly in the gloom.

Quest Updated: Restore the Spear of Nine Spheres

You have learned that the Pearl of Glorious Dawn is the key to the Dragon Gate of Light in Ilia. It is imbedded in the crystal with the fossilized Aesari priestess. Smash the fossil, retrieve the Pearl and return it to the Spear (Part 2 of 3).

Reward: EXP, Mental Skill EXP, Ancient Treasure

"It's a trap." I meandered back over to the giant crystal, keeping a safe distance from it. "It has to be. But... is the Gate in Cham Garai? The Eyrie, maybe?"

I didn't get to finish my thought, because suddenly, my mouth was full of blood.

The stab impact felt like a punch to my back. There was hardly any pain, just the obscene sight of a sword blade sticking out of the front of my chest, through one of the tiny gaps in my armor.

⟦You have taken 150 points of Precise Backstab damage! HP 18/320.⟧

⟦Critical Hit!⟧

[Surprise hit!]

[You are bleeding! 1 HP per second damage for 20 seconds!]

[You are incapacitated!]

[Warning! You are at 17 HP!]

I was dragged back, flailing and spinning around as someone put their boot against my back and kicked me off the blade. I staggered to the side and toppled over, pawing at the bloodstain blooming on my chest, and watched in paralyzed shock as Baldr Hyland bent down to pick up the Spear of Nine Spheres.

Chapter 37

"Oh god." Lucien said from somewhere further back in the room. "I can smell it. Oh Jesus."

"Shut up and quit your whining." There was no friendly warmth in Baldr's voice now, just cold, hard focus. "Let's see here..."

I foamed blood from my mouth, coughing it onto the floor in my efforts to tell him that he was a traitorous, griefing piece of shit. There was no way he could use the Spear, though – it was a soulbound weapon.

Assuming it wasn't, in fact, some kind of player trap.

Baldr picked it up, and swished it down a couple times, like how I'd done when Rutha had first told me to hold it in my hand. "Hey, this is light. And what have we here...? *Restore the Spear of Nine Spheres*? Damn, I knew you were holding out on us, but this is an S-tier quest." Baldr planted the butt of the Spear on the floor, scanning the HUD display I couldn't see.

A nervous thrill passed through my chest. *Holy shit.* Matir was right. The Spear and the quest were loaded. They were either a bug... or that crazy Dev, Ororgael, had set this whole thing up. And Baldr didn't know. "How... how the fuck did you find me?"

"You're on my party history list," Baldr replied, arching one ghostly eyebrow. "I can see you on the map."

I stared at the big man in disbelief. Lucien was wearing rogue gear, not knight equipment, but Baldr was in full plate and a ripped half-cloak. He'd stuffed torn strips of fabric between the plates. I spat blood onto the floor to clear my mouth. "So the whole thing was bullshit. That *entire lecture* was bullshit. What the fuck class are you? Spirit Knight? Is that even a 'real' Knight?"

"I don't think that's any of your business," he said.

I decided to stall for time. "Knights don't sneak."

"I spent six years sneaking around the jungle in a USMC Templar warfighter, squish," he drawled. He didn't turn to look back. "You think old Baldr didn't learn a thing or two about moving quiet while heavy?"

I cleared my throat enough to croak out a suitable one-word reply. "Mother-f-fucker."

He shook his head. "I told you once, and I'll tell you again. Great men take what they want. It's been that way for all of history. Now, an Artifact like this is worth at least a million. I'd have done it before now, but we were being watched."

"Baldr, can we just get this over with?" Lucien whined.

"Sure we can. Step up and kill him, Mr. PK-everyday. Now's your chance to show me what you got." Baldr headed past me to the imprisoned Aesari. "This thing comes with a quest. By the look of things, I'm supposed to free this lil' gal over here."

I almost felt like laughing, though that would have hurt too much. "You don't want to do that. Seriously, this whole thing is s-some kind of player t-trap."

"Uh-huh. Don't think you can Brer Rabbit your way out of this one, Dragozin." I couldn't see his face, but I heard the sneer in his voice.

"Suit yourself. But you tell me how you can just pick up my soul-bound weapon like this." I had one quick-heal item left.

"Game's buggy as hell is why. Damn near lost my leg when I fell through a bridge one time." Baldr glanced back, then advanced to the golden plaque where I'd gotten the first round of information about the Pearl. "Kill him, Luci."

While Baldr was absorbed and Lucien hesitantly moved toward me, I pulled the final poultice from my Inventory and slapped it on. Lucien made a strangled sound and sprinted forward. My health jumped from 6 to 56, but he was on top of me before I could properly react.

He raised a short Japanese-style sword overhead, but I could see the fear in his eyes, the weak grip, the hesitation. He might have been a keyboard warrior, but this was beyond VR. For all intents and purposes, he was about to murder - *really* murder - for the first time. With the smell of blood in his nostrils, he was terrified... and all I needed was a moment of distraction. Something that scared him even more than killing me.

It came to me in a flash of dark inspiration.

"Hey, Luci – you were right. The Alliance nuked your Shard," I rasped.

"What?" He froze, hand shaking. " *What* did you say?"

"Don't talk to him, kill him! You're not on a damn date!" Baldr yelled from across the room. "He's already said too much."

"That blackout before. Remember that?" I lay back, trying not to struggle. The poultice had stopped the bleeding, but I was only regenerating one hit point per second. "The game reset. Can you log out?"

"You're so full of shit." He tensed up, jaws snapping shut, eyes narrowing as he built up to the strike.

"Go ahead and stab me. I'll respawn. I don't give a fuck anymore." I forced myself to keep my eyes locked with his, instead of drifting to the blade. "But you were fucking right. The Pacific nuked us."

"That's... that's ridiculous! I'm still here. I'd have f-felt something." Lucien dropped his voice so that Baldr couldn't hear him. The big knight was lost in a trance some fifteen feet away.

"Look, this is bigger than this game." Some dark part of me was grinning inside. "See if you can log out. And if you can, then you know I'm a liar. *Then* kill me."

"One move. One move, and I'll do it." Lucien's nostrils quivered as he put his knife to my throat and pushed it up under my jaw. He held it there as his eyes became distant and began to scan something I couldn't see. My pulse beat against the edge of the blade, ten beats... and then the thin man's pale face turned the color of milk. "It's gone. It's *gone*!"

"About fucking time," Baldr called back. "Man, that was a trip. Now hang onto your panties, I'm about to crack this thing."

"It's gone. The logout option is gone. There's no one... Temperance is offline. Everyone's offline!" Lucien recoiled in panic. He wasn't a soldier. He was a poor little rich boy who couldn't handle his adrenaline. "Where is it? Why can't I find it. Fuck! FUCK!"

Almost of its own accord, my branded hand shot out like a snake. I grabbed him by the throat and activated *Life for Life*.

Lucien's eyes bugged as the dark energy surged through my body and into his. My Adrenaline Points were full from the damage I'd taken. I burned them like a fuse and sucked the life out of him. It was like a hit of smack straight to the brainstem, and it was FAST - there was no fancy mystical woo-woo, no buildup. Just a burst of dark power,

Lucien's short bleating scream, and the surge of renewed energy and power. I was back to 105 HP.

With a snarl, I pushed him off, pulled the sword out of my back and threw it at him, just as Baldr shattered the Aesari's crystal prison with the Spear.

Lucien dodged the spinning blade, but whatever counter he'd been about to do was cut short when slivers of crystal exploded outward from the entrapped Aesari. There was a split second where we saw her come to life - floating, radiant, like the core of a star. And with it came a one-line system message.

[[Wakey wakey, rise and shine!]]

I didn't even have time to note how weird that was before the explosion threw me, but it threw Baldr further. I spammed Shadow Dance, dissolving and reappearing ahead of the shockwave. Lucien screamed, and Baldr's deeper bellow suddenly stopped as he skidded into a wall, headfirst, and hit it with a dull crunch. We were still partied up, and I could see his HP ring. Empty. As the light shrunk back into the center of the room, I ran over to his corpse, pulled the Spear out of his smoldering hand, and hesitated for a moment before looting him of everything he carried. Gear, clothes, items, weapons: the lot.

The core of light was building up to a second explosion, sucking the dust of the room back into itself.

"Asshole!" I spat on him, uploading his gear to my Inventory, and ran for my life.

My HUD was pinging me as I sprinted out around the bloated body of the dead frog and ran for the exit. There was an exit illuminated by the piercing ray of light flaring out of the crystal room. The great bronze door was still ajar from where Baldr and Lucien had entered, the passage beyond littered with unclaimed junk loot from the frogs they'd killed on the way in. A few of them had respawned, but I didn't stop to whack them. I kept running until my stamina was maxed out and I was out of breath, waited, then kept going. On the way, I pitched the useless junk I'd looted from Baldr on my way through the ruins. He had a lantern, which I equipped to my belt so that I could see, and as I jogged through the ancient flooded buildings, I threw his heavy gear and bloodied clothing down holes and into streams, freeing myself of the dead weight. Only once I was near the base of the Eyrie did I stop running and had a look at my menus and messages.

The '*Restore the Spear of Nine Spheres*' quest was still live. No reward had been delivered to my Inventory or Baldr's. No shiny treasure chest, not even EXP. I checked the weapon, and its stats were the same, except that now it was at 30% durability instead of 36%. There was no explanation, no update, nothing except a horrible sinking feeling I felt in the pit of my belly. The Spear of Nine Spheres was still broken, and the Gates were still unstable. Or were they? Was this thing cursed? Because it definitely wasn't soul-bound.

Hurriedly, I checked everything. Character stats, level, EXP... I didn't have a PK tag, thank goodness. Marching into the Eyrie with the Mark of Matir was bad enough without also being branded as a player killer. I checked my message center, desperately searching the ranks of Devs and checking to see if Temperance was on. They were still all offline. All I had to go off was what Matir had told me.

"...Once, an Architect fell to Earth. His name was Ororgael. Like you, his spirit did not incarnate correctly. Unlike you, he was not rescued from purgatory by one of the Nine, nor by any of the Young Gods of humankind... he was rescued by the Drachan. The other Architects pulled him out of Archemi like a tumor, but cancer has a way of hanging on to the body, doesn't it?"

"Fuck this shit. I just want a goddamn dragon. Is that too much to ask?" I grumbled, hiking off into the darkness.

It was night outside, but the ruins were warm. That meant I was quite deep underground, so I decided on trying to find a way up and out. The cave I'd originally come in from wasn't a good candidate for that, so after making some torches with wood and frog fat, I searched the giant hall. My good mood returned when I discovered one wall that was covered in what looked like a sheet of gray lung tissue. The nodules on it opened and closed like blinking eyes, and at the center of each one was a crescent-shaped spore capsule. These were the Cat's Eye Mushrooms I needed for the Trial, and there were lots of them. I gathered as many mushrooms as I could, holding my breath against the poisonous spores. They'd come in useful for Alchemy later on. I figured I was going to get in trouble for choosing Dark Lancer, so I might as well go the whole way and experiment with poisons. What the commander didn't know wouldn't hurt him, unless he somehow got into my backpack and started drinking random potions.

Even a shallow breath of the gas around the mushrooms left me wheezing, a mild debuff that slowly ticked down as I made my way through the dungeon. Everywhere I turned, there were monsters. Mutated bats, slimes, things with too many mouths... but I didn't fight many of them, because they ranged from Level 6 through to Level 15. Level 15 creatures weren't supposed to exist, no more than the Behemoth Aberration had... the Devs had put a level cap on monsters and players. Something was really screwy. My only guess was that the restrictions had not been installed on whatever the game had booted off during the reset.

After a couple hours of walking and climbing, I was within sight of the outside world. The smell of fresh air gusted through the dungeon and cooled the nervous sweat running down my face as I crouched behind a tumbled block of masonry. Some eight feet away, a Level 15 [[Assassin Bug Drone]] was slowly flying by. Inside the confines of the cave, the wolfhound-sized bug sounded like a helicopter lifting off, wings humming with a deep bass buzz. As it got closer, I held my breath, squeezing the haft of my Spear to otherwise remain still.

The assassin bug drifted up to my right, its carapace gleaming black in the bluish light cast by the luminescent fungi on the walls, and hovered thoughtfully. Then, without any warning, it stabbed down with its stinger barely three feet from where I hid. I heard a squeal, and the monster rose back up with a rabbit-sized rat impaled on the barbed length. It writhed and screamed in its death throes as the bug wheeled around and thrummed off somewhere to enjoy its meal undisturbed.

Mouth dry, I cautiously scrambled out, moving on my hands and the balls of my feet, and kept heading in the direction of the wind.

[[Your Stealth skill has increased!]]

Damn-fucking-right my Stealth skill had increased. In a very un-knightly fashion, I'd been relying heavily on stealth to get through the ruins. With the Spear, I could take enemies two or even three levels above me, and I'd been killing them when it was safe... but there were monsters here even more powerful than Frogger. Along the way, I looked inside of pots and tumbled stone furniture, looting whatever common items I could find. Archemi wasn't so realistic as to deprive the intrepid explorer of loot, and I was able to score torches, linen, interesting molds and fungi, and even a couple of strange-looking silver pieces, which automatically converted to Ilian currency in my Inventory.

It took another forty-five minutes to reach the outside world through a sunken stone archway. Grateful to be alive and outdoors, I scrambled up the broken stairs and vaulted out onto soggy ground, looking around to orientate. I was back in a swampy marshland, much shallower and far more lifeless than the one I'd first entered on the other side of the ruined city. Small hills and shallow gullies rolled on for what seemed like miles into the mist that surrounded me. Looking up, I could see the distant fire burning at the top of Eyrie a mile or two away, and could hear the distinct, far-off cries of Crowned Eagles, the roar of dragons, and the gurgle of stagnant water. Checking my map, I felt my spirits lift. This was the Old Battlefield. I'd made it, with close to twenty-three hours left on the clock.

I found a place to make a concealed camp, but before I settled down, I made sure that Baldr was not somehow in my party. He wasn't - but I hesitated before blocking him. If he was blocked, he wouldn't show up on my radar, and I didn't trust Archemi's systems enough to risk him being completely invisible. It was a good idea to be able to keep track of enemy players.

The situation numbed and exhausted me. I enjoyed PvP in other games I'd played, but I was cooperative by nature. I was always there for my guild before the war, and my platoon during it. When I played old JRPGs or other solo games, I always got attached to the NPCs who were there to support me. They were often more colorful than the main character.

I'd convinced myself that all the HEX-refugees would have every reason to work together. We had common ground. We had everything to gain, because if we passed the Trial, we would all be dragon riders. It didn't matter that there were only three eggs. If all six of us made it, three of us would get a dragon now, and the other three would be able to grind until the next clutch. The only difference was that they'd be a higher level when they got their wings.

Baldr and Lucien's actions bewildered me as much as they pissed me off. Because not only was it pointless, but PKing in Archemi meant you had to be really willing to murder someone. Blood, guts, the smell... it was about as realistic as it got. Lucien apparently hadn't gotten it until he'd seen me go down, but Baldr knew. And he was willing to do it anyway.

I really needed some answers, and I needed to find friends. And as I looked up at the Eyrie, a small dark voice whispered in my ear. *You're not going to find friends in this place. But you will find something.*

With a sigh, I rubbed my face, then started searching for a way to bring Cutthroat to my position. Most games had some form of a mount summoning option. I queried my HUD, and sure enough, a glowing hookwing-shaped icon appeared. When I pressed it, Cutthroat appeared in front of me in the shadowy gloom with a squawk, whipping her head from side-to-side as she struggled to get her bearings.

"It's just you and me, dinobutt." There was nowhere to hitch her, so I took her muzzle off and let her roam while I settled in front of the fire, pulled out my Alchemy tools, and got to work grinding Bonebreak herbs for potions. "Just you and me."

Chapter 38

After scoring some red rashovik from the murk that surrounded us, I was ready to approach my final goal.

The lonely flight of stairs to the temple of Kyrie was narrow and uneven, weaving in and out of the raw stone that surrounded the base of the Eyrie. The shadows of all the flying creatures that called this place home spiraled over the ground as I climbed up to the front of the building, a small castle-like fort carved straight into the rock. The huge double doors were made of the same bronze-colored metal as the ones in Cham Garai.

Feeling bitter and tired, I opened the door just enough to slip inside. It boomed as I closed it behind me, and took a moment to look around the arched room. The church was warm and smoky, lit by the golden glow of a hundred thousand candles. Graceful pillars wrapped by carved wings supported the high vaulted ceiling, and rows of statues marched from beside the door all the way to the altar at the other end. There, a huge round window perfectly framed the yellow orb of the moon outside. The statues were all of women: slender women with elegant hands, their heads lowered, their faces obscured by long floating veils perfectly rendered in marble. Each one of them carried a different item: a book, a globe, scales and a compass, a sword... tools of justice, learning, and wisdom. The room smelled like wax and old roses.

The candle flames flickered as the door shut with a small gust of wind, but quickly settled back to their smooth tapers. At the end of the chapel room, one of the statues moved.

A woman who looked like a pillar of silver veils and robes turned to face me as I advanced. As I grew closer, I could see the suggestion of her face beneath the sheer material. She was older, middle-aged, her hair bound away out of sight. All that was clearly visible of her was her hands, but by moonlight, her outfit made the dim outline of her body seem to glow.

"Welcome, aspirant," she said. Her voice was croaky, but her tone was gentle. "Have you brought the ingredients for the ritual?"

"Yes," I replied.

"And are you prepared to undergo the Trial of Marantha, the gauntlet through which all dragon knights must pass??

"Yes," I said, quickly. "But I-"

"Come with me." She didn't seem to hear the last part. The priestess moved away, her veils billowing out softly behind her.

I hurried to catch up. "Ma'am, before we do this, I need to report something that happened in the field. There was an incident-"

"This is something you must report to the knight-commander," the priestess replied. She sounded benevolent, but firm. "I am not of the Skyrdon, boy. I serve Kyrie alone."

Shit. "Can you send a message up to them? While I'm... uhh... convulsing in agony?"

"If you can write one in the time we have, I will. But we do not have long. Once the infusions are made, they must be administered immediately."

I checked my Inventory for parchment and a pencil or something, but of all the stupid things I was lugging around with me, paper wasn't one of them. Well, there was nothing to do but go through the Trial, come out the other side, and hope I woke up soon enough to tell Skyr Tymos what had happened. "Here... here's the ingredients."

The priestess extended her hands, and I passed over the quest items. She dipped her head in acknowledgement. "Follow me."

She led me through a smaller bronze door into a library, and from there, through another, less ornate oak door and down a flight of stairs. As we descended, the scent of old roses and incense was replaced by a mixture of earthy chemical smells... the faint odors of battery acid and oxidized metal.

She opened the way into a chamber that was lit only by the moon from overhead. A deep skylight focused a beam of soft golden light onto a harsh metal and leather chair in the center of the room, like something out of a dentist-themed horror movie. The sight of it made me recoil. My dad had been a dentist, and I was pretty sure I'd had nightmares about this exact chair.

"This is the chamber where I will administer the Trial," the priestess said quietly. "You will have a few minutes to collect yourself and pray. You are allowed to refuse at any time, with no loss of honor."

"Am I the first to arrive?" I steeled myself and went over to the chair, laying a hand on it. It had a headrest and straps. The padding was in good condition, at least.

"No," she replied. "Another young man arrived before you."

"Pravoslav? Did he make it?"

The woman hesitated, then bowed her head and left the room without replying.

When the door closed, I was left in the near darkness by myself. That's when the nerves finally set in. Weirdly, the first thing I worried about was Cutthroat. I'd left her sniffing around a mostly-empty trough in a crude stable at the base of the Eyrie. She was probably capable of taking care of herself, but... ugh. Then I began to worry about Baldr and Lucien. Baldr's HP ring had been grayed out - hadn't it? If he was dead, he'd have respawned somewhere away from here, because you couldn't take the Trial if you died. Lucien, I wasn't sure about. He'd been caught in the explosion, but I couldn't remember seeing or hearing him after he screamed. I was the second 'young man' to come here, which meant Violetta was still in the ruins... and which also meant that I should be the first to rouse in the event Lucien came here and tried to give a different account of events.

As the anger and bewilderment and anxiety cooled, I found myself thinking back to the past. I sat on the edge of the horrible chair and wrapped a bandage around my branded hand while I brooded on all the things that had led to me being here. The dragons were so close that I could hear them distantly through the walls of this place, their roars and bugles, the thunder of their wings. It was like going into the pod with Steve and Temperance all over again. It was like going home after sitting through an exam at school, the weird mixture of relief, anxiety, and wondering of "did I do everything right? And what do I do now?" It was like being in the transport plane on my first tour. The future was a terrifying dark void. The only things pushing me on were faith and hope.

I balled my hands into fists, feeling them clench and relax, and drew a deep, steadying breath. I wasn't a praying man, but I could get behind hoping for a better future. Loneliness sucked. So did war. Maybe a dragon would be the catalyst for me, propelling me to literal and symbolic heights, or maybe I'd learn that it couldn't do that for me... but either way, I planned to survive to find out.

The priestess came back about fifteen minutes later with a small tray on wheels. There were five glass syringes: two red, one yellow, one white, one gray. All of them except the white one had a shifting, ambient glow. Beside the magical solutions, she had needles and tubing immersed in a vial of clear alcohol, tools for a medieval IV. She was wearing a gauntlet, like the 'witchglove' Rutha wore to perform magic. I stood up restlessly.

"The Trial of Marantha is very dangerous," she said, picking up the tubing and needles and laying them out on a clean cloth to dry. "Only the strongest survive. Not the strongest of body - the strongest of will."

"Then it's good that I'm a stubborn ass," I replied. "Pardon my language."

"You must suffer through the pain and remain conscious as long as you are able." Without commenting on my choice of words, she set up a needle and tube. "This is your final chance, aspirant. If you wish to proceed, shed your weapons and armor, lay down, and rest your head back."

I eyed the chair. Memories of my father rose from the deep, dark past like shadows.

I shucked my armor off, and lay the Spear down on the floor beside the chair. Then I eased onto it, and lay back.

"Focus on your desire to stand before the eggs and serve the people of Ilia." The priestess's voice had shifted to the rhythmic tone of recital. "Focus on your goal of meeting the Matriarch of the Eyrie. Focus on what it will be like when a wyrmling runs to you across the sand of the hatching ground, its eyes full of love and trust. Can you see him? Can you see his eyes? Can you feel his regard for you, you who endured so much pain to be with him?"

I'd never seen a baby dragon, but I could imagine a tiny Talenth, with big blue eyes and little stubs for horns. And I could imagine what it would be like to bond with something like him. It was a powerful feeling, the kind that picked my heart up and made my blood pound. "Yes."

"You don't have to answer me. Answer yourself... feel it until it burns in your heart."

I closed my eyes, and breathed in deeply.

"I will insert the needle and administer an anesthetic." She moved around me in the dark, silk whispering against skin. "It will numb the pain somewhat, but it will make you feel cold and dizzy. After that, you will be given the first of the mana-tainted serums. Once I have begun, it cannot stop, no matter the pain."

I nodded. "I understand."

"Once I begin the spell, do not interrupt me." The woman's hand closed on my arm as she buckled the straps of the chair over my limbs. "Not for any reason. Scream if you must... but do not stop the chant."

Swallowing, I let the waves of fear wash through me. There was no reassurance - only the certainty that yes, this was dangerous, and yes, I probably was going to die, at least for a little while.

The priestess came around to my left side once I was strapped down. "And now, we begin."

The needle was nothing: a cold pinch, a small ache, and it was done. I lay there and stared up at the skylight and the half-visible moon, watching the clouds swirl across its surface. A whole other planet. I remembered Rutha's face when I told her that Archemi was actually the moon to another, larger planet, and that made me smile. I hoped Matir was right... I hoped that anything Rutha was doing on behalf of that crazy dead Dev, Orogael, was being done in innocence.

I felt the priestess ready the IV, and glanced over to see her depressing the plunger on the first of the syringes, the one with the white fluid. It hit my veins like ice, spreading up my arm in a cooling, numbing wave. When it reached my chest, my whole body relaxed, slumping down. I felt distant and strange within a couple of minutes... conscious, but floaty.

There was a clink and rustle, and then the priestess began to drone a soft chant under her breath. The sound rose and fell, rose and fell, and I found myself lost in it as my breathing slowed and my muscles slumped. It was peaceful, even pleasant. I smelled ozone, and then a sharp, bitter, unpleasant smell, like rotten broccoli. Slowly, I looked over to see her attach the darker of the two red vials to the IV. I was sure this was the king's sorrow decoction.

She began to chant louder as she pressed the plunger down, her witchglove glowing out of the corner of my eye. I braced for it, but nothing could prepare me for when it hit. It was like being injected with lava. I jerked like I'd been burned, only to fall back dizzily. As I struggled to remain conscious, to breathe, a mixture of agony, nausea, and a terrible sense of *wrongness* rolled over me like a storm blowing in over the ocean, and when it reached my heart, the agony shocked my mind out of my body.

I fought it, but I only lasted for so long before I threw up and passed out into the black.

Chapter 39

The first thing I felt was water. It rolled down my cheeks, warm and itchy. Irritably, I tried to reach up and brush the droplets away. But nothing happened. My hand lay there, limp by my side. Unmoving.

My pulse lifted with panic. Every heartbeat felt like someone was pressing on a huge bruise deep inside my chest, but I struggled against the heaviness, the inability to move. Something had gone wrong. I was paralyzed.

I tried opening my eyes, but the world was nothing but a dark blurry swirl that turned brown, then red, then black. Sleep rolled me under like a high-speed train... and took me back to the Total War.

The jungle. I was running in a half-crouch, and yelling at the top of my lungs. "Get the fuck down, Spot! What the fuck are you doing! Get your motherfucking head down! Stay close!"

Spot was a dim shadowy blur in the foliage beside me, seemingly unable to duck and sprint at the same time.

"Fuck! Where are they!? Did anyone see where that came from?" Starwars - otherwise known as Private Lucas - called from somewhere further back.

A roar from somewhere to my right. "WHERE THE FUCK IS JOHNSON!?"

...TATATATATAT... The purr-rattle of machineguns boomed around us, seemingly from every direction, but the *spat-spat-thwip* of rounds blowing the leaves and bark off trees were only coming from one direction: southeast.

"Johnson! Where the *fuck* is Johnson!? We have to call this shit up!" Corporal Washington yelled.

"Johnson isn't on fucking COMMO! Starwars is! Why the fuck are you so far behind, Wash!?" I bellowed back.

...spit-spang-brrrrrrrTATATATATAT... The guns sounded almost like toys, or like people slamming dictionaries down onto tables. Lots of dictionaries, lots of tables.

"I was trying to find fucking Johnson! Starwars, call this fucking thing up!"

"Okay! Where are they fucking shooting from? Can you see them?!"

It was just past sunset, which meant that it was already night in the jungle. My vision had narrowed down to a tunnel through my helmet. The radio was blasting off in my ear, I was drenched in sweat, hands hot and white-knuckled around my rifle. It was my first tour. I'd been a soldier for about five months. Somehow I was thinking about nothing and everything at the same time.

...Where is the enemy? Are those tracer rounds? Can they see us? Is anyone hit? Do they have...

-BRRRRRRRRRRRR- I heard wood splinter and crash as a red light lit behind us, and then the awful sound of living wood being torn apart by something with too much strength to be human. The vibrations through the ground had been masked by the tremors in my own body.

Fuck.

They had a Scorpion. Powered armor.

"DOWN! DOWN! GET THE FUCK DOWN!" Screaming at the top of my lungs, I could barely hear myself. I saw Washington trip over the edge of an unseen ravine and faceplant his way down the steep slope, and a moment later, I stumbled over the same edge myself. I slid down on my ass through ferns and plants, overtaken by Spot, who tumbled bonelessly past me and smashed into a rotten log. Panicking and confused, I skidded over to him. "Spot! Fucking hell! Starwars call a..."

Spot's entire face was gone, replaced by a bloody mash.

"MEDVAC." The word came out in a whisper.

Sweat ran down my face.

I opened my eyes.

The ceiling overhead was a curved mosaic of dragons in flight. White dragons, a dark swirling sky, with stars and beautiful glass-like glyphs worked into the patterns around the edge. The light was dim and yellowish, but I could see every variation in tint and hue... the way the tiles shifted between indigo and sky-blue, the tiny opalescent flaws in the glass, the specks of grout that had escaped the artist's notice.

I breathed in deeply, very deeply, unusually so. A prickling rush spread through my limbs, and as my eyes widened, the mosaic came into sharper focus. I didn't have to turn my head to see what was on the dresser beside me - a lamp with a candle burning inside. The fire rippled with a holographic aura that caught the glass and bathed the table in rainbow light. I'd never seen fire like it.

"Easy, now." A low voice said from my other side.

Slowly, I turned my head, trying to clear the cobwebs. It was Skyr Tymos. The old man leaned over me and took a damp cloth from my forehead, setting it aside in a steaming bowl on the dresser beside my bed. The details of the room filtered in. I was laying in an elegant wooden bed under layers of tanned furs. The lamp was on the bedside table by my left, Tymos by my right, and the mosaic overhead.

"I'm alive?" I rasped, blinking away invasive memories of Spot's smashed strawberry face.

"Yes." The Skyr uncorked a small flask and held it to my lips. "And now, your final test. Drink."

I was so nauseated that the odor of the herbal potion made me retch, but I obeyed. While he supported my head, I drank... and cool relief washed through my gut. My breathing steadied, the pain in my chest began to subside. Some of the weakness left my limbs. My gray HP ring filled red to about a quarter, and then began to throb.

"Good," he said. "Can you sit?"

Grunting, I struggled up until I leaned against the headboard. Just that much effort was exhausting. While he prepared a second and third potion, I reviewed my HUD. No fewer than five debuff icons had appeared, their cooldowns slowly draining away. "What was that?"

"Brightlace potion," Tymos replied. "It's toxic to normal men, but you're a dragonman now, Hector. Mana cannot harm you. Here – two more."

He helped me drink the second brightlace potion, which made me strong enough to drink the third on my own. They healed 75 HP and removed three of the debuffs: Fatigue, Bleeding, and Internal Trauma. Lovely.

"I made it." I looked over my hands. I could see the pores of my skin by the light of a single candle. Now that I was healed, I felt... different. Better, stronger. My lungs could draw an obscene amount of air. My heart was slower, my body so light I felt like I would float if I tried to stand. And I could *see*. I felt like I could see for miles. "Holy fuck. I made it."

"Yes, you did." Tymos smiled, and I saw that, too – even though I wasn't facing him. My peripheral vision was now all the way back to my shoulders, even a little beyond that. I could almost look behind my own head.

"Wow." I couldn't think of anything else to say.

"I have vague memories of the day I woke up from the transmutation fever," Skyr Tymos said wistfully. "The knight who kept vigil for me said something I've never forgotten. 'Don't you think this is what it feels like to become a butterfly?'"

Somehow, that was what brought me back. Three crises all pushed their way into my awareness at once. "Skyr Tymos, I need to tell you something. It's..."

I trailed off.

"What?" He waited expectantly.

"It's..." I wracked my brains for what I was supposed to tell him. I *knew* there was something, but when I tried to think of what had happened in the last day, all I saw was fog. I rubbed my face, wincing. "Damn. I can't remember. I can't remember *anything*."

"Amnesia is a common side effect. Don't be alarmed if you're foggy for a few days. The Trial is immensely stressful on the body."

"How long have I been out?"

"Four days," he replied breezily. "A little longer than is typical. We were getting worried."

"I remember leaving the fort, and crashing off Cutthroat in the forest." I frowned, rubbing my hands over my face. I remember..."

Matir. I remembered Matir, and his warnings to me. Alarmed, I checked my quests. By passing the Trial, I'd earned enough EXP to hit Level 7, giving me skill points to spend. The '*Restore the Spear of Nine Spheres*' quest was still there. The revelation was accompanied by a strong sense of dread. I was supposed to tell Tymos about something that happened, but it was all a bright, painful blur. "What about the others? Did they make it?"

Tymos sighed heavily. "We lost one: the large boy, the dark-haired one."

"Pravoslav." I nodded. I hadn't gotten to know him at all, but he'd seemed like a cool guy. "But the others-"

"-Need only concern you when you take your vows," Tymos replied. He got to his feet. "It is time for you to visit the Matriarch. Can you walk?"

I didn't feel like I could, but the only way to find out was to try. Slowly, I pushed aside the covers and shuffled around until I could stand. There was a mirror on the other side of the room. I made that my goal and embraced the suck by tottering over. The first steps were wobbly, but by the time I reached the dresser and peered at my face, I was steadier.

The trial had changed me. The most alarming change was my eyes. I now had the same large, eagle-like pupils as Tymos and the commander, and the iris of my eyes had bleached. They were no longer dark blue, but an eerie pale blue-violet threaded with silver. Looking straight ahead at my reflection, I could see Skyr Tymos almost directly behind me without using the mirror. That felt like it would be a huge advantage in my everyday gaming. *Good luck backstabbing me now, assholes...*

Wait... What?

"Come with me," Tymos said. "And when you meet the Matriarch... please recall our conversation in the garden."

Chapter 40

The human-occupied halls of the Eyrie were smooth and well-made, with tile floors and elegant, austere ceilings, like something out of an Elvish castle. At the core of the tower was something much older and more primeval... and heavily locked down.

The Matriarch's chambers and the hatching sands were at the heart of the Eyrie. There was no way to tell which way was up or down in here. It was very warm, and smelled faintly of sulphur and more strongly of mana. Tymos led me through a gauntlet of doors that burned with wards and magical protections, past a heavily-guarded golden antechamber, and through a grand entry that wouldn't have been out of place in a bank vault, complete with industrial-sized bolts and a great big spoked wheel. We opened that wheel together, and when the door clunked, he pushed it open a crack.

"She is expecting you," he whispered, with a meaningful look at my covered hand. "Be polite... and be careful. The walls here most definitely have ears."

I nodded and slipped inside, entering a huge domed chamber. The ten-foot vault door shut behind me with a boom that echoed through the enormous cave. The air pressed in on me with tropical heat and humidity. Water gathered and trickled down the walls, which glowed with flickering whorls and seams of magical script. At the very end of the cave was an amphitheater of stone surrounding the world's largest sand pit. And there, curled in a tight ball, was the singly most miserable dragon I had ever seen.

The Matriarch should have been beautiful. She was huge – half again the size of Talenth - with a backswept crown of long, slender horns. Her pale scales were like pearls or opals, shifting from opalescent cream to ripples of bright blue, green, violet, and even pink. She was adorned with jewelry. Woven chains, rings, and jewels hung from her horns, nostrils, around her neck, around her wrists and ankles, her claws and the tip of her tail. But when I zoomed in on her – I could do that now - I saw that her neck was swollen, her opalescent hide was grayish and dirty, and she was more than a little overweight. The jewelry, which looked delicate on a creature as large as she was, was made of the same near-impervious bluesteel material as my spear. The links crawled with magical energy, and all I could think of was one of those choke collars some people used on their dogs. Or a shock collar.

Something is not right here. The voice of my intuition screamed.

The dragon's wings sagged as she pulled herself upright, watching my approach with weary suspicion. Her eyes were a brilliant pale violet, dark at the edges and as bright as a lightning strike in the center. Each eyeball was larger than my torso.

There had been no instruction on how to approach her, and I had a feeling someone was watching – and assessing – how I handled the encounter. So when I reached the edge of the sand arena, I bowed from the waist to her in the Korean style, hands by my sides. "Honored Matriarch, I am Dragozin Hector of Tungaant. I'm sorry to have interrupted your sleep this evening. Thank you for taking the time to speak with me at this late hour."

The dragon suddenly seemed more alert. She cocked her head slightly, her winglet crests briefly lifting, then relaxing, and I saw her gaze drop to a level just to my right. My hand. Like Talenth, she could sense the Mark.

"*You are different.*" Her telepathic voice was like rolling thunder... but she sounded old. Sad. Resigned.

"I travelled a long way to be here," I replied, drawing myself up. At my full heroic height of five feet and eleven inches, the top of my head was level with the upper arch of the Matriarch's claws. She could have crushed the life out of me with a single toe.

Her manner shifted toward suspicion. She dropped her wings, shuffling around to reveal what lay just under her chest: the eggs. Three perfect dragon eggs, each one large enough to contain a small terrier-sized dog. My heart skipped. The largest of them was a pure reflective silver. The next largest was a clear azure blue, and the smallest was white. I saw the Matriarch swallow around the lump in her throat. It was off to the side, and looked kind of like an Adam's apple... or a tumor.

"I must get a better look at you. *Orius.*" The Matriarch's booming voice slithered through the air. She could speak aloud.

The blue crystal seams in the walls brightened, and as they did, lights appeared in the air: round lamps of pure energy that blazed to life with pure white light. They sparked and spat, humming like a horde of insects.

"*How terribly noisy these baubles of mine are,*" the dragon spoke in my mind again. "*Noisy enough to obscure eavesdropping, including telepathic eavesdropping... so very inconvenient to those trying to listen in. Such a thing is one of the few freedoms I possess.*"

"*What is... what is going on here?*" I was aghast to hear her breathing rasping in her chest. She had barely moved, but she sounded like a pack-a-day smoker. Now that I had time to look... the muscles around her wings were atrophied and soft. There was no way she could fly. This beautiful, regal creature was a prisoner in her own nest. "*What have they done to you?*"

"*You are not the first to ask,*" she replied bitterly. "*But like all of the rest, you come to make your curtsies and beg my permission to touch my eggs, do you not?*"

"No, that's..." I said aloud, before snapping my jaws shut. "*I thought that's why I was here, but... this isn't what I wanted. Are you a prisoner?*"

She bowed her head down toward me, nostrils flaring. I wasn't exactly a coward, but watching the great queen's muzzle looming down over my head was an unnerving experience. "*I cannot tell you.*"

Something clicked.

It was almost the same thing Tymos had said to me over and over again. I'd encountered this puzzle in tabletop role-playing games before, though not in videogames. My eyes narrowed. "*Wait... You're bound by one of those magic compulsion things, aren't you? A geas? Is that what they're called?*"

"*I cannot tell you. But I can affirm that the... compulsion you describe is called a geas.*" The Matriarch sniffed delicately over me, blowing my hair back with each snort. She moved with grace that was surprising in such an enormous creature. "*But you are too late, Herald.*"

"*Too late?*"

"*You have passed their ritual. Once, long ago, they used to send candidates to me before the Trial of Marantha, but I suppose they learned that lesson. The Trial is the first step to ensuring your 'loyal service'.*" The dragon reared up, the joints in her neck popping stiffly. She was not that old – I could sense that, somehow – but she was fat and sick from being trapped indoors, her muscles unexercised. "*Listen to me, Herald: if you truly do not wish to join in what is being done here, pack your satchel and leave. Tonight. Before you take your 'vows'.*"

What the fuck was going on here? I was starting to feel queasy as I looked around the room. *"You're trapped. They don't let you leave. But... don't the young dragons bond with humans? They seemed happy. Why aren't you...?"*

"They bond, yes. But they are kept ignorant of what cannot be said." The dragon's expression shut down. It was... unnatural. Creatures like her weren't supposed to have a poker face, a game face... but there it was. *"Listen to me. I am supposed to let you touch my eggs, so that your lust for them reaches a fever pitch, and I am supposed to tell you the history of this place: the Skyrdon's version of it. I am to motivate you to swear allegiance to Ilia, to preserve and expand the nation's borders. I shall do so, and you must live up to your mantle and the Dark God's trust in you, Herald of the Hidden Seed. We will see if Matir has chosen well. He has not done so in the past."*

I nodded, waiting.

"Long ago, the Drachan – the Void Dragons – invaded this world." The Matriarch dropped her wings down around us, and darkness swallowed the circle of sand where I stood: a tent of living leather. *"They came in the age when all of the elder races of Archemi had their nations. The nation of the Solonkratsu was in the south of this continent, a region now known as the Shalid. It was a green place: a fertile, beautiful land abundant with prey, ruled by queens and their mates: the great generals, hunting masters, and artificers of dragonkind. And when the Drachan came, they swept through the Aesari and the Catfolk like claws through the hide of a soft-skinned doe... it was* we *who drove them back. It was we, the dragons, who created the Dragon Gates... and we who sacrificed the old gods to the Caul of Souls, so that the Void's blight would never touch our beautiful lands and our precious eggs."*

I listened in the warm darkness, stunned. With her wings covering us and the eggs, I could smell her. She smelled like warm baked bread and hot stone, with an undertone of something sharper. Like orange peel.

"But with our gods gone, we were weakened." The Matriarch bowed her head down toward me, ducking them under the great canopy she had made. *"And the Aesari, who had fled the Drachan like twittering cowards, saw their chance to subjugate those around them and take our learning and our magic. They enslaved us, and they enslaved the humans that the Drachan had bought with them to this world, and they enslaved the Catfolk, and bent us all to their purposes... by warping the same magic we had used to create the Dragon Gates. By taking the life of our gods, and subverting part of their energy away from the Caul so that they could bind us into their service."*

"Are you saying...?"

The Matriarch hissed through her teeth. I shut up.

"It was the humans who discovered the means of subverting this control," she continued calmly. *"You will have heard part of this story already, the tale of Grigori and Sachara. Such clever things, humans are... they found loopholes in the geas the Aesari used to bind all other sentient beings here, and they 'destroyed' them so that we dragons might be 'free'. They freed the Catfolk and themselves. They 'partnered' with us."*

I was now sick to my stomach. "They enslaved you."

"I cannot say," the Matriarch replied.

"For how long?"

The dragon's expression was pained. *"I am the great-great-great-granddaughter of Lirenian, the Diamond Queen. She was the daughter of the goddess Solnetsi, whose great spirit powers the Gate of Glorious Dawn. It lies beneath this monument."*

Solnetsi. Why was that name familiar? My eyes were magnetically drawn to the three eggs resting between her forearms. *"And 'the desert lands to the south'..."*

"Our homeland," the Matriarch replied plaintively. *"Before it was drained dry by the terrible artifacts of the Aesari. They fielded titans of metal made for war... magical machines that sucked the life from the earth, that plow through battlefields and shred flesh-and-blood creatures as if they were drinking water. These are the dim memories passed down to me through my blood, like shadows."*

I was definitely starting to feel sick. *"But... do the Skyrdon... take care of you here?"*

"They ensure that I am fed, and always with egg." The great dragon turned her head away from me, as if ashamed. *"For the good of Ilia, and humanity."*

It took a moment for the implication to set in, and when it did, I ground my jaws so hard I thought my teeth would crack. My wavering desire to join the Skyrdon evaporated in a flash. My hands clenched by my sides, and I dropped my voice to a guttural growl. "I'll kill them. I'll kill them all. If you can tell the other dragons to not retaliate, I'll find the commander and-"

"I cannot, and you cannot. I am myself struggling not to react to your threat against the commander... a compulsion I can neither help nor describe." The Matriarch lowered her head until the tip of her nose was barely a foot away from my head. *"Herald... you are a creature of shadow. Be subtle and be clever. There are no breeding females in the Eyrie other than me, and not for lack of the commander's efforts. And if I am the last Queen born here-"*

Before she could continue, the collar around her neck began to glow blue. She snarled, and her breath knocked me out of my crouch and threw me to the sand, coughing.

The huge dragon snapped her jaws and reared up, pulling her wings back as blue light shot over and through her scales. The big, tumor-like bulge in her neck was very visible as she clawed at the sand with her hind feet, rattling the floor with her weight. I backpedaled as some primal fear overtook me... the fear of a very small mammal in the presence of a reptile the size of a large building.

"That's quite enough." A stern man's voice pierced the air from... somewhere. Like a stadium announcement. "Leave the chamber, novice. The Matriarch must rest."

As fearful as I was of how easily the Matriarch could crush me, I didn't want to leave her. But I saw the desperation in the dragon's huge eyes as she looked down at me, and I understood.

I put my own game face on. And I marched back to the large bank vault doors, where Tymos was waiting for me. The old man looked very tired.

"Come," he said.

He led me out, back through the way we'd come. I waited until we were walking together down an empty, featureless hall before grabbing the old man, spinning him, and slamming him against the nearest wall.

I squeezed the leather straps of his armor until they creaked. "You *knew.* You *knew*, and you went along with it anyway. Why is it that you 'cannot speak', but I can?"

"You haven't taken your vows yet." The Novice Master regarded me calmly. Then I realized. He was able to see behind himself, like I now could. He could have dodged... but he hadn't. He hung without resistance.

"But you took your vows," I hissed. "Even though you *knew.*"

Tymos swallowed, and then did something with his hands: a yank on my little fingers, and suddenly, I couldn't keep my grip on his breastplate straps. He shoved me back, and before I had my guard up, pulled his right glove off.

There, like an old scar, was the faint outline of a Mark of Matir.

Chapter 41

"I knew," he said heavily, pulling the glove back on. "And I listened. Believe me, I listened. You're not *that* special, boy. The Black God has sent more than one emissary to help his daughter. And we went like flies to honey."

"But... you..." I wasn't sure what to say.

"You know what happens to insects when they land in honey." Tymos swallowed. He was sweating like he'd just run a mile in his armor.

'Be subtle, and think.' I frowned. "They drown. It's not just the dragons who are bound under this geas... It's the knights, too."

"I cannot say."

"And this... this geas comes into effect when you take the vows?"

He didn't nod, but he didn't shake his head, either.

I swallowed, looking down at the ground, and only then did I notice my quest journal icon flashing. "Hang on a second."

Tymos crossed his arms, watching with some confusion as I brought up my HUD, which he couldn't see, and checked the notification:

New Main Quest: Darkness Shines on Light Places (1/4)

You have learned that there is a dark secret at the heart of the Order of Saint Grigori: the dragons and many of the knights in the order are bound by some kind of magical enslavement. There is a geas on the Order stretching back hundreds, or maybe thousands of years. Find a way to break the cycle, starting with yourself, and uncover the secrets of Cham Garai.

This is a special quest (Mark of Matir).

This is a sequential quest (1 of 4)

Difficulty: Level 10 (Part 1); Level 50+ (Parts 2 to 4)

Reward: EXP, Fame/Infamy, the Pearl of Glorious Dawn.

I had an option to refuse the quest, but I didn't. I accepted without hesitation, and read over the rewards with a growing sense of certainty. Even if the Spear's quest had been a trap, even if there was no actual reward for completing that quest, this Ororgael guy had somehow screwed the pooch. The Spear was still broken and the Dragon Gates still needed to be fixed. I was the one who'd been handed the bucket of shit, and I'd be the one to pour it out. Whatever had happened in Cham Garai hadn't fixed the Spear, or the Dragon Gates or the Caul they supported. If only I could remember what *had* happened.

Tymos walked me back to my room, but he didn't go inside with me. Instead, he clapped me on the shoulder and stepped away. "Now, you are traditionally given time to meditate before you take your vows. Go in and rest – the ceremony will be held at dawn tomorrow. The eggs are expected to hatch in two days' time."

Great. According to the clock, I had less than eight hours to think of a way to not become a literal slave. I nodded curtly. "Thanks."

He was sweating profusely now, his skin greyish. For a moment, I thought he was about to say something, but his lips sealed back up. He gave me an odd look, and then turned and marched stiffly away.

I sighed and rubbed my eyes as the weight of impending defeat settled heavily over my shoulders. All that work, all that fighting, all the backstabbing and betrayal and... *what? What backstabbing and betrayal?*

I finally felt the ghost of a memory slip in. It was still coming together when I opened the door to my room and walked into a wall of swords.

The knight-commander was dressed in full combat gear, seated in a wooden chair with a sword in his lap. He faced the door like a king seated on his throne. Flanking him to either side were Baldr and Lucien. The rest of the room was taken up by soldiers in dark uniforms and sleek green-black armor, and every single one of them had their weapons trained on me. Most had swords, but there were several crossbows. The bolt heads gleamed red and sticky with poison.

Both Baldr and Lucien were alive, and while sickly, they both looked smug in their own unique ways. The sight of them bought back fragments... enough fragments for me to put together what had happened.

"You murdering pieces of shit," I said, fighting the urge to reach back for my spear.

"The same could be said of you, barbarian." The knight-commander regarded me steadily. "Because not only did you attack your fellow aspirants-"

"Baldr attacked *me*!" Baring my teeth, I took a step forward, and that was as far as I got before the soldiers moved in. The points of the swords pressed against me from all angles. Glancing to either side, I noticed that these hard-faced, crew-cut, leather clad people all had violet titles – [[Mysterious Soldier]] – with small glowing violet skulls next to them. Their challenge rating was far, far above my ability.

Lucien looked haunted and shell-shocked, staring at nothing. He had passed the Trial, but he seemed to have aged ten years. His blond hair was streaked with patches of white, and his red irises had turned bright orange, as intense as an eagle's. Baldr was now a true albino, a ghostly giant of a man with stark white hair and pink eyes. But something else about him had changed. His gaze now bore down like a crushing weight, but the most obvious difference was the glossy pearl imbedded in his forehead, like a third eye. The Pearl of Glorious Dawn... had merged with him?

Arnaud continued calmly. "Not only do we have *two* witnesses to this attempted murder, but we have a further two witnesses who were able to verify that you, Hector, aided and abetted rebels against the rightful government of Ilia."

"Bullshit." I clenched my fists. My chest was tight, and hot. "When?"

"Lyrensgrove," he replied crisply. "And these men and women – faith-militant of the Mata Argis – have extracted eye-witness testimony from villagers who say you waded into battle on the side of the rebels the soldiers were sent to kill. Lyrensgrove happens to be situated in a strategic position, and it was being used by the Kingsmen to ferry supplies back and forth across the river. Grain, tools, medicines."

"It wasn't a battle. It was a massacre by rapers, pillagers, and murderers." Something very dark and very angry was brewing inside me now. It was anger, but it was more than anger. It made me feel... cold. Wolfish. Like I could tear Arnaud and Baldr apart with nothing more than my teeth. My dream of flying dragonback was dwindling into nothingness, but something else was taking its place. Good old-fashioned vengeful loathing. "You aren't a commander. You're a jackbooted thug. You've enslaved the dragons with some fucking magic bullshit."

The knight-commander's face was impassive and eerily lifeless. "The Order is and never will be any of your business. And for the first time in many years, we are going to have to execute someone who passed the Trials. I warned you not to come here, Hector. There is no room here for people like you."

The Mata Argis soldiers moved in. I spat on the floor at his feet... but I didn't lash out. Not yet. Not here. I'd be creamed... and even if I respawned, I'd be ganked, at best.

"You're wrong," I said, as my arms were wrenched behind me. "You're wrong about the Matriarch, and you're wrong about me."

"Cool story, bro." Baldr finally spoke. Smug asshole.

The commander rose, bristling with impatience. "Take him."

"You won't be able to do this forever." I stared at Arnaud over my shoulder as the Mata Argis agents shoved me around toward the door. "And one day, I'll be back, and I'll be bringing the dragons. I'll find a way to tell them, and we'll come for *you.*"

Chapter 42

My wrists hurt, again. Everything hurt. The cell was filthy and dark, and unlike the slave hold of the Arabella, it was wet. The tightly locked stones in the walls grew glowing moss in the seams. Fungi grew in here, too, mushrooms that rose out of the pile of damp straw that was to serve as my bed.

Despite the plant life, the place was unfortunately secure. The wind howled somewhere behind me, and a hidden breeze caused the oily light of the torch outside the bars to flicker and dance. The orange glow wasn't enough to illuminate the back of the cell or much of the hallway beyond the bars, not for normal eyes, anyway. I could see in the dark now, for all the good it was going to do me.

I paced the cell like a tiger, too angry to sit still. My manacles didn't weigh as much as they should have post-Trial, but they might as well have been chained to floor. My ears whined, crackling with every tiny sound in the jail. Boots stomping around, guards breathing, the click of someone clearing their throat, the rustling of mice and rats moving around in my cell and in the cells to either side. I needed to take action, to *do* something, but the only thing stronger than the cell was the crushing, numbing weight of failure.

In all the years of stupid shit I'd done, the drag races and bar fights and speeding, I'd never been to jail, but I had been purposeless. I'd been lonely and without direction. Seeing the effort Steve had made to stay alive and rope me into this, I'd come to Archemi wanting to become something – *someone* – better than what I had been. To find freedom. But after everything I'd done, after the Trials, after the stupid betrayal, it was happening again. My life had been taken from me by some government, again. And not just my life: the Matriarch's, the dragons', and even the knights here were slaves, bound by a conspiracy I'd only begun to scratch the surface of... and even if I *had* succeeded, I'd have ended up like Tymos. I was screwed at every turn. I'd been a pawn all my life, and was *always* going to be a pawn unless I somehow unfucked myself.

The loneliness I'd been fighting ever since the start of the War came crashing over me in that little cell. I'd lost everyone and everything. No family, no friends IRL or within the game. Steve hadn't made it. I was a ghost trapped with other ghosts in some kind of weird virtual purgatory.

And speaking of that, why the fuck wasn't Baldr dead?

The events in Cham Garai were coming back in bits and pieces. Something had happened down there, with the Aesari... but I didn't know what. Just the thought of Baldr's smug handsome face swung me from the deepening apathy back to rage. There were no good guys here. Everyone here was complicit in the Matriarch's enslavement. She needed someone to stand up for her. She needed me to do something.

And in the total darkness of that despair, a plan suddenly germinated and came to life... like a seed.

I ground my teeth together, gathering my resolve. I finally spent my skill points. Manacles couldn't stop me from doing *that*. I had enough to upgrade three of my Dark Lancer abilities to Rank 2, but new abilities didn't open until I reached Level 8. I decided on Shadow Dance, Whirlwind Butcher, and Life for Life. All three abilities had saved my ass multiple times already, and taking them to second rank vastly boosted damage and recharge time at the expense of AP. As I confirmed the levels, my skills and stats swelled. There was the usual surge of knowledge, accompanied by a feeling of greater strength and dexterity. Not just physical, this time. When I checked my sheet, I noticed my Wisdom had boosted by three points. Yeah! Enlightenment, bitches!

I was about to casually stroll over to the bars when a door slammed somewhere deeper in the prison. I heard voices: two - no, three – two lower tones, one higher. A woman. I froze, waiting, as another door opened and the voices became clearer.

"-as well as I do that the word of a traitor is worth nothing more than a sack of triceratops dung! So consider this your last chance before we make your sow of a daughter here start squealing. Where is the Prince's camp?"

"I swear on the gods I don't know!" A hoarse, older man's voice. A familiar voice.

"The gods care little for treasonous old men. Take this girl to the strappado, string her up. I'll need a sharp poker... and go get fresh coals for this thing, they're cold"

"Kira! You bastards, leave her alone!"

My pulse jumped. *You're fucking kidding me.*

"Pa! Pa! No! Don't-" The woman's cries reached a frantic pitch, replaced by gasps from a blow to the gut. Owen bellowed in rage.

I rushed to the front of the cell, trying to see what was happening, but Kira and Owen weren't within view: they were down the hall and around a corner of the dungeon.

"You'd be better off dealing with us than with the Mata Argis, scum." I didn't recognize the interrogator's voice. "Do you want to know what they do to your kind? To those condemned for treason? Do you know what they'll do to your daughter?"

"I'm not a sack of meat, asshole!" Kira cried.

"No! Leave my daughter alone! She's got no part in this, she's a healer-"

"She's a traitor's bitch!" The interrogator lifted his voice in anger. "Now start talking! Where is the camp? Who is commanding the force? How many? Do they have the Prince?"

"Pa, no! Don't tell them anyth-AAAAHHH!"

"Where is the camp!?"

Breathing quickly, I started shaking the manacles, searching for a way out of them. They were snug, but not tight, and they were bolted on with screws that used a tool with a hexagonal head. There was no slipping them, not even if I degloved my wrists and ankles. But they could be used as a weapon.

I gripped the bars on the front of my cell and shook them until they rattled. "Hey! Shitcunts! You want to know where the Prince is? He's screwing Captain Arnaud's mouth while his dragon fucks him in the ass and your mom watches!"

"Who the in the hells is spewing that filth?" I heard the interrogator ask someone else. They were waiting on the coals.

"You heard me! And I've got your fucking Prince right here!" I yelled back. "By the time I'm done with you, you'll be spending the rest of your life in diapers! Don't tell him anything, Kira! It's me, Hector!"

"It's that outlander rebel," the other man - a guardsman, I assumed - replied. He dropped his voice, but my ears were supernaturally sharp now. I could hear every word. "Should I go shut him up?"

"He wants us to kill him. He's Starborn - he'll return to life and come back for us. The imperator warned me."

Whoever was out there, I could probably take them in a fight... unless they were violet-ranked bad guys. I rattled the door, banging it back and forth in the frame. "I can hear every stupid word you're saying down there! Stay strong, Kira! Owen, don't tell them a damn thing! I've got your back as soon as I'm out of here!"

"Fine! Go shut him up!" The interrogator hissed. "Dammit... I forgot he'd passed the Trials. He has a dragonman's hearing."

I almost laughed. Hysterical laughter, but laughter none the less. "Hell yeah, I do! And I'm coming for you, nancy-boy!"

The guards rumbled up the hall in a wave of hobnailed boots and clanking armor, metal scraping on metal. I rolled my shoulders and cracked my knuckles. It sounded like the sweet chorus of freedom.

I closed my eyes, and pictured the Matriarch in my mind. I remembered the dragon's orange peel and warm bread smell, the sound of her wings, the way light reflected off the opalescent curves of her muzzle. *"Ma'am, if you can hear me, you should know that I'm in prison. I'm about to bust out, but I just want you to know... one day, I'm coming back for you. I'm coming to help you. I'm going to take you away from these people."*

The guards stopped in front of my cell, crossbows leveled through the bars. There were four of them, all higher levels than me. Two had crossbows, and two had short, forked spears in their hands. They were wearing Ilian colors, the white seagull on a purple field. They were drawn from the Ilian soldiers who were stationed at the fort. Blackwin's soldiers, not Mata Argis super-troopers.

"Get back!" The guard in the lead snarled at me. "Get back, or we'll pin you to the wall like a cockroach! These bolts have poison on them!"

"Oh no, not *poison*!" I held my hands up and backed away, almost rolling my eyes. "It's not like I just took a bunch of poison and survived a series of hideous mutations to be here!"

"You won't want to have survived anything once we're done with you, dog. Shoot him in the knee!" The captain snapped.

The guard lowered the crossbow and fired, and I triggered Shadow Dance, dashing to the side. The ability didn't allow me to pass through walls, but the bolt flew through the black haze. I dodged the second by rolling back, and got skimmed by the third.

[[You are poisoned!]]

It was just plain old widowberry sap - 1 hp a second for 50 seconds - but I went to one knee with a dramatic cry, clutching the bleeding cut. "Arrrgh! My life of adventuring is over! You guys! Why are you so mean to me?!"

The guard took the chance to unlock and open the door. The first man came in, club raised. I didn't have a spear yet, so I activated Blood Sprint on my fist instead. "Attack!"

My adrenaline points dropped as I rose up with an uppercut, unnaturally fast, and punched him right in the dick.

[[Critical hit! 300 non-fatal damage!]]

The guard's eyes bulged. His face turned cherry red as he fell to hands and knees beside me and vomited with pain.

"Help! Man down, man down!"

"No! Attaaaack!" I rolled under the guard as bolts rained down on us, using him as a human shield until the repeater ran out and the others charged in. When the arrows stopped, I rolled up and pulled the man's weapon off his back – an [[Iron Spontoon]] - then activated Piercing Lance again. I lunged forward at my quickened speed, plowed through the guards blocking the cell door, and blew my way into the hallway. "Yeeeeeeeeeaaaahhh!"

From somewhere deeper in the prison, Kira screamed: a pitiful, agonized shriek of pain.

The guards scattered like pins, shouting in surprise. I threw the spontoon at the back of the man running for reinforcements as the captain closed in on me. The spear nailed the runner with enough force that he lost his balance and fell to the floor, but I didn't have time to see whether he was hurt before steel flashed in my face. I caught the captain's sword with the chain linking my wrists, trapping it in links of rough iron. I twisted the weapon to the side, jerking it from his hands, and pulled him into a headbutt. Nose met forehead, but he was tougher than the other men and it barely hurt him.

I avoided one gauntleted fist, but the follow-up jab caught me across the cheek and sent me stumbling back against the wall. Desperate and dizzy, I pivoted to the side as his other fist slammed into the rock where my head had been. The captain jumped in to pin me bodily to the stone, and that was when I revealed what I had been palming in my left hand all this time: one of the poisoned crossbow bolts. I pulled the captain's head down by the strap of his helmet with one hand, and rammed the sharp bolt into his eye with the other.

The man screamed, stumbling back with a hand over his face. I shoved him into his regrouping men and threw myself to the floor in a diving roll. I scooped up the captain's fallen sword, and turned with a downward blow. The captain fended off the first strike, but not the second - which took his head off his shoulders. The arterial spray soaked the other two remaining guards.

"*Tarn Takhar*, motherfuckers!" I bellowed, and charged in like the barbarian I was.

Chapter 43

Steel clashed, and even though the soldiers were my level or higher, they weren't prepared for this: a pissed off post-Trial Starborn with nothing to lose and everything to gain from kicking their asses. I Jumped through them and stabbed the first guard, ramming the sword up under the edge of his helmet and through the side of his neck. Blood gushed as quickly as his HP ring drained, and then I was on to the next one. The Mark of Matir burned coldly on my skin as we parried, locked swords, and spun around in a circle. He kneed me in the groin, barely missing the family jewels, and wrenched the chain linking my cuffs to trap my sword hand. I struggled, got my guard up, and the guard responded by shoving my hands - and the chain - against my throat.

The commotion was drawing reinforcements, and I couldn't breathe. Wheezing, straining for room to move, I brought both my legs up and got them between us, shoving the burly man away. He growled, but I got back control of my hands just long enough to jab him in both eyes with my thumbs. The man howled. I grabbed his knife from his belt and stabbed: face, neck, under the arms. He dropped to his knees. I grabbed him, and triggered Life for Life II.

Energy drained from him and into me. I drew a deep breath as it flooded my body, and the guard's eyes rolled back in his head.

"Shit. Shit shit shit." Gasping for breath, I pushed him away, then bulk-looted the body, getting some coins, a poultice, and most importantly, a set of [[Jail Keys]]. I used them on the cuffs and fetters, and they fell away, freeing my limbs. Not a moment too soon. More guards were thundering down the corridor toward the hallway slaughterhouse.

Grim and focused, I equipped the guard's greaves, boots, gauntlets, and breastplate, but left off the helmet. The armor was heavy and offered slightly more protection than my old Jack of Plates, but it was something. I raided the others for their HP-restoring food and took off, seizing the spontoon I'd thrown as I ran by.

The corridor around the corner from the cells was wider and taller than the one outside the row of cells, feeding into a large torture room. No fewer than six guards ran at me, swords drawn. Behind them was the interrogator - a tall, bald, lantern-jawed man in a long leather coat. He was holding a glowing poker, standing in front of Kira. She was burned, semi-conscious, her beautiful dark curls had been roughly chopped off. She was also naked, and hanging from a pulley-and-rope contraption by her wrists. That was all I was able to see before the mass of guards was on me.

"Here you go, assholes!" I activated the Mark of Matir, and charged in.

The dark energy washed through my body in a chilling wave. As I closed in, I burned the rest of my AP on Jump, leaping up and out of the way of their lunging swords. I landed on the one helmetless guard in the team, spear-first, and rammed it deep into his neck. Blood sprayed, and the Mark fed greedily, pumping up my HP as I bounced back to the ground.

"Magic! A Heretic! Demon!" someone yelled.

Not quite. But the Skyrdon had gotten what they wanted when they put me through the Trials.

At Level 7, I was able to cut down the remaining five Level 8 guards in a whirl of wood and steel, fueled by rage and grief. After the last man gurgled on the spontoon blade I'd thrust through his mouth and out the back of his head, I pulled it out. I whirled the polearm around my body and turned to face the interrogator.

Whatever he saw in my face terrified him. He was sheet-white, holding the poker like a sword. I looked at what he'd done to Kira, and then to Owen. The healer's face was swollen. He was missing teeth, and tears still poured down his weathered cheeks.

"Please-" the torturer got out one choked word as I ran at him. Whatever else he began to say was drowned out by my furious snarl.

He parried the spontoon once, twice, driven back by the force of the blows. Once the adrenaline hit, the torturer recovered enough to use the poker like a fencing foil. He lunged in past my guard and shoved the burning-hot tool at my chest. It slid along the armor and into my armpit, a shock of hot pain. I ignored it, and used the haft of the spear to flick the poker away, then swung it up to slam the torturer up under his jaw.

He fell back, bleeding from the mouth, and put a hand up to ward me away and protect his head. "No!"

"Life for life." I grabbed him by the face with one hand and rammed the spontoon through his stomach with the other, twisting the weapon even as I sucked the vitality out of him. The energy was cold and hot at the same time, an addictive dizzying rush. The dying man clawed at me, rapidly weakening, and the flesh of his face was like paper when I let go. I pushed him away to collapse on the ground. I should have felt... anything, really, but there was only numbness, and the sensation of something grinning at the world from behind my eyes, a formless predator with very sharp teeth.

Swallowing, I dismissed the Mark, and felt the dark presence recede. In the moment of silence that followed, I felt an odd pressure, the push of telepathic connection.

"Herald, I sense your victory and your impending freedom," the Matriarch said. Her voice was strained. *"You must come to me, before the Mata Argis know you have escaped."*

"Come to you?" I muttered aloud. "How? Where? I don't know where I am!"

"You are in the lower ground level of the Eyrie. Do not fear, I will guide you."

"Okay, hold on. There are people here I have to help."

"As you will. But do not tarry."

"*You*!" The old man stared at me in naked shock as I gazed off into space. "By the Gods! What did you *do*?"

"I just saved your ass. And I'm about to save your daughter's." With a stiff nod, I turned and went to free Kira.

Kira was limp, but conscious. She shook with pain as I turned the winch that lowered her to the ground, but the only sound she made was to whimper when her feet touched the floor. She dropped to her knees as the rope slackened and her dislocated arms slid back into place with a muffled crunch.

"It's okay, Kira." I fumbled with the jail keys, hurrying to unlock her cuffs. "You're going to be okay."

She did not reply, shuddering with the effort to stay conscious.

"Kira!" Owen strained against his chains as I unbound him. He wobbled up to his feet and ran to his daughter, gathering her in his arms.

"Here." I looted the inquisitor's coat and then transferred it back out of my Inventory to my hand, in the hopes that it would clean the garment up a little. It did. I headed for them, coat held in outstretched hands. But to my surprise, Owen flinched away, holding Kira close.

"Please, I beg you!" He looked – and sounded – like he was terrified. "Mercy for her, *missiure*, if not for me!"

"What?" I froze, looking down at him.

"I... I told them everything." The old herbalist trembled. "They made me talk... they were hurting her. I wouldn't have said a word, if not for that, but..."

Oh. So *he'd* been the 'eye-witness source'. Dark anger flared in my chest like an ember, but it was easily crushed. It wasn't his fault. He had no more power than I did.

"Here," I said heavily. "Cover her up. And don't worry about it. I'd have done the same thing for my kid."

Tears streamed down Owen's cheeks. He nodded as he took the coat and tenderly covered Kira's battered body with a layer of warm, heavy leather. She moaned, opening her eyes, but saying nothing.

"We don't have much time." I crouched down next to him. "What happened? Did you know those raiders were soldiers?"

"We suspected they were," Owen said. "But you were a stranger. Our alderman would never tell you. After you left, we had a few weeks of peace, enough to warn the Kingsmen that our days were numbered. Some fled the village... We stayed to help the injured. Then the dragons came. The whole place is gone, Hector. Buildings, fields, everything."

I looked down, and to the side.

Owen regarded me with a touch of defiance. "Now you've seen how the false crown staged its 'revolution'. There isn't anything revolutionary about the warden. He's a thug in the pocket of merchants.

We're northerners and land-bound at that, but even we know he murdered King Rosvin in his chambers by night, all at the command of some wizard and his witch whore."

Rutha. That stung. She and I were going to have a long talk someday soon.

"Listen," I said. "You need to get Kira out of here. Loot the armor off one of these guards, dress Kira like the interrogator, and bluff your way out. It's your only chance."

"You won't come with us?"

I gestured at myself. "I look too foreign. If it's just you two, you have a better chance of talking your way out."

"You're right." Owen looked down at his daughter. "But Kira..."

"I can walk." Her voice was roughened with pain, but she stirred up enough to look at me. "We have to."

"Girl, if you're as badly hurt as-"

"I'm of age now, Pa. Don't call me 'girl'." She turned her warm amber eyes on me. "Thank you, Hector."

"Don't thank me yet. You still have to get out of here." I bounced up to my feet. "And we need to hurry."

While Owen scavenged for disguises, I went to properly search the bodies. Chewing a piece of jerky, I had a look at the Inventory of the torturer. He was carrying a Quest Item.

Note from the Mata Argis to Captain Lorenz

"We are arranging special accommodations for the Starborn in Liren. Under no circumstances should he be killed, if you value your life. Make sure the prison is warded against dark magic. Do not transport him until the fetters have been enchanted and sent to Skyr Arnaud.

- Commander Pavella Blackwin."

"Pavella Blackwin?" I frowned. *A relative of Anya Blackwin?*

"Pah! The Black Bitch, they call her." Owen spat. "She leads the Mata Argis. Come here, help me dress Kira."

"Right." I folded the letter back into my Inventory, and went to assist.

We found some minor healing items, which we split between Owen and Kira, and helmets with visors that concealed their faces. When they left, I locked the jail door and went on a deeper search of the place. My stuff was in a wooden chest inside a small dank room next to the torture chamber, and the Spear leaned against the wall beside it. With the ancient weapon in my hands, I immediately felt better.

"Okay," I thought out toward the Matriarch. *"Sorry. I had to save them."*

"You must go through the sewers," The Matriarch said to me. *"Go down past the cells and underground. There should be a latrine there, a grate that deposits right into the sewer canal."*

"Great." I shook my head, annoyed and amused at the same time. No fantasy adventure was complete without traipsing through the sewers. "How do you even know that?"

"I have my ways, and the knowledge of my mother and her mother before her. This is an ancient place. Please hurry, I cannot hold for much longer."

"Hold? Hold what?" brows creased, I slunk out of the room, spear at the ready. The place was still deserted. Sensing no one, I broke into a jog.

"You will see. Go down to latrine, down through the grate, and descend into the sewers. You will head northeast."

I headed back out into the jail, down the row of cells, and sure enough, there was a locked door that opened into a narrow, damp stairwell. I clattered down through a haze of torch smoke, and the deeper I went, the more pungent the air became. There was no one here, but finding the latrine wasn't hard. The small room was bare, with nothing but an old bucket covered in cobwebs, a crusty, rusted iron grate in the floor, and walls carpeted in fungi. The trickling sound of running water could be heard from below. It looked like it hadn't been used in centuries.

Mucking around in fossilized shit was not my idea of a fun time. No matter how many times I reminded myself this was a virtual reality, the smell of the sewer below was very real. With a sigh, I hauled the grate up and shoved it aside, dropped down, and pulled the cover back over. *"Okay. I'm in."*

The spear on my back throbbed. For a moment, I thought I'd hallucinated the sensation, but then I felt a *push* through the air around me. A small light appeared in front of me in the dark. It was silent but bright, and threw harsh shadows off the walls that sent rats scattering for cover.

"Follow me," the Matriarch said.

The light led the way forward. I brought my spear around, eyes darting from place to place as I jogged along, careful not to slip on the slimy stone. The only enemies down here were rats, quickly dispatched with a couple of spear thrusts if they got too close.

After what felt like hours of scrabbling, the light drifted up a short, slippery ramp and hung by a ladder leading up into the darkness. I slung my spear over my shoulder and started the climb, only to find myself hesitating. The Mark of Matir was making my arm throb: not painfully, but in way that forced me to notice. What if I was walking into a trap? The Matriarch was geas-bound to serve the Skyrdon. If they'd ordered her to lead me here, I was going to climb out and find myself at the mercy of Arnaud and a full wing of Dragon Knights.

"How do I know I should trust you?" I thought. *"There's magic binding you to the Skyrdon."*

There was silence for a few moments. *"I am fighting their control, as I wish I could have done centuries ago. Come quickly - I cannot fight for much longer."*

Shaking my head, I mounted the ladder and climbed to the top. I found a manhole cover there. I pushed it up, and warily slid out into a small, very hot, dimly-lit room. Brass pipes ran along the walls, rows and rows of them. Ancient machinery thrummed in the walls, heard but not seen. A boiler room?

The light danced ahead of me, passing through the door and leaving me in darkness. I followed it, and emerged from a cleverly-disguised side exit into the hatching grounds.

The Matriarch sat rigidly on the sands, her head bowed, her foreclaws dug into the earth in front of her. The air around her was subtly warped, energy snapping and popping as she battled the geas and other enchantments that bound her to her lair. She was alone, as she'd said, and the chamber was completely empty save for the dragon.

"Thank the Nine," she said. She sounded tired.

Being here was a painful reminder of what I would never have. Cautiously, I approached the Matriarch, swallowing against the lump in my throat. "What do you need, ma'am?"

In reply, the dragon extended her neck and head toward me. Her body tensed, and her long throat rippled with contractions as she retched once, then again, like a cat throwing up a hairball. I watched in confusion as her neck bulged, and the tumorous mass moved... a smooth shape that passed up as her jaws widened and she passed up a wet, dark gray-black sphere onto the hot sand.

My eyes widened. It wasn't a tumor or a hairball. It was an egg - an egg half again as large as the white and blue ones that had been warming in the hatchery.

"You cannot know how devastated I was to bear this egg," the Matriarch said sadly. She dipped her muzzle toward it, tongue lashing over it tenderly. *"This is a Queen egg, Hector. One of several I have laid over the centuries. Every time, I have hidden the egg and waited... and every time until now, no one worthy of my daughters appeared."*

"You killed them?" My eyes widened.

"I would not wish this life on my worst enemy," she replied, panting and hunching against the snapping energy coursing over her skin. *"I couldn't let them hatch. I wouldn't allow it. I have never left this lair. I have never seen the sky. No daughter of mine must have her wings clipped, her teeth dulled, or be treated like a breeding sow. Never. That they take the other children of my clan is bad enough. And this one... she will be dark in scale, Hector, a daughter of Matir. The Skyrdon would treat her even more terribly than I for that alone."*

The damp shell was drying, and as it did, the color was changing from a dull gunmetal gray to a polished pewter color, becoming brighter and more metallic. "But if I hadn't come?"

"She would never have hatched," the Matriarch affirmed grimly. *"But a Herald has come, and in you, she will find a worthy companion."*

"You're sure she's...?" I trailed off as, even as I spoke, the egg rocked and chirped.

"Yes." The pearl-scaled dragon snapped her jaws convulsively, squinting against the building pain as she continued to fight the magic binding her. *"I... I will teleport you from here to the stables in the fortress beyond the ruins. It will take the Skyrdon some time to realize where you have gone... e-enough time for you to run. It is too late to help me. But you must... you must give her a better life."*

Struck dumb with disbelief, I stumbled forward to lay my hands on the surface of the egg. It was hot, and the wyrmling inside was kicking, trying to break free through the unnaturally tough shell. But she couldn't - not yet.

The egg fit in my Inventory and disappeared inside the magic hammerspace backpack, but it was heavy and encumbered me to a slow walk. I threw out everything else that wasn't absolutely necessary, then shouldered the struggling burden. When the Matriarch saw I was ready, she bowed her head, her body tense with discomfort. The metal chains and gems danced with power, leaving scorch marks on her pale skin.

"They come," she said. *"I will spend the last of my power to help you. My daughter will hatch soon, perhaps even tonight. Hold her fast to you for the rest of your days, Dragozin Hector. And... thank you."*

"Thank *you*," I stammered. "I'm... I'm honored. I don't know if I'm..."

"You ARE ready. Feelings are not reality, Herald. This is one of the lessons Matir teaches us." The dragon's tone was firm. She lifted her front paws, and the air of the hatching chamber warped, moaning in resistance to the magic that the elder dragon began to weave with her claws. "Mortan... vrath'lass!"

The collar around her neck turned red hot, and the dragon roared with agony - but the spell was cast. The scent of ozone filled my sinuses, and the space ahead of us folded in on itself, sucking back into a 'hole' torn in the fabric of reality.

"A portal," the Matriarch said, her voice strained. *"Go!"*

"I promise I'll come back for you!" I moved for the portal. "I swear it!"

The queen dragon thrashed from side-to-side in pain. Even as I watched, bright blue liquid gathered in the corners of her eyes and trickled from her ears. Blood.

The door to the hatchery opened, and people streamed in, shouting, waving weapons. I glimpsed Arnaud in the lead, his face a mask of shock.

"I... I know you will," the Matriarch's psionic voice was strained and grim with focus as she collapsed. "*Go!*"

There was no time for fear, only action. I half stumbled, half jumped through the portal.

The magic gate sucked me through, and for a moment, there was nothing but a total, bone-piercing cold blackness that ejected me onto the muddy ground outside Fort Palewing's stable. Other than the sounds of the hookwings, it was eerily quiet here, the alarm going up in the Eyrie having not yet reached the main fortress.

I stumbled forward struggling under the weight of the backpack, searching frantically. Cutthroat was back in her default pen, and she came to the door and cocked her head like a dog as I approached.

"Okay, girl. This is no time to fuck around, you hear?" Sweat poured down my back as I attached the nose reins and opened the door, leading the big hookwing out. "Don't cock this up."

Cutthroat made a confused trilling sound in her throat, sniffing the backpack when I dropped the reins and hauled her saddle off the saddle tree. The pack and spear combined was over twice my usual carrying capacity, and every other task was made borderline impossible while I was wearing it - but if I set it on the ground, I wasn't going to be able to pick it up again. I flung a blanket over the hookwing's back, then the saddle, and cinched it with shaking hands. The bridle reins were next. The saurian bird was oddly compliant as I mounted her.

"Hya!" I nudged her in the ribs, and twitched the reins.

Cutthroat started at a walk, slinking out of the stable, and when we reached the courtyard, she picked up her feet and began to run. There were roars from overhead as suddenly, the fortress was shrouded in the shadows of enormous wings.

Dragons. The Skyrdon were here.

Chapter 44

Our only hope was the wild forest that surrounded the fortress, and the ruins that littered it. We were going to have to disappear into the mountains. If we stayed out in the open, we were as good as dead.

"Hiyah!" I slapped the reins, urging Cutthroat to a gallop, and we tore our way through the fortress grounds toward the rear gate. She kept ahead of the bellowing dragons as they circled the fortress. As we approached the gate, my heart sunk. Some guards were milling around in front of the winch that opened the exit. I was going to have to bluff my way through.

"Open the gate!" I yelled, reining Cutthroat back to a lope. "Open the bloody gate!"

"What's going on!" The man closest to the winch called back.

"Thieves disguised as the warden's men stole an egg from the Eyrie! They're escaping!" I had to bring Cutthroat to a prancing, hissing stop, reining her in tightly to stop her from throwing me off in irritation. "I'm giving chase while the commander searches above!"

"Through here? Into the woods? But we didn't... the only people who've been through here was that city inquisitor and his bodyguard."

Holy shit, Kira and Owen had made it out. I shook the spear at him. "And who do you think took the egg? Just open the goat-sucking gate!"

The soldier paused for a moment, features slack, then cursed and began hauling on the gate mechanism. "You there, soldier! Help me!"

As soon as the gate was high enough for me to dash out, I kicked my mount to a run, and off we went.

We pelted out down the road, and as soon as I was able, I turned Cutthroat off the rutted trail and into the trees. The hookwing shrilled with alarm as we careened through the brush in the dark, but she was so focused on running without falling that she forgot to worry about me being on her back. With every stumble and leap, I felt like my shoulders were going to dislocate under the heavy weight inside my pack. I ground my teeth, and hung on for dear life as alerts flashed. Hunger, thirst, exhaustion, and the pee meter. *Thanks, Ryuko. How would I ever remember the need to piss if you didn't tell me?*

Behind us, the fort came to life. Lights went up, sending flickering orange shadows through the blue-green of the forest, but we quickly left them behind. A smarter man probably would have taken a hookwing that was more tractable than Cutthroat, but there was one thing I could say for her: the bitch could run like the wind. She was easily the strongest and fastest beast in the stable, even if she was likely to attack me as soon as I got down off the saddle.

The trees hissed as we flew by them, and dirt sprayed up under Cutthroat's clawed feet. I tucked my head and stood in the stirrups, bent forward like a jockey, and coolly searched my mini-map for anything that could help us. Here and there were small question mark icons, indicating places of interest. There were a small cluster of them not too far from where we were. There was a good chance one of them was a dungeon entrance.

A great rushing sound overheard sent a chill through my chest. I turned to look at the shadow cutting through the trees barely a hundred feet behind us, and drove my hookwing sharply to the left as the air sucked back around us.

A thunderous, superheated blast of fire cut through the forest, blowing up a cloud of burning leaves, splintered wood, and crackling earth in a twenty-foot line that set everything in front and around it on fire. Cutthroat screeched as the dragon blew past, rocking the trees, and I forced her to weave, back and forth, as more wing shadows joined the first.

Fire roared overhead, searing through the greenery. The dragons were burning the woods methodically, setting the forest aflame to flush me out. To get to the ruins, we were going to have to ride through the blaze.

"Ey ey ey ey!" I urged Cutthroat, turning her by the nose toward the leading edge of the forest fire and the cluster of question marks. "Come on!"

The hookwing snarled, slowing and shaking her head, but when I kicked her heaving ribs, she lowered her head like a bull and charged. Flames licked at us from every side as we scrambled across the hot earth, roaring everywhere around us. I held my breath against the smoke, squinting ahead, and nearly lost my seat as Cutthroat leaped over a log I hadn't seen and charged down into a waterlogged gully. Stone plinths loomed out at us through the haze, the remains of ancient statues mostly buried under the muck.

Then, overhead, a huge tree creaked. The wind rushed as it toppled, a flaming pillar headed right for us.

Cutthroat came to a stop with a cry of warning, too sharply for me to hang on. Suddenly, I was flying. My reflexes kicked in just before I hit the ground, and I rolled under the tree as it crashed to the ground, tumbling head over ass and sliding to a hard stop against an outcrop of stone. *The egg!*

The fire was catching up to us, and through the crackling roar of the flames, I heard the resonant, booming cries of the Skyrdon's dragons calling to each other. Shouldering my backpack, heedless of the flashing warnings in the corner of my eye, I staggered up to my feet. "Cutthroat! Heel!"

The hookwing snapped her jaws and tossed her head, but to my surprise, she obeyed. I ran down deeper into the gully with the dinosaur in hot pursuit, staggering under the weight of the egg. We splashed along in fire-heated water that was slowly deepening and getting cooler, and soon, the sides of the gully were above head height. Ahead of us, I saw our goal: an odd, unnaturally-shaped cave entrance shrouded with vines. It took me a moment to realize that it wasn't actually a cave - it was a tunnel, an ancient aqueduct still carrying water from the depths of the half-buried city.

We splashed in, pushing aside vines as we fumbled into the darkness. The light from the fire raging outside lit our way until the tunnel turned, plunging us into the chilly damp I associated with Cham Garai and the swamp. When Cutthroat was close enough that I could take her reins, I gathered them up and led her, nearly blind, into the shelter of the ruins.

While the forest was burning, the Skyrdon wouldn't be able to search for me on the ground. Panting, back aching, I didn't stop until I could hear nothing but the drip of water, the echoes of our own footsteps, and the distant cries of dragons.

We came to a halt in a dark stone chamber defined by the huge patches of glowing fungi that grew on the walls. In near darkness, I slid to the ground and shrugged the pack off, then onto my hands and knees to search around for something to start a fire with.

Then I realized that, since the fall I'd taken in the forest, the backpack hadn't moved. Hadn't chirped. It had gone still, and silent.

"Oh no." My first instinct was to abandon the search for tinder and timber. Then training kicked in. Fire was a priority. If the hatchling was injured or - gods help me - dying, then I needed light to see what I was doing. She needed warmth, because it was cold and wet down here. Cutthroat needed warmth to recover her strength.

I scratched together old wood, vines, and what felt like dead leaves and twigs, clumps of dry moss, and any anything else I could find. I got my flint and tinder out of the front of the pack and struck it over the lightest tinder. My hands were shaking, and it took a few minutes to get it lit, but once I placed the tinder on the wood and leaves, it caught readily.

The room was large, in the shape of an hourglass, and hanging with vines. Aesari engravings were still visible, the walls featuring broad, patterned bands, and the stylized figures of winged, helmeted figures. As soon as I could see, I clambered back over to the pack, brought up my Inventory, and removed the egg.

The pack disgorged it into my lap, where it barely fit. The shell was cooler than it had been in the hatching grounds, and it was no longer moving.

"Fuck!" Shuddering with effort, I carefully shuffled over with it to the fire, and put my ear against the side. At first, I heard nothing... but then a tiny, wet gasp reverberated from inside, a burbling sound, like something suffocating.

"Hang on in there!" I pulled my dagger and wedged it into a crack at the very top of the shell. It skittered away and cut my other hand, but I kept stabbing, flaking the tough material away, layer by layer. Chips became shards, and when I reached the toughened inner 'skin' holding the baby dragon in place, I cut a hole in it, reached in, and began to pull the shell apart with my hands instead. "Breathe, goddammit!"

The dancing firelight shone wetly off tiny black scales: the little dragon's shoulder. I tore at the shell frantically, ears ringing, not even sure I was supposed to be freeing her *now.* Maybe I was killing her by doing this. Maybe she was already dead. My nails were bleeding, but I barely noticed the pain.

At some point, the egg became easier to break down. I opened it about halfway around, and carefully cut away the membrane. The wyrmling's weight began to tear it around the edges of the open shell. It gave way suddenly, spilling the gleaming black creature to the dusty floor. She was fully formed, perfect and beautiful... but she wasn't moving.

Swallowing around a knot of panic, I pressed fingers into her neck, searching for a pulse, and checked her breathing with the other hand. The long, wedge-shaped snout was motionless, eyes sealed, but my fingers found a slow, thready, barely-there pulse. Without a second thought, I levered open the little dragon's jaws and depressed her tongue with my fingers, turning her head. Fluid poured from her mouth to the floor. Once her airway was clear, I stuck my face in as far as it would go, and began CPR.

"Come on, baby. Come on." Three breaths, ten chest compressions. Deep compressions, pumps that would have broken a human's ribs. As I alternated respiration and compressions, Cutthroat slunk over to us and lay on her belly beside the fire, licking her wounds.

I was on the rebound from a compression when the tiny dragon's hind leg kicked. Her awkwardly-thin neck rippled, and she frothed at the mouth, thrashing weakly. I growled, left off, and grasped her jaws top and bottom, forcing her to stay on her side so that she didn't lurch up and breathe the fluid in again. Sweat poured down my face. "That's it... you can do it. Come on, kid! You can do it!"

The wyrmling's tongue lashed, and then she began to cough. Liquid bubbled up from deep inside of her chest, expelled as she panicked and struggled against my hands. She caught my leg with a foreclaw, slashing the leather, fabric and the skin beneath like it wasn't there, but I hung on while the dragon - about the size of a Doberman - unpeeled one wet wing from her flank and began to flap it in the air. She gasped for breath. When her coughing became clearer, I let her go and moved back out of harm's way, chest tight with mingled wonder and relief. The little queen lurched up weakly, still hacking as she pawed at her sticky eyelids.

The dumb thing was going to scratch her own eyes out. I rushed back to her, caught her narrow head and her wrist, so much like a bird's, and pulled her talons away from her face. As she jerked her head away blindly, I used my thumbs to unseal her eyes. The little dragon squawked at the small discomfort, blinking, and then looked up at me. Her gaze locked with mine.

The wyrmling's eyes were a deep, shocking amethyst purple around a core of pure silver-white. A rush of wonder filled me. There was nothing in them but pure, innocent love, yearning that punched through all my grief, my fears, my self-doubt, the pain of betrayal and the lingering sickness of the Trials. Never again would I be alone. She saw me in a way I'd never seen myself, that I *could* never see myself... as someone worth loving.

My dragon's adoration intruded into my mind without words: an empathic push of need, possession, admiration. And with it came a name.

"Karalti," I murmured.

Karalti chirped, and pushed herself trustingly into my arms. She wasn't a black dragon at all. Karalti's scales were a deep, deep indigo, and they caught the light of the fire with every color in the rainbow, gleaming with seams of bright blue and green, scarlet and orange, gold and violet... as if they were made of black opal.

Karalti didn't speak with words, just feelings. She was scared, exhausted, and very cold.

"It'll be okay, Tidbit." I absently reached up to smooth my hands over her head. She still had a small beak - the egg tooth - and her supple skin was as smooth as warm leather. Even her horns, barely more than round nubs hinting at the magnificent crown-like crest she would have some day, were warm to the touch. "You'll warm up. I've got some meat in my pack."

She shivered with shock, clinging to my body with her wings. It was the most natural thing in the world to want to protect her, help her, and any pain her claws might have caused me receded whenever her eyes met mine.

So while the world burned down outside I knelt there, bleeding, soothing her: Karalti the Many-Colored, the Black Opal Queen, and without a doubt the loveliest dragon in all of Archemi.

Read Book 2: Trial by Fire

Want to keep reading? Order Trial by Fire at:

https://readerlinks.com/l/133077

Thank You!

Thank you for taking this journey with Hector, Baldr, Rutha and the crew of Dragon Seed. If you enjoyed Dragon Seed and would like to stay on top of Archemi Online book releases, promos, giveaways and artwork, subscribe to my **LitRPG mailing list**. Your email address will never be shared with anyone, and you can easily unsubscribe at any time.

I run a Facebook group where I often post snippets of the books I'm writing as I write them, so drop by the **James Osiris Baldwin page on Facebook** to connect.

If you really enjoyed reading about Hector and the gang, please consider leaving a short review. Word-of-mouth and book reviews are vital for the success of any writer. **You can click here to leave a review on Amazon (all stores).**

Trial by Fire is being written as we speak, and will be available on the 29th May 2018. You can pre-order it here: **Trial By Fire (All Stores).**

The full first-draft chapters will be posted on my **Patreon** for anyone who joins the $5 tier or above, and snippets will be available for everyone on Facebook. Once Trial by Fire is drafted, I will be serializing it on Royal Road shortly before it is released on Amazon – so keep an eye out. I will be letting my mailing list know when that serial begins.

Speaking of Royal Road and Patreon, I'd like to give a shoutout to all the people who made editorial suggestions and reviewed Dragon Seed on Royal Road. I'd also like to thank all my patrons, especially Eytan, Chris W, Laevus, Liz Copen (who is an author and **writes urban fantasy**), Sylvia, Rebecca, Jami and Erica.

I'd also like to thank Stacy Schonhardt for her awesome editing, my friend R.R Virdi for his endless support and encouragement, and all my other friends and family.

Lastly, I'd like to thank my incredible and talented wife, Canth, for doing what she does and being who she is.

For more LitRPG, check out the **LitRPG/Gamelit Society on Facebook**!

Keep reading to learn about a player race that features prominently in Trial By Fire, the Mercurions, and a little more about the nation of Ilia. At the very end of the book is a link to the concept art for the series.

Tarn Takhar, motherfuckers!

James.

Dev Notes

Archemipedia Entry: Mercurions ⟦Grade A Knowledge⟧

Introduction

Weird living constructs, Mercurions are the inheritor race of Zaunt. The largest island in the north of Archemi, Zaunt is an ancient place that is renowned to be the homeland of the Aesari. Once, it was a green and fertile place straight out of Norse myth, but close to five hundred years of civil unrest has stripped Zaunt down to a bare rock.

Mercurions are flawlessly beautiful, weird articulated humanoids, with sculptural features, silvery skin, white or pale grey floss-fine hair spun from silicone, and precious metal and glass eyes with ringed pupils. Other than their odd metallic skin, they are notable for their wing-like 'ears' – actually a cosmetic feature incorporated into their original design by their progenitors.

Many Mercurions make for unpleasant company: they are a cold, aloof species, keeping to themselves and continuing with an ongoing civil war in their homeland, Zaunt. Mercurions on the Artanese continent fall into four categories: political spies, refugees fleeing the civil war on Zaunt, merchants, and criminals seeking employment.

Mercurions make magnificent assassins, due to their immense physical stamina, cold-blooded impartial natures, and a strong warrior culture. They also have a very strong Artificer culture and are renowned to be the best smiths in the world... but those who have seen the glowing, sigil-covered weapons of war they produce and use on the battlefields of Zaunt report stories of juggernauts, spider-legged constructs seemingly made entirely of blades, and weapons which produce massive explosions. Those same people are usually killed by Mercurion assassins. They have a senate council and no single appointed leader.

Culture

The foundation of Mercurion society is the family. A family's size is its wealth, and so Mercurions naturally form into clans and houses comprised of large families. The houses of Zaunt are called Tlaxican, and they vary extensively in size and power. There is essentially no social mobility within Zaunt. You are born, live and die in your place within the Tlaxican.

The most powerful houses are those which have their own mana well (San'chit). There are three Tlaxican in S. Zaunt and one in N. Zaunt which have their own wells. The three in S. Zaunt have small-ish wells: the one in the North has a Dragongate which surpasses every other well in Zaunt by itself.

Within Tlaxican, there are numerous family units which are called Tlaxi'glica (literally 'lineage') which are analogous to immediate family units. The smallest houses may only have two lineages: the largest have hundreds, or even thousands. This is particularly so in the North, where the vast majority of Mercurions are the children of Tlaxican Quchan ('Chew-chan'), 'The House of Birds', and bear Quchi as their fore-name.

Culture now varies between the two ends of Zaunt, but there remain some commonalities.

Reproduction

A Mercurion child is generally born to three parents, as Mercurions marry in threes. Tlaxican measure their wealth in the number of children they have, the quality of those children, and the reserves of mana they have to create them. To reproduce, Mercurions sculpt their children with a mana-treated silicon elastomer, glass, silicon-carbonite (which is relatively common in Zaunt) and specially softened metals. Their techniques are derived from the technological processes used by the Aesari and Drachan nearly 5000 years ago, and are one of the closest-kept secrets in Archemi.

Mercurions from the richest families are created along very particular clan lines in line with their laws using parts from their ancestors, whereas poorer families tend to craft children less skillfully. This is reflected in the term 'Lixu' - literally 'plain' - which is used to describe people of lower status. Lineage is taken very seriously, and all Mercurions of standing recognize the Tlaxi'glican in their House by appearance alone.

Families within a house have guidelines for crafting their children which must be adhered to preserve the characteristic appearance of that family. Filigree, eye-color, face shape, proportion and body type are all decided by tradition, and the married triad who are crafting the children are generally honored to do so. Appropriating the features of another House or Lineage is considered a grave insult, and the child is scorned as a 'Juchi', a copy, which is analogous to a bastard in human feudal societies. Juchi are created, however: and they are frequently employed as spies and assassins for the duration of their short, violent lives.

Mercurions are a subterranean people: they live in enormous cavern and tunnel complexes which are sculpted into underground cities. Mercurion cities and towns are not dark and gloomy places, but they are often hostile to other lifeforms. Because of their immunity to poisons and [[Stranging]], Mercurion Tsonyan (Cities) are generally built near veins or lakes of mana, and they suffer no ill effects from gas pockets, carbon monoxide, or magical vapors. Because of the near universality of mana and the age of the cities, the buildings sprout glittering crackled covers made of glass dust and mana, as well as crops of bluestone and Stranged fungi and lichen. The resonance would be enough to give a human mage a stroke, though the glittering beauty of Mercurion cities cannot be denied: it would be the most beautiful half an hour of their life, before the Stranging took and their lungs became full of crystallized mana.

Mercurions have some of the most sophisticated, haunting music in Archemi. Their signature instruments include a 27-stringed instrument called a Chiki, the Sasuk (a hammered dulcimer) the Jik (a thumb piano similar to a Kalimba), the Tuntikhi (a kind of metal drum similar to a space drum), the Zai (a harpejji) and the Moun, a quartz cantabile. Every house has a Singer who specializes in music, but all Mercurions are sensitive to sound and are tuned for singing. Their education is primarily musical, with great emphasis on teaching songs, ballads, and lists. Reams of information are memorized musically.

It is thought that the Gate of Eternal Longing, the gate which imprisons the draconic deity Veles, was constructed in Zaunt.

Death

Mercurions are not a long-lived people, as they were created to be shock troops, not a species in their own right. As such, the techniques to create and imbue them are fundamentally flawed. From the time they are born, they gradually slow down as their Seid metabolism decreases. A Mercurion has no 'childhood' to speak of. They are educated in their ways within a year, and the next 30-40 years are spent as adults. No Mercurion has lived past 46, and due to the civil war and various other conflicts, they rarely live past 25 in practice.

It is absolutely vital for them to recover their dead to recycle their matter into the next generation, and often, the times that Mercurions will fight the fiercest is when they are denied the option of retrieval. They attribute great significance to the re-use of materials, with Tlaxi'glican forming from lineages on this basis. Incorporating the previous generation into the new is of fundamental importance, and even in the civil war, battles which have resulted in large numbers of dead have seen ceasefires to allow both sides to collect the dead for reincorporation.

Mercurions have no fear of death, despite being non-religious. The fear of death is actually fundamentally alien to them: their lives are so short and their mentality so communal that the average Mercurion views their own death as the point in which they pass the baton to their family's children and grandchildren. Brave soldiers are commemorated through being recycled into future generations, individuals of which will be named after them for their bravery in combat. Because of their sentience and rapid metabolisms and minds, they do not experience temporal contraction. Mercurions are born, live and die fast.

The recording and passing on of important information in an accurate and accessible manner is another extremely important activity, and for this reason, triumvirate marriages are common. These are usually between two soldier caste members and one scholar or artificer, who is relieved of the duty to sculpt children due to their important work in research, record-keeping, machine construction and scribing.

Archemipedia: Ilia ⟦Grade C Knowledge⟧

Ilia is a large, very old nation which comprises the end of the Garda Peninsula, the westernmost point of Artana. Formerly an absolute monarchy, it endured a decade-long civil war which culminated in the Council of Stewards, the Crown's advisory court of lords, seizing power under the leader of a low-born soldier, Warden Scandiva.

In ancient times, Ilia was home to tribal societies of Meewfolk, who were slaughtered and driven out by the Aesari when they began their migration to Artana from the far north. The city of Cham

Garai was built around the oldest of the dragon gates, the Gate of Glorious Dawn, which is the grave of the great dragon goddess of Light, Solnetsi.

The Aesari were eventually overthrown by the combined forces of Sachara, the Demon Queen of Dakhdir, and her lover and comrade Grigori Skyrr, a human slave who discovered a method to bond and fight with dragons without dying of mana poisoning. The Skyrr name is where the Skyrdon of St. Grigori take their titles from, though it means nothing other than 'laborer' in the language of the Aesari.

Religion

Yea, both Prophets were in accord; Brother and Sister were in accord when they spake: "From many small instances in time, one large result may emerge. If the small things be good, the emergence is good; if the multitude be unfortunate, then the results shall be unfortunate. Strive to perfect the small lest the culmination of your actions crush you."

-The Corpus Harmonia, Axiomata of the Prophetess 4:53

Ilia worships two gods common to the majority of nations in Artana. They are Liric, the Lord of Light, and Kyrie, the Lady of the Law. It is an absolutist, proselyting faith which actively seeks new members and is heavily involved in the law of Ilia and other devout nations. The two deities operate in twin churches. Churches of Liric are referred to as Cathedrals, and churches of Kyrie are generally referred to as Oratories.

The religion operates on the fundamental idea that humans were once higher beings who dwelled in perfection on Erruku, thought to be a world made of gold, where the lore of the universe was stored. Humans fell from grace when they warred against the gods and fell to Archemi, where they were enslaved by demons and used to fight in their conflicts. They were freed from their bondage 2500 years ago by the prophet Esara and her brother Ansin, who commanded magic and was able to control the demons. She was served by Asir - the early Mercurions - and chased the demons from Artana.

For many years, Ilia was a complete theocracy, ruled by a Starborn Primeria and Imperator who were spiritually considered to be brother and sister.

The primary holy text of the church is The Corpus Harmonia, often simply referred to as the Harmonia. It is arranged in five books, which claim to trace the history of all humankind from the Fall through to the present day. It is supplemented by tracts written by every Imperator and Primeria. Imperators are tasked with recording history, and Primerae must review and restore law.

Concept Art

To see all of the concept art for Archemi Online thus far, please visit

http://www.jamesosiris.com/archemigallery

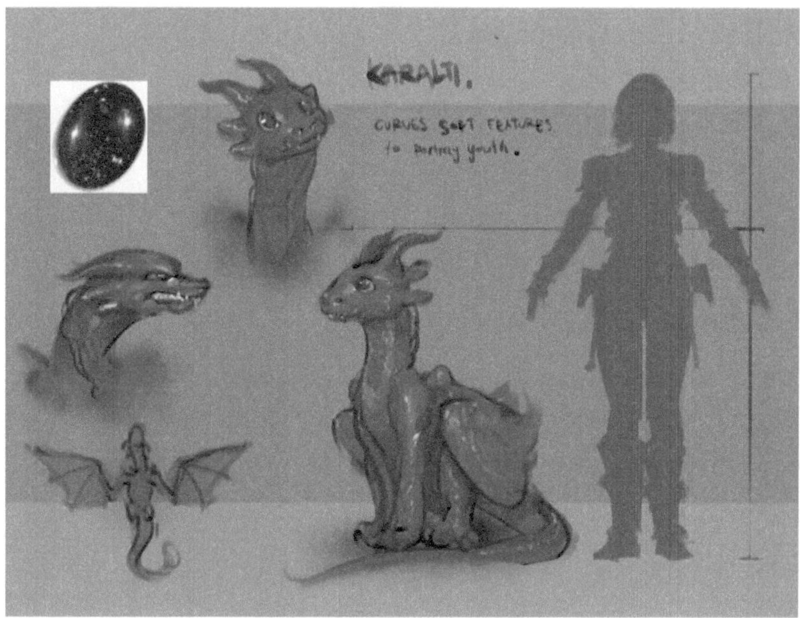

List of James' Books

Hound of Eden Series

Dark, gritty urban fantasy with a cosmic horror twist, join Russian mafia hitmage Alexi Sokolsky as he confronts the mad demons of the abyss, finds redemption, and saves the world. Hound of Eden is an LGBTI series.

Hound of Eden Omnibus (Books 1 – 3)

0 - **Burn Artist** (Prequel)

1 - **Blood Hound**

2 - **Stained Glass**

3 - **Zero Sum**

Archemi Online

A LitRPG saga about a young dragonrider's ascension to greatness inside the virtual world of Archemi.

1 - **Dragon Seed**

2 - **Trial by Fire**

3 - **Kingdom Come**

4 - **Warsinger**

5 - **Spear of Destiny**

Other Titles

Fix Your Damn Book!: A Self-Editing Guide for Authors

The Expanding Universe #1 (Paperback)

The Expanding Universe #2 (Paperback)

www.ingramcontent.com/pod-product-compliance
Lightning Source LLC
Chambersburg PA
CBHW020604310726
48979CB00008B/1332/J

* 9 7 8 0 9 9 4 4 0 7 0 6 1 *